MW01483860

HOPE IGNITES

HOPE IGNITES

Shattered Sunlight Series Book 3

E.A. CHANCE

Darlington
Publishing

Copyright © 2021 by E.A. Chance

All rights reserved.

This is a work of fiction. The characters, names, places, incidents, and dialogue are either products of the author's imagination and are not to be construed as real or are used fictitiously.

No part of this book may be reproduced in any form whatsoever without prior written permission of the publisher except in the case of brief passages embodied in critical reviews and articles.

eBook ISBN: 978-1-951870-10-2
Paperback ISBN: 978-1-951870-12-6
Hardcover ISBN: 978-1-951870-11-9

Cover Design by Dissect Designs, London

❀ Created with Vellum

ALSO BY E.A. CHANCE

Shattered Sunlight Trilogy

SOLAR FURY

HUNTING DAYBREAK

Omnibus Edition

SHATTERED SUNLIGHT SERIES COLLECTION: BOOKS 1-3

E.A. Chance also writes as Eleanor Chance

ACKNOWLEDGMENTS

Thank you to my editor, Joseph Nassise, for his invaluable guidance and encouragement. Also, thank you to my award-winning cover designer, Tim Barber, for his immense talent and ability to see into my mind and create the covers I envision.

I'm grateful to my supportive and loving family who give their time, encouragement, and love in a never ending supply. Love you!

A special thanks to my husband for helping me meet my deadlines! You're the best and I couldn't do this without you!

Last, and most importantly, thank you to all of you, my readers. None of this would matter without you. Your kind and enthusiastic support means the world to me.

CHAPTER ONE

DR. RILEY POOLE hesitated before pushing her shoulder against the operating room door. She was about to perform emergency surgery on her seventh patient in twelve hours. Bone weary, she wouldn't have dared operate under such conditions back when the world was sane. But working under challenging situations was the norm in her life since a global Coronal Mass Ejection struck Earth, killing millions and destroying all vestiges of modern technological life.

Riley was the only orthopedic surgeon qualified to perform such a challenging surgery within a hundred miles of Colorado Springs. The patient would lose his leg if she didn't operate. That outcome would drastically reduce his chances of survival in their resource-starved world, and she couldn't in good conscience resign him to that fate. She took a breath and made her way into the OR.

The man lying on the table was young. Twenty at most. He needed surgery to repair his left femur, where a round from an M-16 rifle had shattered the bone. It had probably been fired by an enemy soldier who was just as young, if not younger. The cause of the wound didn't matter. Riley just wanted to know how much longer the violence would go on.

The United States had split into two countries that were fighting a bitter civil war. The US was ruled by Vice President turned dictator, Aileen Kearns. Like hundreds of despots before her, lust for power was her driving force. Any declared concern for the welfare of her citizens was nothing more than political posturing, which she'd repeatedly proved in her short tenure.

Riley and most of her family lived across the border in the newly formed Western States of America, led by President Lamonte Purnell. He was a wise and benevolent leader, determined to uphold a democratic system of government for the betterment of all his citizens. Everything he stood for directly opposed the power-hungry and self-absorbed Kearns.

The war had dragged on for more than a year, far longer than early predictions. Isn't this always the way in wartime? Riley thought, then asked her equally exhausted anesthesiologist to read off the patient's vitals. Satisfied with his report, she nodded to her surgical nurse and said, "Let's get this started."

As she pressed the scalpel blade into the young man's flesh, the memory of another surgery two years earlier flashed unbidden into her mind. Her oldest daughter, Julia, had been shot in the thigh just weeks after the CME disaster. As Riley worked on her current patient, footage looped in her brain of kneeling over Julia in the dark woods, desperately fighting to save her leg and young life. She couldn't have pulled it off without Coop, a world-renowned thoracic surgeon and the man who later became her husband. They'd only had access to the most rudimentary instruments and supplies and no anesthesia, but by no minor miracle, Julia and her leg had survived the ordeal.

The resident assisting Riley cleared his throat and said, "You're quiet today, Dr. Poole. Is there a problem?"

Riley glanced at him, then smiled behind her surgical mask.

She usually kept chatter going during her surgeries to cut the tension, but she didn't have the energy that day.

"No problem, Sam, and I've told you to call me Riley," she said, aiming to sound more upbeat than she felt. "I'm just keeping my mind focused. This is going to be a long, complicated repair."

"Aren't they all these days?" her nurse asked.

Sam nodded. "You've got that right, Jana. And where do all these boys come from? Barely enough humans exist to keep civilization functioning without sending these kids off to die in a war."

Since the fighting began, Riley had pieced together more bodies than she dared count, but they kept coming. If the two sides didn't stop killing each other, no one would be left alive to populate either country.

"The US has us outnumbered three-to-one, but we're holding our own," Riley said. "Maybe it will be enough to convince Kearns to admit defeat soon. With the world population so decimated, they can't afford the losses any more than we can."

Jana watched her for a moment before saying, "I still haven't gotten used to us-versus-them. It just used to be us, then without warning, catastrophe. My grandparents live in Oklahoma, but I can't even get a message from them. I'm not even sure if they survived the CME. It's insane."

"Jana," Sam said sharply.

Riley glanced up and caught him rolling his eyes in her direction. She knew Sam was afraid Jana's comment had offended her, but she understood. Julia had been missing somewhere on the US side of the border for nearly two years without Riley having a word from her. She blamed herself for that. Driven by the hope of learning the fate of her two younger children, she'd insisted on leaving Julia in Virginia while she and Coop made the treacherous trek to Colorado Springs. Even though she'd made the best decision under the circumstances, she couldn't help second-guessing herself, which had caused countless sleepless nights.

For over a year, their friend, Conrad Elliot, a military intelligence specialist, had used covert assets at his disposal to locate Julia. He'd gleaned occasional bits of intel and learned she was being held in an internment camp with other members of Riley's extended family, but Conrad had failed to nail down the location. Even though the trail had grown cold, Riley hadn't given up hope that Julia was alive.

"It's fine, Sam," she said, finally. "Jana has a right to express her feelings. The CME and war are causing suffering across the board."

"Thanks for saying that, Riley, but I am sorry," Jana said, keeping her eyes lowered. "I'm sure they'll bring Julia home to you soon."

Before Riley could respond, a rush of blood flooded the surgical cavity. Distracted by their conversation and her thoughts of Julia, she'd nicked an artery.

"Pressure's dropping, Doctor," the anesthesiologist said.

Riley refocused all her attention on the patient. There would be time to berate herself over Julia later. She had to close off the bleeder or lose the young man.

"Suction," she said, keeping her voice even.

Sam lowered the aspirator into the field and vacuumed the blood to give Riley an unobstructed view of the artery. She spotted the cut and clamped it.

After waiting for several seconds to verify that the bleeding had stopped, she said, "Pressure."

"Rising," the anesthesiologist said, without taking his eyes from the monitor.

Riley asked Jana for sutures to repair the cut. As she threaded the needle through the vessel, the room went dark. Riley froze while waiting for the backup generator to hum to life. She was relieved to hear the respirator and other machines still operating on their portable batteries.

"Damn, not again," Sam said. "That's the third time the power's gone out today."

Loss of power was a common occurrence in post-CME life but knowing that didn't make it easier to cope with during a delicate surgery. The hospital ran on solar power that was reasonably reliable but not a hundred percent. The hospital's operating rooms and other vital areas had backup solar generators to prevent loss of life, but they hadn't kicked in yet.

"Jana, please find Coop and ask him what's happening," Riley said.

"Yes, Doctor," the nurse said as she hurried from the room.

Riley felt panic churn in her gut when the lights hadn't come on after another five minutes, and Jana hadn't returned. The power outage stirred other memories of the day the CME hit. Riley shook off her fear and snapped back into surgeon mode.

"Sam, get to Coop and tell him we need portable lights ASAP. Then, find out where Jana wandered off to." As the words left her mouth, the lights blinked on, making her flinch. "Never mind. Back to work."

Jana came in thirty seconds later and pulled on a fresh pair of gloves. "Sorry, Riley. I was looking for Dr. Cooper but couldn't find him. A guy from maintenance told me the power would be on in a minute, so I headed back here."

"Don't apologize," Riley said without looking up from her work. "You were following my orders. Did he tell you what happened?"

Jana shook her head and stepped into place at the table. Riley was disappointed at not knowing why the backup generator had failed to come on. But unfortunately, she'd have to wait until after surgery to get the detailed story. Coop was Chief Medical Officer and acting Chief Administrator. He'd worked wonders getting the hospital functioning as well as it did. She trusted he'd have the problem rectified by the time she tied off the final stitch.

———

Riley was running on her last drop of adrenaline when she left the surgical unit six hours later. She was confident her patient would make a complete recovery, even if his soldiering days were over. Her hope was the war would end before he finished his post-surgical rehab, so returning to the fight wouldn't be a temptation. Almost getting his leg shot off should have been enough to cure him of that, but Riley knew the drive of the fighting spirit in these boys. Either way, his would be one more young life saved from war. There were plenty of other dangers lurking in their post CME world, but with luck and common sense, he would live a long, productive life.

Riley made her way to the hospital quarters she and Coop shared on their four-day-on, three-day-off work stints. The twenty-mile trek from her parent's farm where they lived to Colorado Springs took nine hours each way on horseback, so they bunked at the hospital for their shifts. Travel by motor vehicle of any kind had become a luxury of the past. Their access to cars had been limited in the early days after the CME. Later, travel by horse or bike became the norm. They spotted the rare electric car charged on solar power units, but those were the exception. Discovering more convenient, modern modes of travel was number one on the world's priority list.

Riley's life revolved around riding to and from the hospital, performing surgery, then repeating the process. The routine left little time to spend with her three youngest children, but she had no choice. Her skills were in high demand, and she couldn't ignore that responsibility. Not that she wanted to. She was honored and humbled to be called Doctor and contribute to saving and bettering life. But that entailed sacrificing time with her family. She continued to hope the situation would be tempo-rary and that they could all move to a house in town soon. Her fourteen-month-old son, Xav, was growing up fast but hardly knew his parents.

When Riley reached their quarters, she was disappointed that Coop wasn't waiting for her in the bed. He was most likely still dealing with the power-loss problem. She took advantage of the alone time to take a long, hot shower. It was the one luxury she allowed herself. Using valuable and limited power to heat the water wasn't the only extravagance. The other was getting the water that flowed from the shower head.

Their proximity to the Rockies allowed for a sustainable water source. Engineers had figured out how to garner enough solar energy to distribute it throughout the city, but they were still struggling with the problem of ensuring the water was potable. The water pouring over her was clean enough for bathing but not drinking. All water for sanitary uses had to be boiled or treated with purifiers. Under Coop's persistence and his position of authority on the city council, those same engineers had rigged a treatment apparatus solely for hospital use. Regional water treatment was likely years in the future.

The glorious, warm water reminded Riley of how much she'd taken for granted in her old life. Sure, the power had gone out during severe storms on occasion, but no one ever doubted that it would come back on in those situations. Water pipes would burst, or power lines could get knocked down by falling tree branches, but those instances were only inconveniences. Living for two years with cold, tainted water running from the bathroom and kitchen faucets was a different story. She just tried to be grateful they didn't have to carry it from the well into the house.

She stepped out of her shower sanctuary and dried off before pulling her nightgown over her head. As she teased a brush through her curly red hair, she glanced through the mirror to the calendar hanging on the wall behind her. Emily had made it for her as a Christmas gift. Coop must have hung it that morning after she left for her shift.

The sad face drawn with red marker on that day's date caught her eye. Emily must have added the face before giving it to her. Riley set her brush on the counter and went to get a closer look. She hadn't realized what day it was until she saw the drawing on the calendar. It was so simple, but the sight of it twisted Riley's heart into a knot.

She heard the door as Coop came in. Without turning from the calendar, she said, "Do you know what day this is?"

"Seventh of January. Why?"

"It was two years ago today."

Coop came up behind her and tenderly laid his hands on her shoulders. He was quiet for a moment before saying, "How's that possible? It feels like only two months ago in some ways."

When Riley turned to face him, he pulled her into his arms. Resting her head on his chest, she said, "Feels more like ten years to me. Think of all we've been through. Julia getting shot, me leaving her behind, and her getting locked up in one of Kearns' monstrous camps. There was our time as hostages in Branson's compound. Losing Dad last year. Hannah and Brooks before that. The thousands of others who died. If those things weren't bad enough, there's this damned civil war dragging on forever. So much death. So much loss."

Coop stepped in front of her and said, "Look at me." She raised her eyes to his, waiting for the lecture she knew was coming. "I won't downplay the tragedy or loss, but you're over-looking the miracles. You and I meeting at the medical confer-ence in DC and falling in love, smack in the middle of the apocalypse. Getting married and bringing our Xav into the world. We survived that nightmare field trip across the country and arrived home to find Jared and Emily alive and thriving. I know being separated from Julia is a constant black cloud over our lives, but Conrad will find her. He gave his word. I trust him."

"I'm not giving up hope but seeing Emily's drawing to mark the second anniversary of the CME blindsided me." She stepped away and wrapped a throw around her shoulders. "Thanks for hanging the calendar. It was such a thoughtful Christmas gift from Emily. She worked so hard designing and printing it."

Coop kissed Riley's cheek before sinking onto the bed and kicking off his shoes. "That girl never ceases to amaze, much like her mother."

Riley walked back to the bathroom and picked up her brush, once again grateful for Coop's knack of keeping her from sinking into the darkness. "I can reconstruct a shattered leg," she said over her shoulder, "but I never could have gotten the computer and printer working the way Emily did. Of course, the computer's limited without the internet, but I'll take what I can get. It's a relief not having to write my patient notes out by hand anymore. My penmanship is so bad even I can't decipher the records most of the time."

Coop let out a laugh. "No argument from me. Just proves you were destined to be a doctor. How'd your last surgery go?"

Riley dropped onto the bed next to him. "Long, but successful, despite the lights going out at a crucial moment. Why didn't the auxiliary generators kick in?"

Without turning to face her, he said, "Because someone came in and dismantled them."

"What do you mean, dismantled?"

"After the morning maintenance check, someone broke into the generator room and stripped the units for parts. I hate to even think it, but it looks like an inside job, probably to trade the parts on the black market. Security is interviewing everyone on duty who has access to that area."

Riley sat up and crossed her legs, shocked by Coop's news. She'd assumed it was a mechanical failure. "That's sickening. How could anyone who works here stoop so low? If my patient had died in the middle of that surgery because of the power loss, it would have been murder."

Coop propped himself against the wall at the head of the bed and closed his eyes. "I've been thinking the same thing since we discovered the theft. We were lucky not to lose any patients. If we don't catch the thief, I don't know where we'll procure replacement parts. It took superhuman effort to get those generators operational. With these incessant snowstorms lowering main power generation, we could be in serious trouble. Remind me again why I agreed to run this hospital."

Riley moved closer and wrapped her arms around him. "Because you are the perfect man for the job."

"I was the only man for the job."

"That's not true. They would have found someone if you'd said no, but you didn't. Taking on this Herculean task makes you a hero in my eyes. You'll get this problem resolved just like you always do."

Coop brushed a lock of hair from her face and kissed her. "I couldn't manage without you by my side. I hate to tell you this, but I can't go back to the farm with you and Dashay tomorrow. I have to stay and fix this, no matter how long it takes. Will you two be all right on your own?"

"We've done this a hundred times. We'll be fine as long as we don't get stuck in a snowdrift. This may be the worst time for me to ask this, but I was hoping to take a week off. I've been pushing myself hard. I don't want to get burned out, and I need time with the kids. We only took two days at Christmas, and we've hardly seen them since then."

Riley held her breath when he hesitated to answer. She didn't like adding to his burdens, but she knew her limits and that she'd reached them.

"My gut reaction was to say no, which may be coming from a selfish place. I keep it together much better when you're here. But take your break. I'll send for Cameron Andres to come down from Denver. He owes me after that week I filled in for him in November."

Riley let out her breath. "Thanks, Babe. I wouldn't have argued if you said no, but I'm glad you didn't." She reached up and pulled Coop down next to her. "If this is our last night together, we'd better make it count."

"Don't you want to eat first?"

She kissed him with a hunger that surprised her in her exhausted state. "What do you think?"

———

Riley found her friend Dashay Robinson stamping her feet to keep warm near the hospital's makeshift stables the following morning. Riley first met Dashay when they were both hostages in a compound in Virginia. Dashay worked as a nurse in the infirmary and helped Riley treat Julia's gunshot wound. They got separated for a time but stumbled upon each other months later outside Charleston, West Virginia.

Dashay had lost her entire family in the aftermath of the CME, and there was nothing to keep her in the East, so she traveled to Colorado with Riley and Coop. Riley was thrilled when Dashay made her home with them. She'd become like a sister to Riley and had been an enormous help when Xav was born. Coop considered her a vital asset at the hospital and had just promoted her to head of the nursing staff. Riley was happy for her friend but missed Dashay assisting in her surgeries.

Dashay waved Riley over when she saw her trudging towards her through the five feet of powdery snow covering the ground. The sky was cloudless, but the temperature was in the lower teens. The post-CME winters had been brutal, and without the aid of snowplows or blowers, keeping roads and walkways clear was a constant battle. Riley often wondered if the altered weather patterns were similar to what they'd been a hundred years earlier. She hoped rather than believed the changes were temporary.

Their friend, Dr. Adrian Landry, a solar physicist, speculated that the industrial collapse had played a significant role in the drastic climate changes. It could take a decade or more for the surviving humans to know for sure.

Riley made her way to Dashay, who waited with their horses saddled and ready to go. Riley's faithful horse, Biscuit, greeted her with a whinny of welcome. Riley reached up and patted his neck in return. She and that dapple-gray gelding had traveled across the bulk of the country through hellish conditions, and she couldn't imagine life without him. After climbing into the saddle, she nudged him forward with a squeeze of her knees. As much as Riley loved Biscuit, she would have given anything to travel home in a cozy, heated car.

Dashay rode her horse, Xena, up beside Riley and got her into pace with Biscuit. Dashay wore a ski mask and was so bundled in her scarf and hood that all Riley could see of her face were her glittering dark brown eyes.

"You in there somewhere?" Riley called to her in the stillness.

Dashay jumped, then pulled the mask away from her mouth and flashed her brilliant smile. "Just trying to keep my lips from freezing off. I don't know how you can tolerate this cold without something over your face."

Riley grinned and said, "I'm used to it from growing up in Colorado."

Dashay shook her head. "We got snow in northern Virginia, but not nonsense like this. Who in their right mind would have settled here?"

Riley laughed. "You did."

"Momentary insanity. I should have kept heading west until I hit the California coast. I could be lounging on a glorious beach right now, getting a deeper glow on my already gorgeous brown skin."

A cluster of snowflakes stuck to Riley's goggles, so she

brushed them away with her gloved hand. "I doubt it's warm enough for tanning, even in southern California, but that does sound glorious. Let's grab the kids when we get home and ditch this frozen madness."

"Not sure Coop would appreciate you whisking the kids a thousand miles away, but otherwise, no argument from me. We could introduce Xav to the Pacific Ocean."

"What about Conrad?"

Dashay avoided making eye contact as she answered. "I'd need to think before I answer that minefield of a question. He leaves me all the time, so what could he say? Feels like we hardly ever see each other lately."

"He leaves you for his work. It's not out of choice. You know he'd rather be with you."

Dashay shrugged. "Would he?"

"Did something happen between the two of you?"

"No. Nothing. That's the problem. It's always good fun when we're together, but our relationship has never progressed past the fun. To be honest, I don't think about Conrad much when he's gone these days."

Dashay's admission surprised Riley. No one who saw Dashay and Conrad together could doubt their physical spark, but Riley had always assumed their relationship went deeper. After more than a year together, it should have. She thought of Nico Mendez, the army medic held at the compound with them. He and Dashay had been together when they reunited with Coop and her. Tragically, after Nico was attacked by a bear, they had to leave him behind at a hospital in Charleston, West Virginia, to stay ahead of the war. It tore Dashay up to go on without him. He'd planned to catch up once he was recovered, but they never saw him again.

"Are you going to say anything to that?" Dashay asked, rousing Riley from her thoughts.

"Sorry, I was thinking about Nico. Was your relationship with him like it is with Conrad? It seemed like more than a fly-by-night fling."

"Conrad's more than a fling, but to answer you, no, it wasn't the same with Nico. The trauma we endured in the compound and on the road afterward deepened the bond between us, but it started before that. I was still reeling from the CME and my fiancé's death when I got to the compound. Nico got me through, and we became close. When my grief lessened, I realized I wanted more than friendship. When I met Conrad and hooked up with him, I thought I'd have my fun for a few days and never see him again. Imagine my surprise when he showed up at the farm to deliver Biscuit to you. This might sound shallow, but Conrad is...convenient."

"Do you ever think about Nico?"

Dashay shook her head. "I don't let myself. He's gone, Riley. Why should I torture myself?"

Riley saw her point, but it saddened her to see her friend suffering. "Maybe you'll find someone like Coop."

Dashay gave a hearty laugh. "There is no one else like Coop."

Riley smiled. "He is a rare gem, but you know what I mean. Someone right for you."

"Not likely. All the good men are fighting the war, taken by someone else, or dead. Look, I'm not saying I don't have feelings for Conrad. I just don't see him as 'the one.' Is it wrong to stay with him, feeling the way I do?"

Riley had never been in Dashay's position, so it was an impossible question to answer. She and her first husband, Zach, met in college, and there was instant attraction, but neither was looking for a long-term relationship. Their feelings strengthened over time until she couldn't imagine loving anyone else. After his helicopter was shot down over Afghanistan, the thought of getting involved with another man never occurred to Riley until she met Coop. Her feelings for him came out of the blue like the CME and only grew stronger every day.

"Only you can answer that," she finally said. "But if both of you agree on where your relationship is headed, I don't see the harm. Companionship and affection are vital for survival in this world."

"In any world," Dashay said, then snapped Xena's reins to quicken her pace.

CHAPTER TWO

RILEY LEANED against the kitchen counter on the last night of her week's leave, watching her family, relaxed and warm, enjoying time together after dinner. Her sister, Lily, held two-year-old Miles on her lap, trying to get him to stop pestering Jared, who was loving every minute of his little cousin's attention. Lily sat next to her husband, Kevin, who was discussing the progress of the family horse breeding business with Dashay. Emily was attempting to get Xav to finish his peas. Unfortunately, most of them were ending up on the floor or in his mess of blond hair that stuck out in all directions, just like Coop's. Riley's mother, Marjory, sat at the head of the table, looking on as the quiet matriarch. She caught Riley's eye and gave her a faint grin.

Only three things were missing from the perfect scene; Riley's father, who had passed away a year earlier from heart failure, Julia, and Coop. Riley hadn't heard a word from Coop since she left Colorado Springs. That meant the power issues still weren't resolved. Riley was scheduled to head back to the hospital in the morning but wondered if she should wait until she heard from him.

The sound of someone barging in through the front door and stamping snow off his boots startled Riley from her thoughts. Coop poked his hooded head through the kitchen doorway seconds later and said, "Hello, family. Aren't you all just a picture."

Riley and the kids ran to him, smothering him with hugs and kisses while Xav squealed to be set free of his highchair. Coop wrested his way out of the mob, then snatched Xav out of the chair and swung him up to his shoulders. Xav giggled in delight.

"No better sound in the world," Coop said.

"Dada," Xav said as Coop lowered him to the floor.

"Except that," Coop said, then nuzzled his neck with his bearded cheek, setting off a fresh round of giggles. Coop handed Xav to Riley, then pointed toward the doorway. "Didn't anyone notice what I dragged home? I found him stranded and helpless in a ditch."

They all turned to find Conrad laughing as he moved into the room. "I think he has that backward," he said.

Dashay jumped up and planted a kiss on him that even made Conrad blush. She finally pulled away and said, "What are you doing here? I wasn't expecting you until next month."

"I'm here on a special commission from Denver. I traveled down with Coop, but this has to do with Riley."

"Me?" she asked, pointing to herself. "Does it have to do with Julia?"

Coop grabbed two plates and started spooning dinner leftovers onto them. "I put the screws to Conrad the entire way here to get him to tell me, but he says he can only deliver the message directly to you. But it has nothing to do with Julia."

He handed Conrad a plate piled with food and motioned for him to take the empty chair next to Dashay before dropping into the chair opposite her.

As they shoveled the food down, Riley said, "Go ahead. Tell me why you're here."

Coop glanced up at her. "Let the man eat, Babe. We'll talk in the office after we're done."

Coop's tone told her to drop it. She reached for Xav before he grabbed Coop's plate. "I'll get this guy cleaned up and ready for bed. Emily, please give me a hand?"

A ghost of a frown crossed Emily's face before she nodded. Giving Coop a kiss on the cheek, she said, "Glad you're home, Dad. Mom was worried."

Coop raised his eyebrows. "Just Mom?"

Emily shrugged and headed out of the kitchen. As Riley followed, carrying Xav, she said, "Jared, come with us. You need to finish your homework."

Jared didn't even try to hide his disappointment. "Can't I stay with Dad for a minute?"

"Finish your work, buddy. I'll come up and hang out before you go to sleep," Coop said and gave him a fist bump.

Riley glanced at Coop as she herded the kids toward the stairs. He winked at her, but his smile didn't reach his eyes. This is trouble, she thought and did her best to ignore the seed of panic sprouting in her gut.

―――――

Riley fidgeted in her father's desk chair as she waited for Coop and Conrad in the office. Her father had been gone for nine months, but it was still a struggle for her to enter that room. He'd left too much of himself behind. Even his smell lingered. She could forget he was gone when she was at the hospital, but it was a different story at home, especially in his office.

Thomas had been a loved and respected doctor in the region for the thirty years leading up to his retirement. After leaving his career behind, he bought land outside of Colorado Springs and became what he called a gentleman farmer. The memory of that always made Riley smile. Thomas had been content in his last years, and Riley would be forever grateful she made it home before his heart gave out. In her eyes, a better man never walked the earth, except maybe Coop.

She ran her fingertips over the smooth finish of his well-worn desk and said, "I miss you, Dad, but we're good here. Lily and I are taking care of Mom and keeping her too busy to be sad. She's been very brave. I promise not to let any harm come to her if I can help it." The door flew open, and she jumped as Coop and Conrad strode in.

Coop pulled a chair next to hers and lowered himself into it. Laying a hand on her shoulder, he said, "Who were you talking to?"

She shifted her gaze to the framed picture of Thomas on the opposite wall. Coop gave a quick nod and reached for her hand.

"Sit down, Conrad, and tell me why you're here. I can't take the suspense a second longer," Riley said.

Conrad dropped his athletic but weary six-foot-plus self into the only other chair in the room and leaned his elbows on the desk. His sandy-brown hair had outgrown the usual military cut, and he had at least four day's growth of stubble on his chin. As Riley studied his face, she noticed the creases around his eyes and forehead for the first time. He was a powerful man with a commanding presence, but the burdens he carried were taking a toll. She'd always be grateful to him for helping Coop, Dashay, and her cross the border into Colorado more than a year earlier. His actions had saved their lives. It was a debt they could never repay.

He caught Riley scrutinizing him and gave her a half-grin. She looked away, feeling her cheeks redden.

"Before I get to the reason for my trip here," he said, "I wanted to tell you we're making some headway in our search for Julia. It's too early to share the details because I don't want to get your hopes up, but it's promising. I'll update you when the details are more concrete."

Riley squeezed Coop's hand and let out her breath. "Thank you for that. Every tidbit of news keeps me hoping."

"There's no reason to give up hope. Julia's out there, Riley, and she's safe, just like the rest of your family. We're going to bring her home." He leaned back in the chair and crossed his arms. "On to our other business. Two weeks ago, the Minister of Health summoned me to Denver for a meeting."

Coop sat forward and stared at him. "That was the last thing I expected. Why were you summoned to the Health Ministry?"

"I wondered exactly that on my trip to the capitol. The Ministry had petitioned President Purnell to create dedicated medical units to travel to qutlying areas in the WSA, set up clinics, give medical training, and render care where needed. The Minister feels the needs of citizens in rural areas aren't being met and wants to remedy that. The President approved the idea. A panel was appointed to form the department, officially named The Health and Welfare Battalion, or HWB."

Riley couldn't help laughing, despite the seriousness of the conversation. "Who came up with that title? Sounds like a name for Suffragettes."

Conrad chuckled. "Good to know I'm not the only one who thinks so. But despite the name, they're serious about this. As you know, I travel the country extensively in my work. Between current living conditions and the war, there's a tremendous need for this program."

"I agree," Riley said. "That still doesn't explain what it has to do with you."

"They want me in charge of security for the units. It gets dicey out there in the bush. The Minister doesn't want defenseless doctors carrying drugs and other valuable supplies to become targets. I'm here to see you because they want you to sit on the council and lead a unit."

Riley jumped to her feet and stared at him in disbelief. "Are they nuts? After what I went through to get home, they want me to leave my family and journey out into the wilderness? I have a fourteen-month-old son and two other children at home. I hate being away from them for even a few days when I'm on my shifts. Why would I take off to who knows where for extended periods?" She turned to Coop and pointed at Conrad. "Can you believe this?" Coop sat stone-still and avoided her eyes. She put her hands on her hips. "You knew about this?"

He looked up at her with a sheepish grin. "I've heard rumblings about the program, but not the details. You weren't mentioned."

Riley fell back into her chair in a huff. "Why didn't you tell me?"

"I didn't think it had anything to do with us. The Ministry asked for recommendations. I swear I didn't give them your name."

Conrad held up his hands to calm her. "Take it easy, Riley. Coop had nothing to do with this, and I told them exactly what you just said. They want you because of the experience you gained on the road and for your incredible medical skills and knowledge. Most medical professionals around here have never stepped outside their own communities. They're clueless about what to expect in the field. You got on the Minister's radar after that whole Dr. Landry business. You've become somewhat of a legend."

Riley rubbed her face as memories of her harrowing 2000-mile journey ran through her mind. She'd done what it took to make it home safely to her babies. Any mother would have done the same. "This is ludicrous," she mumbled. "Do I have a choice, or am I being drafted?"

"You're a civilian. You have a choice. This isn't Kearns' United States."

She stood and, without hesitation, said, "Then, my answer is an emphatic no!"

Coop put his hand on her arm. "Let's talk about this before

you answer. Maybe you can serve on the council without heading a unit."

She shook her head as she stared down at him. "We'd have to move to Denver. Are you ready to give up your position at the hospital and uproot the kids at a time like this? Denver isn't just an hour car ride anymore. It's a three-day journey each way."

"I don't think they'd go for that anyway," Conrad said. "They'd want you in Denver for six weeks of training and council meetings, but they don't expect you to move there. Coop wouldn't have to leave the hospital. You'd go into the field for two-month stints, then be home for roughly three weeks. Since you'd be on the council, you could assign yourself to a region closest to home. Once the units are running smoothly and experienced, I'm sure you'd have the option to forgo being in the field."

"And how many years would that take? Five? Ten? In the meantime, my children grow up hardly knowing their mother."

"It doesn't sound like it would be that way," Coop said. "Please, I want to talk about this before you give your final answer. I'll respect whatever you decide."

"Sounds like you're trying to get rid of me, Coop."

"Stop it, Riley. You know that's never true."

Conrad stood and smoothed his pant legs. "Dashay is waiting for me. I'll leave you two to discuss this. I don't need your answer for a few days, Riley. Mull it over. I respect the hell out of you, and I won't pressure you. I'll honor whatever you decide."

He went out, quietly closing the door behind him. Riley walked to the picture of her father on the wall. It was taken the day he received a commendation from the governor for his work in support of rural medical clinics. He'd volunteered his time and expertise to ensure every person in the region received adequate medical care. But that had been a different time. It took less than a week to visit every hospital and clinic in the area, not the better part of the year. Still, Riley couldn't help but wonder what advice he'd give her if he were alive.

"Your father was an extraordinary man," Coop said quietly. "His daughter is no less extraordinary. I echo Conrad. I'll honor whatever you decide, but I hope you'll keep an open mind. Not to diminish what you already do, but this is a rare opportunity to make a lasting difference. You know how much I'd hate being separated from you, and the kids would miss you like crazy, but they have your mom and Lily to pick up the slack. You'd leave a gaping void at the hospital, but you have so much to offer the world. I don't doubt for an instant that you're made for this assignment."

Tears welled up in her eyes and spilled onto her cheeks. Coop's words reminded her once more how fortunate she was to have him in her life. She respected and trusted him as much as she had her father. If he was in favor of her taking the position, she had to give his opinion some weight.

She returned to her chair and took his hands. "I appreciate you saying that, but you give me more credit than I deserve. It's not just time away from you and the kids that makes me want to refuse. It's also fear. We know all too well what it's like out there. I'm not sure I have the courage to face that again."

"It won't be the same. Aside from the war, the world has settled down since our days on the road. You won't be as far from us, and if it gets to be too much, you could come home for a time or quit for good. There's always a place for you here."

Riley brushed her tears away and gave him a tender kiss. "What did I do to deserve you?"

"I ask myself that every day," he said and gave her his signature crooked grin. He got to his feet and pulled her into his arms. "Put it out of your mind for tonight. I talked Cameron into staying longer, and Jamison Mackey is filling in for me. Let's enjoy a few relaxing days at home with the kids. You can decide before we head back to Colorado Springs."

"Excellent suggestion." She pulled away, then took his hand to lead him to the door. "What happened with the generator situation?"

"We caught the guys and recovered the parts. It's hard to make a fast getaway in a horse-drawn wagon in five feet of snow. It was someone on the maintenance staff that let the thieves in. I wanted to believe he was desperate for goods to exchange to feed his family. Turns out he was just greedy. Disgusting. But he's gone, and everything's back to normal."

"Normal? I'm not familiar with that word," she said as they climbed the stairs. "Don't forget that you have an appointment with Jared."

"I don't think he'd let me forget." He stopped her outside their room and gave her a hungry kiss. "I hope to have an appointment with you later."

"I'll do my best to fit you in, but don't keep me waiting."

He grinned seductively at her before racing down the hall to Jared's room. As she pushed her bedroom door open, she heard him say, "I missed you, Buddy. What's new?"

Her head was spinning as she dropped onto the bed without bothering to undress. Most days, it took all her energy to keep life running on an even keel. Accepting the position with the Health Ministry felt more like intentionally flipping the boat in roiling, stormy waters. There was no question she had extensive field experience, but others had to exist who were just as qualified. If she refused the offer, she could fail communities in desperate need of medical care. If she accepted, would she be sacrificing the safety of her family and her own sanity? She felt pushed to the brink as it was. Did she have more to give?

She sat up and started unbuttoning her blouse, wishing she'd listened to Coop, and pushed aside the thoughts whirling in her brain. Why did life always have to descend and stir up her little corner of the ocean?

Coop frowned when he came in and saw her on the bed with her arms wrapped around her knees. He sat on the edge of the bed and stared at her. "You don't look like someone eager to engage in amorous activities. What could have possibly happened in the past twenty minutes to make your face look like that?"

She sighed and raised her eyes to his. "I tried to ignore what Conrad told us, but this is too huge. I have a conflicting sense of obligation pulling me between family and responsibilities here and the strangers out there who need my help. No matter which, I'll be failing someone."

Coop put his hands on her shoulders and turned her to face him. "This is so like you, taking the whole blasted world on your shoulders. Listen to me. One, you won't be failing this family if you take the job. Do you think we're incapable of picking up the slack? Two, your decision won't be carved in stone. If it doesn't work, you quit and come home. It's that simple."

Riley shook her head. "Not simple. If I quit, do you really believe they'd just let me walk away?"

"I do. You're not enlisting in the military. You're accepting a job offer. They may have a contractual time period given the training curve and expense. I can't imagine it's for more than a year, and it may be negotiable."

Riley hadn't considered that, so she took a moment to let what he'd said sink in. "That helps. I was picturing myself stuck in the job for ten years. I could try to talk them into a six-month trial. If I'm assigned close to home, it could be doable."

Coop's eyes brightened as he held out his hand for a fist bump. Riley laughed and tapped his knuckles with hers. "That's my girl." He playfully pushed her down onto the bed and straddled her. "Can we tuck this away until morning and have our welcome home flourish?"

In answer, Riley wove her fingers into his hair and pressed his mouth to hers. "How is it you're brilliant enough to always know just what to say?"

He brushed his lips on her cheek and whispered, "Genius, remember?"

"Well, Genius, you've earned my undivided attention."

———

The house was quiet as Riley made her way to the kitchen in the morning. She woke before Xav and was the first downstairs. She held her breath as she flipped on the light switch, then sighed in relief when the lights flickered on. With the dark, stormy days they'd had, it was always a toss-up if there would have enough solar energy stored to power the house. Kevin had installed a wood-burning stove in the kitchen to boil water for drinking during blackouts. Riley was glad she didn't have to light a fire before she could have her coffee.

She started the coffeemaker, then went to the window while she waited and smiled to see that it was a clear, bright day. Blue skies meant frigid temperatures in January, but she'd take it over gray gloom and snowstorms. She swept her gaze over the spectacular view of the grounds. She thought back to how excited they'd all been when her father purchased the hundred-acre estate after he retired. The hundred-year-old farmhouse was ideally situated to give sweeping views of the rolling land and the Rocky Mountains beyond. Before Conrad appeared with his news, she and Coop had been considering a move to Colorado Springs to be closer to the kids when they were at work, but in her heart, she couldn't leave the farm and the warmth of being surrounded by family.

She turned away from the window to get a mug just as Dashay padded into the kitchen in her slippers and bathrobe carrying Xav. He beamed when he saw Riley and said, "Mama!"

Riley took him from Dashay and was rewarded with a slobbery kiss. After wiping her mouth, she said, "Did he wake you? He was asleep when I came downstairs."

Dashay rubbed her eyes and yawned. "No, I've been awake for an hour. When I heard this little bundle of joy chattering to himself, I got up and brought him down so he wouldn't wake anyone else. Please tell me there's coffee."

Riley put Xav down and handed her a mug. "Fresh pot. Why were you having trouble sleeping? I thought you'd be lounging in bed with Conrad until noon."

Dashay poured herself some coffee and carried her mug to the table, then dropped into a chair and propped her feet on another. "You're kidding, right? After the bombshell he dropped last night, I hardly slept. How'd you do?"

Riley strapped Xav into his highchair and scooped a handful of dry cereal onto his tray. He gave her a toothy grin and stuffed a few pieces into his mouth. Riley sat next to Dashay and took a sip of coffee.

"Conrad told you about the reason for coming here? I wish he hadn't until I've given him my answer," she said.

Dashay's eyes widened as she watched Riley. "Don't you think I had a right to know since it concerns me, too? They may not want me on the council, but it's not all about you." She lowered her eyes and stared into her cup. "Sorry for snapping. Sleep deprivation."

Riley stopped stirring her coffee and stared at Dashay in confusion. "How does it concern you?"

"Conrad didn't tell you the Ministry wants me, too?" Riley shook her head. "He's going to hear from me when he gets up. Now I feel even worse for grousing at you. They want me on the nursing staff. I told him I'd only accept if they put me in your unit."

Riley brushed her comment off with a wave of her hand. "Don't blame Conrad. Did he tell you my first reaction was outright refusal?"

"He was stoic about your answer and refused to give me any hints. It didn't occur to me you wouldn't accept the job. Are you saying you're turning it down? Not to add any pressure, but I'm shocked you'd even consider saying no."

"Why, Dashay? Look at my life." She reached for Xav's hand to stop him from brushing all the cereal off his tray. "I'd have to leave this little dumpling, plus Jared and Emily. You know how I already feel about leaving the kids when I go to the hospital for my shifts. It's getting harder every time and having Julia missing makes it worse."

"I get all that but think of the difference you could make. Your country needs you, and sacrifices have to be made in times like these."

"Don't give me that patriotic spiel. You sound like Conrad. I still think of myself as an American. I haven't given up hope they'll dispose of Kearns soon and reunite our countries." She grew quiet for a moment as she stared into her cup. "I understand the necessity for this program and what I can contribute, so stop trying to convince me. I'm going to accept the position."

Dashay gave a whoop, and Xav jumped. "That's the fearless Riley I know and love."

"Not so much. I'm terrified of going back on the road. You remember what it was like last time. I'm shocked that you're in a hurry to get back out there."

Dashay got up to pour herself more coffee. With her back to Riley, she said, "I'd be lying if I said I wasn't concerned, but this isn't our trek to Colorado. Conrad said we'll be traveling with a military escort, and we'll have the provisions we need, so none of that nearly starving to death like last time. He's working on getting assigned to the escort unit." She turned to face Riley. "We won't have that psycho Yeager chasing us, and you won't be pregnant. Those two things alone will make all the difference. Don't forget you'll have me. I refuse to let anything happen to you."

"Knowing that makes all the difference. I wish Conrad had told me last night. It would have saved me some of the angst. I'll give it a shot but no promises that I'll do this long-term. Once Julia is home, that'll be the end for me."

"Makes sense, and I understand." A smile crept up Dashay's

face. "I can't wait to see Coop's look when he finds out he's losing both of us."

Riley smiled, trying to feel as excited and upbeat as Dashay. But she wasn't there yet. The assignment would be life-altering, and it would take time to adjust to the idea. In the meantime, she planned to spend every free second with her children, soaking up their warmth and optimism to replenish her stores. She'd need that to draw on when, once again, she left them in her wake.

———

Riley checked her room for the fourth time to verify she had everything she'd need before heading to Denver with Coop, Dashay, and Conrad. The three days since she accepted the job had flown by in a blur. In Denver, she and Dashay would negotiate and sign their contracts, then spend a month in orientation and training. After training, they'd have two weeks of leave before heading to their first assignment. Riley half-wished she could skip her leave to avoid suffering through saying goodbye to her children twice.

Coop was going along for the contract negotiation and to learn more of what Riley's new position would entail. Once that was completed, he was going back to the hospital, where Riley was sure everything had fallen apart in his absence, as it always did. She was glad he'd have plenty to keep himself busy so he wouldn't worry about her.

It would be harder on Jared and Emily. They'd taken the news that she was leaving like troopers, but she could tell they were struggling to hide their feelings. It hadn't been all that long ago that they had no idea if she was alive or would ever come home. This situation was different, and Conrad had told them they could communicate by radio, but her kids were smart enough to understand that the dangers Riley faced were real. She did her best to reassure them, but she was as concerned as they were.

As if reading her thoughts, Jared came in and hopped up onto the bed. "Emily made me come up here to tell you it's time to say goodbye. She's waiting for you downstairs. Mr. Goodwin will be here soon to take us to school. He's coming in his new wagon. He says it's pretty decked out for a wagon."

Jake Goodwin owned a farm near theirs and had three kids who went to school with Jared and Emily. Parents in the area had banded together to form what they named a Horse-pool. They took month-long turns getting their children to the local school. Riley was glad it was Jake's month.

Riley reached her hand out to Jared and held tightly onto his as they descended the stairs. Emily stood by the front door with her arms folded, quietly watching them. Riley felt more like she was preparing for a funeral than leaving for a new job. When they reached Emily, she wrapped Jared in her arms and held him as tightly as she could without crushing him.

When she finally loosened her hold, he stepped away, and she said, "It's only a month. You'll be so busy helping Nana and Aunt Lily with Xav that you'll hardly notice I'm gone. I'm counting on you to be my good little man."

Jared squared his shoulders and puffed out his chest, showing her how brave he was. When he said, "I will, Mom," Riley's mind raced back to the day she'd left for her trip to DC. Jared had only been six and was her little shadow. She'd never forget how he'd begged her not to go, saying, "You'll never come back." She had come home, but not for almost a year. Seeing his brave face made going easier.

Her voice cracked as she said, "I know. I love you, Jared. Go wait outside for Mr. Goodwin."

He gave her one last look, then held his head high as he marched through the doorway.

Emily rolled her eyes. "So much drama. He's acting like you're going off to sea for three years."

Riley brushed a curly red lock from her daughter's forehead.

"He's sensitive and anxious, like me. Not strong like you. You're so much like your father. Nothing ever fazed him. Julia's that way, too. Wish I had more of that."

Emily barked a laugh. "Julia? She was always such a lazy couch potato."

"Why do you think Coop gave her the nickname Warrior Princess? She lived up to that title and more. Sometimes we don't know what we're capable of until we're pushed to our limits."

"I won't believe that about Julia until she's home, and I see for myself, but I believe it of you, Mom. You're so much stronger than you know. You're going to do great, Red Queen."

Riley pulled Emily to her chest and held her as tightly as she had Jared. "I needed that, Princess Red," she said, using Coop's nickname for her. "When I remember the whiny, stubborn little Emily of two years ago, it's hard to believe you're the same girl. I'm incredibly proud of you, and I love you." She released Emily and was pleased to see tears in her eyes. "No more drama. I'll see you in a month."

Jared poked his head in through the doorway. "Mr. Goodwin's here, Emily. We've got to go."

Emily saluted him and grinned at Riley as she followed her brother outside. Riley closed the door behind them, then leaned against it, sobbing into her hands. Drama indeed, she thought when she regained her composure. She wiped her tears on her coat sleeve and lifted her backpack before squaring her shoulders like Jared.

Coop threw the front door open and stomped the snow off his boots before stepping inside. "You coming, Babe? Jared and Emily are off to school. The wagon's loaded, the horses are saddled, and Conrad's getting impatient. No more stalling. It looks like snow. I want to get as far as we can before it lets loose."

Riley did her best to hide her red eyes as she pulled the beanie her mother had crocheted over her own red curls. "I'm trying to be ready, but what I'm actually doing is asking myself what the hell I was thinking taking this on. Saying goodbye to the kids was brutal. It felt too much like when I left to go to DC before the CME hit. That was supposed to be a week. It turned into ten months of hell."

"I was there, remember? This is just nervous anticipation," he said. "Trust me, you'll be fine once we're on the road."

She stepped toward the door, doubting very much that he was right. She stopped when she heard squeals of delight coming from Xav in the living room. She and Coop hurried to him and found Dashay blowing raspberries on his little round belly. When Dashay stopped, he pointed at his stomach for her to do it again.

Riley caught Coop's eye and said, "This is the prescription I needed. Gloom forgotten."

Dashay climbed to her feet and turned toward Coop as she grabbed her coat. "Who's gloomy?"

Coop tipped his head toward Riley. "Cold feet," he said as he picked up Xav.

Dashay gave a dismissive wave. "We're only going on a little adventure. We'll be back before you can take a breath."

Riley raised an eyebrow. "That's a bit of a stretch, but I'm good to go. It was just a momentary bout of second-guessing what I'm about to do. You ready?"

"I need one more slobbery kiss from Xav before we head out. Where's your mom?"

"Here," Marjory called as she came in from the hallway.

"Nana," Xav said and reached for his grandmother.

Coop blew a raspberry on Xav's cheek before handing him to Marjory. Dashay gave him a quick peck and rustled his hair before following Coop onto the porch. Marjory waited until they were outside before walking Riley to the door. Riley hugged her son one last time, glad to know he was too young to understand what was happening.

She stopped and turned to Marjory before stepping onto the porch. "Is Lily already at the stables?"

"Yes, she and Kevin were gone before I came down for breakfast."

"We said our goodbyes last night, but please give her another hug and kiss for me." Marjory nodded, with tears glistening in her eyes. Riley was glad of the distraction when Xav reached for the string dangling from the hood on her coat and tried to stuff it in his mouth. "Thanks for tending this little whirlwind while I'm gone. It's such a comfort knowing he's in your capable hands. I couldn't leave otherwise. I hope we're not taking advantage."

Marjory patted Riley's cheek. "We've been through this, dear. Getting to spend time with Xav is a gift, and you know how much I love my time with him. Your sister, Lily, is here to help when she's not in the stables with Kevin, and Miles loves playing with his cousin. It often feels like mere moments pass before Jared and Emily come bursting through the door after school. My days pass in a blur, and it helps me not miss your father so much. What more could I want?" Riley thought of all the things she wanted, such as holding Julia in her arms again and not abandoning her other three, but she remained quiet. "I told you this when I started caring for the kids during your shifts at the hospital," Marjory continued. "Why would my feelings change?"

Riley studied her for a moment as she considered her answer. "This is different. I'll be gone for who knows how long. You'll let Coop know if it gets to be too much?"

Xav squirmed in Marjorie's arms, so she put him down, and the two women watched him scamper off to pick up a toy truck.

Marjory put her hand on Riley's arm. "It won't be too much with Lily and Kevin's help, and your father and I managed Jared and Emily with no trouble before you made it home. So, stop worrying and get on your way."

Riley glanced at her mother's hand resting on her arm. "This reminds me of when I was leaving for the medical conference, pre-CME. Remember how afraid I was? I can't recall why now. If

I'd known what was ahead of me..." She stared at the floor as her words trailed off.

Coop stuck his head in the doorway and said, "What's the holdup? Dashay's getting antsy."

"Coming," Riley said and kissed Marjory one last time. "Love you, Mom. See you in a month."

CHAPTER THREE

RILEY PACED in the small waiting area outside the Minister of Health's office. Coop was slumped in a chair with his legs stretched out and his head resting against the wall behind him.

He opened one eye and said, "How can you possibly have enough energy to pace? After that grueling four-day horse ride to get here, I can barely stand."

Riley glanced at him but kept moving. "You know me when I'm anxious. Doesn't matter how exhausted I am."

He drew his feet under the chair and sat forward, rubbing his thighs. "Which leads me to my next question. Why are you so nervous? You already have the job. They're just giving you the details."

Riley ignored his question and said, "What's wrong with your legs?"

"Only sore muscles. I'll never get used to riding a horse. I think I'll retire from surgery and become a mechanical engineer and figure out how to get cars working again. Answer my question."

She dropped into the chair next to him with a sigh. "I'm afraid of the reaction when I tell them I've decided not to take the job."

"Hilarious. You should retire from surgery and become a comedian." When she glared at him, he said, "I listened to you grumbling all the way to Denver. Enough. You accepted the position. You're going through with this."

She let out her breath and stared at the worn pattern in the carpeting beyond the toes of her boots. "What if I can't do the job? What if I don't live up to their expectations?"

"You heard Conrad. He says you're the most qualified person they have. What's with the doubts? You're never this way about your work. You were a rockstar field surgeon."

Before she could answer, the door to the Minister's office opened, and a doctor she recognized from her old life stepped into the waiting area. All the anxiety flowed out of her as she approached Dr. Marcus Ingram to shake his hand. Riley calculated he was in his early sixties, but he looked fit and at least a decade younger than his years.

"It's so good to see you, Dr. Ingram. I don't know if you remember me, but I worked with you for a short time after my residency."

He wrapped her hand in both of his and gave her a warm smile. "Of course, I remember you, Dr. Poole. I'm the reason you're here. When I saw your name on the list of potentials, I told the Minister he had to do whatever it took to get you here. Conrad Elliot tells me it took some doing to convince you."

Coop stood and extended his hand. "I'm Dr. Cooper. Riley's husband."

Dr. Ingram chuckled as he shook Coop's hand. "You need no introduction, Dr. Cooper. It's an honor to meet you. I'm pleased you came with your wife. It's important to have spouses on board with the program, especially one as renowned as you." He gestured behind him toward the office. "Let's go in. The Minister is waiting."

Minister Rosa Alvarez stood as they entered her office. She looked to be in her early forties and not much taller than Riley's five feet, but she had a presence that made it clear she was in charge. Riley admired her composed but welcoming bearing and wondered if it was something she could learn to master. The Minister shook their hands, then gestured to the row of chairs in front of her desk. She waited until they were seated before lowering herself into her own chair.

"I have to say it's a thrill to have two such illustrious doctors in my office," Minister Alvarez said.

Riley glanced at Coop with wide eyes before turning back to the Minister. "Coop's the only illustrious one here," she said. "You must have me confused with someone else, Madam Minister."

Minister Alvarez smiled. "Not according to Dr. Adrian Landry, and no need to be so formal here. Please, call me Rosa. If this were life before the CME, I'd just be another doctor among thousands in the region, and you never would have heard of me."

"The same is true of me. I'm Riley. How do you know Adrian Landry?"

"His appointment as Director of Science and Technology fell under my purview. Before he resigned and left for Fort Worth, we often discussed ways to produce new medications from viable natural alternatives. We became friends over time, and I tried my best to discourage him from leaving, but his family wasn't happy in Denver. During that time, Adrian told me the story of your journey from Washington to Colorado in vivid detail."

"I believe that," Coop said with a laugh. "If there's one thing Adrian is never short of, it's details."

Rosa smiled. "He reveres you as a hero, Riley, but says you'd get mad at him for saying that."

Riley sighed and shook her head. "He exaggerates."

"No, he doesn't," Coop said quietly. "What Riley accomplished is nothing short of miraculous. You couldn't have made a better choice than in selecting her for this post."

"I agree," Dr. Ingram said. "And since we're informal here, I'm Marcus to you. I haven't told you yet that I'm the director of the

Health and Wellness Battalion Initiative. I chair the council. You'll be answering directly to me. You must have questions about what the position entails."

"Hours' worth," Riley said, relieved that they'd moved on from the ridiculous hero worship to the reason they were there. "Please, just start with the basics."

For the following hour, Marcus outlined Riley's duties and responsibilities in detail that even Adrian would have approved. The more Riley heard, the more impressed she was and forgot her early reluctance and misgivings. When Marcus finished his presentation, he stood, and the others joined him.

"Starting at 0800 tomorrow, you'll have a series of meetings with the other members of the council, but we want you in the field for training as soon as it can be arranged. People are suffering and dying out there in the bush. We can't afford to wait."

Riley held her hand out to him. "I'm ready to do whatever you need. You've accomplished an admirable feat creating this initiative. I'll do my utmost to make sure it succeeds, Marcus."

He ignored her hand and hugged her. "Of that, I have no doubt."

———

Riley stifled a groan as she rolled onto her side in her cot. The two weeks she'd spent field training had taught her she'd grown soft in the time since arriving home from her grueling cross-country trek. She thought of countless nights sleeping on the ground, too exhausted to notice the rocks and roots beneath her. It's time to step up my workout regimen, she thought as she stared out into the darkness beyond the tent window.

"You awake?" Dashay whispered from her cot on the opposite side of the tent.

"Unfortunately," Riley said. "Did I wake you?"

Dashay's cot creaked as she turned to face Riley. "No, the

cold did. I'm grateful for the insulated sleeping bags and solar heaters they scrounged up for us, but it's not enough. I ask again why anyone in their right mind would live in this frozen hell?"

Riley climbed out of her sleeping bag and slipped her feet into her tent slippers before retrieving the extra blanket to cover Dashay. "You're just cold-blooded. Do I need to check your circulation?"

Dashay pulled the blanket up under her chin and scooted deeper into her bag. "Thanks. There's nothing wrong with my circulation. It's this damned cold that drags on for days and weeks on end."

Riley got back into her bag and pulled the drawstring to tighten it around her face. "Even I have to admit the cold is lasting longer than usual. Something else to blame on the CME. I'm sure Adrian would have an hour-long discourse to explain it. The cold streak should break soon despite the change in weather patterns. It can't go on forever."

"I'll have to take your word on that. If it's not the cold, why are you awake?"

Riley rolled onto her back and rested her arm over her eyes. "It's the combination of this hard-as-a-rock cot, missing my family, and worrying about Julia. I believe in this program and the work we'll be doing, but it's going to be killer being separated from them, always wondering if they're safe and what they're doing."

"Conrad said he'd have radio communications set up soon. It's not perfect but better than nothing." Dashay was quiet for a moment before adding, "I've been thinking about our Warrior Princess more since we've been out here, too, but I have faith in Conrad. Despite his added security duties, he told me he keeps up with the intel on Julia. I bet we'll hear something any day."

"I've been telling myself that for almost two years, but I'm doing my best to not let go of hope. I wish they'd take out

Kearns, put an end to this war, and piece the country back together. Then I'll just walk in and take my daughter back."

"As Coop says, from your mouth to God's ears. As he also says, try deep breathing to clear your mind. We have to be up in three hours, and we've got a backbreaking schedule tomorrow. You need rest."

"Good. Wearing myself out helps me sleep better than anything else, and it makes the time speed by."

"Speaking of time, keep reminding yourself we're over halfway through the training. In less than two weeks, we'll be on the way home for two weeks of leave before heading to our first assignment."

"That helps. Thanks."

Dashay shifted in her cot and mumbled goodnight. Riley heard her deep, even breathing a few minutes later. She took her friend's advice and tried deep breathing to join her in sleep, but the effort failed. She turned back onto her side and pounded on her lumpy pillow. The only hope she had of peace was the assurance that her family was safe.

———

Julia crouched behind a dumpster in the darkness, straining to hear what the two guards on the opposite side of the street were saying. They were talking about the transfer to a new camp that Julia and her family were facing the following morning. The men said that President Kearns had ordered their internment camp to be closed and all the residents released or transferred to different cities. Residents, Julia thought, scoffing at the use of the glorified word for prisoners, which was what she and her family were.

There was no hope of her family being released since Kearns knew they were related to her mom. Dr. Riley Poole was still on the USA's Most Wanted list. The fact that none of Julia's family had spoken with Riley for almost two years made no difference. It was a case of guilt by association.

All Julia knew was that they were sending her family somewhere southeast of their current camp in Lincoln, Nebraska. It would be their fourth move in eighteen months, each one moving them farther from Colorado Springs. Even worse, they hadn't just transferred them from place to place. The US contingent in charge of the internment camps had split up Julia's group that set out from Uncle Mitch's ranch in Virginia. From the original fifty, only seven were left in her group. She was grateful she'd been able to stay with Uncle Mitch, Aunt Beth, and her cousin Holly's family, but she had no clue where the rest had been sent. Julia's heart broke at the thought that they were probably lost to her forever.

She turned her focus back to the guards. The taller one said camps were being merged and would soon only hold residents considered a threat to the greater society. The rest of the US citizens were being left to rebuild their cities and towns, unsupervised but with government help. He said Kearns was eager for her citizens to transition back to a more stable, everyday life. The other guard laughed at that and said it was more like Kearns couldn't spare the labor force and resources to keep the camps open with the war still raging. She'd rather send people off to fend for themselves.

Julia agreed. Kearns couldn't care less about the welfare of her citizens. She just wanted all the power. Uncle Mitch had heard rumors that communities were rising up to fight against Kearns' oppressive government in the East. They all hoped the rumors were true because that would weaken Kearns and force her to fight a war on two fronts.

The taller guard motioned for the other to keep his voice down. "You know what happens to people caught criticizing our Commander in Chief. Do it again, and I'll have to report you."

The shorter one glanced around to make sure no one was

listening. A knot tightened in Julia's gut. She hated to think what would happen to her if they caught her out after curfew, eavesdropping on their conversation. She leaned closer to the dumpster and tried not to breathe too loudly, but the guard just shrugged and changed the topic to news from the front lines of the war. Julia wasn't interested in that, and she'd completed her mission, so she inched around the dumpster and made a dash for her apartment complex in the shadows.

She heard what sounded like footsteps behind her when she was a hundred yards from her apartment building, so she stopped and checked the area but saw nothing. Not wanting to waste more time and risk getting caught, she sprinted as fast as her legs would carry her until she reached the entrance to her building. She ran inside and leaned against the closed door to catch her breath before heading upstairs to her floor.

Holly glanced up from packing her duffle bag when Julia rushed into the room. "Where have you been? You know you're not supposed to be out after curfew. I was about to go tell Dad to look for you."

Julia hated to lie to her cousin, so she ignored the question and started shoving her few meager belongings into her own bag. The truth would bring on a lecture, and Julia wasn't in the mood. "Did you wear my pink hoodie?" she asked, trying to keep her voice casual. "I haven't seen it for a week."

Holly reached behind her bag and held up the hoodie for Julia to see. "I'll give you the hoodie when you tell me where you were. As if I don't already know."

"If you know, why are you asking?" When Holly scowled at her, Julia dropped onto her bed with a sigh. "Fine. I was hiding letters to my mom with the wagon caravans heading west. Since our jailers are moving us south and farther away from Colorado Springs, I wanted to get letters out with people heading closer to home. I know what you're going to say, so don't bother."

Holly handed the hoodie to Julia and put an arm around her

shoulder. "I won't scold you. I already told you I'm on board with trying to get word to Aunt Riley and Coop. If I was separated from my mom, I'd do whatever it took to let her know where I was. I'm sorry to say this, but I don't think there's much chance of it working after all this time. If your family knew where you were and could rescue you, they would have done it by now. I want to be wrong, but you have to admit I'm right."

"Don't you think I've thought all of that a thousand times, but what's the harm in trying? It's still possible that someone will get one of my letters and sneak it over the border. We've both heard the rumors of people crossing back and forth into the WSA. I won't give up. Besides, what do I have to lose?"

Holly gave her a weak smile. "Not much, but I still don't like you going out alone after dark. Who knows what they'd do to you if you got caught?"

"I'm sorry, Holly. I didn't mean to scare you. I heard two guards talking on my way back and hoped they'd say where we're going. Southeast could mean a thousand different places."

"If you hadn't been out risking your neck, you'd have been here when my dad came in and said he heard they're sending us to a camp near Oklahoma City. It's supposed to be bigger and better equipped than this one, so that's something."

Julia propped her elbows on her knees and rested her chin on her hands. "Oklahoma City? That feels like a long way from home. I should have paid better attention in geography class."

"Dad says it is, but it's closer to the WSA at the Texas border, not that it matters much to us. It might as well be 10,000 miles away."

Julia glanced up at her. "It could mean having access to more people crossing over the border. I'll need more letters."

————

It had taken Coop nearly an hour and seven readings of Xav's favorite book to get him down to sleep, but Coop didn't mind spending the extra time with his son. His responsibilities at the hospital the previous month had kept him away far more than he liked, so he had to take advantage of any time he could get with his family. With Riley away on her first field assignment, Coop felt the pressure even more to fill the void of her absence. He'd been the one to push her to take the job. He had an obligation to shoulder the added weight. It had taken shameless groveling and bargaining to eke out just four full days at home, but it had been worth it.

He gave Xav's cheek a hint of a kiss so he wouldn't wake him, then ran his hand through his hair as he left the bedroom. Picking up the slack was the lesser of his concerns. Worry over Riley's safety was always foremost in his mind. The Health Ministry had gone to great lengths to protect the field units, but life was incredibly unpredictable in the post CME world. With the war, erratic weather, and disease a constant challenge, it was impossible to guarantee Riley's safety or Dashay's. Their training had been thorough, and he trusted Riley's grit and instincts, but more than once, he'd regretted pushing her to go. He'd rest much easier once the Ministry had radio communications working.

Coop was surprised by the lack of the usual household chaos as he made his way downstairs. It was only a quarter to eight, but all he heard was a soft murmur of voices coming from the family room at the back of the house. He'd normally be shushing Jared and Emily to keep them from waking Xav. He made his way to the family room but only found Lily on the floor, reading to Miles. Lily stopped and looked up when Coop walked in and dropped onto the sofa. Miles wriggled off of Lily's lap and climbed up next to his uncle. Coop scooped him up and nuzzled his neck with his beard.

Miles let out a laugh and said, "Again."

"Don't wind him up, or I'll never get him to sleep," Lily said.

"I was just about to take him upstairs. Finally got your little scamp down?"

Coop gave Miles another nuzzle, then said, "It's taking longer every night. I don't know how you and Riley get him down so quickly."

Lily got up and reached for a reluctant Miles. "We don't give in to his demands. Let him know who's boss."

Coop handed Miles to Lily and got to his feet. "We all know who that is. Where is everyone? It's too quiet."

"Mom went to her room after finishing the dinner dishes, and Kevin went upstairs thirty minutes ago. He's got an early start tomorrow to go into town for feed. Emily and Jared aren't in the kitchen?"

Coop felt a twinge of panic, then silently chastised himself. *When did I turn into Riley the Worrier?* he asked himself as he followed Lily into the hallway. The kids knew better than to do anything risky. "Probably in their rooms," he said, sounding less convinced than he'd meant to.

Lily glanced at him and said, "Probably. Might want to check."

Coop bounded up the stairs and checked both rooms, but they were empty. When Lily came up behind him carrying Miles, he said, "How long since you've seen them?"

Before she could answer, the front door banged open. Emily rushed in and yelled, "Dad, come quick. Come see this."

Coop raced down the stairs and ran after Emily into the darkness with Jared on their tail. She flicked her flashlight on and pointed it at a group of ten people huddled twenty yards from the front steps. Coop felt that pang of panic twist in his gut.

"What is this, Emily?" he whispered through his teeth. "Why were you out here? Who are these people?"

A tall man at the front lifted his arm over his eyes against the flashlight beam and said, "Don't scold her, Coop. It's me, Russell Dunne. I'm Mitch's son. Jesse's here, too, and some of the family."

"Julia?" Coop whispered. Russell shook his head as he lowered his arms. Coop stepped forward and threw his arms around Russell. "That's all right, brother." He moved away and studied the group of haggard souls. "You can tell us your story but come inside first. Get warm and have something to eat." Then, turning to Emily, he said, "Wake Nana and tell Lily what's happening. Jared, help me get them into the house."

Russell put his arm around Emily's shoulder for support and went with her into the house.

Jesse wiped at his eyes and patted Coop's shoulder as he passed him. "You can't know what it means to have made it here and find you all alive." Coop caught his eye and nodded. "I'm almost afraid to ask this, but tell me, where's Riley?"

Coop gave him a half-grin. "Alive and well, but not home at the moment. I'll explain everything. Now, get yourself inside."

Jesse nodded and herded his family into the house.

———

Coop looked on while Marjory fed the starving newcomers. Russell had arrived with his wife, April, and their three kids: Mitch, Zeke, and Renee. Jesse had his wife, Sabrina, their twin girls, Drew and Dana, and Sabrina's mom, Gayle, with him. Coop was trying to resist doing the math in his head to figure out how they would feed and shelter all of them. When Julia and the six she was with made it home, they'd be bursting at the seams. He glanced at Kevin and read in his eyes that he was making the same calculations. Coop knew they'd do whatever it took to care for their ballooning family, but it would put a strain on their already limited resources. Their arrival made it even more crucial to make the horse business succeed.

When they'd all consumed as much food as their shrunken bellies could hold an hour later, they moved into the living room. Kevin stoked the fire while the rest got comfortable.

Russell patted his belly and said, "We haven't eaten a meal like that in longer than I can remember, Aunt Marjory. I honestly don't think we would have survived another minute without food. You remember how it is, Coop."

Coop nodded as his thoughts raced back to a time two years earlier. He'd traveled through chest-high snow for weeks with little food searching for Riley. He'd never known genuine hunger before that time, but he and hunger had become good pals since. He marveled again at how fortunate he and Riley had been to survive their cross-country ordeal. He studied Russell's emaciated face and scarecrow limbs for a moment. He hardly resembled the fit, broad-shouldered man Coop remembered.

Russell caught him staring, so he winked and smiled to break the tension. "I'm just glad you heeded my warning not to eat too quickly."

Coop gave a hurried update on events since their last ham radio communication two years earlier. They were thrilled with the news about Xav and were excited to meet him in the morning. They had endless questions about Riley's work and were devastated to learn that there was no news of Julia and the others. Coop told them about Conrad's search for the rest of the family and assured them if anyone could find them, he could.

When he finished, he said, "Now, it's your turn to regale us with your adventures."

"Yes," Marjory said, "and don't hold back on the details."

Jesse was seated next to her on the couch with his arm around her. "We won't, Aunt Marjory. It's no worse than what you've all endured."

Russell leaned forward and rested his elbows on his knees. "A contingent of Kearns' forces captured us just before we reached Memphis. It's a miracle they didn't catch us sooner. It's hard to be inconspicuous with a group of fifty people and livestock. They took us into the city and put us in our first internment camp. That was where we first saw the Wanted Posters for you and Riley. That shook Julia, but she turned it around to her advantage.

She started tearing down the posters wherever she found them and using them to write letters to you and Riley, alerting you to our location. She'd stow the letters with people traveling in and out of the camp. None held much hope of it doing any good, but it gave her a mission to keep her hope alive. She's a remarkable young woman, our Warrior Princess."

Emily eyed her suspiciously. "I still can't picture her being so brave. She was such a lazy lump before the CME."

April smiled at Emily. "And I can't picture her that way. It sounds more like a description of Holly. Julia's survival skills were invaluable, and she always did what she could to keep our spirits up. The younger kids all looked up to her."

"That's surprises me, too, Emily," Lily said, "but you aren't exactly like you were before the CME, either."

Marjory chuckled. "Agreed."

"How'd the group get separated?" Kevin asked, steering the conversation back on track.

Jesse stood and moved to the fireplace. While holding his hands over the flames, he said, "They moved us a few times but kept us together until a Colonel Yeager came into camp and blabbed that we're related to Riley. I don't know how he found out Julia is her daughter, but they rounded up Mom and Dad, Kathryn's family, and Julia and took them to a different camp. That was the last we saw them. They split the rest of us up several months later, but that was just to keep our group more manageable. Fortunately, the ten of us were allowed to stay together."

"Yeager," Coop hissed. "We've had our own fun with him. How did you get free and cross the border in the middle of the war?"

Sabrina joined Jesse at the fire. She closed her eyes at the feel of the heat on her back. "This is delicious. I never thought I'd be warm again." After a few moments, she said, "Escaping was the easy part. As the war dragged on, discipline broke down in the camp, and the guards became lax. Finally, we made a plan and just walked out of camp one day. We were in western Nebraska, so all we had to do was find a way into the WSA through Wyoming. The hard part was evading the soldiers and finding food. Everything in the US is firmly in the grip of President Kearns."

"We saw signs the tide is turning," Russell said. "With the military spread so thin because of the war, Kearns is losing her iron grip. Cross-continent travel and communications are major issues, and as always, lack of resources. I don't know what it's like out east, but the little we saw before we crossed the border gave us reason to hope."

"There isn't much fighting in the North, so we crossed the border there with the help of some WSA sympathizers we met," Jessie said. "They got us over but left us to our own devices on the other side. We were afraid of getting caught and sent back at first, so we kept to ourselves as much as possible. It didn't take long to figure out how different conditions are here."

"How much better," April said. "It renewed my hope in humanity to see how willing people were to share what little they have."

Gayle's eyes glistened as she said, "But we made it. I have to keep pinching myself to make sure it isn't a dream."

Marjory got up and took Gayle's hand. "It's real. Your family is welcome to all we have."

Coop saw that Drew had curled up on the carpet and fallen asleep. "It's late, and you're exhausted. Let's go up and figure out sleeping arrangements. I'll give you all physicals in the morning, then you can take a few days to rest before we get you signed up with the local registry." He stopped and took a few breaths to control his emotions. If Russell's group had escaped and crossed the border, it meant Julia could, too. "Your showing up renews my hope. Riley's going to lose it when she hears the news. Whenever that is."

———

Riley was stalling to avoid giving her patient the grim news that his hand had to come off. He'd waited too long to seek treatment for his frostbite.

Mr. Wallace grimaced from the pain as he said, "What's the verdict, Doc?"

As she continued studying the gray skin, she said, "I'm afraid I need to amputate your hand. The tissue is what we call necrotic. That means it's dead and has to be removed before you lose your entire arm." She looked up and motioned for the nurse to lay him back on the table. His face was ghostly pale, and his breathing shallow from the shock. "Do you understand what I'm saying, Mr. Wallace?"

"Yes, I understand," he gasped, "but you can't cut off my hand. I'm a cattle rancher, and I can't work with one hand. I have five kids. The oldest is thirteen, and my wife passed when the CME hit. There's got to be something else you can do."

Riley walked to the other side of the table and clasped his good hand. "If I don't amputate, you'll lose your arm at the least, and you could die at worst. What would become of your family if they lost you? I would not consider amputation if the situation weren't so critical. But we have to act now."

Mr. Wallace turned his face to the wall and whispered. "Just do it. We'll figure out the rest later, like always."

Riley signaled for the nurse to go schedule the OR before turning back to Mr. Wallace. "You've made the right decision. The surgical nurse will be in to prep you for surgery."

She hurried out before he could respond. He was her fourth frostbite patient that day but by far the worst. Fortunately, she'd been able to debride the dead tissue on the other patients and save their limbs. Mr. Wallace wasn't so lucky.

He was like so many of the patients she'd treated since getting out in the field, desperate, doing whatever it took to hang on. Her work was rewarding and necessary but shifts like the one she'd had that day could be heartbreaking or downright devastating.

She closed her mind to such doom-laden thoughts and went to wash up for the procedure. The surgery would fill up the rest of her shift, and soon she'd be on her way back to camp for a good night's sleep, but Mr. Wallace's life would never be the same. She had no right to pity herself for having to cope with difficult situations. Her life could be enormously worse.

————

Riley yanked her hood down closer around her face as she made her way from the hospital to her unit's encampment on the outskirts of Santa Fe, New Mexico. She'd forgotten her sunglasses in the tent that morning, and the gusting wind burned her eyes.

The fact that it was early April meant nothing. The snows had melted, but high temperatures during the day were still below freezing. The biting wind made it feel ten degrees colder than that. A large percentage of the residents in the area were ranchers or farmers. They couldn't just stay inside during the day, cozying up to the fire. The demands of their work were there, no matter the weather. Many were also running out of wood and coal to heat their homes. If the weather didn't improve soon, she'd have more corpses than patients.

Riley wondered if people back home were dealing with the same shortages. She hadn't had time to ask about conditions in the community during her weekly conversation with Coop and the rest of the family on her radio call home the previous day. Time had been limited, and they'd had more important things to discuss. Her scheduled time slot on the radio had just happened to fall on Emily's birthday. Another one spent apart, Riley thought as she trudged back to camp.

Emily had sounded cheerful and went on about how ecstatic she was to have her cousins with them. The news of Russell's and Jesse's families appearing out of nowhere had been so astounding that Riley was speechless for a full thirty seconds. When Coop asked for the third time if Riley was still there, Dashay took the radio from her and assured him that she was fine. Once Riley recovered from the shock, she spoke with each family member for a few moments. Her favorite conversation was with Xav, who was more interested in pushing buttons than talking to her. She didn't mind because she got to hear the babble of his sweet voice, and that was enough for her. She'd struggled to say goodbye to Coop when their time was over until Dashay reminded her they'd talk again in seven days. Now with six days to go, it felt like an eternity.

Dashay was stretched out on her cot in the tent they shared by the time Riley made it back to camp. She sat up and rubbed her neck as she watched Riley holding her hands out to their small heater.

With her back to Dashay, Riley said, "Don't sit up on my account. You looked so relaxed when I came in."

"I was lying here, trying to remember the feel of that scorching sun when we made the trek from hell across the plains," Dashay said. "I wanted nothing more than to feel a cool breeze on my face back then. Now I'd trade anything for that kind of warmth on my perpetually frozen body."

Riley huffed as she lowered herself to her cot. "You know I prefer the cold, but I'm with you on that. Did winter drag on this long last year?"

"Probably, and the summer was cooler than our first one in Colorado. I never thought I'd miss Virginia humidity. Think this proves what environmentalists had been saying for years about humans causing global warming? The CME wiped out the industrial age. Maybe this is Earth's way of doing a reset."

"Adrian probably has an opinion on that, but scientists might never know for sure. It could be the result of the CME changing the atmosphere, or maybe it's both. I'm less concerned about that cause than the result." She unzipped her coat and stripped off her two layers of sweaters before glancing up at Dashay. "I had four frostbite patients today. Had to amputate the hand on one, a man with five kids whose wife died after the CME. He's going to have a tough go of it, not including the pain. We ran out of morphine today. I prescribed Tramadol and ibuprofen. It won't be enough. None of it will be enough."

Dashay nodded. "I heard. Drake sent word to the welfare council to see what help they can give the Wallace family. He's also pressuring Supply to work harder at scoring us more pain meds. If there are any more in existence around here."

Drake Casco was the unit liaison with leadership in communities they interacted with. He was a small, wiry man with the will to move mountains.

"Good," Riley said. "If anyone can make it happen, it's Drake. I wish I had a fraction of his fierce determination and energy."

"Are you kidding me? If Drake had red hair instead of black, he'd be your doppelgänger. You always sell yourself short."

Riley frowned at her. "He pulled strings to get his husband posted to the unit. They wouldn't have let my family come no matter how fierce I am, and I'm married to Dr. Cooper."

"I hope that was a pathetic attempt at humor. Drake's husband was an Army medic, and you can't compare his one family member to your family of five. Would you honestly want Xav or Jared out here? And your husband can't drop running an entire hospital to follow you around like a puppy."

"I can fantasize, can't I? I'm just hungry, homesick, and concerned about Mr. Wallace and his family. Pain meds aren't the only thing he'll need. The odds of finding a prosthetic hand are next to nil. I hope Drake can dig that out of his bag of tricks."

"We should have been home two weeks ago. Seems our faithful leaders aren't honoring any of the terms of our contracts."

Despite Marcus Ingram's assurances that her assignments wouldn't take her far from home, she hadn't spent a single night within 200 miles of Colorado Springs in the two months since she left. Most nights had been farther away than that.

"You were naïve enough to think they would?" Dashay asked, then gestured to an aluminum plate covered with a cloth on the folding table in the corner. "I had Cook save your dinner. It's cold by now."

Riley groaned with fatigue as she got up to eat her stale meal. "I only care that it's edible."

"It's almost that."

Riley sat on a folding camp chair and pulled the napkin off her plate. She jabbed her fork into the reconstituted slab that posed as meat and reluctantly lifted it to her mouth. Before taking a bite, she said, "No Conrad tonight?"

Dashay dropped back down to her pillow and draped an arm over her eyes. "No, he left this morning on some secret mission for a few days, so I'm all yours."

Riley heard the disappointment in Dashay's voice, but she was secretly thrilled. Though she and Dashay were assigned to share a tent, she spent most nights with Conrad, who served as chief of security for their unit. Riley occasionally enjoyed the peace of having the tent to herself on nights when Dashay was away, but more often, she dreaded the solitude. After lights out, she'd lie in the darkness, unable to sleep, wishing she was with Coop. When Dashay was there, they'd talk for an hour after lights out until they were both too exhausted to keep their eyes open. Just knowing Dashay was on the other cot was reassuring.

After taking a swig of filtered water, she said, "Does Conrad ever tell you where he's going or what he's doing?"

"It's usually hush-hush, but he might be allowed to spill about this mission when he gets back. My curiosity is definitely piqued."

"Do you ever worry about him being in danger?"

Dashay turned her head to face her. "Never. I trust he knows his stuff. He says he spends most of his time issuing orders. Not sure if I believe that part, but he's kept his head attached this long."

"True. I'll never forget that we probably wouldn't have made it home without him." She became quiet for a moment as she ate, thinking of the first time she saw Conrad on a dark road in the middle of nowhere. She'd been convinced that night he was the enemy. She was never more relieved to have been wrong. "It would be exciting to know what he's up to, though. He'll have stories to tell his grandkids someday."

Dashay closed her eyes. "I can't picture Conrad sitting by the fire with a pack of grandkids at his feet. Not sure he's the type to settle down that way."

Riley let the comment drop. Dashay had told her more than once that she hoped for a husband and kids someday, but that Conrad wouldn't be the one. Riley couldn't imagine getting as close to someone as Dashay was to Conrad if it weren't for the long haul. Her thoughts turned to Coop, safe and sound at home with the family, grateful he was in it for the duration.

"I'm glad Coop's not running off on secret missions. It's bad enough worrying about myself without adding him to the mix. The family sounded so great yesterday, didn't they?"

Dashay flashed her trademark brilliant smile. "Did my heart good to talk to them, especially Xav. That's crazy about your cousins showing up at the farm out of nowhere. It buoys my hope for WP and the rest making it home."

Riley pushed her empty plate aside and moved to the cot to unlace her boots. "It's incredible. I can't wait to tell Conrad. He'll probably grill them for details. Even though my cousins haven't seen Julia for more than a year, they can give him intel on procedures in the camps and conditions across the border. Every crumb of information leads them closer to finding her."

"Conrad's obsessed with bringing Julia home, like a bloodhound on the scent. He won't give up on our girl."

"Thanks for reminding me. Sometimes I get locked into the idea that I'm the only one who remembers that Julia is gone. I forget the rest of you want her home as much as I do."

"You shouldn't. When will you get it through that rock-hard

skull that you aren't alone? We're all working with you to bring her home."

Riley gave her a weak smile. "My heart knows that, but I've been spending an unhealthy amount of time in my head lately." She sank into her pillow. "I'm wiped, and I have an early surgery. Mind turning off the lantern?"

She watched Dashay extinguish the light, hoping she'd be able to turn off her brain as easily.

CHAPTER FOUR

COLONEL ORSON YEAGER ducked into the shadows, waiting for the patrol to pass along the Texas-Oklahoma border. In his nearly two years of crossing back and forth over the border, he'd mapped the spots with least surveillance, traversing between the countries with confidence. It was just too much territory for military units to cover. So far, neither side had made efforts to alter surveillance patterns or roadblocks. Sometimes, Yeager felt like he was on a Sunday stroll when crossing the border, but he knew better than to get complacent.

It didn't hurt that his current location had some of the lightest fighting in the civil war. He'd procured uniforms for both sides and changed as needed to pass through the contested areas virtually undetected. When he did happen to cross paths with guards on the US side, he was rarely questioned. They couldn't imagine why anyone would want to sneak into their country.

He'd procrastinated reentering the US for several weeks to avoid reporting to President Kearns. She'd ordered him to stop making unsanctioned trips into the WSA, but he was consumed with finding Daybreak, so he'd ignored her direct orders repeatedly. With cross-continent communications a constant challenge and the military power structure in disarray, it took time for word of his whereabouts to reach the US capitol in Philadelphia. He could complete multiple trips into foreign territory before she was even aware he was gone.

He was required to make regular contact with her even though Kearns had removed him as head of the task force charged with capturing that insane physicist codenamed Daybreak. His new mission was to command a unit conducting routine recon missions along the border area. Since the dismissal, he'd lost interest in staying on her good side. The dismissal had come after Kearns received field reports stating his cover was compromised and that he was obsessed with the Daybreak mission. He'd argued that the reports were exaggerated or outright fabricated by underlings vying for his position. She'd refused to listen to him. No one had more insight into Dr. Adrian Landry than he did. He was determined to complete his mission and prove to Kearns he was still the man for the job. He just needed her to get out of his way.

When the sun slid below the horizon, Yeager made his way to the border fence in a crouching run. The WSA patrol was nowhere in sight by the time he reached the other side. He passed back into his native country and arrived at the first checkpoint thirty minutes later. As usual, there was a new unit of guards stationed at the checkpoint, none of whom recognized him, especially disguised in civilian clothes. When he flashed his ID, the soldiers snapped to attention and escorted him to the nearest camp.

A Sergeant Macon, who looked no more than eighteen, found him a vacant tent, then left him alone. Yeager unzipped his pack and fished out the dirty, crumpled uniform he never would have considered donning in his former life. The last time he'd bathed was when crossing the Red River three days earlier. He would have given anything to shower, but water was a cherished commodity in the dust bowl of a camp, and his gnawing hunger took priority over his fastidiousness.

Once he'd changed, he went in search of his first meal in nearly four days. A skinny private with acne served him measly field rations of pork-and-beans with stale crackers and a peach cup, but it tasted like ambrosia to Yeager. As he gulped down the last of the peaches, a Major approached him in the small, makeshift mess tent.

He saluted Yeager, then said, "If you've finished your meal, sir, I need you to come with me."

Yeager read the Major's name, written in black marker on his breast pocket, then eyed him for a moment before saying, "I'm finished, but what do you need with me, Major Rhodes?"

The Major reached into his other breast pocket and withdrew a folded piece of paper, which he then held out to Yeager. He read the handwritten note, then handed it back to the Major. It was an order for anyone coming into contact with Yeager to immediately take him to their commanding officer.

Avoiding Yeager's gaze, Major Rhodes said, "We received this order two weeks ago, sir. I'm told it comes directly from our Commander in Chief. I'm obligated to escort you to my Commanding Officer."

Yeager stood with a grunt and gestured for the Major to lead the way. He was silent as they made their way across the compound. With the world going all to hell around them, it wasn't a good sign that Kearns had bothered to send out a BOLO notice on him. There was no telling how much time had passed since she issued the order. He hadn't been in direct radio communication with her for months but had hoped to reach out to her first. It couldn't be good news.

When he and Major Rhodes reached the CO's tent, Rhodes tapped on the door before opening it for Yeager to pass. A young Lieutenant Colonel, who Yeager outranked by years and grade, stood when they entered.

"This is Colonel Yeager, sir," Rhodes said. "He's just arrived in camp."

"Thank you, Rhodes. You are dismissed," the CO said.

Yeager caught the disappointment on Rhode's face as he turned to go. Yeager gave him an exaggerated grin when the Major passed on his way out of the tent.

The CO gestured to a folding chair across from him. Yeager lowered himself into it and waited for the younger man to speak.

"I'm Lt. Colonel Mark Dorsey. It's a pleasure to meet you, sir. You're a legend around these parts."

Yeager leaned back and crossed his arms. "I must admit, I'm surprised to hear you're aware of who I am. Why is that?"

"Stories of your exploits to capture our most dangerous enemies have reached us, even here in the middle of nowhere. I'm honored to meet the man in the flesh."

Yeager had steeled himself for a reprimand, so Dorsey's praise threw him off guard. He took a beat to recenter, then said, "I'm flattered, Colonel. Now, can you tell me what this issue is with President Kearns? Must be urgent for her to send orders so far out here to the border."

Dorsey's demeanor changed abruptly. Avoiding Yeager's gaze, as Rhodes had done, he said, "All business I see. Our grand commander has had her all-seeing eye searching for you for weeks. She's not amused that you've eluded her for this long. I'm not privy to the reason she's so fired up to find you, but I gather it's not in your favor. You probably know better than most the price for incurring her wrath."

Yeager gave him a grin that concealed his thoughts. "Not to worry. I can handle Kearns. I've been her right-hand man since the beginning of this madness. So, what's the process to contact her?"

"I'll order Rhodes to escort you to battalion headquarters in the morning. They'll know how to proceed from there. Be prepared to head out at 0700."

Yeager stood and stretched, doing his best to mask his apprehension. "I'll be ready. I'm off to hit the rack. Any chance of rounding up a clean, pressed uniform for me? I'd rather not present myself to the battalion CO in this condition."

"I can probably manage clean but pressed is another matter. I'll get my people on it."

Yeager nodded his thanks, then left without a word. After the deplorable way he'd been forced to live the past several weeks, he could tolerate a few wrinkles in his fatigues.

————

Yeager kept to himself on their three-day journey to battalion headquarters despite Rhodes' unrelenting efforts to pump him for information. He would have relished the three meals a day, a cot to sleep on, and even the companionship if not for the looming prospect of facing up to Kearns. He expected a court-martial and the brig at worst. Anything short of the brig wouldn't concern him as long as he was free to complete his mission to capture Daybreak. If he wasn't behind bars, no one could stop him from stealing back into the shadows. Not even Kearns.

As Yeager and his companions drew closer to Oklahoma City, indications of the military buildup increased. The city had become a central staging area for the war because of its proximity to the WSA border. Yeager's heart still swelled with pride at the sight of his brothers and sisters in arms, willing to risk their lives in defense of their country, even in the aftermath of the CME devastation. He'd known setbacks and had worked as a lone wolf for the past few years, but his loyalty to military command structure remained.

The sun was setting when they arrived at headquarters on the former National Guard base that served as Battalion Headquarters. Rhodes accompanied Yeager to the Battalion Commander's offices. As soon as he handed the Colonel over to this CO, he was dismissed and ordered to return to his outpost the following morning. Yeager was relieved to be rid of him. His new handlers assigned him to temporary officer quarters for the night and informed him the BC expected him back at 0800. He was left to find the mess hall and fend for himself for the following fourteen hours.

After a hurried meal only slightly better than field rations, he returned to his quarters for the first hot shower he'd had in longer than he could remember. He allowed himself an extra ten minutes under the magnificent clean water, then polished his boots and cleaned his uniform as best he could. When he'd finished and stowed his bit of gear, he climbed onto the bed with an actual mattress and closed his eyes. He expected to drop off to sleep immediately but lay wide awake, running through likely outcomes to his encounter with Kearns. Admitting defeat an hour later, he went for a five-mile run, took another shower, then dropped off minutes after laying his head on the pillow.

He woke to the sounds of Reveille being played on actual horns instead of a playback over loudspeakers like in pre-CME days. He allowed himself a moment to smile at the familiar, comforting sound before getting up to dress for his moment of reckoning. He dressed meticulously, deciding to skip breakfast rather than risk being late to report to the BC. He arrived at the waiting room ten minutes early and sat at attention as he waited for the BC's assistant to fetch him. At the click of 0800, the Staff Sergeant stepped in front of him and snapped to attention.

"Colonel Beake is ready to see you, sir," he said. "Please, come with me."

Yeager stood and followed the Sergeant, anticipating another younger Colonel he outranked, but the woman behind the desk had at least a decade on him. She was thin and tall. Her graying black hair was pulled into a tight bun, and her glasses rested on her slender, pointed nose. Beake was an apt name for her.

She remained seated without acknowledging his presence as she continued writing on a yellow legal pad. The Sergeant scurried out, leaving Yeager at attention in front of Beake's desk. Her cold indifference reminded him of treatment he'd experienced with Kearns. Yeager wondered if they knew each other.

After five annoyingly long minutes, she raised her head and locked her eyes on his. "Welcome to my base, Colonel Yeager. Please, sit." Yeager followed her order and sank into one of the three chairs positioned in front of her desk. "We've been searching for you all over the fruited plain. Thank you for coming along willingly."

Yeager raised an eyebrow. "It didn't occur to me to do otherwise. I have no reason to avoid you."

Beake nodded. "True, not me, but every reason to avoid President Kearns."

Yeager shifted almost imperceptibly in his chair. "But I'm eager to speak with her. We've been out of contact for some time."

"Not for lack on her part. I didn't get to be where I am by playing games, Yeager. I see you for exactly who you are, so drop the façade." Yeager relaxed his shoulders and crossed his arms but remained silent. Beake studied him for a moment, then went back to writing. Without looking up, she said, "Present yourself at the communications building for a scheduled telecon with the President at 1200 hours. The Sergeant will instruct you where to go."

Yeager stood and left without waiting to be dismissed. If his situation were as bad as Beake had insinuated, he'd never see her again, and he had nothing to lose. He went directly to his quarters and changed to go for another run before going to the mess hall. He needed a distraction to keep him from thinking about Kearns and to expend pent-up energy. By the time he'd eaten and dressed, the time for his appointment had arrived. He made it to the communications building with five minutes to spare. When he stepped into the radio room, the ten occupants stopped their activities and stared. When he gestured at the patch insignia of rank on his uniform, they all returned to their duties.

A Staff Sergeant stepped up to him and said, "This way, Colonel. The President is waiting."

The Sergeant led him to a chair facing the ham radio rig. Once he was seated, the Sergeant said, "Colonel Yeager is here, Madam President."

"Thank you, Sergeant," the familiar voice of Kearns said. "You are dismissed, and please ensure this conversation is not interrupted."

"Yes, Madam President," the Sergeant said and eyed Yeager as he went out.

"You there, Yeager?"

Yeager sat taller, even though Kearns couldn't see him. "Yes, Madam President. I've been informed you have urgent business to discuss with me."

"Cut the crap, Yeager. You know why you're here. I'm ruling a country immersed in a bitter civil war in the aftermath of a devastating natural disaster. I didn't appreciate having to spend the mental energy and resources on hunting you down these past weeks. You disobeyed my order not to go after Daybreak. Your new orders were to gather intel at the border and report directly to Colonel Beake. You never showed. Where have you been? The truth."

Yeager had rehearsed his response to her question for weeks. He took a breath and said, "I was gathering intel, Madam President. Going undercover and crossing in and out of enemy territory takes time and skill. I have a full report prepared for Colonel Beake."

"What good is that to her? Most of your intel is weeks, if not months old by now."

"Trust me, she'll want the intel I've gleaned." There was silence for a moment, and Yeager felt perspiration beading on his forehead.

"Trust you? Are you giving me orders now? And how can I trust you when you've disobeyed and betrayed me?"

"I would never betray you, Madam. My loyalty is absolute."

"Do you deny you went looking for Daybreak against orders?" she barked.

"I don't deny it, but I only searched for him if my work took me within the vicinity of his suspected whereabouts."

Yeager had lied to Kearns and everyone else for so long that he could do it with practiced ease. He almost believed the lies himself. He held his breath and waited to see if she'd bought his newest fabrication.

"I don't care if you found yourself in his backyard in the course of your duties. You violated your orders and your mission. Daybreak is nothing to you now. I have my best people scouring the WSA for him. They don't need you mucking up the works. I'm issuing a direct order to leave it alone. Can I be any clearer?"

Yeager hesitated before saying, "Understood, ma'am, loudly and clearly, but I'm still hoping to convince you to reconsider. Give me another chance to prove I'm the man for this assignment. As I've said, the reports you received about me were fabricated. I've chased Daybreak across the continent. I know more about him than anyone on the planet. I'll find him and deliver him to your doorstep."

"That response only shows you understand nothing. Going AWOL for weeks on end only proves the validity of those reports. The Daybreak mission is no longer a capture operation. If you comprehend my meaning. That man has caused me no end of trouble and left nothing but death and destruction in his wake. I want him eliminated, but that's no longer your responsibility. Do you understand? Report to Beake for new orders and follow them to the letter. Be warned. Cross me again, and you'll meet Daybreak's same fate. You know too much, and I can't afford loose ends."

The radio static went silent before Yeager could say, "Yes, ma'am." He stared ahead for a moment before slowly getting to his feet. Despite Kearns' threat, he'd gotten off with no more than a reprimand. It was far better than he could have hoped. He returned to Beake's office for orders he had no intention of following. He was still laser-focused on getting his man. He'd show Kearns and the rest. All he needed was time.

———

Riley threaded her unruly hair into a band as she rushed out of her tent. Conrad had sent word to Dashay late the previous night that he was back in camp, and Riley wanted to tell him about her cousins before she left for the hospital. She stepped outside and stopped for a moment to lift her face to the sun. It was probably only forty degrees, but after the freezing cold they'd endured for months, it felt like a heatwave. Temperatures had been climbing the previous few days. She expected it to reach the sixties that day.

After her two-minute indulgence, she hurried across the compound to Conrad's tent. He was coming out with his arm around Dashay as she reached them.

He let go of Dashay and wrapped Riley in a bear hug. After releasing her, he said, "You're a welcome sight, and just the person I was coming to see. I have news you've been waiting to hear for a long time." Her legs went weak in the hope that he'd found Julia. She reached out to Dashay's hand for support. Conrad flashed a smile. It was more emotion Riley had ever seen him express. "We found Julia. We don't have her yet, but we're close on her heels." He reached into his back pocket and pulled out a paper folded to make its own envelope. "Read this."

As she reached for the paper, she realized it was one of her wanted posters from the US. She raised her eyebrows as she took it from him. "I've seen hundreds of these, Conrad. I'd rather not be reminded. Why are you giving me this?"

Dashay let out a laugh. "Always suspicion with you. Just open it and read the back."

Riley's heart pounded as she unfolded the paper. It only took an instant to recognize the handwriting scrawled across it as Julia's. The crumpled and sweat-stained letter was addressed to Dr. Kate Cooper from Colorado Springs. Clever girl, Riley thought at Julia's use of her middle and married names. A letter addressed to Dr. Riley Poole wouldn't have made it ten feet out of Julia's hand. Only people who knew the family personally would recognize the code name. Tears of pride and longing pooled in her eyes as she read.

Dear Mom,

I'm safe and well in a camp outside of Kansas City. I'm still with Uncle Mitch and the rest of the family. They've moved us before, so we may be somewhere else by the time you see this, but I'll keep sending out these letters. I've sent almost a hundred of them, hoping one would get to you someday. I'm going to keep writing them until I'm with you.

I love you, Mom, and I know I'll see you again soon. Stay safe and give everyone a hug and kiss for me.

Love from your WP,

Julia

Riley sank to her knees as she pressed the letter to her face. Julia's fingertips had touched that paper. For the first time in two years, she had a connection with her daughter, even if remote. The WP for Warrior Princess was a nice touch. Julia hadn't lost her fire or hope. That was a good sign.

"Riley," Conrad said softly, "I'm reluctant to say this, but you need to read the date on that letter."

She pulled the paper from her damp cheek and struggled to read through the blur of her tears. The letter was dated eighteen months earlier. Riley's hopes sank. "So long ago. Do you know if she's still in that camp?"

"My people are on the way to find out as we speak," Conrad said. "Even if she's not, it's the most promising lead we've had. For all the chaos across the border, they keep meticulous records. If Julia and your family were moved, we should still have a trail of breadcrumbs to follow. It's just a matter of time now, Riley."

Conrad held his hand out to help her up. She grasped it and climbed to her feet, clutching the letter in her other hand.

Dashay wiped her cheek with the back of her hand, then threw her arms around Riley. "Isn't it incredible? Between this and your cousins appearing out of nowhere, I feel like our girl is already home."

Riley broke free from Dashay and spun around, facing Conrad. "Right, my cousins. I almost forgot to tell you about them in my excitement over Julia's letter."

"No need. Dashay filled me in last night. I'll have one of my guys on the way to the farm to interview your family. Any tidbit of info they might have is another piece of the puzzle. I'm working on getting permission for you to contact Coop before your scheduled day. We may not make a connection since Coop won't be expecting to hear from you, but it's worth a shot."

Riley squeezed Conrad's arm for support. "My head is spinning. After all these months of frustration and disappointment, finally a ray of hope." She read Julia's message twice more before saying, "Where has the letter been for more than a year? How did you get your hands on it?"

"From a captured enemy soldier. I say captured, but it was more a willing surrender. He was a guard at the camp in Kansas City while Julia was there. He got orders to escort a group of prisoners to another camp closer to the border. On the trip, one prisoner dropped the letter. The soldier picked it up and tucked it in his uniform, then forgot about it. When he was captured several months later, the guards found the letter when they searched his belongings. He explained how it came into his possession. The letter made the rounds through our network until it reached Paul Kinlaw. You remember him? He was with Bailey and me that night when we took you from that car accident."

Dashay gave him a playful slap on the shoulder. "Of course, she remembers. Finish the story before she passes out."

"When Paul read the letter, he put together that it was meant for you and contacted me. That's why I left here in such a hurry the other morning. I didn't want to tell you where I was going in case it was a false alarm. God knows we've had enough of those."

While brushing her thumb over the tattered Wanted Poster, Riley said, "After my first husband's tragic death, I stopped believing in miracles. Hell, I stopped believing in everything. All I could do was force myself to get up each day and keep going. Traveling to that medical conference was a gigantic leap for me. I was terrified to get on that plane. It could have been a premonition or just my anxiety. I'll never know. The crucial point is, I met Coop almost as soon as I arrived. No way that was a coincidence. Julia and I wouldn't have survived the CME strike and journey without him. We've all had more than our share of tragedy, like every survivor." She put her arm around Dashay's waist. "But I've also known too many miracles to doubt anymore. Julia's letter reaching me was no coincidence."

"Adrian would probably argue with that," Dashay said. "But not me. Call it what you will. There's more to this existence than our senses can comprehend."

Conrad crossed his arms and studied each of them. "It's too early for my brain to wrap around such deep philosophy. I'll sort it out when I have two free minutes to devote to it. In the meantime, miracle or coincidence, I'm more hopeful than I've been since we started searching for Julia. Keep the letter, Riley. Paul made a mimeographed copy."

Riley gently folded the paper and slid it into her front pocket. "This won't leave my person until my girl is home."

———

Riley was nearly going out of her mind after three more weeks passed with no signs of their unit getting to go on leave. She wasn't the only one. Morale was low, and tempers were high even though the weather continued to improve. Daily temps in the sixties with blue skies were the only things keeping her sane. Conrad had taken off abruptly three days earlier, and there was still no word on Julia's whereabouts. Her frostbite and hypothermia cases had swapped with ranch accidents, dysentery, and insect bites. Her cases passed through the exam rooms and OR in a blur, convincing her more each day that she was overdue for a trip home.

"I'm out of here if they don't give us leave soon," Riley said one night as she and Dashay ate in the mess tent.

Dashay swallowed her bite of reconstituted tomato soup and said, "I'm with you on that, and I don't even have kids I'm dying to get back to."

Riley tossed her fork on the table and dropped her head into her hands. "My assignment was supposed to entail setting up clinics, recruiting medical personnel, and provide training. Instead, all I do is treat patients. Don't get me wrong. I don't begrudge treating these poor people, but I could do this at home. If I'd known this is what the job would be like, I would have refused the job offer."

"You'll have to use that council muscle next time you're in Denver. Convince them to send more medical staff for treating patients to free us up to do what we were sent here to do."

Riley raised her head and was about to agree when she saw Conrad coming toward their table. She jumped up and rushed toward him. She could tell she wasn't going to like what he had to say.

She stopped in front of him and folded her arms. "Are you going to tell me I should sit down before you drop the bad news?"

Conrad ran his hand through his hair, and images of Coop

making that same gesture flooded her mind. I need to see my man, she thought as she waited for Conrad to answer.

He placed his hand on her shoulder and turned her back toward the table. "I am going to tell you to sit, but not because the news is horrific. It's not what you want to hear but not the end of the world either."

"You're stalling," Riley said as she sank back into her chair.

Conrad leaned over Dashay and gave her a kiss of welcome before dropping into the chair beside her. "Give me a second to catch my breath. I just got back into camp and came straight here." He took a swig of Dashay's water, then looked Riley in the eye. "I'm sorry to tell you that Julia's not in the Kansas City camp anymore. In fact, the entire compound was shut down months ago. The only people there now are squatters."

Riley closed her eyes and took three deep breaths. "Just tell me you know where she is now."

He looked away before shaking his head. "My people are digging into it. It appears your family has been moved at least two or three times, but my people have been able to dig up records of the transfers. I have a scheduled radio call with my lead guy in the field tomorrow. He sounded optimistic last time we spoke."

Riley stood and gathered her dirty dishes. "Please, find me at the hospital as soon as you have news." She carried her dishes to the washbasin and tossed them in with a clatter. She made her way to her tent, hoping Dashay would spend the night with Conrad. She was in no mood for small talk.

———

"Dr. Poole," a nurse said abruptly as Riley stared through the hospital window toward the southern tip of the Rocky Mountains east of the city.

Riley had been too absorbed in her thoughts to hear the nurse come up behind her. Without taking her eyes from the window, she said, "What is it?"

The nurse hesitated for a moment before saying, "They need you for a consult in the ER. It's urgent."

Riley dropped her shoulders and turned to face her. "Can't someone else take it?"

"Unfortunately not, Doctor. It's a farm worker with a partially severed leg."

Riley sighed, then gestured for her to lead the way. As they walked to the ER, she asked herself for the twentieth time why she hadn't heard from Conrad yet. When they reached the ER, and she saw her patient's condition, all thoughts of her personal problems vanished. The man had tripped and fallen in front of his horse-drawn plow, startling the horse. The horse took off at a run with the plow behind him, running over the rancher and slicing his leg.

Riley ordered an OR to be readied and went to scrub. For the following four hours, the delicate work of stabilizing the broken femur and reattaching severed vessels and soft tissue were all that occupied her thoughts. When the surgery was complete, she had high hopes for her patient's full recovery.

The operation had filled the remainder of her shift, so she changed into her street clothes and made her way to the exit. Conrad was waiting just inside the main entrance sliding doors. The look on his face was worse than the night before. He led Riley to a bank of chairs in the lobby and motioned for her to sit.

"Should I be afraid to hear what you have to say?" she asked, avoiding his eyes.

"I need to work harder on my poker face around you," Conrad said with a smile. "Part of what I have to tell you is excellent news. The rest will make you furious."

Riley leaned the back of her head against the wall and stared at the ceiling. "Lay the bad news on me first."

"Sorry, can't do that. You need the good news first. We found Julia and your family."

Riley flew out of her chair and stared at him in shock. "Way to bury the lead. Where is my daughter?"

A couple who had been crossing the lobby stopped and stared. "Sit down, Riley, and I'll explain everything." She lowered herself back into her chair without taking her eyes off him. "They're in a camp outside Oklahoma City. She's still with your aunt, uncle, and your cousin Kathryn's family. From what we could learn, they're all as well as can be expected."

Tears stung Riley's eyes, and it was a struggle to get words past the lump in her throat. "Another miracle. And why aren't you on your way to rescue her?"

Conrad stroked his beard for a moment. "Here comes the furious part. I've had to recall my team for another mission. We've been issued top priority orders. Julia's safe in the camp. We'll go for her as soon as we complete this other mission. I'll lead the rescue team to recover your daughter myself."

Furious is the perfect word, Riley thought as her heart pounded in reaction to Conrad's news. "You don't have anyone else you can send?"

He shook his head. "No other operatives have penetrated that far into enemy territory. My men took an enormous risk to get the intel on Julia's location."

"In our entire country, they can't find one other person to lead the other mission? You've been tracking Julia for over eighteen months. Now when you've found her, you're going to let her sit and rot in that camp for God knows how long? How can you sit here and look me in the eye?"

"This is killing me, too, but I don't have the luxury of running off on a personal quest whenever I please. Have you forgotten that we're in the middle of a war in a world gone to hell? I'm an officer first. I have a duty to thousands of people, not just Julia."

Riley's hands shook as she stood and picked up her pack. "I'm familiar with how the military works, Conrad. I'm not blaming you. You've done what you could." She took a few breaths before saying, "Wait, that's not exactly true. You've gone far beyond your call of duty to find Julia, and I'm grateful, but you getting pulled off the rescue is a devastating blow when we're so close. I know you. If you wanted to find a way around this, you would."

"There is no other way, no matter what you believe. There's no shortage of suffering in this world, Riley. Take this as a win and exercise an ounce of patience. Julia's alive, and she's safe. We found her. I'll go for her as soon as I'm allowed." Conrad got to his feet and stood beside her. "Dashay is still here in the hospital. We're meeting up to walk back to camp together. Want to join us?"

"Thanks for the offer, but no. I'm ready to get out of here, and I need time to process this latest setback. I'll see you in camp."

Conrad reached for her but stopped when she flinched. "You'll be all right?"

She gave a quick nod. "Fine. Don't worry about me."

She hurried out, needing to be anywhere but with Conrad. She meant what she'd said. Riley understood how the military worked, but it didn't mean she had to accept it as right. Conrad was duty-bound to follow orders, but there were always ways to sidestep. He'd given in without a fight.

"That had better be one big ass problem that took priority over my daughter," Riley said to no one as she hoofed it back to camp. "I won't accept anything less."

———

"I'm worried about Riley," Dashay told Conrad as she lay with him on the life-raft they'd converted to an air mattress in his tent. "She's hardly spoken to me in the three days since you told her about Julia. It's not my fault you can't ride to WP's rescue. I want her home ASAP too. Why's Riley taking it out on me?"

"Guilt by association. Don't take it personally. Riley said she doesn't blame me, but she needs somewhere to direct her anger and frustration. I've wondered if part of that is to deflect it away from herself. She's the one who left Julia behind in Virginia. What did she think would happen?"

Dashay propped up on her elbow and gazed down at him. "She expected WP to be safe on her uncle's ranch. None of us knew about Kearns then. Riley couldn't have imagined what was coming. Leaving Julia was the right choice with the information she had, and Julia wouldn't have survived that trip from hell to Colorado."

"I'm aware Riley didn't know she was pregnant, but she and Coop should have been patient, then stayed put until after Xav was born."

"And what? Ended up giving birth in an internment camp? How would that have been better? Emily, Jared, and Marjory never would have known what became of them." She rolled onto her back and put an arm over her eyes. "If we're going to play that game, Riley and Julia shouldn't have stepped onto the plane to DC. My fiancée, Darian, and I should have stayed home instead of traveling to visit my parents for the holidays. If we pull at that thread, where does it end? Haven't you ever wondered what you could have done differently before the CME struck?"

She watched while he considered her question. "Honestly, no, but I was single with no ties. Dad passed away when I was too young to remember. Mom lives with my brother and his family. I got all of them out of the US before the border closed. They're in Arizona. I've only seen them once since. They were doing well, all things considered. I live my life without regret, but that doesn't make me insensitive to the suffering of others. I've never met Julia, but I want her out of Kearns' clutches and home with her family where she belongs. I hated breaking Riley's heart."

Dashay brushed his cheek with her fingertips. "You're just a big softie under that tough shell."

He rolled on top of her and pressed his lips hard against hers. When he pulled away, he said, "That's classified. If you tell anyone, I'll have to kill you."

"I'm serious, Conrad. You're a good man who willingly sacrifices for people he doesn't even know. It's not fair of Riley to give us the cold shoulder. I'm going to have it out with her tomorrow."

"That'll have to wait. You have more pressing matters to tend to." After kissing her again, he said, "I have to leave in a few hours. I'll try not to wake you when I go."

Dashay was annoyed to find herself wishing he could stay. Conrad came and went like their relationship had a revolving door. She never questioned that. Her life was so hectic she had little time to miss him when he was gone and accepted what his job required.

"Can you tell me when you'll be back?"

"I would if I knew. Expect it to be weeks, at least, possibly more than a month."

She wove her fingers into his hair and pulled his face close to hers. "Then, we better make this count."

Conrad was asleep minutes after their lovemaking, but Dashay couldn't close her eyes, confused by the intensity of her feelings. She'd been with Conrad for more than a year and thought she'd been careful to guard her heart. But she woke one day to find her feelings had grown stronger. She'd hesitated to ask him if his feelings had changed, too, afraid to hear the answer.

His time away would give her the chance to gauge how deep her feelings ran. If she rarely gave him a thought, nothing would need to change. If she counted the hours until he returned, she'd need to have that talk with him or consider breaking it off. The prospect of that saddened her. Even if their relationship was only casual, it kept her from being alone.

She lay still, listening to his deep, even breathing and allowing herself to savor the feel of his body next to hers, knowing it could be the last time.

Dashay woke with the sun glaring in through the window. She sat up and looked around the tent. Conrad's belongings were gone. He'd been true to his word and left on his journey without waking her. She placed her palm on the mattress where he'd slept. Though he'd been gone for two hours, she imagined she could still feel the heat of his body. She decided that instead of having it out with Riley, she needed to ask her advice as a friend. Maybe Riley could help her sort through her conflicting emotions.

She got up and dressed quickly to catch Riley before she left for the hospital. She ducked into their tent but froze when she saw that Riley's belongings were cleaned out and her side of the tent was empty. All Riley had left was a note lying on the folded blankets on Dashay's cot. She picked it up and sank onto a chair, afraid to read the words scrawled by her dearest friend. She took a few deep breaths to gather her strength before unfolding the note, then began to read.

Dear Dashay,

I've gone off to rescue my daughter. I've been secretly collecting supplies while you were distracted with Conrad for the past few days. I'm sorry for not keeping you in the loop, but I couldn't risk you trying to stop me or telling Conrad about my plans. I'm going to find Adrian in Texas and solicit his help to rescue Julia. He may not be my most courageous ally, but he's good at planning strategy.

I'm the one who took Julia to DC. I'm the one who left her behind, and I'm the reason she's been stuck in internment camps for months. She must be sick with worry over what's become of me. I have so much to make up for with my sweetheart girl. She's as much a part of me as my limbs or heart. You'll understand when you have children of your own one day.

For over two years, my heart has been torn between my children in a never-ending tug-of-war. No clear path forward existed, so I've had to forge my own. I've felt the burden of my decision every day since leaving Julia. The only way to heal the festering wound is to bring her home and make my family and myself whole. As much as I know the rest of you want my girl home, I have to be the one to go. No one else on this godforsaken planet is as driven to see it through.

Please hold off telling Conrad that I've left for as long as possible. Tell Coop I love him and try not to worry. I'll be in touch the instant I get my hands on a ham radio. I apologize for putting you in the middle of this, but I had no choice.

I love you, my dear friend. Don't hate me for doing this. When Julia and I are safely home, I hope you'll forgive me. Take care of yourself and look for me soon.

With deepest affection,

Riley

Dashay lowered the letter to her lap, not knowing whether to cry or scream or laugh. It was such a Riley thing to do, but that didn't make it right. Dashay should have seen what her best friend was up to, but she was too consumed with her Conrad dilemma. She tore the letter into tiny strips, then dropped them into a dented aluminum cup on the table. After digging a match out of her pack, she lit the pieces and watched them burn down to gray ash.

Good lord, Girl, what in the hell have you done?

CHAPTER FIVE

RILEY TRAVELED AS FAR as she dared push Biscuit for the first three nights, covering twenty-mile stretches at a time. They'd hugged the base of the mountains heading southeast and stopped on the third day when she found a shallow cave near an underground spring bubbling to the surface. The cave was hidden between two jagged walls, high enough to keep her location obscured from anyone passing. She'd only found it by chance when she followed a narrow trail that veered off the main road. It was the perfect spot to catch their breath, and Biscuit would have plenty of water and grass.

In the days leading up to heading out, she'd gathered enough energy bars and MRE packets to last the fifteen days until she reached Fort Worth. She mapped out water sources in the area. She estimated she and Biscuit were covered for six days as they traveled along the Pecos River. At Fort Sumner, they'd be forced to turn due east. After that, finding water would be Riley's biggest challenge. With her portable water filter and purification tablets, she'd be able to stretch her supply.

It was a rash, ambitious journey, to say the least. Foolhardy was probably a more fitting description, but Riley was tired of second-guessing her decision to abandon her Julia in Virginia. Her harrowing experiences in escaping the US after the CME taught her that she possessed the survival skills, fortitude, and luck to accomplish this task. There was a strange sort of faith that drove Riley to undertake the arduous and perilous journey. Julia needed her.

She and Biscuit slept through the fourth day, and when no one came for her by the following morning, she decided it was safe to rest for one more day. She needed Biscuit strong for the long haul and couldn't risk wearing him out before they reached Adrian in Fort Worth.

She spent the time in her hidden camp figuring out how she would liberate Julia from the internment camp. She had to admit that her plan was sketchy at best. All she knew was where Julia was being held. Riley had been fortunate enough to evade getting captured and thrown into one of Kearns' camps, so she was short on details for how they functioned. She regretted not pumping Conrad for information before taking off on her quest. He probably would have given what she needed out of guilt for calling off the rescue mission. As it was, she'd have to rely on whatever information she could glean along the way.

Nights were always the hardest on her. During the day, she was moving, planning the next step, worrying about the weather and her horse. At night, she spent hours second-guessing herself. More than once, Riley came close to turning back, but thoughts of Julia locked and suffering in that camp flooded into her mind and strengthened her resolve.

She spent equal time practicing what she would say to Coop when she got the chance to contact him. Riley knew he and the kids would be hurt, furious, and worried. She had flashes of regret for not fessing up that she was going to rescue Julia, but he would have stopped her from embarking on such a reckless enterprise. But it was time to find Julia and reunite her family. Riley didn't have the strength to go on being torn in two, and it was a risk she needed to take.

On the third morning, she rose with the sun and repacked the saddlebags to get back on the road. As she tightened Biscuit's saddle, she murmured comforting words to him, then said, "Thanks for joining me on this new adventure, old friend. I wouldn't have had the courage to go it alone." Biscuit gave a soft whinny of understanding, then lowered his muzzle to her for a piece of dried apple. "You can have two as a reward today, but we have to make these last, so don't get greedy."

He cheerfully munched on the fruit as Riley climbed into the saddle.

"No turning back, boy," she said, then gave him a gentle nudge to get him moving. They were on their way.

———

Riley hunkered down in the decaying remains of a small wooden structure, doing her best to find shelter from the thunderstorm that had blown in without warning. The unstable wall she leaned against quivered under the force of the wind. Two hours earlier, the temperature had been in the seventies with crystal clear skies. She'd stopped for lunch in Vega, Texas, and enjoyed a picnic beside a duck pond. Now, she couldn't see ten yards ahead through the pelting rain. After cursing the belligerent weather gods, she begged the god of her youth to protect her from the storm. She was exhausted after days on the trail and still had a long, hard road ahead.

She pulled her solar blanket tighter until it covered her entirely, but that offered little protection. The wall behind her cracked and popped with the next gust of wind, threatening to break apart on top of her. She jumped to her feet and dashed to where Biscuit stood only mildly perturbed by the weather as he muzzled the wet ground in search of the tender grass. Riley tucked into a ball under him and covered herself with the blanket. She hoped his body would block the wind and that he wouldn't kick her in the head as much as she probably deserved it.

Within ten minutes, the storm blew out as quickly as it came in. Riley climbed out of her blanket and stared at the building where she'd ducked for cover. The entire structure was a pile of rubble. She shivered as the words coincidence or miracle went through her mind, recalling the conversation she'd had with Conrad when he gave her Julia's letter. Either way, she'd survived another day and was ready to get out of her exposed position. She stowed the blanket and got into the saddle, silently praying in gratitude as she lifted her face to the sun.

Her next stop was Amarillo, where she'd be nearing the halfway point. She could melt into the crowd there and stay for a few days to give Biscuit a rest. The first eight days had been long but uneventful despite the storm, but that didn't mean they hadn't been strenuous. They'd found water when they needed it and hadn't run into any unexpected obstacles.

Riley's one nagging concern was that she'd violated the terms of her contract with the Health Ministry by running off without notice. The Health and Welfare Battalion units served under the purview of the military. She'd willingly signed on the line, agreeing to follow military rules even though she wasn't considered an active-duty officer. That meant she was technically AWOL. She couldn't be court-martialed, but the Ministry had every right to lock her up if they chose.

She wasn't expecting that to happen, hoping they'd understand the desperation that drove her to go after Julia. And they needed her as a doctor. Jailing her would serve no purpose. When she returned with Julia, she'd gladly submit to any punishment they saw fit to mete out. Having her daughter home safely was worth any price.

She pushed on toward a village called Wildorado and located a run-down brick rambler with a one-horse stable on the eastern edge of town to spend the night. She wasn't surprised to see the town abandoned, assuming the surviving residents had gathered to Amarillo after the CME. She didn't mind being alone. It meant she wouldn't have to look over her shoulder while she was there.

She dismounted and led Biscuit to the stable. The familiar smells and feel calmed him immediately. Riley was delighted to see bales of dry hay stacked on pallets in the corner and wondered why the previous owners had left them behind. She pulled a handful from one bale and examined it before feeding it to Biscuit. It was dry and appeared fresh, so she gave him enough to last the night, then went in search of water for him. She found an old pump behind the house. After priming the handle a few times, clear water began to flow. She pumped until she was sure it was clean, then filled a bucket to carry to the stable.

After getting Biscuit settled, she went inside to scope out the house. If she found rotting bodies or anything else that made her uneasy, she could bunk with Biscuit in the stable. Even a straw bed would be welcomed after her nights on the hard ground in her tent. She'd even started missing her lumpy cot back in Casper. She tried the back door leading into the kitchen first. It was locked, so she knocked several times to make sure the house was unoccupied. When no one answered, she tried to jimmy the lock but couldn't get the door to open. She spotted an ax in the weeds, so she grabbed it and swung at the doorknob to break it. It popped off with one swing and clattered to the steps.

Riley pushed the door open with caution and surveyed the room before entering. It was silent, and the surfaces were covered with a dense layer of dust. Deciding it was safe, she stepped inside and checked the entire house before stopping to see if the former owners had left anything useful behind. She was relieved not to find any corpses, vermin, or other unwelcome occupants. Other than dust, the house looked like the owners had just stepped out for an after-supper walk.

It wasn't the first time, or even the hundredth that Riley had witnessed such a scene. The former residents had likely perished either when the CME struck or shortly after. Others had discarded the bodies and not bothered to clean out the house. Riley hurried to the kitchen, hoping to find food for herself. Biscuit wasn't the only one who deserved a nice dinner. After opening two cupboards, she smiled to realize she'd struck gold. While such foods as the boxes of pasta and bags of rice had been devoured by hungry mice and other pests, rows of jarred and canned foods still lined the shelves. Riley dug through the drawers until she found a can opener, then sat down to enjoy her feast.

When her belly was full of as much canned beef, corn, and peaches as it could hold, she went to the master bedroom and spread her sleeping bag on the mattress after stripping off the dusty blankets and sheets. She dropped onto her pillow with a sigh and enjoyed her first restful night's sleep since leaving Santa Fe.

———

Riley woke at sunrise and was reluctantly saying goodbye to her one-night oasis by seven. She packed what food she could carry and wished she had a way to haul the beautiful hay for Biscuit. They'd been fortunate to find enough spring grass to meet his needs to that point, but she worried that might not be the case as they traveled further south. She'd considered trying to rig a makeshift sled for him to pull but didn't want to take the time or overtax him. In the end, she gave him enough for breakfast before they started out, hoping they'd continue to find reliable food sources along the way.

They made good time after their night of rest. Riley started reconsidering her plan to camp away from populated areas at night. She hadn't seen a single sign that anyone was following her and wondered if staying in an abandoned house or other building would be safe. She'd reach Amarillo by the end of the day and figured there would be plenty of places to stay in the city.

She was weighing her options in the late afternoon when voices coming from behind roused her from her thoughts. She scolded herself for letting her guard down and steered Biscuit into the scrub off the side of the road. The only cover was a cluster of oak trees fifteen yards to the north. She headed for it at a gallop, hoping she hadn't been spotted.

The travelers were roughly three hundred yards back. Riley must have only heard them because of the faint breeze blowing in her direction. She dug her binoculars out of the saddlebag to try to make out who they were. One thing immediately became apparent. It was a military convoy stretching as far as her eyes could see. It must be an entire battalion, she thought as she lowered the binoculars. She figured they were heading for Amarillo, which made sense since it was so close to the US border.

She dismounted and fed Biscuit dried apple slices to keep him quiet as the convoy passed. The mounted officers led the way, followed by wagons loaded with gear, supplies, and artillery. Riley's heartbeat quickened at the sight of the last wagons with red crosses painted on the sides. Those wagons were followed by line upon line of soldiers on foot. Riley didn't know there were that many people even left in the entire country. Her heart swelled at the sight of so many willing to lay down their lives to fight Kearns in defense of their people.

She also felt guilt pricking at the back of her neck for running away from her duties. The sight of hospital wagons reminded her that though she was a mother desperate to rescue her child, her second obligation was to care for the sick and wounded. A debate sparked in her mind over whether she could fill both at the same time. The convoy was heading in the same direction she was. She could travel with them for a time and treat their people until they parted ways.

She remounted and rode Biscuit back toward the convoy.

When she got within ten yards, a man riding on horseback beside the wagons called out for her to stop. She pulled on Biscuit's reins and squinted at him walking toward her. A knot twisted in her gut when she recognized the markings on his uniform, indicating that he was a military police officer. He motioned for her to stay where she was. She glanced at the sidearm prominently holstered at his hip and froze.

"This might be the end of our adventure," she whispered to Biscuit as he approached.

He stopped fifteen feet from her, then scanned the surrounding area, probably looking for possible traveling companions. Riley took the chance to give him a look. He was muscular but compact. His black hair was close-cropped under his cap, and his eyes were the darkest brown she'd ever seen. When he turned back and locked his gaze on her, she could tell nothing escaped his gaze.

Without even blinking, he said, "Where on earth did you spring up from?"

She pointed at the cluster of trees. "I was taking a bathroom break."

"In the middle of nowhere by yourself? Are you traveling alone?" When she shrugged, he eyed her with suspicion. "What's your name, Ma'am?"

Riley scrambled to come up with a name in case he'd gotten word that she was AWOL. "I'm Dr. Katie Cooper," she said, then flashed him a grin. "What's yours?"

His face remained still as stone. "You're a doctor?" Riley nodded emphatically. "Medical doctor?"

"Yes. Orthopedic surgeon."

She noticed the slightest raise of his eyebrows. "Where are you headed all alone in the middle of the desert, Dr. Cooper?"

Riley had to bite her cheek from smiling when he said the name. Dr. Cooper was Coop, not her. She took a breath and said, "I'm going to visit my brother in Fort Worth."

He studied her for a moment. She could tell by his look that he thought she was insane.

"Are you aware that we're at war?"

"Painfully, sir, but I'm heading away from the border. I've traveled this way many times with no trouble."

He rubbed his forehead. "I'll give you points for courage but not common sense. I wouldn't want my wife out here alone. I should inform you that the southern front lines have shifted east. There's intense fighting all along the Texas border. We're transferring our division headquarters to Amarillo. I'm afraid I can't allow you to travel any farther east from here. You need to turn south."

Riley turned her gaze toward the barren terrain to the south. "I can't go that way. There's nothing out there. I need places to stop for food and rest for Biscuit here and myself."

"You should have thought of that before you left, wherever it is you came from. You'll have to turn back."

"Vega," she said, surprised and disappointed with herself at how easily she could lie. "Turning back's not an option. My brother is sick and needs my help. I have a proposal for you. If you allow me to travel with you as far as Amarillo, I'll help treat your sick and wounded before I turn south. I give my word. I'll stay as far away from the border as I can after that. Believe me, I don't have any desire to be close to the front lines."

"That's a generous offer, but I can't allow it. It's too dangerous."

"I'm perfectly capable of defending myself, and I understand war. My first husband was a helicopter pilot for the Air Force. He was shot down several years ago on the Afghan border. I just want to be a doctor and help your people for a few days in exchange for food and a cot."

He turned and watched the passing convoy. "I don't have time to sit here and argue with you, and we're always short of medical help. Come with me, and I'll try to get it cleared with my superiors. Don't count on it, though. We're not in the habit of conscripting random civilians off the side of the road."

"I'm just volunteering. I'll be out of your hair as soon as I see to the patients."

He turned his horse and gestured for her to follow. She wanted to shout for joy that he hadn't recognized and arrested her. If they agreed to let her tag along, she could travel in safety, and she'd be able to help relieve some suffering. It was a lucky encounter, as long as no one figured out who she was.

As they rode, he said, "You don't strike me as a spy, so I suppose it's safe to tell you my name. I'm Sergeant Cosimo DeLuca. They call me Coz."

"Pleased to meet you, Coz. How can you be sure I'm not a spy?"

"For one, if you were, you'd never ask that question. Two, not too many spies pose as doctors, and three, you seem too smart to be one of Kearns' spooks."

You have no idea, she thought, but said, "I think I'm both flattered and insulted by that remark, but you're right, I'm definitely not a spy. Just a doctor trying to help her family."

She was doing her best to keep the conversation lighthearted as they approached the convoy, but her heart continued to pound. Anyone in the company could recognize her. She regretted not staying hidden or galloping away as soon as she saw the hordes coming.

Coz directed her to the side of the last hospital wagon. Before riding off, he called back, "Ride there. Don't talk to anyone, and don't touch anything."

She chuckled at his command, wondering if he was a father and what she might want to touch. She could feel the stares at her back as they plodded along. She kept her eyes lowered to discourage anyone from talking to her. She was relieved ten minutes later to hear horses approaching from the opposite direction. She raised her head and saw Coz coming toward her with another man. When they were close enough, she could see by the markings on his uniform that he was a Major. The Sergeant had jumped a few grades up the chain of command.

After the two men wheeled their horses and got them into step next to Biscuit, the Major said, "This is a highly unusual situation, Dr. Cooper. Do you have any way to prove your identity?"

Riley had left all her IDs behind in Santa Fe. She shook her head, then remembered Julia's letter in her pocket. She pulled it out and held it up for him to read. "This is the best I can do. It's an old letter from my daughter."

She hoped that he would ask her to open it and expose the Wanted Poster. That would escalate the situation in a hurry.

The Major squinted at the envelope and nodded. "About as good a proof as we can get these days. The Sergeant explained your proposal. I wouldn't consider it under normal circumstances, but we're always in desperate need of doctors. You have permission to stay until you've treated the current batch of sick and wounded. If we can't convince you to sign up after that, you'll be free to go."

"I'd be honored to serve our military that way, but I have family members in need of medical care, and I'm anxious to get back to my children."

"Disappointing, but I understand. Sergeant, see to the doctor's needs," he said as he rode off to return to the head of the column.

"When we reach Amarillo, I'll find quarters for you, then I'll show you to the hospital and introduce you to the medical staff there. We left our most critical patients behind in Albuquerque, but there were too many wounded to leave them all. The ones we're transporting will be happy to see you. Not many surgeons to be found around here."

Riley knew the truth of that. Part of her job was to recruit medical staff, but most doctors were dead, contracting with the military, or assigned to one of the HWB units. Hospitals in bigger cities removed from the fighting had enough general practitioners on staff, but Riley discovered just how slim the pickings were in rural areas. Surgeons were even harder to find.

"I'm willing to do what I can," she said.

"Thanks, doc," he said with a faint Italian accent. "Back to work for me. See you later."

He trotted off, leaving her alone in a crowd of curious soldiers. As much as she'd enjoyed her solitude, it was a relief to have the protection of the convoy. She wouldn't have to sleep with an eye open and her Glock 19 at her side.

———

Dashay felt dread and relief as Conrad strode toward her through the hospital lobby. She hadn't known if or when to expect him, so she was glad to see him safe. The dread came from knowing what his reaction would be when she spilled the news about Riley. No one had heard from her since she took off ten days earlier. Dashay's feelings had swung between being sick with worry and wanting to strangle her reckless friend.

Word of her disappearance had gotten back to the Ministry in Denver. Dr. Ingram had arranged a radio contact and grilled Dashay for the little information she had to give. None of her answers satisfied him, and he made it abundantly clear how much trouble Riley would face if she ever returned. Dashay understood. Dr. Ingram told her that their unit was finally granted a month's leave, so Dashay begged him to not give Coop the news about Riley until she could do it in person. Dr. Ingram said he would honor her wishes but couldn't guarantee word wouldn't get back to him. The whole Ministry was buzzing about it.

The unit had been packing up camp and was heading home the following morning. As Conrad approached her, she wondered if he'd be traveling with them. She hoped more than she was comfortable with that he would be. Consumed with the Riley issue, she hadn't given Conrad much thought. The force of her reaction at seeing him walking toward her meant she had to face up to her feelings.

He held back when he reached her and didn't give her his usual hungry "I'm home" kiss. She hoped it was because they were in a public place.

She flashed him her warmest smile and said, "Welcome home, Babe. I'm glad to see you back in one piece."

He awkwardly put his hand on her arm and gave her a quick peck on the cheek. "Thanks. Are you done with your shift?" When she nodded, he said, "Can I walk you back?"

He was tense when she reached for his hand, and she wondered why he was so formal with her. They'd been together long enough that he didn't need to ask permission to walk with her to camp. "Of course. Since when do you ask?"

He gave her a smile that didn't reach his eyes. "Just trying to respect you. Ready to go."

She started for the door, still holding his limp hand. Something wasn't right, but she was afraid to ask. Had he met someone else, or was he just done with her? If that were the case, why had he come to walk her home? She got her answer as soon as they were alone on the path back to camp. He came to an abrupt stop, then let go of her hand and turned her to face him.

"I heard about Riley as soon as I got back to camp. For such an intelligent woman, she doesn't have a lick of common sense."

Dashay crossed her arms and glared at him. "You know better than most that's not true. Why are you taking this out on me?"

"She left the same day I did. Were you hiding this from me while you were making hot love to me? Did you help Riley get away?"

Dashay acted out of reflex and slapped him hard across the cheek. She'd never struck anyone in her life and immediately regretted it. But Conrad had wounded her with his accusations. While he rubbed the red outline of her hand on his cheek, she said, "Oh my god, Conrad. I'm so sorry, but what you said was like a knife to my gut. Have I ever lied to you? How could you even say those things to me?"

He lowered his head and stared at the ground. "Don't apologize. I deserved that. I'm just so angry with her and concerned. It's bad out there, Dashay. Riley had no idea since she'd been so far removed from the fighting. And then there are all the usual dangers. Aside from the fact that she went AWOL, she knows better than to travel alone. It's bloody dangerous."

"I'm aware of all that. Riley's like a sister to me. If I had known what she was planning, don't you think I would have enlisted your help to stop her? I never would have helped her run away. I've been out of my mind with worry since I found her letter." After Dashay explained about Riley's note, he said, "Do you still have it? Let me see it."

Dashay slowly shook her head. "She asked me to destroy it, so I did. I've regretted it every moment since. They might have been the last words we ever have from Riley." Tears stung at her eyes, so she took a breath to keep control. "I reported what she'd done as soon as I discovered she was gone. They sent a team to track her, but so far, they've come up empty. They can't spare anyone else to follow her to Fort Worth, so they called off the search. All we can do is wait and pray she shows up."

Conrad's eyes widened as he stared at her. "How did Coop react?"

Dashay turned and started walking toward camp. Conrad got into step beside her. "As far as I know, he hasn't heard yet. After Dr. Ingram did his own chewing out with me, I asked him to let me tell Coop in person. Not looking forward to that conversation."

"Should you wait that long? It's already been ten days. He'll be furious if you wait another two weeks until we get to the farm."

"It's partly because I'm stalling and also because, deep down,

I'm hoping she'll be there with Julia when I get home. It's a long shot but possible."

He put his hand on her shoulder to stop her. "No, Dashay, it's not. Even excluding the fact that she couldn't have traveled the distance that fast, the fighting is fierce all along the border in that area. I've seen it. You said she was going to find Adrian. That's the opposite direction from Julia's location. The longer you wait to tell Coop, the angrier he'll be. You need to tell him today. I'll arrange it."

She hated to admit he was right. She'd just been deluding herself. "Make the arrangements, but I want you to tell Coop. He won't yell at you."

She gave her best pouty face, hoping it would help convince him. He burst out laughing and pulled her into his arms. "Who can resist that lip? I'll take the hit. How did you avoid telling him at the last call-in?"

"He'd already told Riley he would be on his way home from the hospital on their next scheduled day, so I didn't bother contacting the rest of the family. They've missed their calls before when one or the other was on the road, so I hoped they wouldn't question it."

He grew quiet for a moment, then kissed the top of her head. "I am sorry for what I said. It was completely uncalled for. You deserve so much better. I should have given you a chance to explain before I lit into you. Forgive me?"

She pulled away and stroked her palm on his sore cheek. "I won't deny it was undeserved, but I'll call us even." She gave him a tender kiss that grew more passionate as he pulled her closer. "Let's make that call, then I'll give you a well-deserved welcome home."

———

Coop flinched when the ham radio crackled to life as they were finishing dinner. His next scheduled call with Riley wasn't for two days. He felt a passing flash of concern, then realized it was probably the hospital.

"I just got home," he said to the family still sitting at the table. "Can't they ever give me a break? I don't care what the crisis is at the hospital. I'm not going back until I'm scheduled for next week. They'll just have to handle whatever the problem is themselves."

"Mama," Xav said and raised his arms to Coop as he passed.

Coop kissed his blond curls. "Sorry, buddy. Not Mama."

He picked up the radio and gave his call sign. Conrad Elliott answered, and the worry returned.

"Hey, Coop," Conrad said. Coop was relieved to hear his light-hearted tone. "Hope I didn't scare you. I don't have news of Riley, but as far as we know, she's safe."

Coop took a breath to center himself. "What do you mean, as far as you know?"

"Ten days ago, Riley left camp alone to go rescue Julia. She didn't tell anyone she was going. Dashay found a note on her bed the following morning, telling us where she'd gone."

Coop was glad there was a chair behind him because his legs gave out, and he dropped into the seat. "What do you mean ten days ago? Why am I just hearing about this?"

Coop noticed the moment's hesitation before Conrad responded. "We have reasons for the delay. I'll explain later. What you need to know is that she was heading to Fort Worth to enlist Adrian's help. She took Biscuit and must have made it there by now."

"Have you radioed him to confirm that?"

"We tried but got no response. We'll keep trying."

Coop's hands began to shake, and he had to remind himself to breathe to keep the room from spinning. "Why, Conrad? What would have triggered her to do something so reckless? You located Julia's location. You were mounting a rescue, and Riley trusted you to bring our girl home. I don't understand any of this." Another pause. "Conrad, what are you not telling me?"

"I was ordered to pull my men off Julia's rescue for a higher priority mission. It wasn't my choice. When I told Riley, I guess something snapped. She was different after that, but she didn't tell anyone what she was planning. No one could have imagined she'd pull something like this."

It sounds exactly like something she'd do, Coop thought, but kept it to himself. "What's being done to find her?" When Conrad gave him nothing but silence, he jumped to his feet with the radio still in his hand. "I'm going after her if no one else cares enough to."

"Don't be ridiculous," Dashay said.

"Why didn't you say you were listening? Afraid to face me?"

"I'm not afraid of you," she said.

Coop knew she meant it. He was the one a little afraid of her when she got fired up, but all he could think about was his wife was in mortal danger, and no one had thought to tell him about it for ten days.

"Conrad will handle this, Coop. Now you're going to listen to me. You will not go off on some half-assed chase after your reckless wife. You're going to stay home and take care of those babies. They don't need both parents running around the country like idiots. We're leaving here tomorrow and will be home in two weeks. If I found out you've done something stupid, you'll have to answer to me."

As much as he hated doing nothing, Coop knew Dashay was right. The kids deserved for one of their parents to be level-headed. "You have my word I'll stay put, but I want promises from both of you that you'll do whatever you can to bring Riley and Julia home. None of us can take much more of this."

"You have our word," Conrad said.

Coop heard Dashay take the radio from Conrad. "You don't

need my promise. I'll do whatever it takes to get them home to you. They're family to me."

"We have to sign off. Keep a clear head and trust us," Conrad said. "See you in two weeks."

Coop clicked the radio off, not wanting to hear more, and dropped his head in his hands. The words, *how could you, Riley? How could you?* replayed on a loop in his brain. When he raised his head, Emily was staring at him with eyes as big as saucers. "How much did you hear?"

"Too much," she said, as her lower lip trembled. "First, I'm going to hug Mom when she gets home, then I'm going to smack her. How could she do this to us after what we've been through?"

Jared came up behind her and put his arm around her waist. "I trust Mom. She made it home once. She'll do it again, and it's a lot safer this time."

Coop glanced at Emily, reading in her eyes that she understood that wasn't true. "She will make it home," he said, "and she'll bring Julia with her. We just have to be strong and believe in her. I think Nana made brownies, Jared. Get us some?"

Jared smiled and ran to the kitchen for their dessert.

"He's so clueless," Emily said.

"Let's keep it that way. The less he understands, the better." He stood and pulled her into his arms. "I've watched your mom accomplish superhuman feats. She wouldn't have run off without a plan. So, I'm choosing to trust her like Jared."

Emily nodded, then pulled away and wiped her cheeks. "I'm not sure if I'm ready to do that, but I trust you. Can you stay home from the hospital until they find her?"

"I'll have to see what I can arrange, but I'll be here as much as I can manage. Don't forget you have the rest of the family to lean on when I'm gone."

"I won't. I'm going to see where Jared is with the brownies. I need lots of chocolate."

Marjory and Lily came up as Emily walked to the kitchen.

Marjory squeezed Coop's hand. "What has my daughter done this time?"

The color drained out of her face as Coop explained.

Lily put an arm around him in support. "I thought she was supposed to be the smart sister."

"We can't be too hard on her. She's desperate to find her daughter. If I were her age, I might have done the same." She reached toward the chair, and Coop helped her into it. "The last time Riley was here, she told me the tear in her heart was growing every day without Julia home. I don't doubt your love for Julia, Coop, but a mother feels a bond for a child with an intensity you can't imagine." She glanced up at Lily. "What if you'd been separated from Miles for two years? What would you do?"

Lily's voice caught as she said, "Move heaven and earth until my boy was back in my arms."

"Those months after the CME when we didn't know if Riley had survived were an agony that I wasn't sure I'd survive," Marjory said softly. "If it hadn't been for Emily and Jared needing me to take care of them, I might not have. We have to remind ourselves this is what Riley's feeling. She saw a chance to go find her daughter and took it."

Coop rested his hand on her shoulder. "I can't know if what I feel is as powerful as a mother's love, but I'd lay down my life for Julia, Emily, or Jared, not just Xav. I'll do my best to give Riley the benefit of the doubt, but she'd better get her cute little behind back here as quick as she can. The kids aren't the only ones I'd give my life for."

———

Riley was counting the seconds until the end of her shift. After three days of bartering and begging, she'd gotten permission to radio Coop. Her scheduled time was in thirty minutes, and if she missed it, she might not have another chance. She'd finished examining and treating the patients for the day, and with fifteen minutes to go, would have just enough time to make it to the communications building. She completed writing her notes in her last patient's chart and was about to head to the locker room to change when the triage nurse ran up behind her in the hallway.

"Dr. Cooper," she said between gasps, "we need you in trauma. I'll explain on the way."

"My shift just ended," Riley said, trying not to let her irritation show. "Dr. McIntyre should be here to replace me."

"He hasn't arrived yet. Please, Dr. Cooper. The patient is critical."

Riley gave a quick nod and struggled to keep up with the nurse as they hurried to the trauma unit.

On the way, the nurse explained the patient's condition. "Gaping chest wound. Artillery hit, I think. I'm not sure how they got him here alive."

Riley's heart sank. Having to take a severely injured patient meant she'd miss her time on the radio, and chest wounds were the most difficult for her to treat. She would have given anything to have Coop there to tell her what to do. She'd learned a great deal about surgeries outside her specialty in the years since the CME, but thoracic wounds were still a challenge for her. She'd do what she could for the soldier, but if what the nurse said was true, there wouldn't be much hope.

When she reached the trauma room and saw her patient, his injuries were every bit as bad as she'd feared. His heart was exposed, and she could see it beating in his chest. His sternum was shattered, and fragments of bone littered the field. Someone, most likely a field medic, had clamped the damaged vessels. If not for that, the patient wouldn't have survived for five minutes.

"OR now!" Riley called out on her way to go scrub.

As she did her best to sanitize her hands with the minimum amount of cleanser allowed, she closed her eyes and pictured the man's wound to plan her surgical approach. The first step would be to clear debris making sure not to leave any bone splinters. If any worked their way into his heart, he could bleed out in minutes from a lacerated vessel. Next, she'd repair the clamped veins and arteries. There were so many, and it was delicate work. If she didn't lose the patient first, the last step would be to rebuild his sternum and ribs. That would mean improvising since the odds of the hospital having what she needed for the delicate work were slim to nonexistent.

All doctors in the post-technological world have been forced to learn innovative ways of treating patients. As time passed and supplies diminished with no hope of replacement, they'd had to get more creative. Riley had been impressed and even amazed at some solutions she'd seen. She often wondered if that was how most medical procedures and tools had been developed in the early days of modern medicine. Without the brains and labs filled with biomedical engineers, doctors had taken center stage in finding answers. Riley knew these skills would only become more critical as time passed. The only hope was that someone would get factories and labs up and running. She was practical enough to know that was years in the future—possibly even decades after she was in the ground.

The other major hurdle was the lack of medications. The few remaining researchers around the country were working to create natural alternatives or manufacture more, but again, there was little hope of that happening soon. The only upside of having a diminished population left on earth was that the medications existing when the CME hit would stretch much further. Many were viable after their expiration dates. Others were not, and there was no way to get more. With their extensive knowledge of medicinal plants, scientists like Adrian Landry were among the most valuable people on the planet. She'd glean what information she could from him as they traveled to save Julia.

She was drying her hands before going to the OR when the surgical nurse came in and slowly shook her head. "We lost him."

Riley brushed past her to get into the hallway. "Let me take a look. There might still be something I can do."

"No, Doctor," she said without moving. "Dr. McIntyre came in while you were scrubbing. He called it. He says there was nothing we could have done."

Riley studied her for a moment, then went into the OR. Dr. McIntyre was leaning over the patient, removing the clamps. "What happened?" Riley asked.

Without straightening, he said, "Do you need to ask? It's a minefield in his chest. We couldn't have saved him under the best circumstances, and these aren't."

Riley stepped to the opposite side of the table and watched him work for a moment. He'd made the right call. With the damage the patient's heart had sustained, it was a miracle he'd survived as long as he had. "A moment of silence, please," she said.

The staff still in the room stopped what they were doing and bowed their heads. After a minute, Riley signaled they could go back to work and left the room.

Dr. McIntyre followed her out and got into step beside her. "Nice touch in there with the moment of silence."

Riley nodded but kept walking. "Just trying to keep a shred of humanity in this insanity. There usually isn't time, but I call for it when there is."

"I'll try to remember that. How did it go today?"

"My notes are on my desk at the nurses' station."

He put his hand on her arm to stop her. "Do you have a minute?"

"I really don't. I'm scheduled on the radio to talk to my husband. We haven't spoken in more than two weeks. I don't want to miss it."

"Husband? I wasn't aware there was a Mr. Cooper."

Riley had felt for the past two days that Dr. McIntyre had more on his mind than a working relationship with her. To put an end to all possibility of there being anything more, she said, "Dr.

Cooper, actually. Dr. Neil Xavier Cooper III. You may have heard of him."

"Are you kidding? He's your husband?" He checked up and down the hallway. "Is he here?"

She smiled at realizing his crush had already shifted to her husband. "No, he's home with three of our four children."

"Dr. Cooper has kids? I heard him lecture about five years ago and got the impression he was single and childless."

Riley turned and started walking again. She couldn't have cared less what the good doctor thought about Coop's marital status and would not let him keep her from him if it wasn't already too late. "Well, he is, and he does. We have four children. The youngest is eighteen months."

He caught up with her, determined not to let her get away. "Eighteen? You gave birth in the middle of an apocalypse?"

"Wasn't planned, but he's the joy of our lives. I really need to go, doctor, and you have patients to see. Can we visit some other time?"

He stopped, and she could feel him watching her leave. "Sure," he called after her. "Any time we're both free."

She had to struggle to keep from laughing out loud, knowing she'd be gone by morning. She'd only stayed the week to get a chance on the radio. Once she'd contacted Coop, she'd sneak away like she had from Santa Fe. Only this time, she'd be far more prepared.

————

When Coop yawned for the tenth time, he laid his pen down and rubbed his face in a vain attempt to clear his head. The grandfather clock in the living room had struck two, five minutes earlier, but going to bed wasn't an option. When Conrad gave them the news about Riley, Coop had set up a schedule with the family to have someone monitoring the radio around the clock. He'd been taking the night shifts since he was suffering from insomnia since learning about Riley.

After topping off his tea, he went back to work on notes for his assistant at the hospital. He'd contacted the Health Ministry to inform them he was going on a leave of absence until Riley and Julia were found. They'd grumbled, argued, and begged, but he'd held his ground. He couldn't function at work while Riley was missing. The Ministry found three temporary replacements to fill in until he returned. He'd teased them that it took three people to fill his shoes, but it also gave him a bit of an ego boost.

With the burden of the hospital off his shoulders, he turned his full attention to the kids and helping Kevin in the stables. The foals would start arriving any day, so he would need everyone to step up and pitch in. Coop was glad of a positive distraction from worrying about his wife.

The sun rose as he completed his thoughts on a proposal for a more efficient hospital waste management system. He was giving it a final proof when the lights on the radio flickered, and it sparked to life. He dropped his pen and moved to the chair in front of the radio.

He only had to wait seconds before he heard Riley's faint voice say, "Is anyone receiving me?"

Coop's words caught in his throat the first time he tried to answer. He cleared his throat and managed to say, "I'm here, babe, and you're alive!"

"It's amazing to hear your voice. Why did you think I was dead?"

Coop laughed at that. He should have known better than to assume she couldn't take care of herself. "Because no one has heard from you in weeks. You pissed me off and scared me to death in one swoop. The kids are sick with worry. Jared might never speak to you again. Where are you?"

"On a military base in Amarillo, Texas. Long story, but I'm healthy and safe. I had to work here for a week in exchange for food, supplies, and use of the radio. I'm leaving today to find Adrian and ask him for help. It's in the opposite direction of the border, but I don't have anyone else to turn to. I confided in two or three people here, hoping they'd help me, but with the war, they all thought my mission was insane. And they aren't granting leave to anyone because of the fighting."

"Riley," he said, interrupting her, "this is insane. What were you thinking? I know you're desperate to save Julia, but this isn't the way. Come home. We'll figure it out together."

"No, Coop. I've waited long enough and relied on too many other people to bring her home for too long. It just doesn't matter to anyone else as much as it does to me."

"I have no doubt of that, but that doesn't mean it's not almost as important to us. And there is the civil war to consider."

"I'm aware. I have a plan. Conrad's people cross back and forth over the border all the time, and we did it once if you recall."

And almost died, Coop thought but didn't dare say it. He was more than acquainted with that tone in Riley's voice. He leaned back in the chair and ran his hand through his hair, knowing there was no point trying to convince her. Experience had taught him that once her course was set, it was etched in stone.

It was one thing he admired most about her and one of his biggest challenges in their relationship. Now, it was a trait that could get her killed and leave him and her children without a wife and mother. The more he thought about the selfishness of her actions, the angrier he got, but he bit his tongue. He did not want his possible last conversation with Riley to be marred by bitterness and resentment.

"Just promise to remember two things. First, we all love Julia and want her home, but not at the risk of your life. Losing both of you would be more than the kids and I could bear. Two, don't be too hardheaded to ask for help. You don't have to do everything yourself. Use that most excellent brain of yours, and don't let your heart make all the decisions. Come home to me. You are my life."

Her voice trembled as she said, "And you're mine, despite how my actions appear. You're taking this much better than I expected. I wasn't sure you'd even speak to me."

"You owe that to your mom for talking some sense into me."

"I'll thank her when I get home. They're signaling that I'm out of time. I'll contact you as soon as I get to Adrian's. Give the kids a thousand hugs and kisses for me. I will come home to you, and I promise I'll stay put this time. Look for Julia and me soon. I love you, Coop."

The connection went silent. Coop wanted to crawl inside the radio and pull her out but would have to make do with trusting her to rely on her instincts. She wasn't making it easy. He was glad he hadn't told her he'd heard from the Ministry. She was in big trouble and would have much to answer for when she made it home. Until then, the point was moot.

The sounds of Xav jabbering in his crib brought him back to reality. For once, he was grateful for the distraction.

CHAPTER SIX

YEAGER WAS ITCHING to make his move. Colonel Beake had assigned him to command a regiment protecting the border in western Louisiana. It had taken three-plus weeks to travel to brigade headquarters in Shreveport. During the journey, he'd played Beake's game and followed her rules with exactness, biding his time until the pieces were in place. After reaching headquarters, he'd waited the two days until his regiment was at the border. His plan was to slip into Texas at night during a break in the fighting. By the time his absence was discovered, he'd be well on his way to Fort Worth, ready to complete his self-appointed mission.

Since his dismissal as head of the Daybreak mission, he'd trained himself to travel long distances on little sleep. His record was seventy-two hours of only stopping for hour breaks to eat and close his eyes for a few moments. He didn't have the stamina to carry that on indefinitely, but it would be enough to get a head start. His men wouldn't be able to go after him once he crossed the border, but it would only be a matter of time before Kearns ordered Beake to send an infiltration unit after him.

The trickiest part would be avoiding the assassination team Kearns had in the field tracking Daybreak. Yeager could only guess at who'd gotten the assignment. His best hope was that it wasn't someone he'd worked with, or crossed paths with, in the past. No matter what, he had to be the one to take the shot. The Daybreak had been his mission from the beginning, and it was up to him to see Dr. Adrian Landry get what he deserved. Once he'd made the kill, Yeager was convinced all would be forgiven, and he would resume his place as Kearns' right-hand man.

At three in the morning, he left his tent and calmly strolled through the camp. He casually made his way to the camp boundary and waved to the first set of sentries when they snapped to attention on seeing him, creating the illusion he was out for an early morning stroll. He repeated the process as he passed the three other guard posts along the perimeter. On his second circuit, none of the guards paid him any mind. He meandered through the camp until he reached the darkest, most secluded area along the perimeter and pulled the wire cutters from his pocket.

He'd snipped the last stand and stepped through when a sentry called out to him. He quickly slipped the cutters back into his pocket, then shined his flashlight toward the man.

The guard drew his sidearm and held up his other hand to block the glare. "Who's there? Drop that light and show yourself."

Yeager raised both his hands and glared at the young Corporal. "It's Colonel Yeager. Lower your weapon and get over here. Someone has cut through this fence."

The guard hurried to Yeager's position and examined the opening in the fence. "This is fresh, sir. I passed by here thirty minutes ago. The fence was intact."

Yeager gave the ground leading away from the fence a quick flick with this beam. "There are tracks leading into the woods. Whoever did this can't be far ahead. Let's get after them."

The guard took point, and Yeager got into step behind.

When they'd gone fifteen yards, the Corporal stopped and swept his light across the ground. "I don't see any tracks, sir. Whoever it was must have changed directions. Should we split up, sir?"

"No, that would leave us vulnerable. We don't know how many there are. There's only one other way they could have gone. We'll track back in that direction. Let's go another quarter mile."

The Corporal stared at him for a moment as if he disagreed with Yeager's plan, but he said, "Yes, sir."

He took off in the same direction, and when they reached a small stand of trees, Yeager lifted his gun and brought it down on the back of the young man's skull. He dropped in a heap. Yeager waited a moment to make sure he'd stay down. He spotted dark liquid pooling around his head, wondering but not caring if the boy would survive. If the blow to the Corporal's head hadn't been fatal, and he regained consciousness, Yeager counted on him to report that they were attacked from behind, and the attackers must have taken Yeager captive. A Colonel would be much more valuable to them than a Corporal. If he didn't regain consciousness, that was no concern of Yeager's. He had a mission to complete and couldn't let concern over the Corporal's welfare stop him.

When sufficient time had passed, he stomped the dirt in the area to give the illusion of a struggle, then created three false trails leading from the clearing. Next, he used a branch to wipe his footprints and backed out of the area before taking off at a full run. It would take a day or more for the guards to track his route if they found it at all. He'd hoped to rebind the wire so no one would locate his exit point, but he couldn't risk being seen, so he was forced to let that go. His escape time may have already been cut by hours. He could run twenty miles without needing to stop. By then, he'd be out of reach of his pursuers. The next any of them heard of Colonel Yeager, his mission would be accomplished.

———

Sergeant Nico Mendez took advantage of the lull in the fighting to take one of his customary strolls across the border. He'd crossed into the WSA often enough to make it second nature. He had established a routine of leaving his horse, Fred, in the paid care of Diego Moya, a resident in the nearly nonexistent town of Temple, Oklahoma, close to where he was stationed as an Army medic on the front lines of the war. Once across the border, he'd travel on foot to his buried cache of food and clothes, change into civilian clothes, then walk to the ranch of his friend, Santi Hernandez. He paid Santi a monthly fee to care for his other horse, Lucio. Nico told Santi that if he ever went over four months without showing up, Lucio was his to keep. Santi readily agreed to the arrangement.

After leaving Santi's ranch, Nico would ride the ten miles to Burkburnett, Texas, and mix with local residents for a day or so. The town reminded him of his home in Farmington, New Mexico, even though it was much smaller. It grew harder to leave with each visit. He'd become acquainted with some locals, including a couple of young, attractive women. One of them reminded him of Dashay. Some nights, he'd fantasize he was with her. He'd been tempted to stay in Burkburnett for good, but he knew he could never live with being a deserter, despite his growing disillusionment with the Kearns dictatorship.

He'd bristled under the treatment of the military as food and clothing rations continued to be cut. Worse, he briefly worked as a medic in two internment camps. If conditions were bad for the military, they were abysmal for the prisoners. Sometimes he wished the WSA forces would win the war and rid the US of their rogue president. The day would come when he'd have to decide where his true loyalties lay and stick with it. In the meantime, he'd dedicated himself to doing what he could to ease the suffering on his side of the border despite his growing misgivings about his president.

As he rode Lucio to Burkburnett that day, he was disappointed to see the growing WSA military encampment just outside of town. US forces had beaten back the latest assault, and he hoped they'd given up and moved north. He'd visited the base to the south in Wichita Falls more than once, just to get a gauge of their strength there. He wondered if it was time to pay another visit.

———

The two weeks Riley spent in Amarillo had been a welcome break from roughing it, but she was grateful to be back on the road and was enjoying the return to solitude. The few acquaintances she'd made had been kind enough to stock her up with provisions to add to those she'd obtained from the military. Coz had been the most generous. She saw in his eyes that he would have liked to be more than acquaintances. He was a good man, and if it hadn't been for Coop, she might have considered it.

In addition to the donated provisions, Riley had helped herself to a few of her own. She'd hoped her thieving days were behind her, but she justified her actions by telling herself she'd earned those supplies by offering her surgeon skills far longer than planned. She'd swiped medications and other medical supplies that would come in handy for trading and bribes. As drugs became scarcer, their value grew. They might be just what she needed to buy her way to Julia.

Her time in Amarillo had erased her fear that the military was going to snap her up at every turn. If the Ministry hadn't caught up with her on the enormous military base, they never would. She decided it would be safe to travel along the major roads and through the larger towns. It would cut her travel time and make it easier to keep her supplies stocked. Even so, she planned a route that would keep her away from the border fighting. It was slightly longer in miles but would prevent her from getting caught up in the conflict.

A week out of Amarillo, when Riley was on the northern outskirts of Wichita Falls, she found a secluded place to camp on the banks of a river. Before getting underway the next morning, she decided to allow herself a quick swim. She relaxed in the river for almost an hour, figuring it would take that long to wash off the grime of the road from the past week. When her skin began to pucker, she climbed up the bank and started for the pile of driftwood where she'd draped her clothes. She took a step and heard the rattling sound in an instant before she felt a searing pain below her right ankle. She shook her foot and looked down just in time to see a six-foot diamond-backed rattlesnake slither back into the water.

Her foot began to swell immediately, and the pain was excruciating. She crawled to her clothes and quickly dressed before wiping away the excess venom. After grabbing antiseptic from her pack and applying it to the bite area, she covered the wound with a small bandage. Her foot and ankle would swell up to the size of a watermelon before long.

By the time she finished treating the bite, she was sweating and shaking uncontrollably. Gratefully, she'd loaded her belongings onto Biscuit before taking her fateful swim, or she would have had to abandon them. Her only hope of survival was to get to a hospital as quickly as possible and pray they stocked antivenom. This was one medical emergency she couldn't treat herself.

"You know better than this, Poole," she said as she struggled into the saddle. "Get me to a hospital, friend," she told Biscuit as she felt the numbness spreading through her body. "No matter what, don't let me fall. I'll never make it back up."

Her faithful friend couldn't understand a word she said, but it didn't hurt to ask. She pulled the map from the saddlebag and spread it across the saddle. It would take roughly two hours to make it to Wichita Falls if she kept Biscuit to a steady but sensible pace. She roped herself in just to be safe, then braced herself and snapped the reins. She had no time to lose.

————

As Nico guided Lucio toward Wichita Falls, he became more concerned and strangely pleased at the size of the WSA military buildup. He estimated the number of enemy troops was large enough to at least form a battalion. He wondered if they were mounting one last push to take the border. If they succeeded, it would mean his post would be on the WSA side. He'd have no objection but didn't like that it would mean numerous casualties. If he were taken prisoner, he could surrender. It was more honorable to surrender in battle than desert. If they didn't take him as a POW or enlist him in the WSA force, he might be able to make his way home to Farmington and his family, who probably thought he was long dead.

He was envisioning the scenario when he looked up and saw a horse trotting toward him. Something about its color and gait looked familiar. As he drew closer, he could make out a redheaded female rider draped over the saddle. He thought he recognized the rider, but he couldn't believe what he was seeing. It was Riley on Biscuit. He closed his eyes, then looked again to make sure, thinking his fantasizing made him see things that weren't there. He snapped Lucio's reins and galloped toward the oncoming horse. They didn't have to go far to verify he was right. It was Biscuit and Riley.

He steered Lucio alongside them and reached for Biscuit's reins. "Whoa, boy," he said and pulled both horses to a stop. Fearing the worst, he dismounted and grabbed for Riley's arm to take her pulse. It was weak but beating. He let his breath out in relief, then patted the back of her hand.

"Riley, it's me, Nico. Can you hear me?" She lifted her head slightly and gazed at him in confusion. "Do you know who I am?" When she gave a quick nod, he said, "What happened? What's wrong with you?" She shifted her hand and pointed to her ankle. It was swollen to the size of a grapefruit and black and blue all around the bandage.

When he asked if she had fallen off Biscuit, Riley gasped, "Rattlesnake bite."

"Hold on. I'm going to get you to a hospital. They'll have you fixed up in no time."

He took hold of Biscuit's reins and remounted Lucio. He was afraid the horse wouldn't follow, but he got into step with Lucio without resistance. It was the first time he'd ever seen Biscuit cooperate.

As they rode along as fast as Nico dared go, a string of questions flowed through his mind. What was Riley doing alone on the Texas border in the middle of a war zone? Where were Coop, Dashay, and the rest of his former traveling buddies? What had she been doing going barefoot in a snake-infested area? She knew better. What were the odds that he'd cross paths with her for the third time in the middle of nowhere? They had to be microscopic. Whatever the odds, he was glad he'd found her when he did. She wouldn't have survived much longer, and it would be touch and go as it was. In the end, he was grateful for the chance to pay her back for saving his life after he was attacked by a bear.

———

Riley woke in a clean bed to the worst pain she'd known in her life. Every inch of her body throbbed. She was clearly in a hospital but had no idea how she'd gotten there. All she knew was that if someone didn't give her relief in a hurry, they might as well let her die. She moved her head as little as possible to find the nurse call button but couldn't find it. Her only other option was to call out for help. She gathered what was left of her strength and opened her mouth, but all she got out was a croak. She sensed movement from the corner behind her, and a second later, a man she vaguely recognized leaned over her.

"Welcome back, friend. You had us scared for a minute," he said.

"I know you," she said in her raspy voice. "Who are you?"

"It's Nico. Bet I'm the last person you expected to see. I saved your life, so we're even."

"Nico? It can't be. Am I dead? I hope this isn't heaven."

He let out a deep laugh that warmed her to her toes. It was Nico, but how could it be?

"You're alive but just barely. Biscuit brought you to me. You're in a hospital in Wichita Falls. Rattlesnake bite. Remember?"

The memory of her swim and getting bitten flooded over her. She'd survived, at least so far. She was far from out of the woods. "Give the details of my prognosis and treatment, then I guess we both have some explaining to do."

"Gladly, but first, you need water."

He lifted a plastic jug with a straw to her lips. She drank long and deep, feeling like she could never get enough. When the jug was empty, she said, "More, please."

"Give that time to settle. Your stomach needs to adjust." He set the jug down, then pulled his chair closer to the bed. "You have tissue damage to your ankle, but it's not permanent. It'll heal. It looks like your major organs took a beating but also no permanent damage. I won't kid you, Riley. It's going to be a long recovery, but it should be complete. You'll have to be patient, which, if I remember right, is something you suck at."

She gave a weak laugh followed by a groan. "Don't make me do that. Laughter clearly isn't the best medicine in this case."

"Fair enough." He watched her for a moment before saying, "I've thought of all of you every day since we parted ways in Charleston. Are you real or just my imagination?"

She lifted her hand to his. "I was thinking the same about you but feel that. I'm real."

"Tell me every detail of what's happened to you these past two years."

"You first, while I recover my strength. I'll need more water."

She closed her eyes as he stood to fill her jug. Her mind was reeling from the effects of the venom and at discovering Nico was alive. And he'd saved her life. More than coincidence.

He returned with the water and held it up for her to take another draft. While she drank, he said, "Most of the past two years have been a tedious repeating cycle, but my story didn't start out that way. Kearns' forces attacked Charleston the day you left. I worried you hadn't made it out alive. You obviously did."

"The others, too. We got out just in time."

"A few days later, three men came and kidnapped me from the hospital in the middle of the night. They took me to a secret bunker just outside the city. That was my first encounter with a man named Colonel Orson Yeager."

Riley cringed at the mention of that horrible man. "Unfortunately, I recognize that name."

Nico sat forward and pressed his fingertips together. "I figured you would. I've seen the posters. Did you have a run-in with him?"

"The answer to that is a major part of my story. Finish yours first."

He nodded, then closed his eyes as he continued. "Yeager questioned me for days while my wounds healed, but I told him nothing. Eventually, he realized I wouldn't crack, so he stopped, but he confiscated the map of your route to St. Louis that Brooks gave me. That's how Yeager knew who you were and where to find you."

"Don't blame yourself. There was nothing you could do, but this answers why you never caught up with us. How did he know who you were?"

"I later found out that one of Branson's goons informed on us, but I don't know which one. Yeager was after Adrian. It was guilt by association."

Nico's revelation answered so much. Coop and Dashay were going to be stunned when she told them. "What did Yeager do when he was through with you?"

"Simple. He sent me back to my unit, and I never saw him again. When the WSA was created, and the war started, I put in for transfers until I made it to the front lines. I've been serving as a medic in forward areas since."

"Then, what are you doing on this side of the border? And why didn't you just go home to your family in New Mexico?"

He sat back and crossed his arms. "I have one answer for both questions. Even though I hate what Kearns has done to our country, I'm still a member of the US military. I couldn't bring myself to be a deserter. I sent a letter to my family that I'm alive and well. I'm not sure if they got it, but I had to try. I believe America will be restored once Kearns is gone. There's a growing swell of opposition to her reign of tyranny, and I've seen the massive buildup of your forces along the border. If our two sides combine their strengths, Kearns doesn't stand a chance. The day is coming when our country will be whole. I honestly don't know if I'm on the right side or what the right side is, but here I am."

"I admire your dedication, but it's misplaced, and that doesn't explain what you're doing here. Are you a spy? I thought you were a medic."

"I'm no spy, and I'm still a medic. To maintain my sanity, I make my little trips across the border when I get the chance. I've made friends over here. There are times I consider staying, but my misplaced sense of duty sends me back over the border. It's rough over there, Riley. Aside from the CME, you wouldn't recognize the US anymore. It's a tragedy that one person can wreak so much havoc."

Riley looked down at her hands clasped over her stomach. "Trust me, I know."

"Enough about me. I'm dying to hear your story."

"I don't have the strength to tell you all of it now. There's so much. I'll just give you the highlights if you can call them that. I have to tell you first that we lost Brooks early in our journey. He fell off a bridge to his death just west of Charleston. It was a horrific, freak accident."

Nico gave a low whistle. "Sorry to hear that. After everything, he only survived to fall off a bridge to his end. Tragic."

Memories of that traumatic day fought their way to the surface of Riley's mind. Two years had passed, but at times, the wound still felt fresh.

"We pushed ourselves to keep going. Short version, Adrian's family had moved on to Fort Worth by the time we reached St. Louis, so he traveled with us to Colorado. Coop and Dashay got typhoid. Coop almost died, but we figured out what was wrong with him just in time. We spent time in an Amish community. We made a harrowing escape across the border, one step ahead of Yeager, and got home just in time for our son, Neal Xavier Cooper IV, to arrive. We call him Xav, and he's the joy of our lives."

Nico's eyes brightened. "Congratulations! That's the best news I heard in a year. I'd hoped the baby survived but was afraid to ask."

"He's incredible. Jared and Emily are great, too. It was quite the reunion. My mom is still with us, but Dad passed a year ago. His heart gave out. I'm grateful I got time with him before we lost him."

Nico laid his hand on hers. "Me, too. How about our Warrior Princess? I bet she was glad to get home. How's her leg?"

Riley's breath caught at the mention of Julia, and it took several moments for her to respond. "Julia still hasn't made it home, Nico. She's the reason I'm out here. I'll give you all the details later, but we just found out Julia and some of my other family members are being held in one of Kearns' camps in Oklahoma City."

The color drained from Nico's face. "*Dios mio*, Riley. I worked in one of those camp's infirmaries for a few months. You're right to want to get Julia out of there. I'll tell you, they work the residents hard, and they're stingy with the food and supplies, but they don't hurt them if that puts your mind at ease."

"I'm aware. I've gotten intel from my sources."

Nico's eyebrows shot up. "You have sources? What are you into, Doc?"

The last thing she wanted him to know was that her source was Dashay's longtime lover. "Long story. I'll tell you later, but this is why I'm on my way to Adrian in Fort Worth. I'm going to enlist his help in rescuing Julia."

"Are you still talking about Adrian Landry? He's the last person I'd expect you to turn to for mounting a rescue. Why not Coop or Dashay or just anyone else? The way I remember it, Adrian's pretty much useless for anything but endlessly jabbering on about plants and planets. And hell, Riley, he's partly responsible for Kearns becoming president."

"Most of that's true, but he's not the same man after our cross-country ordeal. I'm sure you heard that he finally fessed up about Kearns' betrayal on the day of the CME. I was in the room when he told President Purnell what happened that day. He was appointed Science Minister or whatever his title is. He's confident and more fearless now. You wouldn't recognize him."

Nico shook his head. "I never thought I'd see Riley Poole coming to Adrian's defense. You two were always butting heads. I'm glad he's grown into a decent man, but I still don't understand what he can do for you that Coop or Dashay can't."

Riley wasn't ready to divulge her own desertion, so she scrambled for an explanation Nico would accept. "Coop runs the hospital in Colorado Springs, and he's taking care of the kids.

Dashay and I serve on a traveling medical unit providing aid in rural areas. When we heard about Julia, I got leave to go get her. Adrian was the only person I could think of who has resources and people we'd need for the mission. He's not bad with strategy either."

She couldn't tell by Nico's blank expression if he's bought her story or not. He hesitated for several seconds before saying, "That makes more sense, but Fort Worth is a long way in the wrong direction."

Riley's lip quivered as she said, "I haven't seen Julia for two years, Nico. I'm desperate, and I didn't know where else to go. Now, I'm stuck here with this blasted snake bite."

Nico stood and checked Riley's monitors. "Take three slow, deep breaths, Riley." While she obeyed, he gently reached for her hand, and she noticed him resting his index finger over her pulse. "You need to stay calm. Getting worked up will delay your recovery. Seems I remember you saying that to me after the bear attack." He raised his shirt to expose the scars. "I owe you my life. I'll do what I can to save our WP, but your job is to focus on getting well. I'm going to let you rest. I'll make sure someone is monitoring you at all times, and I'll come back in a few hours. You still need to tell me all about Dashay."

He leaned down and kissed her cheek, then left her to rest. She continued taking slow breaths until she felt her heart rate slow. He was right that she needed to keep calm. That was vital to her healing. She wasn't sure how Nico could help save Julia but knowing she wasn't alone was enough to bring her peace for the present. The rest would have to wait.

———

"Who's that sitting up in a chair?" Nico asked as he came into Riley's room the following morning. "You're looking better by the hour."

"The mean nurse made me get up," she said and winked. "Have a seat." He turned the other chair around and straddled it. "Where were you last night?"

"I came by earlier, but you were out cold, and the mean night nurse wouldn't let me anywhere near you."

"I think they sedated me, not that I minded. My pain has diminished considerably except in my ankle, and my heart rhythm is stabilizing. My blood still isn't clotting as well as I'd like, and my BP is all over the place."

"I told you, patience. You should be dead. Keep that in mind."

"I haven't forgotten. I don't care what you say. I owe you."

"All I did was ride up by coincidence and lead your horse to the hospital. You operated on me in a park after a bear attack then kept me alive to get me to a hospital. What I did doesn't compare."

"I'm grateful no matter what you say." A young woman came in with her breakfast of oatmeal and a peach cup. There was even a packet of brown sugar on the tray. Riley's stomach growled at the sight of it. She stirred the sugar into the steaming cereal and took a heaping mouthful. After gulping it down, she said, "You know, a bowl of oatmeal saved my life when I was starving to death once."

"Don't think I've heard that story. What adventures you've had, Riley Poole. Quit stalling and tell me about Dashay."

Riley stopped with her spoon in midair and stared at him for a moment. She knew his questions would come and decided to be straight with him. After swallowing the oatmeal, she said, "She was miserable after we left you in Charleston, then Brooks died a few days later. It was a horrible time. If she hadn't been distracted with taking care of me, I don't know if she would have survived it, especially so soon after losing her parents and fiancée in the CME. But you know Dashay. She rallied, and I wouldn't have survived the trek without her. She never forgot about you. Nico, she still loves you."

Riley caught the faintest smile before he lowered his head. "She hasn't moved on? As much as I still love her, I always hoped if she survived, she'd find someone else to love eventually. I never expected her to be alone forever."

"I didn't say she was alone." His head snapped up, and he stared at her in anticipation. "She's had someone in her life for eighteen months, but it's never grown into more than a casual relationship. Conrad's a good man, but she says he's just convenient. Those are her words, not mine. I think it's because she can't let go of her feelings for you. She wants that kind of love again and hasn't found it with Conrad."

"That makes me feel relieved and sad at the same time. I'm glad to hear she still loves me, but I want her to be happy. She deserves that after what she's lost."

"What about you? Do you have anyone in your life?"

"No, it's not possible with my job and as much as I get transferred. I've had my occasional fling, but nothing more than that. Dashay ruined me for other women. No one else will ever measure up to her."

"I won't argue with that." Riley put her spoon down and sat forward. "Come back with me, Nico. I respect your loyalty to the service, but thousands of soldiers have come over to our side. You can do just as much good fighting alongside us. No one would question it, and you and Dashay could be together. You're meant for each other."

"I couldn't sleep last night thinking about that. I decided if you told me Dashay still loved me, I'd consider going. I'd love to see my family again, too. Let's get you well, and save our Warrior Princess first, then I'll decide."

Riley grinned at him despite the pain in her facial muscles. "I feel better already just hearing that."

"Don't jump the gun, Riley. We have a long way to go. Dashay wasn't the only thing I thought about last night. I came up with a way to help with Julia." His words were what she'd hoped to hear.

She leaned forward, giving him her full attention as he continued. "I'm going to push for a transfer to Julia's camp. I've been on the front lines for more than a year, so I don't think my superiors would balk at changing my posting. I've never asked for a transfer. If they approve, I'll keep an eye on Julia and your family and be your man on the inside. I'll do whatever I can to get them out of that camp. You work on getting them across the border. I know the best places to do that."

Riley didn't try to stop her tears of gratitude spilling down her cheeks. "I hardly know what to say, Nico. Saving my life isn't the only miracle from running into you. I'll find Adrian and get him to recruit whoever he can to our cause. We'll be there waiting for your signal. How are we going to communicate? I'm not sure if Adrian has a radio."

"Let me work that out. I've made lots of allies. I told you yesterday. Your only job is to focus on recovering."

"Knowing you're helping with Julia is all the medicine I need."

"As nice as that sounds, we both know it's not true. You're going to be weak when they kick you out of here. The fact you nearly died and ended up in the hospital is enough proof for me you can't do this by yourself. I refuse to let you travel to Fort Worth alone, but I have a trusted friend named Santi Hernandez, who I'm sure I can talk into watching out for you. He's a good man."

"No need to worry, Nico. I won't give you grief on this one, and I appreciate it. The snake bite ordeal gave me enough of a scare to admit I need friends by my side on this quest."

Nico stood and kissed her cheek. "Glad to hear you're coming to your senses. Finish your breakfast. I have to head back to my unit in the morning, but I'll start the transfer process as soon as I get there. I have other arrangements to make in the meantime. I'll come back to say goodbye this afternoon. We're going to do this, Riley. We'll find your girl."

"I believe that, little brother. I've missed you."

He gave a quick nod on his way out and said, "Me, too, big sis."

Riley wished she had the strength to jump out of her chair and dance for joy. Crossing paths with Nico was the break she'd hoped for, and it reinforced that she'd done right in going after Julia on her own. Victory was still in the hands of the Fates, but she'd been handed a fighting chance.

CHAPTER SEVEN

CONRAD FOUND Dashay feeding Xena hay by hand in the stables. He came up behind her and laid his hand on her shoulder. "I've been looking for you. Why'd you run out after dinner?"

With her back to him, she said, "I needed time away from the clamor to think. I love those kids to death, but sometimes I need a moment of peace."

Conrad leaned against a stack of hay bales and folded his arms. "You've been distant since I got here yesterday. I'm hoping it's Riley."

She fed Xena the rest of the hay she held, then turned to face him. "Isn't it always Riley? I'm going to throttle that girl when I find her."

Conrad blew out the breath he'd been holding. "That's a relief. I thought you were going to send me packing."

"You thought I'd spend the night with you first? You know me better than that."

He gave her a sheepish grin. "I do. What is it about Riley, then? You said when you find her. You meant when you see her, right?"

Dashay shook her head. "I meant what I said. Coop hasn't

heard from Riley since she contacted him in Amarillo three weeks ago. She should have been at Adrian's for more than a week, but we haven't heard from either of them. Something's wrong."

"This isn't news, Dashay. You're just repeating what Coop said this morning."

"Let me finish. I have been trying to find an easy way to tell you something, but there isn't one, so I'll just come out with it. I'm not going back to my unit."

Conrad rubbed the stubble on his chin and glanced up at her. "You mean tomorrow morning as scheduled?"

"No, I mean indefinitely."

"You planning to go AWOL, too?"

She sat next to him on the hay bale. "I contacted the Ministry a week ago. I told them I needed to stay here to support Coop, which is only partially true. I put in for an extended leave of absence. I tried to resign, but the council wouldn't accept that. That was actually a relief. I'm not ready to quit the HWB. I love the work, but I'm useless to them with Riley missing. I heard back from them yesterday. They granted my leave. I'm going to find Riley."

Conrad jumped to his feet. "Over my dead body. You're not setting foot off of this farm."

She smiled up at him. "You think you could stop me?"

"Don't force us to find out."

"Sit, Conrad. I'm hoping to talk you into coming with and bringing along a few members of your team."

"We're a long way from the front lines, so you may have forgotten, but we're in the middle of a war. I can't just take off on a whim."

"Give me some credit. I've been thinking this through for more than a week. This war has been going on for two years. It may go on for two more. I'm not belittling the work you do, but aren't you entitled to some extended leave? You've only had scattered breaks here and there, like the four days they generously granted you this time. Put in for an extended leave. Let's go find Riley and Julia. I know you've felt responsible since you had to pull your guys off the rescue mission. None of us blame you for what Riley pulled, but this is your chance to fulfill your promise to bring Julia home."

Dashay could see the wheels spinning in his brain as he thought over her proposal. She'd at least gotten through to him. She had no intention of running off like Riley had, but she was determined. If Conrad couldn't or wouldn't go, she'd find someone else who would.

"Give me a day to mull it over," he finally said. "It's a big decision."

"Why do you think I had such a hard time telling you? While you're mulling, think about this: I'm not just doing this for Riley. I'm doing it for Coop, too. He can't do it himself, and I wouldn't want him to. Those kids need him here, but it's killing him not to be able to go after Riley. I'm going to do what he can't. I owe that to him."

Conrad put his arm around her. "You're an incredible woman with an enormous heart. How'd I get so lucky?"

"Not luck. Fate. You're a good man, Conrad, and I feel just as fortunate. I hope you know that."

He stood and helped her to her feet. "Let's get out of this barn and go upstairs so you can show me."

She took him by the hand as they walked out of the stables. She was learning more each day how much he meant to her and was grateful to find he felt the same.

The orderly held the wheelchair in front of Riley, waiting for her to sit. She was capable of walking to the exit on her own and had resisted getting in the chair, but he wouldn't relent.

"It's hospital policy, Dr. Cooper. You should understand that."

She lowered herself into the chair in a huff. "It's not like I could sue you if I fell. Just get this over with." When they reached the lobby, she said, "I'm sorry. You're just following protocol. You know what they say. Doctors make the worst patients."

He barked a laugh, then cleared his throat. "I heard you've been a model patient."

"Then someone is lying." She lifted herself out of the chair slower than she had hoped to. Her recovery was complete, but she still felt residual fatigue. That would only fade with time. "Thank you, Pete. Go. Celebrate being rid of me."

She was through the door before he could respond. She turned in time to see him rushing away down the hallway. She let out a hearty laugh as she walked toward Biscuit. He was waiting ten yards from the entrance alongside a gray quarter horse with his rider, Nico's friend, Santi Hernandez.

When Santi saw her approaching, he dismounted and walked toward her. When they reached each other, he said, "It's good to see you walking on your own, Dr. Cooper. According to Nico, it was dicey for a bit."

"Hello, Santi. It's good to see you again, and I told you to call me Riley. We're going to be traveling together for some time. There's no need to be so formal."

Santi gave her a slight bow. "*Muy bien*, Riley. Your belongings are packed, and we're ready to go if you are."

"More than ready, but I need to get reacquainted with my boy first." She rested her ear against Biscuit and wrapped her arms around his neck. "Oh, how I've missed you, my friend. Thank you for getting me to Nico." Biscuit pressed his neck against her head and gave a soft whinny. She went to the saddlebag and found the last slice of dried apple. "This will have to hold you until I can make more. It may be a while." She turned to Santi and waved him over. "I'll need your help to mount. My right leg is still weak."

It took a few tries before Santi practically had to push her into the saddle, but she finally made it.

He scratched his head and said, "We'll have to find a better way to do that."

"I second that," Riley said between gasps for air. "Thank you, Santi, and not just for hefting me into the saddle. I know you have a ranch and family to care for. Taking me all the way to Fort Worth is no small sacrifice."

Santi climbed onto his horse and snapped the reins. Once they were moving, he said, "I have four brothers and their families to look after the ranch while I'm gone. You also have a family, Doc... Riley. Nico told me your story. Incredible. It's my honor to assist you."

Riley gave him a nod. "Let's just pray for an uneventful trip to Fort Worth. I've had enough adventures for ten lifetimes."

Santi crossed himself, then whispered, "Amen."

———

Coop and Dashay looked on as Conrad finished tightening the wagon straps.

"I'll ask this once more," Coop said. "No way I can talk you out of this?"

Dashay reached up and kissed his cheek. "It's cute that you'd ask, but you know my answer. Don't you want us finding your wayward wife and dragging her back here?"

Coop pulled her into his arms. "I need Riley home as much as I need air, but I hate the thought of two more people I care about out on the road. Promise you'll be careful."

Dashay moved away as Conrad came up the porch steps. "I'll bring all three of your girls home. Hopefully, the rest of the family, too. You'll be bursting at the seams here."

"I forgot to tell you in all the excitement of packing," Dashay said. "Kevin just signed the deed for the neighboring property. He's been working on it for a year. The previous owners moved to the city and abandoned the land. Kevin had to wait for the allotted time to pass before he could claim it. Russell and Jesse are starting work on the renovation of the farmhouse next week. We're going to have quite the homestead here soon."

"You and I should stake out our claim as soon as we get back," Conrad said and winked at Dashay.

She caught Coop's raised eyebrow but let Conrad's comment pass.

"You better get going before the kids come out for another round of goodbyes," Coop said.

"Please, no more of that," Dashay said. "I barely survived the last round."

Conrad pounded Coop on the back. "See you in a month."

Dashay climbed onto the wagon seat and took the reins as she waited for Conrad to join her. She gave Coop a quick wave as she turned the wagon around the drive and didn't dare look back. She'd been antsy to get on the road since they got word Conrad's leave had been approved five days earlier. Now that they were moving, she was getting cold feet. To distract herself from her growing uneasiness of the unknown obstacles ahead, she turned her thoughts to Conrad's comment about the two of them staking their own homestead. Had he been joking? Was it a roundabout marriage proposal or just an offhand remark? She was tempted to ask but wasn't sure she wanted the answer either way.

They rode to the main highway in silence, each lost in their private thoughts.

Dashay flinched when Conrad finally said, "This trip reminds me of a VHS video my father rented when I was young."

She stared at him for a moment, then said, "What movie?"

"I think it was called, It's a Mad, Mad, Mad, Mad World. I'm not sure if I have the right number of Mads."

Dashay smiled at the memory of seeing the film as a child. "I remember. How does a madcap treasure hunt compare to what we're undertaking?"

"Not an exact analogy, but it popped into my head. Riley's

chasing Julia. We're chasing Riley. The Ministry is chasing Riley. Kearns' people will come after us if we cross the border. Caught me as slightly madcap."

"I get what you mean, but this isn't so much a comedy as a drama."

"As long as it doesn't end as a tragedy."

"Way to jinx it." Dashay pretended to spit on her knuckles three times.

Conrad stared at her like she'd lost her mind. "What was that?"

She gave a faint smile and shook her head. "Never mind. Will we find them and bring them home alive? You made some bold promises to Coop, but we both know this is a long shot. I've been trying not to let myself face it, but Riley might not be alive."

"I've considered every scenario like I would for every mission. Of course, I've considered that Riley could be dead. If that's the case, we'll bring her home to bury her next to her father. The odds of that are slim. She's on our side of the border. The roads are relatively safe. The most likely reason we haven't heard is that she didn't find Adrian and doesn't have a way to notify us. Or a hundred other reasons. We'll find her trail and get our answers."

Dashay kissed him and said, "That helps. I'm just letting myself get into my head. Thanks for agreeing. I know your CO wasn't too happy about you taking off on this madcap treasure hunt."

"He'll get over it. I reminded him that Riley and Adrian are still at the top of Kearns' most wanted list. Julia's her daughter. He agreed with my point that Kearns could order her people to use Julia as bait and approved the mission. I honestly believe they would have done that by now if they were going to, but it got me the permission and resources I needed."

Dashay snapped the reins to get the horses to step it up. "Let's go make you a hero."

———

Riley reined Biscuit to a stop, then reached into her pocket for the worn slip of paper with Adrian's address he'd given her before resigning his position in Denver to settle permanently in Fort Worth.

Santi rode up beside Riley and handed her the map Coz had given her as a farewell gift in Amarillo. As she studied it, he said, "Close yet?"

She held up her finger, signaling for him to wait. She'd carefully mapped their course before leaving camp early that morning. Adrian lived near a lake and nature preserve on the western edge of Fort Worth. They'd been able to skirt the edge, which saved them hours of traversing the massive city and reduced the risk of interaction with the locals.

When she was sure of the direction they needed to head, she looked up and nodded. "Just over five miles after we cross the bridge. I'm looking forward to getting out of this saddle and sleeping in a bed."

Santi gave her that smile that veiled his thoughts. She knew he was glad they'd arrived without incident, but she was sure his thoughts were of getting out of unfamiliar territory and home to his family. She folded the map and note, then shook Biscuit's reins. He took off at a quick pace as if he understood they were close to the end of their journey.

Riley was grateful the trip had been uneventful, but that hadn't meant it was easy. She'd been plagued by pain and overwhelming fatigue from her snake bite. Being recovered enough to leave the hospital hadn't meant she was cured. Complete recovery could take weeks, if not months. She judged by her symptoms that it would take her that long, but she was glad they'd need time at Adrian's to rest and plan their strategy. Once they were on the road again, her strength would be recovered.

After crossing the bridge, they wound through neighborhoods

until they found Adrian's street. Her heart pounded in anticipation of seeing her friend and in fear that she might not find him. She needn't have worried. As they approached his address, she recognized him walking from his house to a wagon parked in the driveway. He was carrying what looked like a load of bedding. Biscuit whinnied when he recognized him and took off at a gallop. Riley would have tumbled out of the saddle if she hadn't been gripping the reins.

Adrian spun toward the sound of Biscuit's shoes on the pavement. Clearly not realizing who it was barreling for him, he dropped the bedding in the dirt and raced for the front door.

"Adrian, stop," Riley called. "It's me, Riley, and Biscuit."

He froze mid-step, then slowly turned to face them. Riley had to tug hard on the reins to slow Biscuit down. Adrian was Biscuit's favorite human, and the feeling was mutual. Adrian's eyes widened when he realized it was Riley and Biscuit. As he hurried toward them, Biscuit stretched his neck out for a hug while Riley dismounted. Santi held back, quietly waiting for the friends to get reacquainted.

Once Adrian had given Biscuit a loving welcome, he turned to Riley and pulled her into a suffocating hug. "You are the last person I expected to see. What are you doing here?" Before she could answer, he pointed at Santi. "Who is that?"

"I'll explain my reasons for trekking all this way once I've had a chance to catch my breath." She turned and gestured with her hand to Santi. "This is my new friend Santi Hernandez. Santi, this is Dr. Adrian Landry."

Santi gave Adrian the same veiled smile and dipped his chin.

Adrian stared at Santi with a blank expression, then said, "Pleasure," before shifting his gaze back to Riley. "Now, explain."

Riley sighed, then said, "You never change. Aren't you going to invite us in first and offer us food and water? What kind of host are you?"

"Right. Not much to offer, but this way," he said and motioned for them to follow.

Santi dismounted, and he and Riley tethered their horses to an enormous oak tree in the middle of the front yard. Biscuit made his displeasure clear when Adrian entered the house.

"Sorry, boy," Riley said, "but you're a bit tall to fit through the door."

He hung his head as she left him to go inside after Santi. The scene that greeted them in the house was the last thing Riley expected. Boxes and household items were scattered all over Adrian's sizable great room, but the area was devoid of furniture. She turned to Santi with raised eyebrows. He just shrugged. Riley felt a flicker of panic in her gut. If Adrian was in the middle of a move, helping her find Julia would be the last thing he'd be prepared to do.

The two of them left the front room and went to join Adrian where he was banging around in the kitchen. When they came in, he gestured for Riley to take the only chair, then moved a three-legged stool next to it for Santi. He waved it off and leaned against the wall with his arms folded.

"Where are you going? The ministry set you up nicely," Riley said as she watched him scoop what looked like cold vegetable soup into camping bowls. "What could make you abandon this gorgeous house?"

He handed each of them a bowl, then dropped onto the stool. "Someone's after me, Riley. We're bugging out before they get to my family and me."

Riley took a bite of the soup to keep from rolling her eyes. For such a rational scientist, Adrian had a tendency toward paranoia when it came to his personal safety. She studied him for a moment while she carefully chose her words. She was glad to see him looking so fit. He'd been suffering from exposure and injuries from a severe beating the first time she met him. He'd looked so frail and mousy then. When she saw him again months later, he'd recovered his health but was suffering from malnutrition. Seeing him so robust made it difficult for her to believe he was the same man.

She took a slow breath before saying, "I won't deny that Kearns would still love to have your head, but you've been living safely in the WSA for two years. I doubt she'd waste the resources to come after you now."

He looked her directly in the eye, which was not something Adrian usually did. The action showed her he was seriously concerned.

"You're wrong, Riley. I'm not imagining this, and you don't know that woman like I do. I've gotten word some shady men have been questioning associates in Denver. A colleague in my old office contacted me by radio last week. He said two men grilled him about me for an hour. They claimed they were interested in one of my research papers, but they asked too many questions about my personal life and location."

"I admit that *does* sound suspicious," Riley said. "Did he tell them anything to compromise you?"

Adrian shook his head. "He had nothing to tell them except that I left Denver a year ago. My colleague called the authorities to report this contact. When the authorities looked into it, they had vanished. He wasn't the only one they questioned. Anyone less suspicious and who doesn't know my history might have told them what they were fishing for. Kearns is after me."

What he'd told them sounded like much more than paranoia.

Adrian glanced at Santi and checked the room to make sure no one was listening before whispering, "I'm taking my family to California. We've been telling our friends that we're moving back to Denver. Kenzie and the girls are off saying goodbye to friends and family. We're leaving at sunrise tomorrow."

Riley stared at him in disbelief. What he'd told her didn't sound like paranoia. His wife Kenzie must have believed the threat was real to pull up stakes and make such a drastic move.

Riley still wasn't convinced it was Kearns who was after him. But maybe someone else might have been. Adrian definitely had his enemies. Riley had once counted herself one of them. "Couldn't it be someone else looking for you? You're a well-known physicist and flora expert. Maybe someone needs your expertise and is searching for you."

He stood and began pacing the kitchen. "Why wouldn't they have told the people they're questioning that? My friend would have willingly told them where I am if that were the case."

That made sense, but there was another possibility. "You haven't made new enemies, have you? You do have a tendency to rub people the wrong way. Remember how we met?"

He stopped pacing and put his hands on his hips. "Thanks for the vote of confidence. Although, Kenzie said exactly the same at first."

She got up and put a hand on his shoulder. "You know I think the world of you now. If I didn't, I wouldn't be here."

"Why are you here, Riley?" She sank into her chair and told him the entire story, starting with her cousins showing up at the ranch and the letter from Julia. He gave a low whistle when she finished. "With Conrad on the job, I thought your Julia would have been home long before this, but you were out of your mind running off alone like that."

"More desperate than crazy. What would you do if one of your girls were held captive in Kearns' camps for all this time, Adrian? Would you sit back waiting for others to bring her home?"

Adrian pondered her words for several seconds. "Makes more sense when you put it that way. I'm truly sorry I can't help. I wouldn't be alive and reunited with my family if it weren't for you, but why didn't you radio that you were coming? I could have saved you the trip."

Riley sank back into her chair and stared at the floor as the weight of failure threatened to crush her. She hadn't thought farther than getting to Adrian. It hadn't occurred to her he wouldn't rush to her aid.

"I couldn't tell anyone I was leaving, so I had no way to find out how to contact you. I don't know where to go from here, Adrian. I can't do this alone, and Santi needs to get back to his ranch. Nico is across the border, waiting to hear from me. He sends greetings, by the way. I have one contact in Amarillo, but he's a long shot."

Adrian rubbed his chin as he became lost in thought. "There might be one option," he finally said. "I have two nephews in their early twenties who live nearby. They're both sharp as tacks but experts at getting into trouble. They're also fearless and always seeking adventure."

Riley glanced up at him, feeling a faint ray of hope. Two strapping and adventurous young men might be exactly what she needed. "Do you think they'd help?"

"I can all but guarantee they will, and Kenzie's sister will be thrilled to have them constructively engaged. It'll do them good to put all the pent-up energy to positive use for once."

Riley jumped up and gave him a hug. "Thank you, Adrian. I may be able to recruit more helpers along the way, but this is a start."

"I'll even supply the gear and supplies you need. We can only carry so much in the wagon. We'll go ask them after you've had a rest. I don't mean to offend you, Riley, but you look like hell. I can't believe you traveled across the country pregnant without getting a single injury, then you go and get a snake bite. Get yourself upstairs and rest in Brittany's bed. Santi, you're welcome to a bed, too."

Santi gave a slight bow. "No, thank you. I don't need rest. I'll check on the horses."

"Sleep can wait," Riley said. "I need to contact Coop and let him know I'm alive. Then I want to meet your nephews. Point me in the right direction if you can't go with us."

Adrian squinted at her. "Are you sure? I'm no medical doctor, but you look like you can barely stand."

Riley crossed her arms. "I don't need to stand to ride Biscuit. It might take work to get me into the saddle, though."

Adrian held up his hands in surrender. "I know better than to argue with you once you've made up your mind. I haven't packed the radio yet. I'll set you up, then leave a note for Kenzie explaining why the wagon isn't loaded."

Riley kissed his cheek. "Thank you, friend. My entire family will be indebted to you."

"No, Riley. I haven't begun to pay back what I owe you. Not sure I ever will."

————

Riley hadn't been wrong about needing help getting into the saddle. It took Adrian and Santi ten minutes of maneuvering to get her perched on Biscuit.

"You're staying up there until we're back at the house. I don't have the strength to repeat that today," Adrian said as he mounted his horse, Brooks.

Riley found it morbid that Adrian would name his horse after the friend they lost on their cross-country journey, but it was such an Adrian thing to do.

"Agreed," she said, between gasps for air. "Would have been easier to use ropes and pulleys."

Adrian got Brooks moving while Riley and Santi guided their horses into position behind him. She was so exhausted from mounting Biscuit that it was all she could do to cling to the saddle. While she rested to regain her strength, she rehashed her radio conversation with Coop. While he'd been hugely relieved to learn she was alive, she couldn't mistake the coolness in his voice, no matter how much he tried to mask it. She knew him too well to be fooled but didn't fault him. She'd had plenty of time to imagine how furious she would have been if he'd run off without telling her. She hoped that when she showed up with Julia in tow, all would be forgiven.

She told him of her snakebite and hospital stay. He was thrilled to hear she'd run into Nico and enlisted his help. She filled him in about Adrian's situation and her hope of the nephews joining her quest.

The news that Dashay and Conrad had left the farm to search for her was surprising. She couldn't imagine Conrad doing such a thing and knew Dashay had to be the driving force behind the decision. Riley was relieved and infuriated at the same time. She'd ordered Dashay not to come after her. She promised Coop she'd leave a note for them at Adrian's and keep a lookout for them on the road. She reassured him that if anyone could find her, it would be Conrad.

She didn't make promises about when she'd contact him next, having no idea when that might be but said she'd do her best to get in touch whenever she scored access to a radio. He explained how they were leaving the radio running day and night with someone monitoring it at all times. It comforted her knowing she could reach him any time she got her hands on a ham radio.

His tone had relaxed some by the time they said goodbye, but he wasn't his usual jovial self. He had the weight of caring for the kids and the rest of the family and managing the hospital, all while his wife was traipsing all over the Southwest. He had to be stretched to his limit. She vowed to get Julia and herself home in one piece, reminding him she'd never failed at anything when she was determined. That got a laugh from him, at least.

After professing their love and signing off, Riley broke down and feared she'd never stop crying. Adrian came to her rescue by announcing that if she wanted to meet the nephews, they had to go. She'd pulled herself together and got ready to move to the next step in her mission.

When she was strong enough to carry on a conversation, she

rode Biscuit up beside Adrian and said, "Tell me about these nephews. What are their names? How much farther to their house?"

"Last question first. We'll be there in five minutes. The boys are Kenzie's sister's only children. Reece just turned twenty-two. Brady is eighteen months younger, but they could be twins. Brady reminds me of that kid Kip, Jace's nephew in Madisonville. Remember him?"

Riley raised an eyebrow. "How could I forget? He helped save our lives. If your nephews are half the young man Kip was, I'll be in safe hands."

Adrian gave a quick nod, then continued. "Reece was just starting his mechanic training when the CME hit. Brady was in high school, but he's good with his hands, too. It's been a challenge for my sister-in-law to keep them occupied, but she refuses to let them sign up to fight, no matter how much they beg. Their father was killed in a ten-car pileup when the CME struck."

"I'm sorry to hear that," Riley said. She meant it, but the words rang hollow. Adrian held himself directly responsible for a modest percentage of CME deaths. Riley didn't disagree, but it hurt to see him suffer for it. They'd never know which lives could have been saved if he'd had the courage to stand up to Kearns. He'd have to live with that burden for the rest of his life.

Adrian shook it off and said, "She's kept the boys close, but their friends are all off fighting the war, so those two ended up with too much free time on their hands. Their mom may jump at letting the boys help you, as long as we don't let on how dangerous it could be."

"Mums the word, but she'll probably figure out that if Kearns' hounds are after you, they could be after me, too."

"They would have captured you by now if they were. You haven't exactly been hiding your whereabouts."

Riley shivered at the thought of Yeager's spooks showing up at the farm and taking her children. It was bad enough Kearns had Julia in her clutches.

"Besides," Adrian went on, "you didn't cause Her Awfulness any trouble. Yeager was only tracking you across the continent because you were with me."

What Adrian said made sense, but that didn't erase all doubt that Yeager could be searching for her, too. "All good points," she said. "I'll trust your judgment just this once."

Adrian nodded in satisfaction. "That is a miracle." He reined Brooks to a stop outside an average middle-class house in the center of the block. "Here we are."

He dismounted and tethered Brooks to the porch railing. Despite the trouble she'd had getting into the saddle, Riley wasn't about to stay mounted on Biscuit. She swung her leg over the saddle and slid to the ground before Adrian could stop her. When he glared at her, she shrugged and started for the house. Santi held back by the horses as she and Adrian stepped onto the porch.

She paused when she realized he hadn't followed them. "You're not coming in with us?"

He gave her his veiled smile. "This doesn't concern me. I'll keep a lookout for banditos."

Riley chuckled as she followed Adrian inside, then wondered if maybe Santi wasn't making a joke. "Might not be a bad idea," she whispered.

"Hello," Adrian called from the empty living room. "Anyone here?"

"In here," a voice Riley assumed belonged to one nephew came from the back of the house.

They followed the sound to a den and found the two of them lounging on couches with comic books. They each sat up and stared at Riley.

Without taking his eyes from her, one said, "Hey, Uncle

Adrian. I thought you bailed for California already. What are you doing here?"

Adrian glared at him. "You're not supposed to talk about California in front of strangers, even if I'm in the room. Both of you, on your feet now." They obeyed their uncle, scrambling to their feet in a hurry. "Don't you know you're supposed to stand when a lady enters a room?"

Riley was stunned by Adrian's authoritative tone, unaware he had it in him. She'd always seen him as more of a groveler. "Seriously, Adrian," she said, "I'm not the queen."

Adrian flashed her a look to silence her, then turned back to his nephews. "This is *the* Dr. Riley Poole who saved my life."

The nephew closest to Riley gave her a half-grin. "So, this is the famous Riley? Forget being a queen. Uncle Adrian talks about you like you're a goddess."

"Hush! That's Dr. Poole to you," Adrian snapped. "Riley, these are my nephews, Reece and Brady."

Adrian had been dead on about the boys being two peas in a pod. If it weren't for the fact that Reece was four inches taller and wore an earring, Riley wouldn't have been able to tell them apart. Each had their light brown hair pulled into ponytails and wore metal band t-shirts and cargo shorts. They reached six feet in height and were thin but muscular. Reece, the oldest, was the one who'd spoken. His disdain and lack of respect for Adrian were palpable. Riley wondered if Reece blamed Adrian for his father's death, or if he was just an arrogant, spoiled brat. Brady wasn't quite able to achieve the same level of contempt, but Riley sensed that there was no love lost between Adrian and the boys.

"Honor to meet you, Dr. Poole," Brady said, with what appeared to be genuine respect. She hoped he wasn't just putting on a show for his uncle.

Riley gave them the warmest smile she could muster and said, "I'm glad to meet you, Brady and Reece. Mind if we sit?"

Brady and Reece dropped onto one couch. Riley sat next to Adrian on the other.

"Where's your mom?" Adrian asked as soon as they were settled.

"At the market trading vegetables," Reece said. "She won't be home for at least another hour."

"And you didn't go along to help her?"

They shrugged in unison, then Brady said, "She told us she didn't need us."

Probably because she thought you'd just get in the way, Riley thought. Witnessing the nephews' attitudes was making her second guess the wisdom of traveling with them. Their behavior might have had more to do with their feelings toward Adrian than their characters. She reminded herself that it took months for her to even tolerate the man.

"I was hoping she'd be home to hear what we have to say," Adrian continued, "but I don't have time to wait. Dr. Poole's been on a long, arduous adventure to get here. Her daughter's being held captive in one of Kearns' camps in Oklahoma City. She needs help to free her and other family members. Since my family is leaving in the morning, I told Dr. Poole you two might help her." He stopped and glanced pointedly at the comic books. "It's not like you have anything else to do."

Brady's eyes brightened, and he sat up straighter. Reece watched them, trying to mask his interest, but Riley could tell he was intrigued.

"Seriously? A real live rescue mission?" Brady asked. "That sounds awesome."

Reece elbowed him in the ribs. Brady fell back against the cushions, rubbing his side. He glared at his brother and said, "That hurt."

Reece folded his arms and watched them with a blank expression. "It might be an interesting way to pass the time but sounds risky. What's in it for us?"

Adrian started to answer, but Riley held up her hand to stop him. She wasn't about to let this snit of a boy get the upper hand after what she'd been through. She leaned forward with her elbows resting on her knees and gave Reece a steely glare.

"There's nothing in it for you except the chance to help a fellow human being. This isn't a negotiation, and I don't have time to satisfy your curiosity. If you're not a hundred percent committed to helping me save my daughter, stay here. If you want to do something noble for another person and go on an adventure, join me."

Reece's eyes widened enough for Riley to see she'd gotten through to him.

"I told you she's not someone to mess with," Adrian said. "What's your answer?"

"Come on, Reece," Brady said. "You talk all the time about how bored you are and want to take off and see the world. This is our chance, and we'd even get to cross the border. It's better than sitting around here chopping wood and pulling weeds in the garden."

It wasn't exactly what Riley had hoped to hear, but maybe she'd expected too much. Adrian got to his feet, so she followed, hoping to force Reece to decide. They really didn't have time to haggle.

"I'll provide all your gear and provisions," Adrian said. "All you have to contribute is your muscles and willing hands."

As Reece mulled it over, Riley said, "Just know this isn't a game. Lives are at stake. If you commit to going, there's no turning back if it gets too hard. I expect you to see it through."

Brady jumped up and held out his hand. "I don't care what Reece does. I'm coming. When do we leave?"

While Riley shook Brady's hand, Reece slowly got to his feet. "I'm in, too. We won't let you down, Dr. Poole."

Riley extended her hand to Reece, who hesitated for an instant before shaking it. "Perfect," she said. "To answer your question, Brady, we leave in two days. I'm recovering from a snake bite, and I need rest before we hit the road. You two can also help me gather supplies. I have a friend named Santi who will travel with us for the first few days. After that, we're on our own until we cross the border. I have help lined up on the other side."

"Sweet," Brady said. "This is like being in a spy movie. We'll do whatever you need."

Reece frowned at his brother. "Grow up. It's nothing like that."

"Reece's right," Adrian said. "It's more serious. I better hear a good report about you two from Riley after the mission."

"Or what?" Reece asked as they heard the front door close.

A woman Riley guessed to be the boys' mother strode into the room and said, "What is this, Adrian? Who is that man in our front yard?"

Adrian put his arm around her shoulder. "Don't worry, Chrissy. It's safe. This is my friend, Dr. Riley Poole. The man in the yard is her traveling companion."

Chrissy stared at Riley for a moment, then said, "The Riley you're always going on about? She's smaller than I expected."

"Chrissy," Adrian said, "that was rude."

Riley laughed and held out her hand. "No offense. I get that all the time. It's nice to meet you."

Chrissy shook her hand, then said, "I apologize. The way Adrian spoke of you, I pictured you seven feet tall, not five."

"Told you," Reece said.

Chrissy turned to Adrian and said, "I'll ask again. What are you doing here? Shouldn't you be home packing?"

Riley's gut tightened. This woman had the power to put a stop to her plan. She'd go alone to get Julia if forced to, but only as a last resort. Reece and Brady might have an overabundance of attitude, but that could be useful down the road.

Adrian's earlier boldness faded as he hemmed and hawed to explain their presence. Riley jumped to his rescue.

"I'm the reason we're here, Chrissy. I need your sons' help." She explained about Julia. "I'm desperate. Reece and Brady have agreed to come with me."

Chrissy swung around to face Adrian. "How could you even put this idea into her head? You'd let my boys go off and leave me all alone to manage here? I won't even have your help. I can't believe you'd do this to me. I'm sorry about your daughter, Dr. Poole, but my boys aren't going anywhere."

Reece stepped in front of his mother and stared down at her. "You can't stop us, Mom. We're grown men, and didn't you raise us to put others above ourselves? Where's your charity when it's inconvenient? We didn't sign up when our friends were going off to fight like you wanted. We're not missing out this time. You can get Cousin John's kids to pull your weeds and chop the wood. We're going to help Dr. Poole rescue her daughter."

Riley was as stunned as any of them at his outburst, but she couldn't help wondering if it was sincere or just a way to get out from under his mother's thumb. She wasn't happy to rob Chrissy of her sons, but she had other family members nearby and wouldn't be alone.

She stepped closer to Chrissy and rested a hand on her arm. "I haven't seen my daughter for two years. For most of that time, I didn't even know if she was alive. I wouldn't take your boys if this weren't my only option. It won't be forever. They should be home in less than a month. As one mother to another, I give you my promise that I'll do everything in my power to protect your sons and send them home safely to you."

Chrissy's eyes glistened as she gazed at Riley. "I can't imagine what you've gone through. Adrian told us the story of how you had to choose to be separated from one child to find the others. He told us he thought Julia would be home by now. It's heartbreaking to hear that she's not. I'll lend you my sons, and may God go with you all."

Brady pulled his mom into his arms and gave her a tight hug.

"Thanks, Mom. We would have gone anyway, but I'm glad you're on board."

Chrissy pulled away and held her arms out to Reece. "What about you?"

Reece gave her a quick hug. "Enough of this. We're not babies. Come on, Brady. Let's start packing."

Before they left the room, Riley said, "Come by the house in the morning so I can give you the details. Thanks for agreeing to join me. You don't know how much it means to me."

"I guess we'll find out," Reece said as he left the room.

———

Adrian's family did their best not to wake Riley the following morning as they finished their last-minute packing, but there was no avoiding it. She made her way downstairs in the dawn light and helped carry the last of their belongings to the wagon. When the time finally came to go, she and Adrian faced each other, not knowing how to say goodbye for the last time.

"You're always welcome with us in California," Adrian said, then blew his nose on an enormous red handkerchief. "An old college friend I ran into in Denver gave us his father's orange groves in a place called Fallbrook, about twenty miles east of Oceanside."

"Orange groves. The perfect place for you," Riley said, then gave him a warm hug. "Forgive yourself and be happy, my friend. It's time."

Kenzie put her arm around Riley's waist. "Just what I keep telling him. Maybe he'll listen to you. I'll be praying for you to get Julia home safely and Chrissy's boys, too."

"You all treat them like they're five," Adrian said. "They need some toughening up." He stood taller and puffed out his chest. "Look what it did for me."

Kenzie kissed Riley's cheek, then climbed on her horse. "Sun's up. It's time to go."

Adrian put his hand on Riley's shoulder. "The house and everything in it are yours. Stay there whenever you need a break from the cold. Give my love to Dashay and Coop."

"I'll do that. Safe journey," Riley said as she watched Adrian climb into the wagon seat and ride off to his new life. When he glanced back at her, she gave a peace sign, then turned and walked to Biscuit, who was pitching a fit at not getting to go with Adrian. She patted his neck and fed him an apple slice. "We'll visit him someday, boy, but we have other work to do first."

Santi came up behind her. "It looks like Adrian left everything you need for three rescue missions. We won't be able to carry most of it."

"I wish we had another wagon. It's just going to go to rot here," she said.

"Scavengers will take it long before then. When are those boys coming?"

"Probably not for a few more hours. I'm going back to bed in the meantime. Please wake me when they get here."

Santi gave a quick nod, then went to stow his bedroll. She'd tried to get him to sleep in the house, but he refused, saying someone needed to be lookout. "I wish you were the one coming with me," she whispered as she climbed the stairs to her bedroom.

————

The room was warm and bright when Riley woke. She glanced at her watch and was shocked to see it was past noon. She climbed out of bed and pulled on her clothes before bounding down the stairs. She raced around, checking rooms for the boys or Santi, but the house was quiet. As she headed for the front door, she heard angry voices coming from the yard. She stepped onto the porch to find Santi and Reece in a heated argument.

She rushed down the steps and pushed her way between them. "What's going on here?"

Santi backed away, and his lips tightened into a line. His face was as still as stone, but Riley couldn't mistake the fire smoldering in his eyes. Reece was glowering at him, breathing heavily and clenching his fists. If Riley hadn't appeared when she did, they might have come to blows. Brady stood under the tree several feet away, silently watching the exchange but doing nothing to stop it. It was clear he was afraid to cross his older brother.

Riley pointed at Reece. "You first."

"This little man thinks he can give me orders," he said, practically spitting the words. "Isn't he just the illegal hired help?"

Riley jammed her finger in his chest. "He was born on this soil, but that's beside the point. He owns more land and goods than you can imagine. He wouldn't even consider hiring the likes of you to work his ranch. If I see you raise your voice or fist to him again, you'll have to deal with me and trust me, you don't want that. Do whatever he tells you as if his orders are coming from me. Understand?"

Reece took four steps back with his hands raised. "I didn't sign up for this. I'm the one helping you."

Riley started for him again. "Then get out of my sight. So far, I'm not seeing the help."

Brady inched his way between them and put his hands on Reece's chest. "Calm down, Bro. Don't blow this for us. All he did was ask you to water the horses. We do that all the time at home. It's not a big deal."

The four of them stood frozen in place as they waited for Reece to respond. For Riley, everything rested on what he did next.

Reece lowered his shoulders and took a deep breath before walking up to Santi and extending his hand. Santi hesitated half a second before accepting it, but the fire in his eyes remained. "I'm sorry. I'm just not used to anyone but my mom giving me orders. It won't happen again."

Santi gave a quick nod, then walked around to the backyard.

"Get these horses watered," Riley said before following after Santi.

When they were out of earshot of the boys, Santi leaned close to Riley and whispered, "Send them home now. I've seen plenty of boys like that Reece. He's trouble that can't be tamed. Brady's fine, but he'll follow his brother."

"I'm not disagreeing with you," Riley said, "but I need them. I've handled worse than Reece. He seems to respond to me, and maybe he just needed to test his boundaries. We'll give it a few days. If he causes any more trouble, I have no problem dumping him on the side of the road, despite what I told his mother. He's a man, not a boy. Let him fend for himself."

Santi studied her for a moment, then nodded. "I'll trust your judgment, but I'm keeping one eye on him. His mother should have sent him to war. They would have taught him what discipline is."

"Agreed." She blew out her breath and relaxed her shoulders, hoping the incident was behind them. "What do you need me to do?" she asked as they walked back to the front of the house.

"We need to repack the gear to see what has to come and what you can do without."

The four of them spent the rest of the day working in a quiet truce. While they ate the last of the stew Adrian left behind for them that night, Riley said, "We need to get an early start. I want to push as hard as we can before we part ways with you, Santi, so I can find out if Nico left me word. I'm feeling stronger today, so after another good night's sleep, I might get into the saddle by myself."

"Gracias a Dios," Santi said and crossed himself. "I don't care how *pequeña* you are. My arms are too sore to lift you onto that horse one more time."

"And I've lost enough of my dignity." She looked at Reece and Brady. "Do you two have questions or need anything before I head off to bed?"

They shook their heads.

"We're good, Dr. Poole," Brady said.

"Your uncle's not here. Call me Riley. I'm going to say good-night to Biscuit and head upstairs. See you at sunrise."

They said goodnight in unison, and Riley was glad to see Santi heading for the stairs to sleep inside. She told him he'd better take advantage of the soft mattress while he could, though he'd be home to his own bed long before she would.

Even after her long nap, Riley dropped off to sleep as soon as she tucked the sheets under her chin, but her blissful oblivion didn't last. A sound she didn't recognize startled her awake at two. She bolted upright and scanned the room while she got her bearings. When she was conscious enough to stand, she slipped her feet into her sneakers and tucked the gun into her waistband before gingerly stepping into the hallway. She expected to come face to face with Yeager or one of his men, but the hallway was empty and the house silent. She checked Santi's room first, but he was out cold. She went to Brady's room next, but he was snoring away under the covers.

She made her way to Reece's room at the opposite end of the hall and wasn't surprised to see his bed empty. She'd passed the bathroom on her way, but the door was open with no one inside. She craned her head out the window to see if Reece's horse was still tethered with the others, but he was missing. She turned and leaned against the windowsill. Reece's gear was still piled in the corner, so he hadn't left for good. The most likely explanation was that he'd forgotten something at home and went to retrieve it, but Riley's gut told her the reason wasn't that innocent.

She considered going in search of him but realized she

wouldn't be too broken up if he wasn't back by the time they were ready to hit the road. She certainly wouldn't hold up, waiting for him to make an appearance. She could make the trip with only Brady, but she wasn't sure he'd be willing to go without his brother. If all else failed, she could head to Amarillo and try to enlist Coz's help. The odds of him deserting his post were slim, no matter how infatuated he was with her.

She yawned and decided endless speculation was pointless. Morning would bring the answers she needed. She went back to her room, hoping for a few more hours of sleep, but lay awake tossing and turning. She missed Coop and her children, fretted about the unknown dangers ahead, and berated herself for leaving Colorado Springs. *What were you thinking, Riley Kate?* she asked herself as the sky turned from black to gray. She heard the front door as she climbed out of bed to dress. Reece was back from wherever he'd spent the night. One problem solved. How many more to go?

CHAPTER EIGHT

RILEY'S TROUBLES started right out of the gate. Reece endlessly pushed the boundaries, and Riley was afraid it was just a matter of time before he and Santi would square off. He pestered Santi every chance he got, trying to goad him into losing his temper, then chaffing when his ploys failed. Reece was strong with an overabundance of testosterone and no self-discipline. It was a volatile formula. Riley and Brady hoped Santi and Reece wouldn't come to blows. Fortunately, Santi had the patience of Mother Teresa.

Brady did his best to distract his brother or convince him to let up, but his efforts didn't make a dent. Riley found herself caught in the middle of the fray, playing referee. Whenever she threatened to abandon Reece on the side of the road, he'd shape up for a time, then go right back to his campaign of harassment and torment.

If Riley had felt fatigued on the way to Fort Worth, she was pushed to the brink of exhaustion on the way out of it. To avoid the military buildup and fighting at the border, they'd taken a more westerly route. That meant adding two travel days to the trip before the point where Santi would turn east toward his ranch. Adding more chances for Reece to go after Santi was the last thing Riley wanted, but she feared getting caught up in the war more than dealing with Reece's asinine behavior.

As they neared the spur where Santi would leave them to return to his ranch, Riley wasn't sure whether to be relieved or concerned. With Santi at her side, she knew Reece wouldn't dare do anything to threaten her. Without that buffer, she wasn't sure which side Brady would take if Reece came for her. She hoped that once Santi was out of the picture, Reece would forget his vendetta and turn his focus to helping her rescue Julia. She didn't dare allow herself to consider the alternative.

As Santi was saying goodbye, he pulled Riley away from the others. "I've warned you, and I will one last time. Send these boys home. You're in more danger with them than without."

"You may be right, friend, but I'm not ready to be on my own yet. I'm only alive now because Nico happened to come along when he did. I'm not completely recovered from the effects of the venom. My reflexes are slower, and I have much less stamina. I'm not too proud to admit I'm afraid to travel alone."

"There's no shame in that. I agree it's not safe to travel by yourself. It's your choice of companions I'm questioning."

She glanced at Reece and Brady, impatiently waiting for her to finish saying goodbye to Santi. "Unfortunately, those two are my only choice at the moment."

"*Then, vaya con Dios, mi querida amiga.* I hope to cross paths with you again."

"I have a feeling you will. Please, get word to Nico that I'll do my best to meet him at the drop point in a week."

"I'll pass on your message and pray for you. Find your daughter and get her home safely."

He turned Lucio toward the East and left Riley staring after him. She was tempted to dump the brothers and wait it out on Santi's ranch until she could come up with another way to get to Julia. She probably would have if he weren't heading in the wrong direction. She watched until he and Lucio were just specks on the horizon, then turned to find the brothers silently staring at her.

"Where to next, Boss?" Brady asked.

Riley turned Biscuit around, and at that moment, they looked like college boys getting ready to take a road trip. She silently chided herself for letting her fears get the best of her. It must have been the pressure of the constant animosity between Santi and Reece. These were Adrian's nephews. He hadn't hesitated to recommend them to her as travel companions. He wouldn't have if it meant putting her in danger. These young men had lost their father. She understood the weight of such a loss. They were merely products of the CME, not dangerous outlaws.

"Northward we go," she said with a smile.

The boys rode their horses up alongside her and chatted about what lay ahead. The tension drained from her shoulders as she listened. Even if they were immature and obstinate, she was still relieved to have their company after the weeks she'd spent alone after leaving Santa Fe.

"Where are we stopping tonight?" Reece asked, startling her out of her thoughts.

Riley took out her list she'd made of possible stopping points along the trail. "A place east of Wichita Falls called Lake Kickapoo. We should reach it before sundown, so we'll have time to fish. I need fresh food after eating this dried stuff for days."

"Lake Kickapoo," Brady said with a laugh. "What kind of name is that?"

"I think it's from a Native American tribe."

"Let me see where it is on the map," Reece demanded. When Riley just stared at him and didn't reach for the map, he said, "Please."

As she handed him the map, she said, "That's better. Your mother seems like a good person. I'm sure she taught you manners."

Reece shrugged as he unfolded the map. Riley watched him

locate Wichita Falls and trace with his finger to the lake. He measured the distance between his index finger and thumb, then frowned. "That's thirty miles from Wichita Falls."

"That's by design," Riley said. "There's a large military presence there, and we need to keep our distance. Is that a problem?"

"Are we going to spend the whole trip in the sticks? I want to get a glimpse of the action."

Riley took the map from him and stowed it in her saddlebag. "This isn't a vacation. If you want to go sightseeing, do it when the mission's complete. You can travel back to Fort Worth any way you'd like. I'll be on my way to Colorado."

"Fine," Reece said. "I just didn't know we'd be hiding from everyone like cowards."

"Not everyone, Reece," Brady said, "just the war."

"Right," Riley said. "I've seen fighting up close and stitched enough soldiers back together to last a lifetime. You don't want any part of it."

"I'll decide that for myself after we find your daughter," he said, then snapped his horse's reins to get her moving faster.

Riley kept Biscuit at his same steady pace, not wanting to wear him out. If Reece wanted to ride ahead to let off steam and tire his horse, that was his problem.

Brady rode in silence for several minutes before saying, "I'm sorry about my brother. It's not you. He hasn't been the same since Dad died after the CME. He got worse when all our friends left to go fight. He's always pushing our mom. I hate it when he does that. She says he's just a hothead, but you don't need to be afraid of him. It's all show. He's never hurt anyone, except when he gets in fights after he knocks back a few beers."

Riley kept looking forward as she said, "I believe that, but his behavior is getting old. Fortunately, I won't have to deal with the drinking on this trip. I pity your mom having to put up with him on her own."

"I do what I can to be a go-between. That works most of the

time. He loves Mom. He just doesn't like her telling him what to do. He says he's an adult and can make his own decisions."

"There's truth in that, but she's probably afraid to lose him after everything that's happened, and it sounds like she needs his help. Maybe he'll get the wanderlust out of his system on this trip and settle down at home."

Brady shrugged but remained quiet, and Riley had a feeling Brady had his doubts about his brother settling down. Some people never did, like Conrad, but he'd found a constructive way to channel his energies. It could be that the military was precisely what Reece needed.

———

Dashay tried to stifle a yawn as she watched from her chair while Conrad carried on a conversation with the MP ten feet away. They'd reached the base in Amarillo at two in the morning. The guard had insisted on dragging them to the Military Police office, even though Conrad had all the proper papers and badges. They'd waited in the cold, hard chairs for thirty minutes before someone came to get Conrad. She could see him through a window but couldn't hear what he was saying. She was relieved when he finally smiled and shook the MP's hand before coming back to join her in the waiting area.

He sat next to her and rested his head against the wall. "They're arranging quarters for us. Just a little longer, then you'll get to sleep in an actual bed."

She tried to curl up, but the chair was too small. "Not a moment too soon."

A Corporal who looked like he was fifteen came to get them ten minutes later. He led them to an old building that reminded her of something out of Soviet Russia, but she didn't care as long as it meant she got to sleep. The room he took them to was small, with two twin beds that reminded her of her college dorm.

The Corporal handed Conrad a notecard and said, "This is where your horses and wagon will be stabled. Breakfast starts at 0600 in the mess hall. Enjoy your rest, sir."

Dashay collapsed on her bed without bothering to undress. "Does he expect us to get up in two hours to eat?"

Conrad chuckled as he sat on his bed to unlace his boots. "No, that's just when it opens, but they probably only serve breakfast until 0800. This isn't a hotel after all."

She groaned as she tried to get comfortable on the stiff mattress. "I'm acutely aware of that. Don't wake me for breakfast. I think I'll survive until lunchtime."

She must have fallen asleep before he had time to answer. The next thing she knew was waking to light streaming in through the open curtains. They'd pushed hard on the trip to Amarillo, hoping to gain ground on Riley. Dashay had assured Conrad she was up to the grueling pace, but that morning every muscle and joint disagreed. She reached for her windup clock and wasn't shocked to see that it was twelve-thirty. After forcing herself into a sitting position, she turned to look for Conrad. His bed was neatly made in military fashion, and his belongings tidied. She hadn't heard a thing.

After dressing in a hurry, she left a note for Conrad before going to find the mess hall. She arrived just in time for the end of lunch service. She carried her bowl of stew with some kind of questionable meat to an empty table. She was pleased to find that what the stew lacked in appearance, it made up for in taste. She wolfed it down, then went back for seconds. She savored the second bowl and was just finishing when Conrad came in and waved at her.

He came to her and kissed the top of her head, then said, "Let me grab some chow, then I'll fill you in on what I've found out so far."

Dashay drank down the rest of what passed for juice while she watched him get his food. Conrad was easily the most handsome man in a room full of strapping men. She'd been attracted to him from almost the first moment she saw him, even though she thought he was taking her as a hostage.

Soon after, they'd engaged in what she thought would be a harmless fling. When they said goodbye, she never expected to cross paths with him again. He appeared out of nowhere months later and had been a part of her life since. Even so, she still harbored feelings for Nico, which had always been an impediment in totally investing herself in the relationship with Conrad.

Without either being brave enough to acknowledge it, their relationship had made a subtle shift since they left the farm. They still hadn't expressed love for each other openly, but she felt certain he felt it as much as she did. Her question was, who'd be the first courageous enough to admit how they felt? She hoped it would be Conrad.

He brought the food back to her table and sat across from her. When he frowned at the slop in his bowl, she said, "It's better than it looks."

Trusting her opinion, he took a huge mouthful and gulped it down. "You're right. Glad you told me because I was about to pass and go for a power bar." After downing a few more bites, he said, "I went to the hospital first to ask around about Riley. As usual, everyone I spoke with had nothing but praise for her and wished she hadn't left. No one there has seen or heard from her in almost a month. When I asked if anyone else might know where she could be, they all pointed me to the same person, an MP named Cosimo DeLuca. I'm headed to the MP office next."

Dashay wondered how early he'd gotten up to have made that kind of progress already. She'd gotten used to how well he functioned on little sleep, but that was a stretch even for him.

"You've been busy. I'm not even all the way awake yet. Did you even bother to sleep?"

He took a bite, then winked. "I got two quality hours. I told you we're playing catchup. Riley wouldn't be able to travel very fast on her own. That gives us an advantage. After we find this Sergeant DeLuca, I'm going to request time on the radio to touch base with Coop. He may have heard from her."

"I'm ready when you are. If we get what we need today, when do you plan to get back on the road? Should we take a day to rest the horses?"

His look told more than words could have. "I'm considering stashing the wagon here and picking it up on the way back. We need to move faster, and pulling the extra weight is harder on the horses. Can you get by traveling with less stuff?"

"Easily, as long as we come back for it. We'll need it to get Riley's family home. It's likely we'll be getting them out of there with just the shirts on their backs."

"I'll make sure of it." He stood and picked up their dirty dishes. "I'm good. Let's find DeLuca."

Their search didn't take long. Sergeant DeLuca was just coming off his shift when they reached the MP office. His eyes brightened when they told him who they were.

"Is there anything you can tell us, Corporal?" Conrad asked.

"Everyone calls me Coz, sir. Riley's incredible and hot. I think we kind of had a thing. I tried to get her to stay."

Dashay gave Conrad a questioning look, then said, "Did she happen to mention that she's married?"

"Sure. What's your point? It sounded like her old man wasn't too happy with her for taking off. He should have understood her need to find her daughter."

"Give it up, Corporal," Conrad said. "You don't have a sliver of a chance there, and what's with going after married women?"

"With so few women left, I have to take what I can find." He eyed Dashay for a moment before saying, "What about you?"

Dashay shivered. "That's disrespectful to Riley. And, *in your dreams*."

Conrad took a step toward him. "She's with me."

Coz raised his hands in surrender and took a step back. "Just making a joke, sir. As far as Riley is concerned, all she said was that she was going to Fort Worth to find a friend. I haven't seen or heard from her since."

"Did she mention the route she was going to take?" Conrad asked.

"Yeah, I'll show you. Wait here."

"He's something else," Conrad said once Coz was out of earshot. "Think there's truth to something between him and Riley? She wasn't acting like herself before she took off."

"Are you insane? If there is one thing I'm sure of in this life, it's that Riley would never cheat on Coop or anyone else. Even if by some impossible fluke she did, it wouldn't be with a player like Coz."

"Aren't you being a little hard on him? Sounded like bravado. Most guys like to see themselves as God's gift to women."

"Why are you defending him? He came on to me with you standing right here."

Conrad put his arm around her and gave her a hungry kiss. "Why wouldn't he? You're incredible and hot, too."

She pulled away and gave him a playful slap. "I think he's rubbing off on you."

Conrad was still laughing when Coz came back with a map. He pointed out the route he'd recommended to Riley. It had been solid advice, directing her away from the action on the front lines. But he hadn't told them anything they didn't know.

"We appreciate your help, Corporal. We'll give Riley your regards."

"And stick to single women," Dashay called back as they went out into the sunlight. "Now, do we follow her tracks or take the quickest route to Fort Worth?"

"I say we go for speed. Are you up to getting on the road today?"

"Yes. My gut's saying we need to hurry, and I want to find my friend. Let's hit it as soon as you contact Coop."

They made their way to the communications center and got top priority use of the radio after Conrad flashed all the right badges.

"Impressive," Dashay said as a Private directed them to the radio. "I enjoy being with a man who can open doors."

"Stick with me, Babe. I'll take you places."

They took the chairs in front of the radio, and Conrad adjusted the dials to Coop's frequency. They didn't know who would be manning the radio on the other end or if Coop would even be home, but at least they'd make contact with the family. Whoever responded would get word to him.

It didn't take long before the radio crackled, and Coop answered with his call sign. "I'm so glad to hear from you. I have news. Where are you?"

"In Amarillo following Riley's trail," Conrad said. "We're checking to see if you've heard from her before we get back on the road."

"Eight days ago," Coop said. "There's a whole story about Adrian, but that's for another time. Don't bother going to Fort Worth. Riley's headed north. She may not be far from you by now, but I have no way of knowing where. Dashay, there's something you need to know."

"Sounds serious, Coop. Spill it."

Coop told them about Riley's snakebite and Nico saving her. When he finished, Dashay whispered, "Nico Mendez? Our Nico is alive?"

She stared straight at the radio but could feel Conrad's eyes on her. She'd told him about Nico and imagined he wasn't thrilled to find out her old flame was in the neighborhood.

"He's not just alive. He's stationed just over the border in the US and is going to be our man on the inside. Riley couldn't give more details but promised to update us as soon as she could. She wasn't too happy with you two for going after her when she told you not to."

"She has no right to be mad at us. But good thing we didn't listen," Dashay said. "She has two more soldiers accompanying her on the quest, but I don't know much about them."

"More promising news on that front. She's not traveling alone. She's with a friend of Nico's named Santi and two of Adrian's nephews. You should stay put. She could be heading toward you."

"You might be right," Conrad said. "If she contacts you, connect her with us. I'll get details to you on how to do that as soon as I can. Glad we reached out, or we could have ended up on even more of a wild goose chase."

"Still could be. She didn't say she was headed to Amarillo. That's just my guess. Keep in touch, and we'll get all the pieces in place." The connection grew quiet for a moment, then Coop said, "For the first time since getting WP's letter, I feel like we have a chance of bringing her home."

"Me, too, Coop," Dashay said. "Sounds like someone's on our side making that happen."

The communications tech gave Conrad the wrap signal, so he took the radio from Dashay. "Our time's up. I'll be in touch tomorrow. Same time, then we'll go from there. Stay safe."

He signed off and thanked the techs before walking with Dashay back to their quarters. They sat on their beds facing each other, waiting for the other to speak.

Conrad finally said, "What Coop told us is a lot to process. I can't believe Riley almost died from a snake bite. Talk about a coincidence with Nico showing up when he did."

Dashay raised her eyes to his. "Is that really what you want to talk about?"

He sighed and slowly shook his head. "You must be in shock after finding out Nico's alive."

Dashay rubbed her arms even though the room was warm. Her mind had been racing since hearing about Nico. Not only was he alive, but it was likely she was going to see him soon. It wasn't how she pictured a reunion with him.

"I'm not sure what I'm feeling," she said softly. "It hasn't sunk in yet. But know this. Nico and I haven't seen each other for two years. I still love him on some level, and I'm beyond thrilled to know he survived, but that doesn't mean I'm going to run back into his arms the second I see him. You and I have far more history than Nico and I ever did. Even though you and I haven't discussed our future or even where our relationship stands now, I have strong feelings for you. I promise not to abandon what we have without serious thought and discussing it with you."

Conrad blew out his breath in relief. "Good to know. I appreciate you telling me. I'll give you whatever space you need to figure it out if the time comes."

She got up and moved next to him. "Thank you. I know that wasn't easy for you to say."

Conrad gave her a tender kiss. "For now, we need to figure out what we're going to do about Riley. Coop's right that we should stay for at least another day, but we can't hang out here indefinitely, hoping to hear from Riley. She might not be heading back here. She may not have access to a radio, and I have no idea where to look for her."

"Can we decide all of that tomorrow? For the first time in longer than I can remember, every second of my time isn't scheduled out for me. It's a beautiful day. Let's go say hello to the horses after dinner, then find a quiet place to enjoy the sunset."

"Sounds perfect. You always know just what to say." He moved her braids aside and brushed his lips on her neck. "We have some time before dinner. I know how we can spend it."

She turned and kissed him passionately before pulling him down with her onto the bed. Until she had decisions to face, she planned to enjoy every minute with him.

———

Julia waited in the scorching sun with a hundred other people for their weekly food allotment. Uncle Mitch or Aunt Beth usually took turns getting their order, but they were both down sick with what Kathryn called dysentery. Kathryn had stayed home from her job in the stables to care for them. Her husband, Clint, went to the stables where they both worked, hoping to make up for Kathryn being absent so their food allotment wouldn't be docked. The amount they got for the seven of them in their cramped apartment kept shrinking. Julia wondered how long it would be before their jailers stopped giving them any food at all.

The line moved forward, so Julia tugged on the wagon she and Holly had scavenged from the city dump. She was tempted to sit in the wagon, but it would waste what little energy she had in trying to get out of it when the line moved. Instead, she leaned against one of the concrete posts that lined the walkway leading to the Food Distribution Center entrance. That's what the people who ran Oklahoma City called it, but the building used to be a music hall before the CME. She'd always grumbled when her mom dragged her to classical concerts when she was younger, but she would have given anything, even her wagon of food, to spend one night sitting in a comfortable seat listening to music with her mom.

She was closing her eyes to imagine the two of them sharing time in the air-conditioned hall when she spotted a man waving to her from where he stood half-hidden in the shade of some trees. Something about him looked familiar, but she couldn't place him. She'd met so many people in the years since the CME that it was hard to remember all of them. Her gut tightened when he wouldn't stop waving at her, fearing the guard might see him and punish her. She looked away for a minute, but her curiosity won out, and she peeked back in his direction. He was holding up a white poster with five words written in black marker.

Julia-Nico-Here-When-Done

She gave an almost imperceptible nod, then stepped closer to the man in front of her and stared at his back. She forced herself to wait two minutes before daring to take another peek, but Nico was gone.

She'd only known Nico Mendez for a few days while she was in a compound infirmary in Virginia after she got shot in the leg. He was a medic there and had been very nice to her. The only other thing she knew about him was that he traveled with her mom and Coop for a while until he was mauled by a bear in West Virginia. She knew Dashay had been in love with him and was sad when they had to leave him behind. If Dashay loved and trusted him, she could trust him, too.

It felt like time stood still as she moved with the line to get her food. When she reached the distribution tables, her heart pounded so hard she was afraid the people doling out the food would notice, but they hardly looked at her. Once she had the paltry food ration, she hurried out to find Nico. She went to the spot where he'd held up the sign, but he wasn't there. Her heart sank in fear that he'd been caught. She moved through the park another hundred feet until she found him sitting near a dried-up fountain. He acknowledged that he'd seen her, then got up and started walking away from the food center across the park. She pulled her wagon behind him until he led her to a spot that hid them from both sides.

Nico gave her a bear hug and said, "I wasn't sure you'd remember me and come to find me. It's so good to see you." He stopped and rubbed his chin as he looked her over. "You're taller, but you're too thin. How's the leg?"

She did a little dance to show him. "It hurts when it's cold, or I have to walk a long way sometimes, but mostly it's fine. What are you doing here, Nico, and how in the world did you find me?"

"I literally ran into your mom," he said, then told her the rattlesnake story.

"I can't imagine Mom letting herself get bitten by a snake. Guess you two are even now."

"I found her just in time. She's fine and on her way to break you out of here. I got transferred to your camp to help her."

Julia gasped. "What? How does she know where I am?"

"She got one of your letters. It took eighteen months, but it made its way to her. It was a brilliant idea." Julia started to tremble, and her legs got weak. Nico led her to a bench and helped her sit. "Are you okay? Is it lack of food?"

She shook her head and didn't try to hide her tears. "I'm just so happy. After so long, trapped in here like animals, we get to go home. I can hardly believe it." She turned to him and grabbed his arm. "Can you come with me to tell my family? They won't believe me."

"I'd love to, and I'll do what I can to make things easier for all of you until we get you out of here, starting with getting you more food. It may take a few weeks, so you'll all need to be patient and go about your lives as normal so no one will get suspicious."

"One thing we can definitely be is patient." She wiped her face, then caught Nico smiling at her. "What?"

"You're so grown up. You were a little girl last time I saw you."

"I had no choice but to grow up." She stood and picked up the wagon handle. "Let's go now. Uncle Mitch and Aunt Beth are sick. Finding out about you will make them feel better."

"Let me pull that," Nico said and took the wagon handle from her. "I'll examine your aunt and uncle and get them whatever treatment and meds they need."

"Thank you, Nico. They treat us like dogs in here and don't care if we live or die." She grew quiet for a moment before saying, "Do you know anything about the rest of the family that was with us? We don't know what happened to them after they sent us to separate camps."

As they walked, Nico told her about the cousins making it to the farm and updated her on all the news Riley had shared with him. Her step grew lighter with every word.

———

Yeager had grown impatient by his third day of casing Daybreak's house and seeing no sign of him. He'd seen various people he didn't recognize entering and exiting carrying boxes or household articles. None of them seemed to live in the house. He mulled the possibility that his target had gotten spooked and hit the road but couldn't imagine how that could be. Yeager hadn't shared his plan with another living being and hadn't seen even a hint of the team Kearns had assigned to replace him.

Concluding it was time to act, he emerged from his hiding place. Squaring his shoulders and donning his signature in-charge attitude, he strode across the driveway and pounded on the front door.

An averaged size man in his mid to late thirties swung the door open twenty seconds later. He looked Yeager up and down, then said, "May I help you?"

Yeager deliberately folded his arms and narrowed his eyes. "Who are you?"

The man balked and put down the moving box he carried. "You first." When Yeager didn't budge, the man said, "Why should I tell you? You're the stranger here."

Yeager softened his stance slightly. He wouldn't get anywhere by arousing suspicion. He gave a practiced congenial smile but remained ready to pounce. "Fair point. I've been sent from Denver to act as personal protection for Dr. Adrian Landry. This is his house, isn't it?"

The man visibly relaxed. "It is, but I'm sorry to say you're too late. He told us he'd been recalled to his post in Denver. He and his family left about a week ago. You must have passed each other on the road. We're old friends of the family. Adrian told us to help ourselves to whatever they couldn't carry in the wagons."

It took all Yeager's strength not to punch the man, even though it wasn't his fault he was too late to catch Daybreak. It was that petty Colonel Beake's fault for sending him to Shreveport. He doubted Daybreak was headed to Denver but couldn't fathom where else the man would take his family. His only option was to travel north and hope he caught up to him.

"That's unfortunate," Yeager said, regaining his composure. "I was unavoidably detained."

"We're just about finished, and the sun's setting. You're welcome to sleep here tonight and get a start in the morning. You'll probably be able to catch him since a single rider can travel much faster than a family with a loaded wagon." He craned his head out through the doorway. "Where's your horse?"

Yeager pointed his thumb behind him. "In a stable up the road. Thanks for the offer. I think I will stay here tonight."

The man let him in, and Yeager kindly helped the family carry the rest of the loot to their house four doors up the block. They offered him a satisfying dinner of chicken roasted on a spit, a salad from vegetables in their garden, and flatbread. Though the food was simple, it was the first home-cooked meal he'd eaten since before the CME and tasted better than he remembered food could. He took the leftovers they offered and thanked them profusely before heading back to Landry's house.

He had no intention of staying the night. He waited until every resident in the humdrum neighborhood was dead asleep, then retrieved the horse he'd hidden in an abandoned movie theater and made his way north. He pushed the beast as fast as he could go. If he rode him to death, he'd just find another to take its place. All that mattered was catching up to Daybreak before he reached Denver. If that's where he was headed.

———

Riley lay awake in her tent, listening to Reece and Brady muttering to each other by the fire. She wanted nothing more than to drift off into sweet oblivion for eight hours, but a good night's sleep had become a forgotten luxury. In the three days since parting with Santi, she hadn't had more than two or three hours per night. Still not recovered from the snake bite, Riley wasn't sure how much longer she could go on without proper rest.

She'd woken just after midnight the night Santi left to find Reece riding away from camp. She'd stayed awake the rest of the night waiting for him to return. As she was getting dressed in her tent before going out to get the breakfast fire started, Reece rode back into camp, tethered his horse, and went to his tent to sleep. He didn't emerge until eleven, despite Brady's repeated efforts to wake him. Fuming from him making them late getting on the road, Riley finally dumped a cup of cold water on him. Reece shot up and cocked his fist, then backed down when he realized what was happening. When he finally came out for coffee, his breath reeked of booze. Riley had it out with him, warning that if he pulled that again, he was done.

To her immense disappointment, the pattern repeated itself the following night, except Brady went with him to a local village that time. Riley didn't smell alcohol on him when he came out of his tent at ten the next morning. She assumed Reece had taken him along as the "designated driver" of sorts. When Riley repeated the water trick the second morning, Reece sat up and aimed a small-caliber handgun at her. He hadn't left Fort Worth with a weapon, so she could only guess he'd stolen it somewhere along the way. She backed out of his tent. It was the last straw. She asked Brady to separate their gear from hers so she could go on without them. Reece came out and ordered Brady to stop. He apologized to Riley and told her he was just goofing around.

Riley pretended to accept his apology but insisted he give her the gun. His eyes flashed as he hesitated for a moment before reaching into his waistband and handing the weapon over to her. She behaved as if the incident was forgotten but secretly began planning her exit strategy. She berated herself for not listening to Santi, but she'd felt trapped with no other choice. Now she was trapped in a worse way and was far more afraid of Reece than any rattlesnake.

That third day passed with Reece cheerfully cooperative, but Riley didn't buy his act. She lay in her tent that night, waiting for the boys to either sneak off or go to their tents so she could make her escape. But they just kept jawing away by the fire. As hard as she tried to fight it, her exhaustion got the best of her sometime around one. She woke with a start three hours later to the worst situation she could imagine. Reece and Brady had taken off with all their provisions. They'd only left her with Biscuit, her tent, and the contents inside. They'd even taken her packhorse.

Riley sank onto a log next to the fire and gave herself time to cry it out before figuring out what she was going to do. She still had her horse, enough food for two days, and two guns. The boys only had a three-hour head start on her, and they were slowed by the packhorse. Biscuit wasn't the swiftest of horses, but he'd always gotten her where she needed to go.

While she waited for the first rays of sunlight, she loaded her gear on Biscuit, speaking words of encouragement and feeding him the last handful of the apple slices that Adrian had given her. He seemed more relaxed at being alone with her. When there was just enough light to see the road ahead, she mounted her faithful horse and headed for the nearest town, hoping to find the boys passed out at a local bar. As the sun rose, their trail became easier to follow. She was grateful they hadn't thought to mask their tracks.

She made it to the town by lunchtime and headed for the only bar she could find. The boys were nowhere to be seen. She told her story of woe to the few locals she came across, but none of them had seen Reece and Brady. After taking time for a quick lunch and bathroom break, she took out her map to figure out her next stop. By that point, there were too many hoof prints for her to track the boys any farther.

She studied the map, searching towns along the route she'd

planned out for her rendezvous with Nico. She could make the next town just after nightfall, but before heading that way, she asked herself which direction the boys were most likely to take? Rescuing Julia or finding Nico didn't matter to them. Reece had clearly only come along to get out from under his mother's thumb and sow his wild oats. He'd complained incessantly the day they passed the outskirts of Wichita Falls. They could have headed that way, but it was in the opposite direction. She didn't have time to backtrack.

She had a decision to make. Did she go after the boys and try to recover her belongings or let them get away with what they'd done? It was possible to scavenge supplies as she went, hoping Nico had left provisions for her at the drop point. She'd made a promise to Chrissy to send the boys home safely, but she hadn't bargained on Reece threatening her with a gun and robbing her. From that moment on, she owed their family nothing.

As she stared at the map, trying to decide where to go, an elderly couple approached and watched her for a moment before the man said, "Excuse me, ma'am. Berle Johnson told us you're looking for a couple of young fellows. We thought we might help."

With nothing to lose, Riley gave them a warm smile and repeated her story. "I was trying to figure out the most likely direction they took. Any ideas?"

"I think we may have seen the boys you're tracking," the man said. He went on to give detailed descriptions of Reece and Brady. "We run a shop up the street with our son. They came in earlier and traded some of those military meals for a map. They were looking for a town big enough to have rooms for rent on the way to Amarillo. We directed them to Vernon, a town of about fifteen thousand that serves as our county seat northwest of here. They're only three or four hours ahead of you and looked a little worse for wear. If you get my meaning. Leave now, and you'll catch them by nightfall."

Riley reached down and shook his hand. "That was kind of you to help a stranger. How can I thank you, sir?"

"Catching those boys is all the thanks we need. I'd recommend having some backup standing by when you confront them. The older brother looks a bit rough."

"I'll keep that in mind," Riley said as she waved and rode off to her showdown, hoping it wouldn't end in a shootout.

———

Weak from her illness and so many days without sleep, Riley could barely stay in the saddle by the time she reached the outskirts of Vernon. She'd pushed poor Biscuit hard, afraid of missing Reece and Brady. Regardless of how their confrontation ended, she'd need to stop for a few days to regain her strength and give Biscuit time to rest. None of what she'd done would be worth it if she died on the side of some dusty road in the middle of nowhere. Vernon was the biggest town she'd entered since leaving Fort Worth. They'd likely have rooms available in exchange for goods. If she recovered her supplies, she'd have plenty to offer. If that failed, she'd find an abandoned house and hole up until she was ready to move on and finish her quest alone or head to Santi's ranch for help.

She rode down the main street in the darkness, scanning for the three horses, hoping the boys hadn't been smart or sober enough to think to hide them. They wouldn't be expecting her so close on their heels, so that gave her the advantage. The streets were quiet except for dogs barking and chatter coming from families gathered in the yards to enjoy the nice evening. As Riley neared the northwestern edge of the city, a sound she hadn't heard for two years floated toward her in the still air—a band playing country music. She followed the music to a bar and grill called The Broken Spur. It was lit up with strands of white lights outside and lanterns inside. If Reece and Brady were in Vernon, that was where they'd be.

Their horses weren't tethered in front, so she rode behind the building and was rewarded with the sight of all three horses grazing in a patch of grass behind the bar. She was tempted to tie them to Biscuit and ride out of town with the spoils, but she didn't want to leave the boys destitute, and their horses didn't belong to her.

She slid out of the saddle, then walked to the packhorse and grabbed hold of his reins. As she led the reluctant horse toward Biscuit, two men and a woman came out of the bar and stared at her in the dim light. One man was the size of a mountain and dressed in biker clothes. His bushy beard reached halfway down his barrel chest. The other man and the woman looked slightly younger, probably in their early forties, and normal human size. They were dressed in biker clothes, too.

The normal-sized man stepped toward her, but she ignored him and worked at tethering the packhorse's reins to Biscuit. She did her best to hide the fact that she was terrified of what they might do to her.

"I don't remember seeing you inside," he said, "and I'd remember you. What do you think you're doing?"

Without stopping, Riley said, "Recovering my stolen property."

She stepped toward Brady's horse to unstrap a saddlebag that belonged to her. The man put his hand on her shoulder to stop her. She shrugged off his hand and stepped back.

"Prove this horse belongs to you," the woman said.

"I can't, but the brothers who stole it from me are inside this bar, I believe. Go ask them."

The man gripped her upper arm and practically dragged her toward the door. "You ask them."

Riley's heart pounded so hard she had to gasp for air. She wanted to say she'd go along willingly but couldn't form the words. Once they were inside, he released her arm and nudged her forward. The band kept playing, but every head turned toward them.

"What's this, Lou?" the bartender asked.

The man who'd dragged Riley inside rubbed his chin. "We caught this tiny snip of a redhead trying to steal a horse. She says it's hers but can't prove it."

"Just take her to the sheriff," someone called from a table near the band, and the bar patrons exploded in laughter.

Riley didn't get the joke but didn't care. Weak as she was, she'd reached her tipping point, and the fire of years of loss and frustration surged up from her gut. She was leaving with her property if she had to take down every person in that bar to do it.

She swept the drinks and food off the closest table, sending them crashing to the floor, then grabbed an empty chair to climb on top. The people seated at the table cursed and clamored, but she stared them down until they were quiet. "Sorry. I'll replace those," she whispered. Then, she raised her voice to the rest of the room. "That horse is mine, and the thieves who stole him are in this bar." She motioned with her hand to silence the band, then swept her gaze over the bar until she spotted Reece and Brady hiding at a back table. Her eyes narrowed as she pointed. "There they are."

Riley hopped off the table, and the crowd parted to let her pass as she strode toward the boys. She had them cornered. Reece appeared unconcerned but sweat glistened on Brady's forehead. By the number of empties on their table, she could tell they'd been at the watering hole long enough to even the playing field.

Brady's voice trembled slightly as he said, "Hey, Riley. Glad you caught up with us. We were just getting a head start."

"Shut it," Reece snapped at his brother. "What do you want, Riley?"

She leaned over him until she could feel his foul breath on her skin. "I'm here for what's mine. Did you think I wouldn't track you, ignorant punk?"

Reece sprang out of his chair and backhanded her across the cheek in one smooth motion. The force sent her flying into the crowd behind her, and her head struck the edge of a chair. She didn't lose consciousness but was so stunned that she lay paralyzed on the floor for several seconds as the crowd erupted around her. When she regained control of her muscles, she sat up in time to see the man-mountain lifting Reece by his collar. While the attention was on them, Brady squeezed through the crowd and dashed out of the bar. Riley saw two men chase after him before turning back to Reece. She tried to stand, but her legs wouldn't hold her. Two women standing above her each took an arm and helped her to a chair.

"How dare you strike a woman?" the gigantic man said. "Did you steal her horse and gear?"

Reece tried to answer, but the man-mountain was holding him too tightly at the throat, so he just nodded as his face turned from red to purple.

"You're choking him to death, Bobby," someone behind Riley said. "Put him down. He's not going anywhere."

Bobby lowered Reece to a chair. Reece raised his hands to his throat, gasping for breath. Even after what he'd done to her, Riley's doctor brain kicked in, and she was relieved to see his color returning to normal.

"You've probably bruised his trachea," she told Bobby.

Bobby spun around to face her. "Only bruised? I was trying to crush it. Why do you care about this punk after what he did to you?" When she didn't respond, he looked to the crowd and said, "Someone get her a towel. That cut's going to need stitches."

Someone shoved a dirty towel into Riley's hand. She dropped it on the table and tore a strip of fabric from the bottom of her t-shirt. After pressing it to her cheek, she said, "Can you breathe, Reece?" He glanced up at her and nodded. "Can you speak?"

"Barely," was his hoarse reply.

The bar customers watched the exchange in stunned silence.

Ignoring them, Riley said, "Good. Lift your chin." Reece tilted his head back, exposing the bruising. "Keep a cool, wet cloth on that and don't speak for at least three days. Longer if it's still swollen and painful."

The man called Lou, who had dragged Riley into the bar, pushed his way forward and said, "What is happening? I thought the redhead was the bad guy."

Reece pointed at Riley. "Doctor."

Riley said, "I need someone to go after that other boy."

A man standing beside Riley elbowed his friend and said, "We'll go."

Riley nodded, then grimaced as pain shot up her cheek. "Great. His name's Brady. Tell him I want my stuff back. Bring me the black bag with the red cross on it." As the men hurried out of the bar, she lifted her eyes to Reece. "I'm ordering you to go straight home and tell your mother what you've done. I'll be checking with your Uncle Adrian to make sure you do. If you don't, I'll send my powerful friends to take care of you. You know I'll do it." She cocked her thumb at Bobby. "Or I can just let him deal with you. Your choice."

When he didn't move, she slid her gun from the holster and aimed it at his forehead. "If I ever see you again, I'll forget I'm a doctor. Get out of my sight." Reece stumbled out of the bar with his hand to his throat. As soon as the bartender slammed the door behind him, Riley gently laid the gun on the table. "Good thing he didn't know I forgot to load that this morning."

One of the men who'd gone after Brady came in with the medical bag and set it on the table next to the gun. "Is this the right one?"

She swallowed and said, "Yes. Thanks. Does anyone have a mirror?"

The woman who'd been with Lou and Bobby when they

confronted her outside the bar said, "I have one in my bag." She dug in her oversized shoulder bag and pulled out a makeup mirror. "Will this work?" Riley gave a slight nod. "Name's Harper, by the way. Harper Mitchener. My boys here are Lou Holtz and Bobby Wise."

"Nice to meet you, Harper," Riley said, thinking the situation ranked as one of the most surreal in her life. "Can you please hold that mirror where I tell you while I work?"

Harper crinkled her nose. "While you work on what?"

"Your friend Bobby was right. From the amount of blood on this cloth, I think my cut needs suturing, so I'm going to stitch it. Unless there's another doctor here."

The people standing around Riley glanced at each other, then shrugged.

"I'm a CNA," a young woman behind Bobby said. She stepped around him and smiled at Riley.

"Have you been drinking?" Riley asked.

"Just one beer."

Riley patted the table. "It'll have to do. You can sit here and assist me. What's your name?"

"Brittany Mills, Doctor."

"Just call me Riley. Unzip the bag, please. Let's get started."

Brittany and Harper sat across from Riley, and Brittany withdrew items from the bag as Riley instructed. They disinfected their hands thoroughly with whisky from the bar, then each pulled on a pair of surgical gloves. As Brittany opened and laid out the suture kit, Riley told Harper how to angle the mirror so she could see to work. She cleaned the area around the cut on her left cheek just below the temple as best she could, then injected a local anesthetic directly into the cut. Her eyes watered from the pain, blinding her momentarily. She had to stop until they cleared.

The bar patrons stood mesmerized at the sight of Riley performing the medical procedure on herself. In order to deflect her focus from the pain and heavy breathing from the audience, she imagined herself in her sterile OR back home, closing a patient after surgery. It didn't help even a little, but she kept going.

She glanced up to her left and said, "Someone better catch that man in the red plaid shirt before he passes out."

As she said it, a man over six feet tall swayed, then tipped backward. Two other men caught him in time and gently lowered him to the floor.

"Good catch," Brittany said. "If you'd missed, the doctor might have had to stitch old George, too."

There was a quiet murmur of laughter, then the bartender said, "Everyone, come to the bar and settle up. Time to clear out for the night, folks. Bar's closing early."

"Come on, Bart," one of the customers grumbled, "don't kick us out just when it's getting good."

Bart pointed toward the front, then crossed his arm. The patrons gathered their belongings amid groans of disappointment and headed up to the counter to settle their bills.

The man who'd been with Brittany kissed her cheek and said, "See you back home. I'm proud of you."

Brittany beamed as he left the bar. Only Bobby and Lou stayed with Riley and her helpers. The two men took the table next to them and watched with rapt attention as Riley closed the wound in her cheek. The laceration was larger than she'd expected until she remembered that Reece always wore a heavy ring on his right hand.

He'd told her in one of his rare congenial moments that it had been his father's Notre Dame class ring. He'd always hoped Reece would follow him at his Alma Mater, but Reece wasn't interested in college. He'd said he was fascinated with cars and never wanted to be anything other than a mechanic and own his own shop someday. Riley asked him if he had ideas about how to make existing cars work after the CME. He'd shrugged and said he'd never had time to think about it because he was too busy pulling weeds in his mom's garden.

Riley responded that if he told his mom he wanted to be a mechanic for the military, she might have let him go because he'd be in home territory. His eyes had brightened at the thought. Riley hoped Reece would remember the conversation when he got home. If he could get some military discipline, there might be hope for him.

Her hand holding the needle trembled slightly at the memory of the blow that had caused the cut she was stitching. Riley tried to rationalize that it had just been the booze driving his behavior, but she'd spent enough time with him to know that wasn't the case. She was lucky he hadn't done something more damaging to her while they were on the road. Reece had serious anger issues and needed the right guidance to shape him into the man he had the potential to become. Unfortunately, that man didn't seem to exist in his life.

She lowered her hand, then closed her eyes and took a few slow breaths.

"You okay, Doc?" Bobby asked.

She opened her eyes and studied him for a moment. "Not sure," she whispered. "Doing this under the best of circumstances would be a challenge for any doctor, but I've been through more than you can imagine in the past few weeks."

He leaned back in his chair and crossed his arms over his barn-sized chest. "Try me," he said. "Can you talk while you sew?"

"I'll try."

"Tell us your story. Bet it's a good one. Start by telling us how you ended up with those two punk thieves."

She asked Harper to readjust the mirror, then threaded the needle through her skin with a steady hand. "To tell you that, I have to go back much further."

She began her story by telling them about traveling to the medical conference in DC just days before the CME, then took them through the highlights, including crossing Adrian's path and getting separated from Julia. She finished stitching her wound just as she caught them up to getting Julia's letter and her adventures since rushing off to her rescue.

"I don't think anyone could write a novel with a more compelling story," Harper said.

Riley gestured for her to hand her the mirror. "Hasn't been great living most of it," Riley said as she admired her work.

As Brittany dressed the wound, then repacked the medical bag, she said, "But you found love again, and you have your little Xav."

Riley gave her a warm smile. "Thanks for reminding me it hasn't been all bad."

"What are you going to do now?" Lou asked. "You're in no shape to go back out on the road, especially alone."

"I'm going to find a bed to crash in for a few days. I'll figure it out after that. Any idea where I can stay?"

The bartender pressed a key into her hand. "I have some rooms I rent in exchange for food or supplies. You can have one on the house as payment for the floor show you put on tonight. Nothing interesting has happened in this town since the CME. People will talk about this for weeks, at least. I'll send one of my servers over in the morning with breakfast."

As she was leaving, she stopped and said, "I told those people I'd pay for the drinks and food that I tossed on the floor. They didn't look so happy with me."

The bartender gave her a wink. "I'll take care of it."

Bobby picked up her bag and said, "We're staying in one of Bart's rooms, too. We'll show you the way."

Lou helped Riley to her feet. She was unstable for a moment, then got her balance. She squeezed the bartender's hands. "I'm deeply grateful." He waved her off as if to say it was nothing. Riley walked out with the others and thanked Brittany before she headed down the road. "Is it far?" she asked Bobby. "I'm not sure I can mount my horse."

"Just a few blocks. You strong enough to walk? If not, I can easily carry a little wisp of a thing like you."

"That's a kind offer, but I think I can manage." As she tethered the packhorse to Biscuit, she noticed that the men who'd retrieved her gear from Brady had loaded it for her. "Kind people in this town," she whispered, then gestured for Bobby to lead the way.

———

Riley feared her skull would split apart from the pain. The scene at the bar flooded into her brain as she lifted her fingertips to the stitches in her cheek. The skin was warm and swollen. Add concussion and infection to my growing list of maladies, she thought. She carefully opened her eyes and looked around the small, tidy room without moving her head. The only furnishings were the bed, an easy chair, and a simple pine chest of dressers. The sheets were spotlessly white and were covered with a beautiful handmade quilt. If not for her splitting headache, she would have felt like a queen after weeks on the road.

She only had vague memories of Harper helping her clean off and change before climbing into the bed. Everything after that was a blank. She could tell from the shadows that it was late afternoon. She bent her elbows to push herself up but stopped when fireworks erupted in her head. She slowly lowered down to the pillow, hoping someone was nearby to help her to the bathroom before her bladder ruptured.

"Hello. Is anyone there? Please help me." Her words came out as a croak, and she wasn't sure if anyone would hear. There was a tap on the door a few seconds later. "Come in," she called, cringing from the renewed round of pain.

Bobby came in wearing the same outfit he'd had on in the bar except for a different Heavy Metal band shirt. His bulk filled half of the small room.

Harper followed him in and squeezed around him to step next to the bed. "It's a relief to see you awake. You had us worried," she said with a smile.

Riley squinted at her. "How long have I been asleep?"

Bobby leaned against the wall and folded his arms. "Day and a half."

It felt like only hours to Riley, and she grew more concerned about the severity of her concussion. "Do you have a doctor in town?"

"He's been in to see you twice. He's the one who gave you the IV," Harper said, pointing to the bag hanging from an IV pole.

Riley hadn't even noticed the line connected to her arm. "What's he giving me?"

Harper shrugged. "We didn't ask, but everyone here seems to trust Dr. Mueller. Is there anything you need?"

"The license plate of the truck that hit me and a bathroom before my bladder bursts."

"Can't do anything about the truck, but there's a bathroom next door," Bobby said.

"I'm not sure I can stand."

Bobby crossed the room in one step, threw back the covers, and lifted her into his arms. "Not a problem." He carried her to the bathroom and sat her on the toilet. "You're on your own for the rest. Let me know when you're done." He turned and left before she could thank him.

Harper had come in behind him and closed the door. "Want me to stay?"

"Please. No need for modesty here."

Once she was finished using the bathroom and was back in bed, Harper brought her chicken broth and bread that she said Dr. Mueller had ordered her to eat. She finished every bite, surprised at the strength of her appetite.

Harper reached into her pocket and pulled out a baggie with

two white tablets. "Dr. Mueller said you could have these after you ate."

She dropped the pills into Riley's palm. Riley inspected them and was overjoyed to see they were Oxy tablets for her pain. She popped them into her mouth and washed them down with the rest of her apple cider.

Harper picked up her empty bowl and headed for the door. "We'll leave you to rest."

"I've had enough of that for the moment. Please stay unless you have somewhere else to be."

Bobby laughed at that. "We never have anywhere else to be."

Riley wasn't sure why that was funny, but she was glad her new friends weren't going to leave her alone. Before Harper dropped into the chair, Riley asked for the two IV bags to find out what Dr. Mueller was pumping into her. Harper handed them to her. Both bags were more than half full, so the doctor must have come in not long before she woke. She turned them over to read the labels. One was Vancomycin, a broad-spectrum antibiotic, and the other was a saline solution to keep her hydrated, just as she'd expected. She was impressed that he'd been able to get his hands on the antibiotic. Now, if only the good doctor had more painkillers in his bag of tricks. She held the bags out for Harper to rehang them.

Harper took the only chair, so Bobby sank to the floor and crossed his legs. Riley wondered what it would take for him to get back on his feet.

Before any of them spoke, Lou poked his head through the open door. "Mind if I join the fun?"

Riley waved him in, unexpectedly glad to see the third member of their clan. Her feelings surprised her since Lou was the one who'd forced her into the bar. If he hadn't, she could have ridden off alone with her horses and belongings, and Reece wouldn't have been able to injure her. Still, her gut told her that running into these three was more than coincidence. Lou nodded his thanks, then came in and dropped next to Bobby.

"I'm grateful for all you've done for me," Riley said. "How can I thank you?"

"Let's call it even," Lou said. "It's my fault you're in this condition."

"It's not your fault. I provoked Reece, knowing he was capable of something like this. Has anyone heard what happened to them?"

Bobby shook his head. "Not a word, and good riddance. You should have shot him."

Riley touched her cheek. "He didn't deserve to die for slapping me. He's just a screwed-up kid. I'm hoping this whole incident scared him straight."

Harper watched her for a moment. "You're more forgiving than I'd be."

"Like I told you in the bar, we have a history."

"What's next after you're recovered?" Lou asked.

Riley wasn't sure how to answer. She was days behind schedule and could be laid up for days more. Nico had probably given her up for lost. She was so close to Julia but farther away than she was when she started. Coop, Dashay, and everyone else had been right. Heading off alone and unprepared had been foolish. She'd learned nothing from past experiences.

She sighed and sank into her pillows. "I can't do this alone. I think it's time to pack it in and go home. How far is it to Amarillo?"

Bobby sat forward and said, "You're not alone anymore. We've talked while you were sleeping and want to offer to help rescue your daughter, if you'll have us."

Riley was stunned and slightly leery of their offer. She'd jumped off into the wilderness, hardly knowing Reece and Brady after Adrian had vouched for them. That had turned into a disaster. She knew nothing about the people sitting in her room other than they'd been kind to her, expecting nothing in return. They had clearly been bikers before the CME but had been decent, patriotic Americans. It didn't mean they were dangerous, but for once, she decided not to make a rash decision. She had questions. If they weren't willing to be upfront about who they were, she'd know how to proceed.

"First," she said, "why would you take the risk to help me like that? What's in it for you?"

Bobby gave a laugh that shook the walls. Riley scowled at him, not seeing the humor in her question. He held out his hand and said, "Forgive me. You caught me off guard. You have been through the wringer, haven't you?"

"I've been stung more than once." She touched her fingers to her cheek. "Case in point."

"Fair enough. I'll ask a question in answer. Would you do it if our places were reversed? Not expecting anything in return?"

"Without hesitation."

He turned up his palms to her. "As would we."

She gave him a half-grin. "Very well. Next question. Were you members of the Hells Angels or something like that before the CME?"

The three of them broke out laughing. Riley was confused but waiting for the laughing to stop.

"We were as far from that as you can get," Lou said. "We're members of a national motorcycle club that fights to stop child abuse. Or we used to be before the CME." He took a card from his wallet and handed it to Riley. "Still have my membership card."

Riley read the ID, then handed it back to him. "I actually heard of this group in the course of my work."

Bobby raised an eyebrow. "Does that change your opinion of us?"

"What you've done for me was already doing that, but this helps. Do you blame me for asking?"

Harper stood and adjusted Riley's pillow. "Not a bit. It was a fair question. So, what about our offer?"

"If I decide to continue my quest after I'm recovered, I'd be honored to accept your help and have your companionship. I have a feeling you have stories of your own that need telling, and I'd have plenty of time to listen."

Lou spat in his palm and held his hand out to her. "Deal. As soon as you're well, we head off on our next biker gang adventure."

Riley crinkled her nose at his spit-covered palm. "Do I have to touch that?"

"Please don't," Harper said, then elbowed Lou. "I told you to stop doing that. It's disgusting."

Bobby gave his booming laugh and got to his feet. "Your word is good with us. We'll start gathering supplies and making plans while you recuperate. Getting well is your only concern right now."

Riley could feel the pain pills kicking in, so she closed her eyes and said, "That's an order I'm grateful to obey."

CHAPTER NINE

Riley waited in hopeful silence for Dr. Mueller to clear her for travel. After a week of lying around feeling useless, she was itching to get back on the road. She'd been a model patient and followed the doctor's orders to the letter, which was a novel experience for her. The result was that she felt like her old self for the first time since before the snake bite, despite the ugly gash on her cheek. She'd have to remove the stitches herself in three or four days, but that would be nothing compared to suturing them in herself.

Another upside to her week of convalescence was that it gave her the chance to get better acquainted with her new friends. Lou and Harper had met in the American Motorcyclist Association years earlier. They'd started out as friends, but over time, their relationship had grown into more. The two of them met when Bobby was a UFC fighter. By that time, he'd been in the sport long enough to become a championship fighter.

One night after a fight, Bobby fired his manager for skimming off the top of his winnings. Lou and Harper had attended the fight and heard Bobby needed a new manager, so they offered their services. They'd continued in the partnership with Bobby until he suffered one too many concussions and was forced to retire.

The three of them had invested their winnings well and had earned enough to live comfortably, so they joined forces with the motorcycle club's crusade to fight child abuse. Bobby had even served as their spokesperson for a time. They were living the life until the CME hit while they were on the road near Dallas. They'd traveled around since, doing what they could to help people in need. Riley was grateful they'd been on hand to come to her aid in the bar.

"Well?" she said when Dr. Mueller continued to scratch away incessantly on his notepad. "What's my prognosis?"

He turned and looked at her over the top of his glasses. "You seem fit enough to travel, but don't overdo it. The infection in your wound is still healing." He reached into his pocket and handed her a packet of oral antibiotics. "Those are expired, but only by three months, so they should still be effective. You may still suffer residual effects of the snake venom and/or that concussion. Wish I could do a CT or MRI."

Riley jumped to her feet, not even trying to conceal her delight. "My head's fine, Walt. I didn't hit the chair hard enough to do lasting damage, but I promise to behave myself."

Walt extended his hand to her. "I'll hold you to that. Good luck finding your daughter."

She took his hand in both of hers. "Thank you for taking such attentive care of me. Please, do the same for yourself."

"You know how it is," he said and waved as he went out, leaving her alone. She walked to the mirror above the dresser and studied her healing wound. It wasn't a bad sewing job, given the circumstances, but she'd have a permanent scar. She grinned at her reflection in satisfaction. Forget Red Queen. I'm the Warrior Queen. She laughed at the thought as she reached for her backpack. Coop's going to love that.

"What have you got to laugh about?" Harper asked as she came in.

Riley pointed to her cheek. "Just admiring how badass I look with this. People have been underestimating me my entire life. Maybe the scar will make them think twice."

"I hate to tell you it might take more than that, but I get what you're saying. People take one look at my tats and clothes and assume I'm a drug dealer or some other kind of criminal. Like you did." Riley started to protest, but Harper held up a hand to stop her. "I'm not blaming you. We all make snap judgments based on appearance. If there was less of that in the world, we'd all get along much better. I'll certainly never underestimate you again."

"Because I sutured my own wound?"

"That was impressive, but I'm talking about the way you stood up to Reece."

Riley put her pack on her shoulder and started for the door. "That was nothing. You should have seen me the time I took out an armed guy the size of Jason Momoa."

She followed Riley down the hallway. "I've got to hear that story. As you said, we'll have plenty of time on the road." She stopped midway down the stairs and sighed. "Man, I miss my ride."

Riley looked up at her from the bottom step. "I miss my car for convenience, but your motorcycle was a huge aspect of your way of life. I bet that's rough."

She bounded down the rest of the steps, then opened the door for Riley. "Horses just don't cut it, but we've adapted like everyone else. Biker gearheads are still looking for a way to get bikes to run without gas. No luck so far."

"If they figure it out, I hope they can adapt it for cars. I'm sick of it taking days to cover ground that used to take hours."

"I hear that."

Harper headed down the street so fast that Riley had a hard

time keeping up after her week of lounging in bed. "Where are we going?"

"Lou and Bobby are waiting for us at the Spur," she said, giving the nickname for the bar where she'd had her showdown with Reece. "The horses are loaded and ready to go."

Riley slowed, not feeling keen to reenter that particular establishment. "I'll wait outside," she called to Harper.

Her new friend turned and waited for Riley to catch up. "Come in. Bart is giving us a sendoff breakfast." When Riley stopped, she said, "The bar is closed. We'll be the only ones there."

Riley's thoughts flashed back to the early days after her first husband's death when she suffered a panic disorder and was terrified of even leaving her house. Facing multiple terrors after the CME had cured her PTSD, ironically, but there were rare times when those familiar pangs of panic sparked to life. She was mildly surprised that contemplating going back to The Broken Spur brought on a mild panic attack.

She contemplated the bar's sign for a moment. After reading it a few times, it struck her as funny. She was a broken spur in ways, but somehow, she'd continued moving forward. She squared her shoulders and marched past Harper toward the bar. She was the Warrior Queen, after all.

Harper shook her head as she got into step beside her. "You are a puzzle, Red."

"So, I've heard," Riley said as they reached the bar. She pushed the door open without hesitation and went in like she owned the place.

The five of them laughed and chatted as they enjoyed a delicious meal of veggie omelets and homemade bread with honey butter. Bart even had freshly squeezed orange juice.

As he cleared away the dishes, Riley said, "So what's this plan you've been hinting at all week?"

The other three gave each other loaded glances and avoided Riley's gaze.

Bobby finally said, "We'll tell you as we get closer to our first stop."

"And where is that?"

"Gainesville," Harper said.

Riley raised an eyebrow. "That's in the opposite direction of where I was going. What's that way?"

"If we tell you that, you might not come," Lou said. "I give my word it's not dangerous."

Bobby folded his massive arms and looked her in the eye. "Do you trust us?"

She paused to ponder his question before answering. She balked at the idea of going into a situation blind, but if the three of them wanted to harm her, they'd had plenty of opportunities. Her options were to go along with them and take her chances or go home and organize help there, which could take weeks, if not months. She hated the thought of making Julia wait one minute longer than necessary to get free of that dreadful camp. Everything else was secondary.

"My gut is telling me to trust you, but I'll only go with you on one condition. I need to go to the cache site my friend set up. He might have left crucial materials for me there. It's not much of a detour." Bobby glanced at the others, then gave a quick nod. Riley got to her feet and shouldered her pack. "Then, when do we leave?"

———

Riley and her companions searched the area beside the highway for an hour before Bobby located Nico's marker.

"Over here," he yelled as he waved his red handkerchief.

Riley was relieved but cringed at his bellowing. They were close enough to the border that they'd spent the past three days dodging patrols, convoys, and skirmishes. The area they searched was clear of other people, but that didn't mean Bobby's voice wouldn't carry. Riley was a hundred yards away from Bobby and hurried to him as quickly as she could navigate over the rough terrain.

By the time she and the others reached him, he was clearing away the pile of rocks which concealed a compartment lined with decaying wood underneath. It looked like an old root cellar, but Riley didn't see any indications that there had ever been dwellings in the area. She couldn't imagine how Nico had found it and made a mental note to ask the next time she saw him. He'd marked the spot with a tattered white rag tied to rusty barbed wire. Anyone passing would have mistaken it as a pile of discarded junk.

"What's in there?" Riley asked as she leaned over Bobby's shoulder.

He held his arm out and ordered, "Flashlight."

His command made Riley wonder if that was how she sounded in the OR, barking orders to her assistants. She had to bite her cheek to hide a smile as she retrieved her penlight.

Bobby raised an eyebrow at the tiny light. When Riley shrugged, he shined the beam into the hole. "I'll have to jump down there. Get the ropes ready to haul me back up."

Harper put a hand on his shoulder to stop him. "Wouldn't it make more sense to lower Riley down? We'll never lift you out of there."

Bobby glared at her for a second, then said, "Fair point."

Riley was still stunned that they'd found the stash and was excited to see what Nico had left. She could hardly contain herself as she climbed into the ropes for them to lower her down. The hole was only six feet deep, so she didn't have far to go. When her feet touched the packed dirt floor, they loosened the slack, and she reached for the packet closest to her feet. When she cut through the duct tape with her pocketknife, a sheet of paper fell out. Riley unfolded it as fast as her trembling hand would work.

She had to remind herself to breathe as she shined her light on the page.

Dear Katie,

If you're reading this, we're one step closer to getting your girl home. I also hope it means you found Adrian. I got the transfer to Julia's camp, so this is the last time I'll be able to cross the border before heading to my new assignment. I was able to get my hands on some materials that will help you cross the border and enter the camp. You'll understand when you see what I've included.

I'll be ready for you when you arrive. I'll take good care of your girl and family in the meantime. You know I'll protect them with my life. Stay safe on the road, and I look forward to our happy reunion.

All my best,

Nico

It was better than Riley could have hoped. She wiped her tears, then folded the letter and tucked it into her pocket next to the one from Julia. It was just a matter of time before they would be together in person.

"What's the holdup?" Lou called down to her.

"It's all good," Riley said. "Drop more rope down for the packages. Won't take a minute." Fifteen minutes later, Riley and the three packs Nico left were back topside. "We'll open these later," she said. "We're too exposed. Let's get out of here."

They replaced the cover to the cellar just in case they'd ever need it again, then got out of there in a hurry. They reached a wooded area near a creek at sundown and stopped to set up camp for the night. Once they'd eaten, they opened the packs from Nico as they relaxed around the fire. He'd left guard uniforms, badges, and forged papers for crossing the border. Riley was impressed at how well Nico had pulled it off. He was an Army medic, not a covert agent like Conrad. But how he'd done it didn't matter. What mattered was that the goods he'd left would make it that much easier to save Julia.

He'd also included MREs, medical supplies, and prescription

drugs. The provisions would come in handy for bartering or bribes if need be. She just hoped she wouldn't need to use them for treating their own injuries.

Harper picked up a vial of morphine. "And you were worried about us being drug dealers."

Riley snatched it from her and returned it to the pack. She kept her eyes lowered as she said, "My friend is a medic. I'm sure he obtained these through legal means."

"Sure," Lou said. "I don't care how he got his hands on them. They'll come in handy where we're headed."

Riley glanced up from stowing the rest of the goods. "And where is that? There's no reason not to tell me now."

Bobby combed his hand through his gray-streaked beard. "It'll be better to just show you. Let's get sleep. We've got another long day tomorrow."

Riley was tired of their evasions, but she was too worn out to argue. There would be time for that during their long hours on the road. She said goodnight and went to her tent to reread Nico's letter. It was such a comfort to know Julia had a champion. She didn't doubt that Uncle Mitch and the rest of the family had done what they could to care for her but having a man Riley trusted on the inside made all the difference.

She took Julia's letter out next and read it for the hundredth time. She had it memorized, but something about seeing her daughter's handwriting made her feel closer to her. She kissed the paper before folding and stashing it under her pillow. *I'm on my way, sweetheart. Just hang on a little longer.*

———

Yeager had miscalculated on his plan to run his horse to death and just find another one. Horses had become a much more protected commodity and stealing them was becoming trickier by the day. He'd ridden two horses into the ground since leaving Fort Worth and had been on foot for a week. He was covering less ground each day, slowed down by the weight of his gear and the blistering heat. He'd made his way into a hick town called Henrietta, hoping he'd hit the jackpot and make it out with a ride and a packhorse after he rested up for a day. He wasn't happy to lose ground on Daybreak, but he was human and could only push himself so far.

He stashed his gear in some brush while he cased the town for an abandoned house. If he couldn't find one, he'd settle for a barn or even a shed. He'd been tempted to find a room to rent in exchange for supplies, but his provisions were running low, and he couldn't afford to give them away for luxuries like running water and a bed. The most he was willing to trade for was one hot meal.

It only took an hour for him to find a three-room brick house on the southeastern edge of town. There was a tire-sized hole in the roof over one room, but he could avoid that part of the house. He walked the two miles back to his stash and hid out until after sunset before returning to his makeshift lodgings.

The front room was filthy with garbage and debris, but the kitchen and one bedroom were virtually untouched. He stowed his gear and unrolled his sleeping bag on the mattress before heading into town for dinner. No one gave him a second glance as he searched for a place to eat. The town was on a major highway, so they probably had strangers passing through daily.

He found the local watering hole by following the sounds of a band playing country music. He went in, took a table in the corner, and waited for the server to take his order. As she sauntered up to his table, he guessed she couldn't be more than eighteen, the age his youngest would have been if she hadn't died in the CME. The girl took his order with bored detachment and left him to listen to the band. They were one of the better ones he'd heard on his journey, which mattered little to him because he loathed country music.

After a satisfying meal of a ground beef patty and potatoes smothered in gravy, he dragged himself back to the house but forced himself to stay awake. At two in the morning, he made his way to nearby farms he'd scoped out earlier to search for a horse to steal, but every time he got close, dogs would bark, alerting their owners to his presence. This was an issue he'd faced before, so it was pointless to keep trying.

He walked into town but met with the same result, except no one seemed to pay attention to the dogs. He heard a few people calling out to hush them, but no one paid the least bit of attention to Yeager. He eventually located two tan geldings tethered in a yard on the northeastern edge of town. All he had to do was spend the day resting, then gather his spoils and be miles away before anyone realized the horses were gone.

He woke just after ten to sunlight streaming into his room. He'd had a solid six hours of sleep and felt more rested than he had in weeks. He rewarded himself with another hot meal in town. All his dinner the night before had cost him was two unopened boxes of matches and a four-pack of batteries. He expected breakfast to be cheaper since eggs were a common commodity.

He made the walk into town and was nearing a diner when he spotted four riders coming toward him. Three looked like bikers. One of them was as big as a barn. The fourth was a tiny redhead who looked utterly out of place with the other three. The horse she rode was a dappled gelding that looked familiar. He looked closer at the rider as she passed. They locked eyes, and he instantly knew why he recognized her horse. It was Riley Poole, one of Daybreak's compatriots. She snapped the horse's reins and yelled "yah," then took off at a gallop. She'd clearly recognized him, though they'd never seen each other in the flesh. Her three companions stared him down, then took off after her.

Yeager looked around in a panic, hoping to find a horse tethered in front of a shop on the main drag, but there wasn't a single one. He raced down the side streets but didn't have any luck there, either. His one sure hope of capturing Daybreak was galloping away from him, and he couldn't find a damned horse. No matter what it took, he couldn't lose her. As he'd learned from bitter experience, she was an expert at evading him. He couldn't let that happen this time.

———

"Riley, hold up," Bobby shouted. "He's not behind us."

Riley was reluctant to stop, but she knew Biscuit couldn't keep up his pace much longer. She reined him in and steered him toward a small stand of trees next to a pond. She dismounted to let him catch his breath. The others rode their horses up to join her.

The four of them looked on silently while the horses recovered and took some water.

Lou finally stepped in front of Riley and glared at her with his arms folded. "What in the hell was that about?"

"That man was Colonel Orson Yeager. He chased me most of the way across this country for the better part of a year. The friend I went to see in Fort Worth, Adrian Landry, is number one on Kearns' most wanted list. He couldn't help me with Julia because he was bugging out to California to get away from someone who was searching for him. Adrian told me it was Yeager, but I didn't believe him. Now I know he was right." She paced around for a moment, then bent over with her hands on her knees. "This is bad. So very bad."

Harper rubbed her back, then said, "Take a breath. We won't let him get to you. We know how to deal with his kind."

"And you escaped him before," Bobby said. "How good a tracker can he be?"

Riley straightened and shot him a look. "Thanks."

Bobby shrugged. "That didn't come out right."

"I looked back while we were galloping off," Lou said. "I don't think he's got a horse. At least he didn't have one on hand. It looked like he was trying to find one to chase after us."

Riley rubbed her forehead and took up her pacing. "I hope you're right. You don't know Yeager. This guy doesn't give up, and he's probably not alone. Adrian was a pet project for Kearns. We thought she'd given up after so long."

Harper put a hand on Riley's shoulder to stop her. "Wait, you said Adrian Landry? Dr. Adrian Landry from the posters?"

Riley was hesitant to answer her. She'd forgotten about the propaganda war Kearns waged against Adrian in the early days after the WSA spread the word about her crimes. To Riley, he was just Adrian, not the person in the center of political intrigues as others saw him. If people only knew the real Adrian the way she did, they'd find that laughable.

"I remember hearing about him," Bobby said. "You never told us that's who you crossed the country with. What other secrets do you have, Dr. Cooper, if that's your actual name?"

"It is. Well, it's my married name. I go by Dr. Poole at home. Poole was my first married name."

Harper's eyes widened. "You're the Riley from the posters."

Riley nodded as she slowly took Julia's letter from her pocket and unfolded it. The three of them stared at the sketch of her for a moment, then burst out laughing.

"Not only a drug dealer but an outlaw, too," Bobby said when he caught his breath. "I can't believe you were worried about coming with us. None of us has ever been on a wanted poster."

Riley tucked the letter back in her pocket. "I'm glad you're enjoying this, but it's not even a bit funny. Yeager's a dangerous psycho. More psycho than Kearns. My sources tell me he's part of her inner circle."

"Your sources?" Lou looked at Harper while pointing his thumb at Riley. "She's got sources."

Bobby folded his arms. "Who are you, Dr. Riley Poole?"

Riley took a few slow breaths. "Enough. You've had your fun. We need to figure out what we're going to do about this. Yeager could derail the mission to save my daughter, and there's no way I can lead him straight to her. Now, do you understand why Nico went to such lengths to create that drop point? This may be an adventure to you, but it's life or death to me. If you want out, I understand. I'll make my way on my own. That was my plan from the start."

"Back the train up, Doc," Harper said. "This won't scare us off the mission. Knowing your secrets makes me more committed to helping you. Have you forgotten the mission of our club? Trying to end child abuse. We've run across our own share of scumbags like Yeager."

"Amen," Lou said. "I believe our current destination will give us the perfect cover from your Colonel Yeager."

Harper gave a playful tug on Riley's ponytail. "First, we've got to do something about this red mop of yours."

"What will altering my hair matter?" Riley asked, fingering her curls. "Yeager got a good look at the three of you, and you're kind of hard to miss, Bobby."

Bobby looked down at his chest. "Fair point. We'll figure it out as we go. We'd better get out of here before that Colonel is back on our heels."

They checked the map and plotted a fresh course to Gainesville before remounting. Riley's uneasiness grew with each mile as memories of her harrowing escape across the border two years earlier plagued her thoughts. Her current situation was completely different, and Yeager didn't know of her mission or where she was headed. If they could stay ahead of him, or better yet, lose him, her fears might be for nothing. Fingering Julia's letter in her pocket, she reminded herself that she couldn't let Yeager be a distraction. Nothing in the wider world meant a thing compared to rescuing her baby.

CHAPTER TEN

DASHAY WAITED outside the radio hut at the border outpost for Conrad to finish his call with Coop. The room was too small for both of them, and the major who'd arranged the call for Conrad hadn't looked so happy about the idea of Dashay joining him. It hadn't been the first time she'd been excluded from calls or discussions since they left Amarillo, but she wasn't offended. Conrad was the one with the clearance and creds. She was just along for the ride.

She glanced up when she saw him emerge from the hut. His face told her all she needed to know.

He caught her looking at him and took off his baseball cap, then scratched his head. "No luck."

Dashay felt tears threatening but fought them off. There would be time to lose it when they were alone in their tent instead of in the middle of the busy compound. "Coop hasn't heard from Riley?"

"Nothing, and he didn't sound good. He says he's quit trying to keep the kids' spirits up. It's been almost nine weeks since she left Santa Fe. I can't say I blame him. I know how I'd feel if you'd been missing for weeks with no word."

While it touched Dashay to hear him say that, it didn't ease her disappointment or worry. "So, what's our next move?"

"Tracking Riley at this point serves no purpose. She left Adrian's weeks ago and could be anywhere by now. Finding her will have to be put on the back burner. Maybe we'll cross paths at some point since we're heading the same direction." He hesitated and looked away before saying, "I think it's time for you to go home, Dashay. I'll arrange an escort, then put together a team to go after Julia. I have the backing of my superiors. They'll get me across the border. I can do the rest from there."

Dashay stepped closer and made him look her in the eye. "What are you saying? You're just shipping me home after coming this far? No way I'm showing up on Coop's doorstep without either his wife or stepdaughter."

"I have training for this type of operation. You're a nurse." She glared at him, debating whether he deserved a slap for his condescending comment. Before the debate ended, he gently laid his hands on her shoulders. "I'm sorry. You know I respect the hell out of what you do, and I respect you, but this mission will be dangerous. I'd hate myself if anything happened to you."

She relaxed and took a breath. She didn't doubt his sincerity, but she hadn't come so far to turn tail and run. "It isn't as if I don't know what it's like over there. Have you forgotten my months of evading Kearns' bloodhounds? And with a pregnant woman no less?"

"I haven't forgotten. That's how we met." He lowered his hands. "You understand that once we cross that line, we're on our own, right? If we're captured, we'll end up in a camp, at best, right along with Riley's family."

She slid her arms around his waist and pulled him closer, ignoring the curious glances of the soldiers passing behind him. "Don't worry, I understand, but you won't let that happen. I have to take this risk. I owe that much to Riley."

His lips tightened into a line. "Then, if you're determined to do this, I need to make a few more calls. We're going to need backup."

"Whatever it takes." She stepped away but grasped his hand before he turned to go. "Hey, this is going to work. We trust each other. I know how to take care of myself. See you back at the tent."

She waited until he entered the radio hut before turning to go. She had put on a brave face, not wanting Conrad to see that the idea of crossing the border terrified her. He'd done it numerous times, but she'd only crossed once, heading in the opposite direction. That had been one time too many. She'd meant that she'd do whatever it took to help Riley and Julia, but that didn't mean she wasn't afraid. She just hoped that when the time came, she'd be able to summon the courage to equal Riley's.

Two days with no sign of Yeager hadn't been enough to convince Riley they'd escaped him. The others kept telling her to relax, but she knew her pursuer well enough to be certain they were nowhere near out of the woods. Riley was Yeager's only link to Adrian, and now he had her in his crosshairs.

"Riley," Harper said, making her jump. "Did you hear me? We're stopping for our siesta." Riley gave her a blank stare. She hadn't heard a word. "You've got to get a grip, Red."

She reined Biscuit to a stop, then dismounted and led him to a small grove of trees lining a creek. "It would help if you told me where we're headed."

"Doubt that," Lou said, "but we'll be there tomorrow. Just be patient for a few more hours. Once we arrive, you won't need to worry about that pesky little tail of yours."

Riley was skeptical that a place existed that could hide her from Yeager, but she let the matter drop. As she set up her spot for their three-hour break to avoid the worst of the heat, she said,

"Where will you go once we find my family? You're welcome to come with us to Colorado."

"Too cold in your neck of the woods for me," Bobby said. "I'm a Vegas boy. I get chills if the dial dips below sixty."

"We consider that a heatwave," Riley said with a laugh as she untied the handkerchief keeping the sun off her neck. She wiped at the sweat to keep it from running down her back. "You must be loving the weather today, Bobby. I'd guess it's close to a hundred."

He lowered his bulk to the hard ground and leaned against the trunk of the biggest oak tree. "It's a touch on the warm side today, even for me."

"At least it's dry," Lou said as he unrolled his sleeping bag onto a tarp. "I don't miss the humidity in Philly, where I grew up. You'd think the damp air would cool you off, but it saps the energy right out of you."

"It was the same in Baltimore," Harper said. "I loved the winters there, though. They could be brutal if we got a nor'easter, but it was the summers that got to me. My parents were school-teachers and had summers off, so we'd spend them at our lake house in Vermont. I never appreciated that until I got a summer job in Baltimore before I left for school. I thought I'd melt every time I stepped outside."

Riley recalled her conversation with Dashay when they wondered if they'd ever know what it was like to be warm. That seemed like only days earlier instead of months. A wave of home-sickness washed over her as she remembered her friend. That brought up thoughts of Coop and the kids. Xav had probably changed so much since the last time she saw him, and she feared he wouldn't recognize her when she finally made it home.

Riley had already made a vow not to spend any more nights away from her family once she had Julia home safely. She'd resign her commission from the Ministry as soon as she returned home and renew her efforts to convince Coop they needed to move to Colorado Springs to be near the hospital. With her cousins having shown up at the farm and with the additional family she'd bring home, her mom, Lily, and Kevin would have plenty of hands helping with the horse business and farm. They'd have more room in the house without Riley's family of six taking up space. Emily would love to be closer to school and having friends living nearby. It was the perfect solution for all of them.

She laid back on her bedroll and stared up at the afternoon light blinking through the leaves. "When this is all over, come spend your summers with us if the Vegas heat gets unbearable. There are plenty of damsels in distress to rescue in Colorado."

"You've got it, Red," Harper said. "I'm dying to meet this famous husband of yours."

"If he still wants to be my husband. I'm going to have some serious damage control to do when I get home."

Bobby yawned and said, "All will be forgotten the second you show up with Julia in tow. Besides, he'd be a fool to let go of a woman like you."

"Quit your jawing," Lou said as he stretched out on his back and tipped his baseball cap over his eyes. "We need sleep if we want to hit our mile quota tonight."

Riley followed his lead and closed her eyes. "Just one more question. How do you find these perfect places to stop?"

Harper was lying next to Riley and rolled over to face her. "We mapped them along our route, so we know just how to time our stops like we did when we biked. It's saved us hours of time and aggravation on our travels."

"We don't stay in one place for long," Bobby said. "These trails and rest stops have become our home."

"I have a bonus question. Last one," Riley said when Lou glared at her. "What took you to Vernon?"

Harper rolled onto her back and covered her eyes with her arm. "You're better off not knowing," she said softly.

"Please, tell me," Riley said. "There's not much in this world that shocks me anymore."

"We and some of our old buddies busted up a child trafficking ring we'd been tracking for almost a year," Bobby said. "We found a brother and his two younger sisters who'd lost their parents in the CME. Their grandparents are in Vernon, so we dropped them off there. They were shocked to find out the children were alive and sickened to hear what had happened to them. Those kids are going to need massive amounts of TLC."

"I'd hoped the CME had put a stop to such horrors like child trafficking."

"In some ways, it's worse since there are so many vulnerable kids with no one looking out for them. That makes it easier for bad guys to get away with it," Harper said.

Riley shivered. "Revolting. The world is lucky to have people like you working to put a stop to it."

"We all play our part," Lou said from under his cap. "Can we please sleep now, Riley?"

"You have my permission."

Riley turned onto her side and curled into a ball. Of all the ways life could have gone after the CME, Julia having to spend time in an internment camp wasn't the worst, but Riley was more motivated than ever to get her home. Needing to get what rest she could, she worked through her deep breathing exercises to calm her thoughts and drifted off faster than she expected to. After what felt like five minutes, Lou was shaking her shoulder to wake her.

She sat up and rubbed her eyes. "It's time to go already?"

He shook his head and whispered, "No. It's only been two hours, but Harper heard Biscuit whinny and got up to check on him. When she did, she heard a horse whinny back. She crawled to the top of the rise with binocs to check it out. There's a lone rider in the valley behind us. Could be anyone, but we'd better move, just in case it's your stalker. He's far enough away that we can make some headway if we get a move on."

Riley jumped up and rolled her bag, then stowed her gear in

record time. The four of them were trotting off ten minutes later. The blistering heat would tire the horses in a hurry, so they wouldn't be able to move for long, but the rider behind them would have to rest his horse, too. Chances were, he'd use the rest stop they'd vacated minutes earlier. They'd done their best to remove any signs they'd been there recently. Their tracks wouldn't be traceable since the dry, packed ground was covered with hundreds of hoof prints from riders that had passed that way. Still, Riley was on edge, waiting to turn any second and find Yeager coming for her.

Lou led the way with the rest following in a silent chain behind him. After two miles, he turned due north and guided his horse down a bank into the shallow creek. The water would cool the horses' hooves and hide their tracks. They kept to the creek until it became impassable after ten miles before returning to solid ground. Bobby kept an eye out for the lone rider but saw no sign of him, which brought out a collective sigh of relief from the group. As they searched for a new spot to stop and rest, Lou crested a plateau with the others close behind. He pointed out a stand of trees in the valley below, and they nodded in agreement. The sun was setting by the time they'd finished setting up camp.

"I hate to miss prime nighttime travel, but the horses need to rest and feed," Bobby said. "We'll take six hours. No fire. It'll be too easy to spot from the plateau."

"Too hot for a fire anyway," Riley said as she collapsed onto her bedroll.

Lou rolled a log to the edge of their camp. "I'll take first watch. Riley, you're next, then Harper. Wake us at two. That should give us time to reach the farm by sunrise."

Riley turned her head to face him and said, "Farm?"

Lou chuckled at her. "Nice try, Red. Get some rest. You'll have your answers soon."

———

Riley got four hours of restful sleep and was grateful to be traveling at night out of the heat. There was a full harvest moon in a cloudless sky. If her mission hadn't been so urgent, she would have enjoyed the view more. She counted the time since she ran away from Santa Fe. She was distressed to realize over three months had passed. For all she knew, Conrad's team had already rescued Julia, and she was waiting in Colorado for her mom to come home. Riley's first order of business was to get her hands on a radio ASAP to find out what was happening at home.

"They wouldn't happen to have a radio at this farm we're heading to, would they?" she asked, breaking the silence.

"They do," Bobby said. "You have to trade to use it. I'm sure we have something they'll want."

"I usually offer medical treatment as my currency," Riley said. "I haven't run across a community yet that wasn't in need of my services."

"That should work," Harper said, then chuckled. "Although, they're a pretty healthy bunch."

Riley sighed in exasperation, loud enough for all three to hear. "Enough with keeping me in suspense. Who are these people, and how much farther?"

As they reached the top of a bluff, Lou tipped his head toward the east as the sun rose over the horizon. "We're here."

Riley followed his gaze, and her eyes widened at the sight of acres of cultivated fields spreading out before them. She studied the various crops, easily identifying the corn and wheat, but couldn't make out the plants growing on two acres at the southern edge. She took out her binoculars to get a better look and had to check twice.

She slowly lowered the binocs, and without taking her eyes from the scene, said, "Please tell me that's hemp."

Bobby avoided her eyes and scratched his head, which Riley recognized as his tic for discomfort. "Some of it is. Some of it's a close cousin to hemp."

Riley lifted the binocs back to her eyes. "You're trying not to say marijuana."

Bobby grinned at her. "Pretty much."

Riley took a beat to keep herself from speaking the thoughts running through her brain. "So, the three of you thought bringing me to a bunch of pot farmers was a good plan to rescue my daughter, especially considering what you guys do?"

"Not just pot farmers," Harper interjected. "They grow various crops which are helping to feed communities in the area."

Riley stared at her, wondering how she'd jumped headlong into trouble. Again. "That's not an answer. What *am* I doing here?"

Lou gave up trying to hide how hilarious he found her reaction and burst out laughing. "You should see your face." When she narrowed her eyes at him, he held up his hands in surrender. "Before you go getting all virtuous on us, I seem to remember you engaging in a little drug dealing of your own."

"That's different. I'm licensed to prescribe those drugs. I don't grow them in my backyard to sell them to users."

Bobby rode his horse in front of Riley and wheeled him around to face her. "We're getting off-topic. There's a reason we brought you here. These farmers are a co-op that, yes, happens to grow pot, but they're decent people who are taking care of their neighbors. It might interest you to know that they're in negotiations with the WSA government to help in the production of natural medications, but that has nothing to do with our plan."

Riley loosened her grip on Biscuit's reins and relaxed her shoulders. "You have my attention."

"These farmers don't consume the pot they grow, except in small amounts, but they do sell it to customers across the border. Regardless of your moral objections, they have clients in strategic positions who purchase their wares. This gives them the ability to cross back and forth across the border without interference. Now, do you understand why we're here?"

Riley looked down at her hands resting on the saddle. "It's dawning on me, but that doesn't mean I'm good with it."

"Listen to me, Riley," Harper said. "We debated about this ad nauseam while you were recovering in Vernon. They've helped us chase more than one bad guy across the border. We'd never put you in danger. They're good people willing to help those in need. If you can keep your moral judgments in check, they might surprise you."

"You're asking me to overlook their international drug dealing activities because they're such nice people?"

"You're overreacting," Lou said. "We're not asking you to smoke or sell the drugs. Wasn't weed use legal in your state before the CME?"

He had her there, but she said, "Lots of legal activities exist that I choose not to engage in."

"Bottom line," Bobby said, "it doesn't hurt our cause if our enemies are too high and mellow to pay attention to us."

Riley rubbed the sweat from her forehead. "I'm too exhausted to keep arguing about this. I'll listen to your plan. This won't be the first time I've ignored my ethics or morals for the sake of my family's survival. You asked me in Vernon if I trusted you. I do, so I'm placing my life, and those of my family, in your hands."

"We expected more of a fight," Bobby said. "Maybe we should have told you earlier."

Lou winked at Riley. "That would have made it too easy for her to run."

Bobby flicked his hand at him. "Shut it, Lou. Here's the plan, Riley. We're going to ask them to allow us to go on their next cross-border sales run as one of them. We'll need to change up your entire look."

Riley looked down at her four-year-old designer boots, her brand-name cargo shorts, and a trendy, pre-CME t-shirt. "What's wrong with my clothes?"

"Everything about you screams Soccer Mom, not Zen weed farmer," Lou said.

"And we've got to do something about that hair, Red," Harper said. "It's too recognizable."

Riley told them about cutting off her curls and dying her hair black to trick Yeager. "I could go the opposite way this time and bleach it, but I don't want to chop it. Maybe just a trim."

Harper fingered Riley's ponytail. "I could try to straighten it some."

"Let's get there first," Lou said. "We'll discuss hairstyles later."

Riley did her best to ignore the knot in her gut as they rode closer to the farm. Lou could have been right about her overreacting, but it wasn't just the marijuana farm. It was becoming all too real that soon she'd be crossing back into Kearns' world. She'd known from the beginning that this was where her journey led, but facing that reality filled her with dread. She reminded herself that it also meant she was getting close to Julia. If all went well, she and Julia would be on their way home for good.

———

Events moved at breakneck speed from the moment Riley and her companions reached the farm. The farmers were on board with Bobby's plan from the moment they heard Riley's story. The problem was, they were scheduled to make the next delivery across the border in thirty-six hours. That left little time to prepare.

A few of the women in the co-op donated clothes for Riley that were a better fit for the mission. Harper helped bleach, trim, and straighten her hair. She started by cutting her braids off halfway down, so her hair fell to her shoulders. The result was more appealing than Riley's short, black-haired disguise had been.

When they finished, Harper stood back and admired her

work. "Not a bad look for you, Red. You might keep it once you're home."

Riley studied herself in the hand-held mirror. "I'll have to see what Coop has to say about that. He loves my red mop. Why don't you have to change?"

"Who would question a couple of bikers selling weed?"

Riley set the mirror down and shrugged. "Fair point."

"Speaking of Coop, it's time for your radio call."

Riley had earned time on the radio by successfully delivering the baby of a woman who was in labor and experiencing complications when they arrived. She also volunteered to provide exams for the children and a few adults experiencing various maladies that their natural remedies couldn't cure. After that, they were willing to give her the world.

As she crossed the co-op compound with Harper, she thought of the people she'd met in the few hours since they arrived. They were like most of the people she met in her crazy travels across the continent. They loved their families and were concerned about their welfare. They worked to support themselves and make life better for the others in their community. While Riley didn't condone some of their activities, she understood they were trying to make the best of a difficult situation. She felt guilty for condemning them before laying eyes on them and remembered her conversation with Harper in Vernon about making snap judgments. She clearly still had work to do.

They found the converted barn with the antenna mounted on the roof. The tech in charge of working and maintaining the radio ushered Riley inside and pointed to a chair at the table.

When he explained how to make the call, she said, "Thank you, but I'm familiar with how this works." She gave the call sign for the radio at home, then gave hers. Silence greeted her. She repeatedly tried for three or four minutes, growing more concerned by the second. It was her last chance to contact the family, possibly until she arrived home. She took a few deep breaths to slow her heart rate, reminding herself that they hadn't heard from her for weeks and weren't expecting her call.

She gave the call signs again and nearly jumped out of her chair when she got a response.

Her mother repeated her callsign before saying, "Is that you, sweetheart?"

Riley's voice caught as she said, "It's me, Mom."

After several seconds of silence, Marjory said, "We've feared the worst. What a relief to hear your voice. Where are you?"

"Near Gainesville, TX. How are you, Mom? How are Coop and the kids? Are they there?"

"What in the world are you doing in Gainesville," she asked, ignoring Riley's questions.

"I'll explain everything. What about Coop and the kids?"

"I'm sorry, dear, but Coop's at the hospital. I'll send Kevin or one of your cousins with word that you're alive as soon as we end our call. He's not doing well, though. Sick with worry over you and Julia. He'll be overjoyed to hear you called."

Tears stung at Riley's eye at the thought of the pain she'd caused Coop. He was one to mask his emotions and make a joke out of everything, so if his suffering was obvious to her mother, it had to be bad.

"The rest of us are fine," Marjory continued. "There's so much to tell you. Lily's pregnant and doing great. Due in November. I'll get the kids as soon as you tell me what's happening with you."

"That's great news about Lily. I'm crossing the border tomorrow to go after Julia and the rest of the family. If all goes well, we'll be home within a month."

"That's wonderful news, dear. Are you going alone? Did Dashay and Conrad find you?"

The familiar knot tightened in Riley's gut at the news that Conrad and Dashay hadn't returned home or found her. "No, Mom. I'm hoping we'll meet up outside Julia's camp, but I'm not traveling alone. I've made new friends along the way who are helping me. You don't have to worry. We're taking every precaution."

"That's a relief. Hold on while I grab the kids."

Riley did her best to hide her trembling hands from the tech as she waited for her mom to return. The next thing she heard was Emily squealing in delight.

"You're not dead, Mom!" she said in a rush. "I was so sure you were. For a while, I was worried about you, then I wanted to punch you the next time I saw you. After that, I started planning your memorial service."

"Hello, sweetheart," Riley said, laughing and crying at the same time. She loved that Emily always blurted whatever was on her mind. She caught the tech turning away to wipe his eyes. "I don't blame you. This was the first time I could get to a radio to contact you."

"I got over being mad at you when I thought you were dead. This is so exciting! Did you find Julia? Are you coming home?"

"I'm on my way toward Julia now. We'll be home in a month or so. I won't be able to call before then, but don't worry if we take longer to get there. You know how it can be."

"Don't worry about it. Just bring my sister home. Love you, Mom. Here's Jared."

"Love you, too," Riley said, but she wasn't sure Emily heard.

As Riley waited for her oldest son to come on the line, she heard Jared and Emily's muffled voices and knew Emily was trying to convince him to talk to her. How many times would she have to win Jared's love back before he gave up on her?

"Hey, Mom," he said, without emotion.

"It's so great to hear your voice," Riley said with as much enthusiasm as she could muster. "You can't imagine how much I've missed you."

"Missed you, too." Riley was elated to hear the touch of sincerity in his voice. "Did you really get bitten by a rattlesnake?"

"I did. It wasn't fun. I got hit in the face, too, by some jerk. I have a cool scar on my cheek."

"Seriously?" Jared said, sounding impressed.

"Yeah, and I stitched the cut myself. I'll tell you all about it when I get home. It won't be much longer, and I'll be bringing Julia home. We'll all be together again, and I promise I won't leave you anymore."

"You won't?" she heard Emily say. "You're quitting the HWB?"

"I am. I need to be with all of you as much as I can. I can't live with being away from all of you anymore." She was on the verge of losing control, so she took a few gulps of water. "My time is up. Tell everyone I love them and that I'm fine. Give Xav extra hugs from me tonight."

"We will, Mom," Jared said. "I love you. Get home as fast as you can."

"I promise. Love you. Goodbye."

Harper came in and helped her out of the chair. "It's someone else's turn now. Let's go to your room until you compose yourself."

Riley untied her handkerchief, then wiped her face and blew her nose. "I'm good. Just been holding that in for so long. It was a bit overwhelming to hear my kids' voices. Let's get out of here and get my daughter. I want to go home."

"You've got it, Red. We leave at sundown."

As they walked to the house where their temporary rooms were, Riley ran her hand through her hair and said, "You need a new nickname for me. Red doesn't make sense anymore."

"I don't care what color your hair is. You're Red to me."

Riley chuckled. "Not sure if that's a compliment or not."

Harper shrugged and dropped onto her bed when they reached their room. "You ready for this?"

"So ready. I'm not even afraid anymore. I meant what I said. I'm ready to go home."

"Good. Let's get a few hours of sleep before our final mission chitchat."

Harper turned toward the wall, and Riley heard her deep, even breathing, minutes later. Riley envied her, knowing there would be no sleep for her. She laid on her pillow and did her best to rest as she ran through her conversations with her mom and the kids. All that had been missing was getting to talk to Coop and hearing her Xav's baby chatter. We might find a radio along the way, she thought, knowing she was fooling herself. The only way they'd have access to a radio was if one magically appeared on the side of the trail. Until they were back on WSA soil, she'd have to be content with her memories.

———

Riley leaned over and studied the map their leader, Simeon, had spread across the table. Simeon was about five-nine, with a slim build, but Riley could see the definition of his muscles through the lightweight sleeves of his hemp shirt. Riley guessed it from working hard in the fields. Not unlike the Amish she'd spent time with on her trip to Colorado. Simeon's straight blond ponytail reached nearly to his waist. He had calm, even manners and kind eyes.

"Your journey to Oklahoma City will take a week, minimum. There are water sources along the fastest route, but not much else, so you'll need to ration your supplies. The border between Texas and Oklahoma runs through the middle of the Red River. The only ways to cross are these three bridges. We've tried all three, but these two add too many miles to the trip." He pointed to the far western and eastern bridges. "We head up the middle."

"How do we cross? Isn't the bridge heavily guarded on both sides?" Lou asked.

Simeon grinned at him. "That's why you need us. We have arrangements with the guards on both sides. As long as there are no skirmishes going on when we're ready to cross, we're good."

"The border's been quiet, probably due to the heat," Simeon's brother, Harry, said. "Makes our job easier."

"Once we're on the other side, we'll all travel with you for a day or so, then just Harry will go on with you in case anyone gives you trouble," Simeon continued, then reached up to put his arm around Harry's shoulders. "I expect you to get my baby brother back to me."

Riley almost laughed at his use of the word baby. Their faces were nearly identical, but that was where the similarity ended. Harry was at least five inches taller than Simeon and had hair almost as red as hers. He was bigger-boned and had a smile as broad as his shoulders. Riley was sure having Harry along would keep everyone's spirits high.

"I'll do everything in my power to make that happen," she said.

Simeon smiled and patted Harry's back. "Riley, Bobby tells me your friend on the inside gave you documents and uniforms to enter the camp?" She gave a quick nod. "If the weather holds, and you don't run into wandering patrols, I don't see you having a problem reaching your daughter. What are you going to do once you get your family out of the camp?"

Riley ran her finger over the map. "We'll head due west back to Texas as quickly as we can. I don't know what their physical conditions will be. My aunt and uncle are in their late sixties. They were pretty fit from working on their ranch the last time I saw them, but I have no way of knowing what they've done to them in that camp."

Bobby reached over her and pressed his index finger to a spot on the border. "Cross here near Sweetwater. I'll be waiting there for you."

Riley turned to look up at him. "What do you mean you'll be waiting? You're not coming with us?"

"I can't, Red," he said, shaking his head. "I'm too conspicuous, and you'll need a man on this side once you're across."

Even though what Bobby said made sense, Riley was disappointed with the news. "I'm sorry to hear that, but we'll have to do our best to make do without you."

Bobby gave her a bear hug that nearly knocked the wind out of her. After putting her down, he reached into his vest pocket and pulled out one of her cut braids. "I have this to remember you by, not that I need it. Just make it back into the WSA. I'll take over from there."

Riley gave him assurances that she'd do her best and thanked him for everything he was doing for her. Bobby turned from Riley and gave Harper an even tighter hug. There was a low ripple of laughter that signaled the end of the meeting. The group crossing the border finished last-minute packing, then said their goodbyes and took to the road. Riley reflected on the change in her opinion of these people as they left the farm, then looked over her ragtag group of traveling companions. Her group was composed of two bikers, six New-Age pot farmers, and a Soccer Mom orthopedic surgeon.

"Not exactly the Fellowship of the Ring," she said, just loud enough for Harper to hear.

"What are you mumbling about, Red?"

Riley shook her head, then raised her chin as she readied herself to face the forces of Mordor.

CHAPTER ELEVEN

YEAGER CROUCHED near the edge of the cornfield, listening intently as one male and one female farmer discussed the departure of members of their commune to sell their prize marijuana crop two days earlier. Yeager had tracked Riley and her biker pals to the commune and spent the past day spying for information. Gathering intel could save him days of heading in the wrong direction on the road. It hadn't taken long for him to learn that Riley had been there but was already gone. It was imperative that he discover her next destination, hoping he could arrive ahead of her.

Yeager's legs began to cramp, so he dropped to his knees and wiped the sweat pouring from under his baseball cap. He wasn't thrilled about having to hide between the sweating corn stalks in the hottest part of the day, but he could sense that he was zeroing in on what he needed. As he watched the couple work, he wondered how they seemed to tolerate the heat so well. Probably high, he thought.

He'd heard of these types of farmers who made a living by keeping guards and soldiers in the US supplied with weed. He admired their resourcefulness but was disgusted by their exploitation of their neighbors across the border. He was also ashamed of those same weaknesses in his comrades-in-arms, expecting them to hold themselves to a higher standard. They never would have gotten away with such behavior before the CME. Yeager shook his head in sadness at how the world he once knew had gone to hell on so many levels.

He shook his head to clear his distracting thoughts and aimed his focus back on his unwitting informants.

"Do you think she'll rescue her family?" the woman said.

"I do," the man answered. "The Doc's smart enough to outwit those simpletons across the river."

Bingo, Yeager thought, leaning in to hear more.

The woman stopped and leaned on the handle of her hoe while she wiped her face. "Not everyone in the US is as easy to fool as those idiot guards along the border. They have a long way to go. Who knows what they could run into, and some of our people are with them."

"Harry's the only one going all the way to OK City. No one will mess with him."

Yeager fell onto his back between the stalks, wishing he could shout for victory. He had his answer. Riley was going for her daughter, Julia, in one of Kearns' infernal camps in Oklahoma City. A plan sprouted in his brain that would get him to Riley, who would lead him to Daybreak. All he had to do was wait for nightfall to sneak out of the field and hit the road. He'd travel much faster as a lone rider than they would as a group. He had his shortcuts and his IDs that would open any door, too. The end was finally in his sights.

———

Julia had done her best not to give up on her mom, but when weeks passed with no sight of her or any word that she was on her way, it got too hard to keep her hopes up. Life was much better for them with Nico there, but that wasn't the same as having her mom show up to rescue them. Nico had come by four days earlier to tell them he was working on a way to get them out and send word to her mom. Julia was all for that plan. Even if her mom was coming, it would be easier for her if they were already free.

Julia had watched for Nico's flashlight signal from the grassy area in front of their apartment for the past three nights, but he hadn't been there. She wasn't too worried since sometimes they went for a week without seeing him. He could be busy working on his rescue plan. She'd just have to be patient a little longer.

"Julia, come away from the window," Aunt Beth said. "You have homework and staring outside won't bring Nico any faster."

Julia lowered the blinds and sank onto the couch. "What's even the point of school if I'm going to be a prisoner for the rest of my life?"

Uncle Mitch looked up from the notepad where he'd been scratching notes about something all evening. "You won't be here for the rest of your life. People are working on getting us out. If that doesn't work, Kearns won't be president forever. Maybe someday, the two countries will be one again, and there won't be any more camps. Keeping us locked up serves no purpose and costs her in supplies and labor. If Kearns set all the prisoners free, we could help grow crops and contribute to the economy in other ways."

"That would make too much sense," Holly said as she came into their tiny living room from their even tinier kitchen. "Kearns probably thinks we'll all run away to the WSA, which we so would."

"Not everyone would leave for the WSA," Aunt Beth said. "Most of the other detainees are from these parts. They have no reason to leave."

"Except that Nico says life is so much better in the WSA. We can't be the only people who know that."

Uncle Mitch put his finger to his lips, then whispered, "We shouldn't be talking this way. The walls might have ears."

Julia rolled her eyes. "I seriously don't think anyone gives a crap about us anymore. I'm not sure anyone even remembers us or why we're here. If we just walked out of the gate one day, no one would even notice or miss us."

"I wish that were true," Kathryn said. "Unfortunately, the walking out of the gate part is the problem. If you know a way to do that, Julia, I'd love to hear it."

"I bet Nico does," Julia said.

Uncle Mitch looked back down at his notepad and whispered, "We're all counting on that."

Kathryn picked up the pair of Holly's shorts she was mending. While she worked, she said, "I thought you liked school, Julia. The teachers here are so much better than they were in our first two camps."

"I like biology and math, but US history seems pointless. English is not bad, but I don't like Mr. Ceder. The way he looks at me creeps me out. And I guess it's hard for me to care about grades when Nico might get us out of here any day. It's not like my transcripts will transfer to my new school."

Holly held her hand up for a fist bump. "Good one, Cuz."

Kathryn went on, ignoring Julia's comment, "You'll still need the knowledge you're gaining. You were saying last week you might want to be a doctor like your mom. Eventually, they'll get electricity and universities running. You'll need to glean as much as you can before that happens."

Aunt Beth tapped Julia on the shoulder. "Excellent point."

"Fine, I'll go do my homework."

As she stood to go to her room, someone pounded on the door. Julia started for it, but Holly's dad, Clint, put his arm out to stop her. He motioned for her to move away, so she crossed the room and stood behind Uncle Mitch.

Clint looked through the peephole, then let out his breath and opened the door. "What's with the pounding, Nico?"

Nico rushed into the room and pointed to the door, "Close and bolt that." Once Clint had done as he ordered, Nico turned to the rest of the family and said, "I don't have much time. One of my contacts just got word to me they're moving you to a new camp in the morning."

Julia ran to him and grabbed his arms. "No, they can't! What if my mom's coming? She won't know where to find us."

Aunt Beth gently peeled Julia's fingers from Nico and nudged her away to give him space.

"Did your contact tell you where they're sending us, or why?" Kathryn asked.

Nico ran his hand through his hair, keeping his eyes lowered. "Wichita, Kansas. We don't know why. My contact said it was a sudden decision."

Uncle Mitch stood and stepped closer to him. Keeping his voice low, he said, "Are they moving others or just us?"

"Your family and two or three others. My contact assured me he'll do whatever he can to get me transferred with you. He's good for his word, but if he can't, I'll get there on my own." He motioned for Julia to come closer. "I'll leave a note for your mom at the spot where I told her to meet me when she got here. She'll find it and will come for you. You know your mom. She doesn't let anything get in her way." He turned to face the others. "Don't lose hope. This is just a minor setback. I have to go, but hopefully, I'll see you in the morning."

He was gone before any of them could say a word. Julia stared at the door until her legs went numb, and she collapsed in a heap. Holly and Kathryn ran to her and did their best to comfort her as she sobbed into her hands. She'd stayed strong for the rest of them for so long, but this was too much. Someone must have found out her mom was coming, and now they were sending them farther away from the border.

None of it had mattered. Nico finding them hadn't mattered. Her mom running away from everyone hadn't mattered. She wasn't yet sixteen, but all she saw of her future was years as a prisoner in a stinking camp. No boyfriends. No husband. No children of her own. No life as a surgeon working alongside her mom. Her life was over before it had even begun.

Riley did her best to appear bored as they neared the checkpoint on the WSA side of the bridge, but her heart pounded so hard she was afraid it would be obvious to everyone. The way her journey had gone, she was sure the guards who'd been bribed to let them through had been switched out with new ones who would send them packing back to Gainesville. She shifted her focus from the guards to the river flowing beneath them. That brown water and the guards were the barriers keeping her from Julia.

"If it isn't Sandy," one guard said, in a heavy Texas accent. "Haven't seen you for a while."

The way he was eying Sandy gave Riley the impression she may have shared more than her crops with him.

"You know how it is, Sarge," Sandy said and rode her horse up next to him. "I'm here now."

"What do you think of this heat?"

Sandy gave him a seductive look. "The sun's not the only thing that's too hot."

Riley gritted her teeth to keep from saying seriously like Julia used to. In Riley's opinion, Sarge wasn't any woman's idea of hot.

"Well, aren't you sweet?" Sarge said. "What takes you over the bridge so early in the morning, as if I don't know."

"Just going to sell our crops, as usual," Sandy said, putting on an innocent air. "I'll be back in a few days. Will you be here?"

As Riley witnessed the exchange, she imagined Conrad would love to have Sandy on one of his teams.

"Wouldn't miss it." Sarge motioned for the guard behind him to raise the barrier arm, then waved for Sandy and her companions to pass. When Riley and Lou reached him with Harper behind them, he said, "Who are these three? I've never seen them before."

Sandy wheeled her horse around and rode back to them. "They're just new members of the commune. We're showing them the ropes."

Lou smiled and winked as he chewed a piece of hay, and Riley gave what she hoped was an alluring look. Sarge gave her the creepiest grin she'd ever seen and waved them on.

"Hope to see you on the way back, too," he said to Riley.

She kept her eyes forward, pretending she didn't know he was speaking to her. She was afraid it would be too hard to hide her revulsion if she turned and looked at him. They'd made it through the first barrier, but her hands were still shaking by the time they reached the middle of the bridge.

"I think I'm going to be sick," she told Harper.

Harper laughed as she passed her. "Just pretend you're in a bar fight, Red."

Her friend's joke eased the tension, reminding her she'd stared down and even taken out some of the scariest people she could imagine. A measly border guard was no match for her. At least, that was what she told herself. She sat straighter in the saddle until the sight of the guard hut at the far end of the bridge caused her courage to waver. The worst consequence at the WSA checkpoint was getting sent home. The other side could mean getting arrested or worse. Riley took a breath, struggling to keep her fears from gaining ground.

Two guards, a young man, and a woman, waited for them behind the barrier. They reminded Riley of the kids standing guard outside Madisonville when she was racing to save Coop and Dashay from dying of typhoid. She'd been prepared that day to run over anyone who got in her way. She was ready to do the same for Julia.

The young woman approached them and dipped her chin. "Simeon. It's been a while."

Simeon gave her a warm smile. "Hello, Zoe. We've been harvesting the early summer crops. We need to get them to our arranged buyers as soon as possible. They won't stay fresh for long in this heat."

"I'm sure you don't need to worry about the freshness of what you're delivering," the male guard said with a laugh.

"Good one, Noah," Harry said, "but we're delivering several kinds of produce on this run, some fresher than others. Are you going to let us pass?"

"Who are they?" Zoe asked Simeon, tilting her head toward Riley, Harper, and Lou.

Simeon smiled at the three of them like a proud father. "The newest members of the commune. We're just teaching them how this works."

Noah narrowed his eyes at the new additions. "We weren't notified you were bringing extras. You should have sent word ahead before just showing up with them. We have a process."

Riley noticed Simeon's smile fade a touch. He clearly hadn't expected to be questioned.

"Bernie assured me we'd have free crossing rights, and you know full well we have different crews for each trip. It's never been an issue."

Noah stood taller and crossed his arms. "Those three don't look like your usual delivery drivers."

"We get all kinds," Simeon said, dropping the grin entirely.

Zoe stepped closer to Noah and pulled her rifle off her shoulder without raising it, but the gesture spoke volumes to Riley. "Those three need to turn around and go back where they came from. The rest of you may pass."

"No," Harry said, stepping closer to her. "That's not part of our arrangement. All of us are going to cross."

Noah lifted his rifle, aiming at Harper, and Zoe followed, pointing hers at Lou. Riley's heart was in her throat, and she had to fight to keep from turning Biscuit around and galloping back across the bridge. Nothing else but her drive to get to Julia could have stopped her.

"Bernie's not here," Noah said, keeping his voice even.

Simeon locked eyes with him and didn't flinch. "Seems you've made an arrangement of your own. Bernie will be interested to hear this."

Zoe scoffed. "Bernie's so mellowed from your prized product that all he cares about is his next high, so go ahead and narc on us."

Riley was stunned to see Simeon and Harry calmly slide their hands to their waistbands. She'd thought they were pacifists. She should have known drug dealers would never travel unprotected, especially in the wild west.

Simeon's smile returned, but it didn't reach his eyes. "Noah, none of us wants trouble. And is it wise to challenge us? We outnumber you three to one, and we're on horseback."

Noah stuck two fingers under his tongue and gave an earsplitting whistle. Within seconds, twelve riders came out from behind a crumbling barn off the side of the road, ten yards past the end of the bridge. They were all uniformed and armed. Simeon's people should have realized such a strategic checkpoint wouldn't be protected by only two guards. This is the end of the line, Riley thought, trying not to tremble herself out of the saddle. She wished she'd listened to that earlier voice urging her to gallop to safety.

A smile crept up Noah's face. "What were you saying about being outnumbered? If my math is right, looks like two to one, our favor."

Riley's three other companions drew weapons she didn't know

they carried. She inched Biscuit behind the others as she worked to retrieve her handgun from the holster. Her hands shook so violently it took some doing. The sound of loading a round into the chamber was deafening in the tension-laden silence. Harper rolled her eyes at her. Riley mouthed sorry without removing her gaze from the guards aiming rifles at them.

"Let it go, Simeon," she whispered just loud enough for him to hear. "It's not worth any of you getting killed. We'll try another way."

"What's she saying?" Noah called to them.

Without bothering to keep his voice lowered, Simeon said, "This isn't about you, Riley. We made a contract with these people. They've betrayed that. They're a bunch of lying snakes."

Riley cringed, wondering why Simeon was doing his best to incite a gunfight, but that was the last straw for her. Getting herself killed wouldn't help anyone. She tugged on the reins to wheel Biscuit around and get the hell out of there.

One of the enemy guards yelled, "Where do you think you're going," then fired at her without waiting for an answer.

The round struck one foot from Biscuit's front left hoof, then ricocheted off the pavement and sailed over the railing into the river below. Biscuit reared up on his hind legs, nearly unseating her, but Riley tightened her legs around him and clung to the saddle horn and reins while trying to keep a hold on her gun. Biscuit dropped down after a few seconds but continued to dance and fidget in panic. Riley patted his neck and whispered calming words as she struggled to calm herself, hoping that shot was only a warning.

"Hold your fire," Noah shouted, then turned to Simeon. "You should have listened to your companion. I'm accepting your comment as a confession of bribing a US official. I'm taking you and your comrades into custody. If you resist, we're authorized to subdue enemy citizens by any means we deem necessary."

Simeon didn't lower his weapon. "And how are you planning to take us?"

"What kind of pacifists are you?" Riley whispered.

Sandy turned her head slightly to face her. "Who told you we're pacifists?"

"There you go stereotyping again," Harper said and chuckled nervously.

Riley swung around to face her. "Glad you think this is a joke. Am I the only one who sees all those guns aimed at us?"

"We have guns pointed at us all the time," Harry said. "Comes with the job."

Riley holstered her weapon and lifted her hands. "I surrender. Please don't shoot me."

"Put your hands down," Simeon said evenly, keeping his eyes on Noah and Zoe. "I won't let you do this. They'll kill you."

Riley ignored his order and kept her arms raised.

"She'd be dead already if that's what we wanted," Zoe said. "We accept your surrender. Keep your hands visible and slowly ride toward us."

Riley gently tried to get Biscuit moving, but he wouldn't budge. "My horse is spooked," she called to Zoe. "Give me a sec."

Harper moved her horse closer to Biscuit. Keeping her voice lowered, she said, "Are you insane?"

"Utterly," Riley answered.

"You can't turn yourself over to these people. Have you forgotten Kearns is searching for you?"

"These people don't know who I am," Riley whispered. "They think I'm some random weed dealer. This will get me across the border in one piece. I haven't done anything wrong, so they might let me go, but if not, I'll figure that out later. This is better than getting killed in a firefight on this bridge."

"What's the holdup?" one of the guards at the back shouted.

Harper raised her hands. "Then, Lou and I are going with you."

"What?" Lou said. "I didn't sign up for getting arrested."

"Won't be the first time. Or probably the last," Harper said.

Riley slowly shook her head. "No, I can't let you do this. I got you into this mess. I'm getting you out." She tipped her head toward Harper and Lou and said, "I'll come quietly but let my two friends go. Their only crime is falling in with the wrong group."

"Don't listen to her," Lou said as he guided his horse next to Biscuit. "We're coming, too." He took the reins from Riley, then got his horse moving. Biscuit got into step behind him without resisting. Lou turned back to Riley and winked. "No lip from you."

"Harry!" Simeon snapped at his brother. "Do something."

Harry moved his horse perpendicular across the bridge, blocking Lou and them from crossing. "I'm sorry, but you three know too much for us to let you go," he said.

In the next instant, one of the guards fired, but it wasn't a warning shot. There was a dull thud, and Harry's horse went down beneath him. Harry climbed off and ducked behind his fallen horse.

With the guards distracted by Harry's movements, Riley saw their opening. "Now," she said just loud enough for Lou and Harper to hear.

Lou tossed Biscuit's reins to Riley, then got his horse moving at a gallop. Riley and Harper followed his lead toward the far end of the bridge. The guards moved aside to let them pass, and they were across in moments. Riley had expected to feel a stray round pierce her spine every second as they moved and was shocked to escape unscathed.

Deafening sounds of gunfire filled the air as four guards corralled them toward the barn where they'd hidden earlier. When Riley spun in the saddle to see the battle going on behind them, the guard closest to her growled, "Keep moving. Nothing you can do for your friends now."

She obeyed but was devastated to think of what could be

happening to Simeon and the others. She'd tried to convince him to abandon their plan and find another way into the US, but he'd refused to listen. She prayed he hadn't paid for that stubbornness with his life.

———

The guards led the three of them to a border outpost two miles beyond the bridge. It was little more than a collection of fifteen, one-person tents, three larger tents, and the horse corral surrounded by a barbed-wire fence. The two sentries guarding the gate perked up as Riley's captors motioned for them to admit them with their prisoners.

Once inside the fence, they ordered Riley and the others to dismount and hand over their weapons. Riley complied without resisting, then stood motionless as one guard got a little too friendly while patting her down.

Lou caught what was happening and tried to pull away from the guard who was patting him down. "Watch the hands, buddy. Show the lady some respect."

The guard shrugged. "Got to get what I can when I can."

"Cretin," Harper mumbled.

The guard clicked his tongue at her, then said, "You three wait on that bench by the tree while we get orders for what to do with you. We weren't prepared to be taking prisoners today."

Riley dropped onto the bench, then watched in dismay as the guards removed the saddlebags from their horses and carted them off to the biggest tent.

Once the guards were out of earshot, Harper said, "Still happy you surrendered, Red?"

"Yes, without question. You heard that firefight as we rode off. That situation wasn't going to end in any other way. I thought Simeon's people were peaceful pot farmers."

"They are, but that's not the same as being pacifists," Lou said.

"In their line of work, they have to know how to defend themselves."

Riley considered his answer before saying, "What happened back there wasn't self-defense. What was that breaking the contract business? Simeon should have just let it go and backed off. We could have found another way across the border."

Lou studied her for a moment, then said, "Think it through, Riley. It's kind of an 'honor among thieves' deal. If Simeon pays a bribe in exchange for certain concessions, he can't just let the other side get away with breaking the contract. He must enforce the terms of the agreement. He couldn't let that upstart, Noah, change the rules on a whim."

"This whole situation has my head spinning. In the world I know, Noah would be considered the good guy."

"Then by association, the creep who just tried to feel you up is a good guy," Harper said.

Riley closed her eyes and massaged her temples with her fingertips. "Trust me, I understand life's not black and white, but I guarantee there are men like him on both sides. My point is none of this makes sense. I'm just relieved we're alive and on US soil."

Lou put his arm around her shoulders. "Yes, we are, Red, and that much closer to your daughter."

As two of the guards headed towards them, Harper whispered, "Or that much farther away."

————

Dashay stood on Xena's left side in the early morning shadows, psyching herself up to climb into the saddle. It had taken five nights for Conrad and her to travel from Amarillo to Shamrock, Texas, their last stop before meeting Conrad's agents at the border. Temperatures had soared higher each day, and she began to doubt she'd survive the trip. She was barely able to stay in the saddle by the time they'd ridden into Shamrock the previous day.

It hadn't taken much to persuade Conrad to trade some of their precious supplies for a room and a few hot meals at a motel with solar power. After savoring the luxuries of a refreshing shower and a clean mattress, she'd slept soundly for eight solid hours before Conrad shook her awake. If not for the urgency of their mission, she would have ignored him and slept for three more days. Instead, she forced herself out of the last bed she'd sleep in for weeks and got ready to get back on the road.

Conrad came up behind her and wrapped his arms around her waist. While brushing his lips on her neck, he said, "You smell so good. I could just devour you."

She turned in his arms and rested her head on his chest. "It's amazing what a long, hot shower can do, but didn't you get enough last night?"

"I'll never get enough of you."

Dashay gazed up at him, then gave him a lingering kiss. "Sure we can't stay for another day? I'm having a hard time convincing myself to get on that horse."

"If my team wasn't waiting at the border, I'd agree to another week. I know you're exhausted, Dashay. I am, too. We need to keep reminding ourselves that Julia and Riley are depending on us."

Dashay blew out a long breath. "How could I forget? Help me up, please," she said.

Conrad put his hands on her waist and helped her as she climbed into the saddle. He waited for her to settle, then mounted his horse, Steve. As they headed east, he saluted and feigned an Irish accent, said, "Farewell, Shamrock. Thanks for the memories. We'll not likely pass your way in the future."

Dashay chuckled as she rode Xena up beside him. "I give it a five. I wouldn't quit your day job."

"Excellent advice."

They rode in silence for thirty minutes as they watched the sun rising in the East. As she'd done many times, Dashay reflected on what she'd taken for granted before the CME struck, especially the sun. Their star made life possible but had destroyed it just as quickly. She'd heard people say Mother Nature had performed a reset on Earth to counteract the damage humans had done. Still, Dashay wondered if the disaster had only been the normal rhythm of life in their universe. Adrian Landry had explained how numerous global CMEs had struck the earth in the past and would as long as the solar system existed. If another hit their world at its current state of technology, or lack thereof, no one would notice.

"You're far away," Conrad said, rousing Dashay from her thoughts.

When she raised her head to respond, she spotted movement under a tree on the side of the highway. She pointed to the tree and said, "Is that a person?"

Conrad raised the binoculars that hung around his neck. After a few moments, he handed them to Dashay. "You need to see this."

Dashay put the binoculars to her eyes and stared in shock at the hulking behemoth dressed in biker clothes leaning against the trunk of the enormous elm. The man spotted them and climbed to his feet as they approached.

"Look at the size of him," Dashay whispered. "Is he one of yours?"

Conrad chuckled. "I wish. Keep your guard up. We don't know where his loyalties lie since we're so close to the border."

"That was a waste of a perfectly good warning," she mumbled.

The man stepped in their path and crossed his arms over his barrel chest. Conrad reined Steve to a stop ten yards from the man. Dashay did the same as she tried to ignore her heart pounding in her throat. She and Conrad could have galloped around him, but it was too big a risk since they had no idea if he was armed. Dashay would have bet good odds he was.

"Good afternoon, sir," Conrad said. "We're just passing through. Is this your land?"

The man uncrossed his arms and combed his beard with his fingers. "I'm not sure it's anyone's land anymore. I'm just taking a rest under the only tree around here big enough to give me shade." He glanced at the road behind him. "The only thing past here is the border. You planning to cross?"

Conrad grinned, but Dashay could see his muscles tense. "Would it matter if we were?"

"A yes answer would tell me a lot about you."

"We're not crossing. Just meeting friends who've been scouting supplies for us," Dashay said, flashing her brilliant smile. "I'm Chante. This is Carlton. We're from Amarillo."

"Judging by your accent, I'd wonder if you've ever been to Amarillo."

"She meant we're from Amarillo now," Conrad said. "We left the US just before the border closed and made Texas our new home. What's your name?"

"Bobby," he said, still looking skeptical of every word they'd said.

Conrad dipped his head. "Nice to meet you, Bobby. Do you live in Shamrock?"

He shook his head. "I'm from nowhere."

Dashay raised an eyebrow. "No one's from nowhere."

"Fair point. Then I'm from everywhere."

"This is getting us nowhere," Conrad said. "We don't want to keep our friends waiting. Enjoy your rest, Bobby."

He prodded Steve to get him moving, and Dashay followed suit with Xena, hoping Bobby wouldn't try to stop them. She blew out a breath in relief when he walked back to his spot under the tree. Dashay chastised herself, assuming the man was dangerous just because of his size and dress. She hated it when people made snap judgments about her based on her skin color.

She took a few deep breaths to relax before hurrying Xena to catch up with Conrad. She watched out of the corner of her eye as Bobby lowered himself to the ground, then leaned against the tree with his arms folded. He caught her watching him and gave a wave. She smiled and waved back as she passed his horse, who was tethered to a neighboring tree. She glanced at the saddle and bags, looking for weapons. What she found made her breath catch. An unmistakable braid of Riley's hair was bound to the saddle horn by a green tie Marjory had crocheted.

"Conrad, stop," she cried, then dismounted and ran to Bobby's horse.

Bobby got to his feet faster than Dashay thought possible for a man of his size. He ran toward her, but Conrad reached her at the same time.

Dashay untied the braid, then held it up to Bobby's face. "Where did you get this?"

He snatched it out of her hand and tucked it in his pocket. "None of your business."

Conrad maneuvered Steve between Bobby and Dashay. "Answer her question," he ordered.

"No. She's the one who owes me an explanation for touching my personal belongings."

Dashay pushed her way in front of Steve and put her hands on her hips. She didn't care how big the brute was. She was going to get the truth out of him. "That braid belongs to my friend. Her mother crocheted the tie. I'd recognize it anywhere. How did you get it?"

Bobby scratched his head. "My friend gave it to me willingly. As a gift."

Dashay stepped closer and glared up at him. "Your friend? What's her name?"

When Bobby hesitated, Conrad said, "He's lying."

"I'm not. My friend goes by two names. I'm not sure which one to tell you."

"You probably shouldn't have told us that," Dashay said. "Is one of them Katie Cooper?"

A smile crept up Bobby's face. "You know her?"

Dashay, unwilling to get her hopes up, put a hold on her emotions but hoped that Bobby's smile meant her friend was nearby. Still, it didn't compute why Riley would voluntarily give up her braid to this brute of a man.

"Better than you can possibly imagine," she said. "Tell us her real name."

"Dr. Riley Cooper. We call her Red."

Conrad jumped to the ground and moved beside Dashay. She noticed he kept a hand on his hip above the holster. "Why do you have Riley's braid?"

"Not until you tell me who you really are."

Dashay glanced at Conrad, not sure what to do. For all they knew, Bobby had killed Riley and taken her braid as a trophy. After a moment's reflection, she realized if that were the case, telling him who they were wouldn't matter.

When Conrad gave a quick nod, she said, "We're her friends Dashay and Conrad. We're looking for her. How do you know her? Is she alive? Where is she?"

Bobby gave Dashay a hug that nearly crushed her. "Riley told me about you and your crazy trip across the country with Yeager chasing you. Last I saw Riley, she was alive and well, but do I ever have stories to tell you."

Conrad visibly relaxed and dropped his hand away from his sidearm.

Dashay said, "When did you last see her?"

Bobby gently laid his plate-sized hand on her shoulder. "A week ago. I'll tell you everything you need to know, but not here. I've staked a claim at a house two miles away. Join me. I'll cook you a hot breakfast."

Dashay glanced at Conrad. She believed Bobby's claim of being Riley's friend, but that didn't mean they should divulge the purpose of their mission. And one thing Conrad had told him was true. They had people waiting for them at the border.

Conrad motioned that he'd answer and said, "That's a kind offer, but we do have friends to meet. Will you ride with us and tell us about Riley?"

Bobby combed his beard while he mulled over Conrad's offer. "I suppose I can do that, but I'll need to grab supplies. My house is on the way."

Conrad looked to Dashay for confirmation. When she nodded, he said, "Deal. Lead the way."

Bobby mounted his horse that matched his size and gestured for them to follow. He led them north, a short distance from the highway, then turned back to the East. After twenty minutes, Bobby steered his horse to an adobe bungalow hidden by a stand of trees. Dashay hoped they were right to trust Bobby and that he hadn't brought them to the secluded area to rob and kill them where no one would ever find their bodies.

He hopped off his horse and bounded up the three steps to the porch but stopped before going in. Turning to them, he said, "You're welcome to come in while I pack. It'll just be a few minutes."

Conrad gave a one-shouldered shrug before dismounting. Dashay climbed down but made sure to tuck her handgun in her waistband before entering the strange man's house. They cautiously made their way up the steps, then entered the surprisingly cool, darkened house. The kitchen and front room were all one space. One door led to what Dashay guessed were the bathroom and bedroom. The only furniture was a sagging sofa, a hand-hewn rocking chair, and a small, worn table with two chairs. The place was shabby but tidy.

"When a place like this looks like a palace, it's time to go home," she whispered. "We need to find Julia and Riley in a hurry."

Conrad reached up and gently massaged her shoulder. "That's the idea, Babe. Just hang in a little longer."

Bobby came out with a bulging pack on his shoulder. "I'm good to go. Anyone need to use the facilities before we hit the road?"

"You have running water?" Dashay asked, crossing her fingers in hopes of a positive answer.

Bobby gave a slight nod. "The previous owner rigged a mini solar system just for the pump. There's no other power in the house, but with running water, what else do you need?"

"Amen to that," Dashay mumbled as she pushed past him into the bedroom.

After using the bathroom and flushing the toilet three times just for the fun of it, she soaped her hands and let the water run over them for two minutes, savoring the feel for what may be the last time for weeks.

Conrad raised an eyebrow when she finally joined them in the front room. "Just taking some little girl time," she said, then went out and mounted her horse.

When they hit the main road and turned east, Conrad said, "With that nice little house of yours, what were you doing out in the heat under that tree?"

"Just people watching. All kinds pass this way since it's a major interstate. And to be honest, I don't have anything better to do."

"I'd love to know what that's like," Dashay said. "I don't think I've been bored once since the CME hit. Tell us about Riley."

Bobby gave a low chuckle. "She's quite woman."

"He does know her," Conrad said to Dashay.

Bobby told them about the bar incident with Reece and Brady. "There she was with blood gushing down her cheek, but she was still worried about Reece. Then, she sat there calm as could be and stitched her own wound. I used to be a biker and UFC fighter, but I've never seen anything like that."

Dashay couldn't hold back her laughter. When she caught her breath, she said, "That is so Riley. What happened after that?"

"It took her a week to recover from the injury. My friends and I got to know her during that time and offered to help her save Julia."

He explained his child rescue mission with Lou and Harper, then told them of Yeager, Nico, Simeon, and the commune.

Dashay and Conrad stared at him in stunned silence until Dashay said, "You sent Riley across the border with drug dealers? Are you insane?"

"Trust me, it's not what you think. Riley wouldn't have gone otherwise. She was reluctant until she understood what these people do. They use their customers strategically to help the needy in both countries. They're good people. I trust them completely."

"I guess that's something coming from you, considering your mission," Conrad said, "but I'm still leery of the entire plan. Too many variables."

Bobby shrugged. "Impossible to avoid these days. I'm here on the border waiting for Riley to return with my friends and her family, but that won't be for a few more weeks. Now, tell me what you're up to."

After hearing Bobby's account, Dashay knew they could trust him with the truth. She shared their Julia rescue plan, then said, "We should join forces. Come with us. We can always use more muscle."

"What if we miss them and Riley shows up looking for me? We have no idea what condition they'll be in when they get over the border."

Conrad rubbed his chin. "You equal two of my guys. I'll post them at the border and have them radio if Riley makes it over before we find her."

Bobby beamed at them. "I'm game. Let's go find our girls."

Dashay gave a whoop and pumped her fist in the air. "Now, it's a party!"

Having Big Bobby, as she nicknamed him, along for the venture raised her spirits. Having him and Conrad significantly increased their chance of success. The three of them chatted about Riley and Julia as they made their way to the outpost just inside the Texas border where Conrad's unit would be waiting. They arrived at noon, and for once, Dashay hadn't noticed the sweltering heat.

The sentry recognized Conrad and waved the three of them into the compound without asking for his ID. He directed them to the command tent, then radioed with his walkie that Conrad was on his way. The team was waiting by the time they reached the tent.

Conrad's deputy, a wiry man with a medium frame and shiny shaved dome, held out his hand and said, "We're relieved to see you, Boss. Riggs was getting worried."

"Sure it wasn't you, Jordan?" Conrad said as he shook his hand.

The man named Riggs stepped forward. He was the same height as Jordan but bulky and as pale as Jordan was dark. Dashay couldn't figure out how he managed to stay that pale with all the time he must spend in the sun.

"Don't let him fool you. Jordan's been crying himself to sleep every night over you," he said. "Good to see you, Chief. We have news."

Before he could go on, a woman behind them said, "It's about stinking time, Elliott. I was about to give you up for lost."

Dashay recognized that voice at once. She spun around to give her a quick hug, then said, "Bailey, it's great to see you. How long has it been?"

"Almost two years since I saved your butt at the border." She leaned back and looked Dashay up and down. "Damn, girl, how do you manage to look so amazing even out in the field?"

"It's my superpower," Dashay said with a laugh. "Conrad didn't mention you'd be on this mission."

"That's because he didn't know." Bailey grew serious and turned to Conrad. "There are developments. You up to a briefing, or do you need some beauty sleep?"

"Now," he said. "Riggs, please get Dashay and Bobby some chow and a place to rest." He gave Dashay a quick peck on the cheek. "I'll catch up as soon as I can."

She squeezed his hand and joined Bobby as Riggs led them from the tent, ignoring her rising fear that Bailey's news concerned Riley or Julia.

———

It felt like Riley had been asleep for five minutes when someone shined a flashlight in her eyes and called her name. She pretended not to hear, but the woman kicked the end of her cot.

"Get up, Ms. Cooper. You have ten minutes to dress and pack. We're moving you to a permanent camp in Oklahoma City. We need to cover ground at night to beat the heat."

Riley sprang to her feet as soon as her brain processed the news. Her captors were taking her to Julia! She looked at Harper's cot, but it was empty, and her belongings were gone. "Where's Harper?" she asked the guard.

"Up and ready half an hour ago. Get moving."

As the guard strode from the tent, Riley threw her clothes on and started shoving her belongings into her pack. The guards had confiscated all their other provisions but allowed them their personal belongings. Riley fingered the letters from Julia and Nico in her pocket. I'm coming, sweetheart, she thought as she hurried out to find Harper and Lou. A three-quarter moon lit the cloudless sky, so it didn't take long to find them standing near a half-loaded wagon. Lou handed her a power bar and canteen when she reached them.

She gulped down a bite of the power bar and said, "We're going to Oklahoma City. Did they tell you?"

"We heard," Lou said without enthusiasm.

She raised an eyebrow at him. "What's with the attitude? They're taking us exactly where we want to go."

"As prisoners," Harper said.

"But Nico's there. He'll get all of us out of the camp."

As Lou picked at his teeth with a sliver of wood, he said, "You have a lot of faith in your friend. Are you sure you're not overestimating his abilities?"

"No, I trust him completely. If anyone can get us out, it's Nico."

Harper stared at her with doubt evident in her eyes. "Hope you're right, Red. All I know is they're taking us further into enemy territory. It was one thing when we were going of our own free will. This is the worst possible scenario."

Riley laid a hand on her arm. "You have nothing to worry about. We'll be free and on our way home in no time."

Lou gave a snort. "From your mouth to God's ears." Riley spun to face him. "What?" he asked with a shrug.

"My husband always says that." She set the canteen down, then leaned against the back of the wagon and folded her arms. "I haven't seen him in months or talked to him in weeks. He wasn't doing well the last I heard. I'm not sure if he'll take me back when I get home."

"We've been through this, Red. He'd be a fool to send you packing," Harper said. "All will be forgotten when you arrive with Julia and family in tow. I've seen it happen more times than I can count."

"Then, I'll have to trust you on that." She looked around, searching for the people who would be taking them to the internment camp, but didn't see anyone. "I thought they were all fired up to get out of here. Where is everyone?"

As if on cue, five people, three men and two women, including the one who woke her, headed toward them.

"Get in the back of the wagon," the man who appeared to be in charge barked.

"What, we're not riding our horses?" Riley stammered.

"What horses?" he said, sneering at her. "Get in and no more lip."

Riley was too shocked to protest. She'd assumed they'd give their horses back to ride. She threw her pack into the back of the wagon and climbed in after it. The tears dripped down her face as she dropped onto a stack of bedrolls. Biscuit had been her faithful horse and friend for more than two years, and she couldn't imagine going on without him.

She covered her face with her hands and muttered, "Poor Biscuit. He'll think I abandoned him."

Lou sat next to her and put his arm around her shoulders. "I know how you feel. As crazy as it sounds, Strider was like a brother to me. I hope they'll treat him well."

Harper threw her pack down and slumped to the floor of the wagon. "Chalk up three more losses to this damned war."

"Look on the bright side," Lou said. "We're getting out of this stinking camp, and we'll have an actual place to live."

"Quiet down back there, and sleep while you can," the other woman guard said. "It's going to be a long and bumpy ride."

Riley leaned against Lou and cried in silence as the wagon driver got the horses moving. She felt silly for blubbering over a horse and a daft one at that, but Lou was right. Biscuit had been more like a member of the family. To comfort herself, she turned her thoughts to Julia. She'd see her daughter in a matter of days. Nothing mattered more than that.

———

Dashay was afraid she'd be sick when Conrad recounted the briefing. Riley had been captured during a shootout while crossing a bridge into Oklahoma. An unknown number of Bobby's friends had died in the battle. If that wasn't bad enough, Julia and Riley's family had been transferred to Wichita, Kansas. It was three hundred miles north and might as well have been on another planet.

"It's too much," she whispered. "Whenever I'm sure we're on the verge of victory, we end up in worse shape than when we started. What are we going to do, Conrad?"

Conrad sat next to her on the cot. "Don't bite my head off, but I think we should revisit the idea of you staying here. I can arrange an escort back to Amarillo. You'd be safe waiting there for me. Border guards on both sides are on high alert, and skirmishes have broken out all along the front lines."

Dashay remembered how furious she'd been the first time Conrad suggested she stay behind. This time, all she felt was sadness and desperation at the thought of being alone.

"I understand that you're only thinking of my safety, but to be honest, there's nowhere I want to be but by your side. Both of us have held our emotions close to the chest, but I'm tired of playing that game. I love you, Conrad. I don't expect you to say it back, but I needed you to know. Because of that, I'm going with you, and that's final."

Conrad wrapped his arms around her and pulled her to his chest. "I can't tell you how long I've waited to hear those words. I love you, too, and have for I don't know how long. My feelings have only grown stronger as we've made this trek together. I never said anything because I didn't want to pressure you."

Dashay lifted her head and gazed up at him. "For a couple of brilliant people, we can be pretty dense."

Conrad kissed her, then said, "No question about that. I want you by my side every minute, but I don't want to deliberately put you in danger. I feel like that's what I'd be doing if you come on this mission. I couldn't stand to lose you, especially now that I know how you feel."

"I'm a grown woman, doing this of her own free will, so I release you from all responsibility. I promise to stay out of the fray. I'm not like Riley, who rushes headlong into fire."

"And trust me, I'm grateful for that. We'd better tell Bobby what happened before he hears the news from someone else. Then, I can let both of you in on the plan at once."

Dashay stood and held her hand out to him. "Not looking forward to that conversation. I hope Harper and Lou survived."

"There's only one way to find out. Let's go find them."

She turned her thoughts from war and mayhem to the fact that Conrad had finally expressed his love for her. Knowing how he felt gave her the courage to face whatever lay ahead.

CHAPTER TWELVE

Julia pushed her history textbook across the table and rested her chin in her hands. It had been impossible to concentrate on her schoolwork since they arrived in Wichita two weeks earlier. The trip from Oklahoma City had been hot and miserable. Her mood hadn't improved even though the family was assigned a more spacious and nicer house than their cramped apartment in OKC. The furniture was in better condition, and they even had their solar power. Those things made daily life easier, but all that mattered to Julia was that her mom thought they were in Oklahoma.

They hadn't seen Nico on the journey or heard a word from him since getting to Wichita. Uncle Mitch had told her to accept that he hadn't been able to get the transfer to their new camp. No matter what Uncle Mitch said, she would never believe that. Nico had promised to do whatever it took to get her family home. She had faith in him and refused to give up hope like the rest of the family.

Her belief in their imminent rescue did nothing to make daily life easier to tolerate, though. They lived through one drudgery-filled day followed by another. Kathryn constantly reminded her that she needed to keep up with her studies if she wanted to be a doctor like her mom. Julia was beginning to realize that was a hollow dream. Even when they did make it home, there wouldn't be any universities where she could study medicine, so what was the point. Her mom could probably teach her rudimentary medical skills, but that was a far cry from becoming a surgeon.

In the meantime, it took all her energy to force herself to do her history, English, and math homework. The only subjects she had the slightest interest in were biology and chemistry. Still, she had to suffer through the other assignments.

"Did you finish your homework already?" Aunt Beth asked as she came into the dining room where Julia was studying.

Julia sat back and folded her arms. "No. I see no point in studying the US government. Kearns has abandoned the constitution and created a dictatorship. What good will knowing any of this do me? Even if the country ever goes back to the way it used to be, people might come up with a whole new system of government. It's all propaganda anyway."

Beth sat next to her and put a hand on her shoulder. "True, but that's the world you'll grow up in. If you want to make it better, you need to know how governments function."

Julia looked up at her and smiled. "That's the first time anyone has explained it in a way that makes sense. Thanks, Aunt Beth." She reached for her book and found her place on the page.

Beth stood and kissed the top of Julia's head. "That's high praise coming from you. Glad I could help," she said as she went back to the kitchen.

Julia had nearly finished her studies an hour later when she heard a faint knock on the door. She sat still and waited before answering it, wondering if she'd imagined it. When there was a slightly louder knock a few seconds later, she ran to the door and peered through the peephole. She was thrilled to see Nico standing on the porch and opened the door. He stumbled in over the threshold and collapsed at her feet.

"Hurry, close and bolt the door," he gasped.

She did as he asked before calling for her aunt and uncle. She knelt at Nico's side and stared in shock at the sight of cuts and bruises covering his face and arms. He was filthy and smelled terrible.

"What happened to you?" she cried as Uncle Mitch came in and helped him limp to the couch.

"We'll get to that later," Aunt Beth said. "What can we do for you, Nico?"

"Water first, please," he whispered. "Water, bandages, clean clothes, and food."

Holly hurried to the kitchen and filled a large glass to the brim with filtered water. Nico downed it in seconds and asked for more. Holly brought him two more glasses.

When he finished the third one, Uncle Mitch said, "That's enough for now, or you'll make yourself sick. Help me get him to the bathroom, Clint, then find him some clothes."

Mitch and Clint lifted Nico off the couch and practically had to carry him to the hallway. Julia paced in the living room while waiting for her uncle and cousin to clean and dress his wounds. Aunt Beth heated a plate of their leftover dinner of chicken and vegetable soup with fresh bread.

Nico was able to limp to the table on his own thirty minutes later. The family quietly surrounded him at the table and watched silently as he ate. Julia noticed how he cringed each time he lifted the spoon to his mouth.

When he'd finished, Aunt Beth said, "Would you like strawberries and cream?"

Nico looked up at her in gratitude and said, "Sounds delicious, but my stomach needs time to adjust. I haven't eaten more than berries and plants for five days."

Julia leaned closer to him and wrapped his bandaged hand in both of hers. "What happened to you?"

"Julia, let the man rest," Clint said.

Nico raised a hand to stop him. "It's fine. The food, water, and aspirin have revived me a bit. I'm sure you remember that I put in a request for a transfer. Well, my superiors decided that instead of sending me to Wichita, they'd transfer me to St. Louis. I tried to appeal, but someone reported that they'd seen me entering your house more than once. They grew suspicious, so that put an end to Wichita. I pretended to let the matter drop but finally decided I'd had enough of Kearns' and her military, so I deserted. Military Police chased me for five days before losing my trail. All I was left with is the clothes on my back."

"What a nightmare," Kathryn said. "I hate to think you did this for our sakes, Nico. Conditions are much better here for us."

"I didn't only do it for Riley and your family. I've been straddling the border for months, trying to pick sides. When I got the news they were transferring you again, I made my decision. I couldn't stand by watching the atrocities Kearns' lackeys were committing and do nothing. So, I'm going to fight her from the WSA now. That woman needs to be taken down."

"But how did you know where we were?" Julia asked.

"I scouted the camp at night to get the layout, learn patrol schedules, and guard positions. I slept in a garden shed during the day with the rakes and shovels. At nightfall on the fourth day, I found the stables where I hoped Clint would be working and got lucky. I followed him home from work but had to hide until after dark. I wasn't sure I'd make it until it was safe to sneak to your door."

"We're grateful you did," Mitch said. "Stay here for as long as you need."

"No," Nico said, trying to push himself to a standing position, but his arms and legs wouldn't hold his weight. He fell back onto the chair with a groan. "I refuse to put you in more danger. Give me a couple of days to regain my strength. I'll find myself a hideout. I'm good at disappearing. Then, I'll work on getting all of you out of here."

"Recover first, then we'll figure out the rest," Beth said. "For now, you can have Julia and Holly's room. I'll make up the couches for them."

Nico started to protest, but Julia put a finger to his lips to silence him. "We're not allowed to argue with Aunt Beth. Holly and I don't mind taking the couches. It'll be like a slumber party."

Nico pushed himself up again but took his time until he was on his feet. He pulled Julia into his arms, struggling to control his emotions. "You're the best little sister I could ask for. I'm going to get you home to your mom and Coop. I promise."

Julia leaned her head against his chest so no one could see her tears. "I know you will, Nico, and you're the best big brother. I never gave up on you, and I never will."

———

Riley thought she'd go out of her mind by their eighth day on the road. She lay in her sleeping bag on the hard floor, trying to block out sounds of the drunken orgy raging ten yards from the tent she shared with Harper. Their escorts were in no hurry to get to Oklahoma City, clearly enjoying the freedom from their superiors. The five of them would stumble out of the party tent at around three each morning, get everyone loaded up, then drive from four to ten. The trip should have taken more than six days, but Riley estimated it would take two weeks at the rate they were going.

"They're at it again," Harper said from across the tent. "I don't know how much more of this I can take."

A quiet tap on the tent canvas interrupted their conversation. "You two awake?" Lou whispered.

"How could we sleep?" Harper said. "Get in here, and don't bother to whisper. They wouldn't hear you if you screamed."

Lou ducked into the tent and spread his sleeping bag between Riley and Harper. "I have an idea," he said once he was settled. "Once they're smashed tomorrow night, let's take the horses and make a run for it. They won't notice we're missing for hours and wouldn't be able to come after us without the horses."

Harper rolled on her side to face them. "The thought has crossed my mind. We could load the horses but leave the wagon and head for Wichita Falls. They wouldn't expect us to go back the way we came."

"Go that way if you want," Riley said. "I'm going on to Oklahoma City. They definitely wouldn't look for me in the North."

Lou propped up on his elbow and glared at her. "That's crazy talk, Riley. Did you forget the trouble you got into trying to travel alone last time?"

Riley rubbed the snakebite scar, then shook her head. "How could I? But that was different." She sat up and rested her elbows on her knees. "I haven't seen my daughter for more than two years. I've run into nothing but obstacles on this trip, but we're so close I can taste it. I can't turn back now. Come with me or not, but I'm going."

Harper let out an exaggerated sigh. "I don't know why I keep forgetting how stubborn you are, Red. If you refuse to turn around, we have no choice but to go with you. We've signed on for the duration."

"That's the plan, then," Lou said. "We wait until the revelry gets going full bore tomorrow night, then make our move. We'd better get some sleep for all the sitting around we have to do until then."

Riley laid back on top of her sleeping bag and smiled in the darkness. "I'm grateful. I was willing to go alone but hoped I wouldn't have to."

"It'll be my first daring escape," Harper said. "I'm looking forward to it."

Riley gave a quiet laugh. "Not mine. I don't recommend it unless absolutely necessary, which this is."

"Then, we'll have to get it right. Thank us once we're out of here."

"Easy with Red as our ringer," Lou said. "Now, hush. All this talk is drowning out the carousing."

———

Yeager congratulated himself as he approached the guards standing watch on the internment camp perimeter. He'd made it to Oklahoma City without so much as raising an eyebrow. There had been the one unfortunate altercation with Colonel Mosley at Fort Sill. Yeager had dispatched him and taken his identity in one stroke. Now, he was on the verge of taking Riley Poole's daughter as bait to lure her into his trap.

He'd lost track of that pesky, redheaded doctor on the US side of the border, but he knew who her traveling companions were and where they were headed. He'd be ready when she came for Julia. It would be the final step to capturing Daybreak. He'd turn the wretch over to Kearns, accept his reward and accolades, then fade out of the picture on his perfect piece of land to live out the rest of his days in peace.

The guards came to attention and saluted when they saw the Colonel insignia on his uniform. He had to bite his cheek to keep from smiling. He'd missed the reverence and respect his rank afforded.

"At ease," he said, feigning casual indifference.

"Good evening, Colonel Mosley," one of the sergeants said, trying to hide his discomfort. No enlisted men appreciated an unexpected visit from a high-ranking officer.

"Evening. I need one of you to accompany me to the Dunne quarters. I have special orders involving the family."

The two sergeants gave each other a quick glance. Then, the one who'd spoken first said, "Meaning no disrespect, sir, but are you certain you need the Dunne family?"

"Of course, I'm certain," Yeager barked. "Why?"

The other sergeant straightened and said, "Our records indicate that the Dunnes were transferred to Wichita, Kansas, three weeks ago, sir. I could be wrong, but I haven't seen any of the family members for some time, sir."

Yeager swore under his breath, then said, "Who ordered the transfer?"

"Colonel Beake, sir."

That was the last name Yeager wanted to hear. He swallowed his revulsion and pasted on a friendly demeanor. "Thank you, Sergeant. I'm acquainted with Colonel Beake. I'll have a word with her in the morning to see if we can straighten out this miscommunication. Carry on."

"Yes, sir," the sergeants said in unison as Yeager turned and left them staring after him.

As much as he wanted a comfortable bed and a hot meal, he couldn't dare show his face at Battalion Headquarters since someone might recognize him. Instead, he retreated to the abandoned house he'd been holing up in on the outskirts of Oklahoma City. He needed a change of strategy and to prepare for his journey to Wichita. He was disappointed at this latest obstacle but didn't have the luxury of letting it knock him off course. He'd never been to Wichita, so no one would recognize him there, which could be a plus. All he needed was patience, cunning, and enough supplies to get him to his next destination.

———

"Stop fidgeting," Harper said as she sat on a fallen log watching the sunset with Riley. "It won't make time pass any faster, and you might arouse suspicion."

Riley took a deep breath and massaged her neck. "You say that like any of them pay the least bit of attention to us."

"True, but it's making me jittery, so knock it off."

Riley grunted and said, "Bit snippy, aren't you?"

"Do I have to separate you two," Lou asked as he came over carrying a canteen for each of them.

Riley gladly accepted the offering and took a big swig. "I'm parched. How'd you get our jailers to part with those?"

Lou dropped onto the log on the other side of Riley. "I didn't think to ask. Just helped myself. I overheard talk of them retiring to the funhouse tent. It may not be long now."

"Hey, you three, time for lights out," their most obnoxious guard named Corporal Boone called from across the camp.

Lou saluted, then said, "Sure thing, sir. On our way."

"I told you to stop calling me sir," the guard snapped.

Lou smiled and gave him a nod. "I can guarantee I'll never do it again," he mumbled as the three of them headed to their tents. Lou held the flap open for Harper and Riley. "Start packing as soon as you hear the party get rolling. I'll meet you at the horses."

Riley tussled with her sleeping bag before getting what passed for comfortable, then ran through their getaway scenario in her head. She pictured the escape step by step as Conrad had taught her to do. It helped calm her nerves to imagine them taking the horses and leaving the drunken guards with no way to come after them. It would be so simple. She wondered why they hadn't tried to escape sooner.

Once they were free of the camp, they would reach Oklahoma City in thirty-six hours. Once near the internment camp, they'd change into the uniforms Nico had left and clip on the fake IDs that their captors had failed to find in their packs. She'd be at Julia's door an hour later.

"Two days," she whispered.

Harper stirred and said, "What are you mumbling?"

"Sorry. I didn't mean to bother you."

"What bother? I'm lying here wishing this crazy plot of ours was already behind us. Should I be worried that you've started talking to yourself?"

Riley smiled, but it was too dark for Harper to see. "Not yet. I was thinking that I'm going to see my daughter in two days. It doesn't seem real. She was thirteen when I last saw her. Now she's almost sixteen. She won't be the same person. What if she's changed so much that she can't relate to me anymore?"

"You've both changed, but your feelings for your daughter haven't. It'll be the same for her. When we return children who've been living in hellish conditions to their families, it normally takes two minutes for them to feel like they've never been separated. Julia's been with family members who love her and hasn't suffered the kinds of abuses I've seen. Trust me, she'll be overjoyed to see you."

Riley wanted to believe she was right, but she couldn't help thinking how Jared had avoided her when she returned after her cross-country ordeal. It took more than two minutes for him to forgive and warm up to her. Julia was older and understood the situation, but it could be awkward. Not that it mattered to Riley. She just wanted to hold her daughter and never let her out of her sight.

The drunken singing and laughing grew more boisterous in the party tent. "How much longer should we wait?"

Harper sat up and switched on her flashlight. "We should give it another hour. We want to make sure they're good and sauced, but I'm going to pack. I can't stand lying here doing nothing."

"I'm with you," Riley said and reached for her pack.

It only took them five minutes to gather their meager belongings. Harper huffed and clicked off her light. "Now, what do we do to pass the time?"

"Tell me about your family. You never talk about them."

"Some things are better left buried. Growing up was no fairytale for me. What I would have given to have a mother like you."

"I didn't know. Is that what motivated you to join the motorcycle club and rescue abused children?" Harper's silence told Riley all she needed to know, so she changed the subject. "How come you don't sleep in Lou's tent? I'm capable of taking care of myself."

"We don't doubt that you can, but we didn't want you to get lonely, and it's safer no matter how tough you are. Lou and I have seen the way some of these scumbags eyeball you, and we can handle spending a few nights apart now and then. We've been together for a long time."

"I appreciate it. The nights can get long out here."

They continued talking about their lives and experiences until they could hardly hear each other over the ruckus.

Harper got to her feet and shouldered her pack. "I think it's time."

Riley glanced at her trusty watch that had managed to keep working through all her adventures. She'd often wondered if she'd be able to find a replacement battery when hers died. It read 3:30. If they could get away from camp within the next thirty minutes, they'd have eight hours of good riding time before it got too hot.

"I'm good," Riley said and led the way out of their tent.

They skirted the camp perimeter to where the horses were tethered and were relieved to find Lou waiting for them. He'd saddled the five horses and loaded the saddlebags with whatever he could grab without being seen.

"Glad you made it," he said. "Riley, you ride Sally. I'll take Fable, and Hope is for you, Harper. The other two seem docile enough to follow as packhorses. Saddle up."

Sally was taller than Biscuit, but Riley had become an accomplished rider and could mount without help. Her heart pounded as she settled in, though they hadn't met with the least resistance or even notice. Lou tapped his heels on Fable's sides to get him moving. The other horses got into line behind without any urging.

This is too easy, Riley thought as they headed out of camp toward the main road. Didn't she deserve to have one of her plans go off without a hitch for once? A rifle shot rang out as she thought it, and Corporal Boone stepped into their path.

He rested the rifle on his shoulder and gave a sarcastic laugh. "I'll give you marks for effort. Did you think we're a bunch of morons who'd leave camp unguarded?"

Lou raised his hand. "I'll field that question."

Corporal Boone leveled his rifle at Lou. "Such a comedian. Get off those horses, now. Then hands raised."

When Riley's feet hit the ground, she was tempted to kick herself for jinxing the operation. *I couldn't leave it alone,* she thought as she reached for her pack.

"Leave your belongings," Corporal Boone ordered. "You've just lost all your privileges."

"Privileges?" Lou said as he took a step toward Corporal Boone. "What would those be?"

Corporal Boone was on him before they had time to react. He knocked Lou to the ground, then began kicking and punching him with unbridled fury. Riley and Harper struggled to stop the beating, but they were nothing more than gnats to him. In desperation, Riley picked up the rifle Corporal Boone had dropped. *You are a moron,* she thought as she swung the butt against his head. Corporal Boone dropped to his knees but didn't stay down. He sprang to his feet and snatched the gun from her. When he aimed it at her, she raised her hands in defeat.

Lou groaned on the ground behind them.

Corporal Boone yanked a bedroll free from Sally's saddle and dropped it on the ground next to Lou. "Get that thing on a blanket and drag it back to camp. Don't leave your tents without permission. I'll be watching, and I have no qualms about doing the same to either of you." He took hold of Fable's reins to lead him off and whistled for the other frightened but obedient horses to follow.

Riley and Harper dropped to the ground on either side of Lou, and Riley immediately snapped into doctor mode. She assessed his external injuries in moments. He had multiple lacerations on his face, and his nose was broken. Lou was lucky that

Corporal Boone had missed his eye sockets and hadn't struck him hard enough to fracture his skull. She examined his neck, spine, and limbs for breaks but didn't feel any. He had at least three broken ribs but no punctured lung that she could hear. If he had internal injuries, there would be little she could do to treat him.

She untied her neckerchief and pressed it to the worst of his cuts before climbing to her feet. "Let's get him to our tent. I'm not sure what I can do for him without my pack. Should I risk asking Corporal Boone if I can just have my medical supplies?"

Harper tore a strip of fabric off her shirt and gently wiped the blood from Lou's face. "I'm torn, Red. I want to do whatever we can for Lou, but that Corporal Boone has serious anger issues. He might beat the daylights out of you just for asking."

Riley opened the bedroll and spread it on the ground next to Lou. "Let's get him to the tent and then decide."

"How do we get him on the blanket?" Harper asked as she stood. "I'm afraid we'll injure him worse if we try to lift him."

"Just leave me here to die," Lou said through his rapidly swelling lips. "It's what I get for shooting my mouth off."

"Nonsense," Riley said. "You're not dying, but this might get you to keep quiet next time. Harper, stand next to me and help me roll him on his side." Harper moved beside her by Lou's legs. "On three." She counted off, then they rolled Lou onto his left side. Riley quickly pushed the blanket under him before rejoining Harper. "Now, roll him back onto the blanket."

"I think I've seen this on TV medical dramas," Harper said as they adjusted to get Lou on the center of the blanket.

Lou grunted when they each took a corner and began dragging him toward camp. "It must be more fun to watch than participate in."

"Good to see you still have your sense of humor," Riley said. "We'll do our best to avoid roots and rocks."

"Much appreciated."

Riley's back and hands were throbbing in protest after the

half-hour it took to drag him to their tent and get him situated. She didn't dare complain, knowing how much more painful it must have been for Lou. Riley surveyed the tent in the dim moonlight, hoping she'd left something useful behind, but there was nothing to help Lou.

She pulled Harper to the side and whispered, "I have to risk begging Corporal Boone for supplies. If I don't treat Lou, we run the risk of infection at the very least."

"I can hear you," Lou said. "Don't you dare speak to that brute. The state he's in, he'll pummel you for looking at him funny."

Riley walked back to him and put her hands on her hips. "Stop me."

"You should know better than to tell Red not to do something," Harper said. "If you insist on doing this, stay inside the tent doorway and call him to you. That way, you'll still be obeying his orders. That might inch you toward his good side."

"He has a good side?" Lou said and tried to laugh at his joke, but all that came out was a gasp.

"You hush and save your strength. Doctor's orders," Riley said, then stepped to the tent opening to look for Boone. He was sitting on a camp chair in front of his tent. She waved her arms over her head to get his attention. "Corporal Boone, may I speak with you. It's an emergency."

"Shut it," Boone said, then went on picking his teeth.

"I think Lou is dying," she yelled above the noise from the party still raging on the other side of the camp. "You don't want his death on your head, do you."

"Couldn't care less," Boone shouted back at her. "Leave me alone."

"You might not care, but the First Sergeant might have something to say about you killing one of his prisoners."

"Holtz was trying to escape. He had it coming."

"Keep going," Harper whispered behind her. "At least you've got his attention."

"But that's not your call to make, is it?" Riley shouted.

Boone bolted out of his chair and made a beeline for their tent.

Harper picked up the broken branch she'd dragged back to camp on Lou's blanket and held it behind her back. "We've stirred the hornet's nest," she said as she stepped behind Riley.

Boone stopped three feet from Riley, panting like a bull. He unholstered his handgun and aimed it between her eyes. "I told you to shut it unless you want to join your friend. What's one more dead Waster to us?" he said, using the US slang for WSA citizens.

Riley tried to raise her hands in surrender, but she was frozen with fear. She stood statue-still as he grumbled, "That's more like it," and lowered his gun as he turned to go. When his back was to her, she spotted a dark, wet stain on his green t-shirt. She raised her eyes to the back of his head where she'd hit him with the rifle. His hair was matted with sticky blood.

"Your head is cut," she said, just loud enough for him to hear. "Where I hit you."

He reached up to feel the wound, then pulled his hand away and examined his blood-covered fingers. "I'll be damned," he said as his knees buckled.

He fell face down in a dead faint.

Riley let out the breath she'd been holding. "Doesn't matter how big or fierce they are. Some men just can't handle the sight of their own blood."

"What's happening?" Lou said.

"Boone fainted at the sight of a little blood," Harper said with a laugh. "You going to finish him off, Red?"

"No time. He's coming to. I think we can use this to our advantage." She helped Boone to a sitting position, then held him down by his shoulders when he tried to get to his feet. He didn't resist. She squatted in front of him and said, "Take your time, or you'll go down again. Do you want me to examine your wound? I'm a doctor."

Boone's eyes widened as he stared at her. "You are? How come you never said?"

"It didn't come up. I'll stitch that cut if you let me treat Lou." He watched her for a moment, then nodded. "Excellent. I'll need our packs. Where are they?"

"Wait. What kind of doctor knocks a man in the head, then stitches his wound?"

Riley stood and stared down at him. "Only me. This isn't my first time. Where are those packs, and I could use some of that never-ending supply of alcohol as a disinfectant."

"The packs are still strapped to the horses. Take what you need of the booze. They won't notice. Don't try anything, though. I still have my sidearm, and I'm not too far gone to miss my mark."

"Got it," Riley said as she ran off to get her supplies.

After depositing the packs in the tent, she reluctantly made her way to the party tent, wishing she could close her eyes, but she was worried for nothing. All four of them were passed out in a heap on their cots. There was a clutter of military gear, empty whiskey bottles, food containers, and at least one bong scattered around. Riley hadn't even noticed the camp had grown quiet while she was talking to Boone. She grabbed the only unopened whisky bottle and hurried back to the others.

She used cotton thread and a sterile sewing needle to close Boone's wound, which only needed two stitches. She was tempted to shoot him up with the last of her sedative, but it would serve no purpose. It was too late for them to escape with Lou in such bad shape. She decided to keep that plan in reserve.

After she and Harper helped him to his tent, Riley rushed back to treat Lou's injuries. She used her last sterile suture kit on his wounds and had just enough silk for the twenty stitches he needed. Her next worry was his nose. His left nostril was completely blocked. She could reduce the fracture back into place but worried the pain would be unbearable.

"I can give you a local," she told Lou, "But, it might not be near enough to dull the pain. It's your call."

"Will it fix his pretty face?" Harper asked.

"It'll be close to the original."

Lou grimaced as he reached up and felt his nose, which had swollen to twice its size. "Do it. I can't breathe through my nose, and it's killing me."

Riley shined her penlight up his nose. "That's from the swelling. It could take a week to get back to normal."

Lou scrunched his eyes. "Get it over with."

Riley used the last of her Lidocaine to numb him, then found a blunt metal probe to help her reduce the fracture back into place. "Take a few deep breaths. Scream if you need to. We won't judge."

After Lou took his breaths, Riley inserted the probe into his right nostril and pressed against it with her fingers on the left one. She heard a click before Lou cried out in agony. She removed the probe, then gently inserted sterile gauze into his nostrils.

She smiled down at her brave patient. "All finished. You were a champ. I probably would have passed out from that much pain."

Harper kissed his cheek. "I'm impressed. I almost tossed my dinner."

Lou closed his eyes and went back to deep breathing. After a minute, he said, "I may vomit and pass out. No chance you have any pain meds?"

"Sorry, those are long gone. The best I can do is ibuprofen. It will help, and your nose will feel much better in a few days. It's your ribs I'm worried about. I'm sure our jailers will force us into that wagon once they're conscious. We're going to have to find a way to stabilize you, or a bone could puncture a lung. I treated that condition in the field once and have no wish to repeat it."

"We'll figure it out once he's in the wagon. We should get what sleep we can in the meantime. I'm whipped."

"Lou beat you to it," Riley said when she heard Lou's deep, even breathing.

Once they were both on their sleeping bags that Riley had retrieved from the horses along with the packs, she put her lips to Harper's ear and told her how she'd almost sedated Boone.

"I would have," Harper whispered. "What stopped you?"

"Lou, for one. We would have had to lift him into the wagon without causing him more injuries, hitch the wagon, and be long gone before anyone woke up."

She felt Harper watching her before she said, "Makes sense. And number two?"

"Boone isn't worth wasting the last of my good meds, and I wasn't sure I was ready to go down that road. I dosed a man in the past to escape from a similar situation with Coop and Julia. I almost killed him. Ironically, he later became a dear friend."

Harper chuckled at that. "Nothing you say surprises me anymore, but that's a story I must hear."

Riley hesitated before saying, "I'm not sure I'm ready to tell it. He's dead but not by my hand. A freak accident."

"I'm sorry. Sometimes I forget how much loss we've all suffered." She grew quiet for a moment, then said, "Don't beat yourself up for doing the right thing. Unfortunately, the lines get murky in this world."

"I'm glad to hear you say that. I find myself closer to crossing all the time. I need to bolster the boundaries." She yawned and rolled onto her side. "See you in a few hours."

———

Boone's shouting across the camp invaded Riley's fitful dreams, startling her awake three hours later.

"Who did this?" he shouted.

"Can't that guy give it a rest?" Harper asked as she sat up and rubbed her eyes.

"I should have knocked him out when I had the chance," Riley mumbled as she got up.

"Get out here, Doctor. Now!"

As Riley headed for the tent door, Harper climbed to her feet and grabbed her broken branch. "Wait for me. You're not facing Boone alone."

Riley pointed at the makeshift weapon. "What good will that do against his gun?"

"Better than nothing. Let's go."

Riley ducked out of the tent into the blinding sunlight. She slipped her sunglasses on in time to see Boone barreling straight for her. Harper stepped in front of her and raised the branch. Boone pushed her aside and leaned his face close to Riley. She almost retched from the foul smell of his breath.

"I'll ask again, what kind of doctor are you?" he hissed between clenched teeth.

Riley leaned away from him, reaching for Harper's stick. "I don't know what you mean. Is it your head?"

"Murderer! You killed her. Are you planning to pick us off one by one?"

"Killed who?" Harper said. "We haven't left our tent since Riley patched your head."

"That's when she did it when she went for the booze." He grabbed Riley's forearm and yanked her toward the party tent. "Come see your handiwork."

Harper caught up with them and brought the branch down hard on his wrist, but Boone was too jacked up to notice.

Riley tripped and lost her footing. Boone kept going, dragging Riley by the arm.

"Please let me go," she cried. "I'll come with you. You don't need to drag me."

Boone released her hand. She fell to her knees, then recovered and scrambled to her feet. As she hurried to keep up with him, she said, "Tell me what's happening. Who's dead?"

He turned and sneered at her as he kept walking. "Don't say that like you don't know. It's Corporal Bowen. My Stace. She's dead."

Riley pushed past him and rushed toward the party tent. Russo, Murdock, and Ayers sat on camp chairs in the shade beside the tent. Corporal Ayers quietly sobbed into her hands. The other two sat in stunned silence, staring into the distance. Riley ignored them and ducked into the tent. Private Bowen's body lay face down in a half-dried puddle of vomit. The smell of that and escaped body gasses was overwhelming in the stuffy tent. Riley covered her nose and mouth with her neckerchief, then opened the windows and flap.

She stepped out to let it air before she examined the body and said, "Who found her? Give me the chain of events. She was passed out but breathing when I went in to get the whisky."

"Don't answer her," Boone barked. "She's just saying that to look innocent. You killed her."

"That makes no sense," Harper said. "She could have killed you when she was treating your wound. She could have done the other four in when they were passed out last night. Hell, we could have killed you every night since we've been on this trek. Why would Kate kill Bowen now?"

Boone started at her, huffing with his fist clenched. Riley could tell it angered him that Harper made so much sense.

She stepped closer and said, "You know she's right, and I'm not in the business of murder. I do my utmost to save lives, not take them. I believe Private Bowen died from other causes. Allow me to examine her. It's the only way to get the truth."

Boone stared at her for a moment, processing her words, then his breathing slowed, and her fingers relaxed. "Fine, but I'm not letting you out of my sight while you check her over."

"That's a bad idea after your fainting spell last night," Harper said.

First Sergeant Russo pushed himself out of the chair. "You're not in charge here, Boone. Want to explain what happened last night? You were on the watch. And what fainting spell?"

Boone straightened and met Russo's eyes. "I stopped our three prisoners from escaping." His eyes narrowed as he pointed at Riley. "They resisted, and that one got my rifle and knocked me on the back the head with it, cutting my scalp in the process and knocking me out for a second. She told me she's a doctor, so I made her stitch me up. She got whisky out of your tent, so I thought she killed Bowen."

Riley glanced at Harper and gave an almost imperceptible shake of the head to warn her not to contradict Boone's story.

The Sergeant stabbed his finger in Boone's chest. "You let that tiny snip of thing get her hands on your weapon?"

"The three of them overpowered me, Sergeant. I gave Holtz a good beating for his insubordination and took my weapon back as soon as I came to."

Riley was amazed at how adeptly Boone had invented an altered version of events, but she kept his secret. "Sergeant Russo, the Corporal was on the verge of killing Holtz until I reminded him that he needed to clear it with you first," she said.

Russo spun around and glared at her. "He doesn't need you defending him." Riley bowed her head and stared at the ground in pretended contrition. "Let me get this straight. You smashed Boone in the head, then stitched him?"

Without raising her eyes, she said, "He was beating Lou. I had to stop him."

"Why didn't you tell me you're a doctor?"

She slowly raised her head and looked him in the eyes. "Why should I?"

"Get in there and deal with Bowen, Doctor," he ordered. "I'll be in shortly. Boone, I'll deal with you later. Go back to your tent and wait for me. Harper, please return to your tent as well."

Riley went back into the tent as he turned to Murdock and Ayres, rubbing his forehead. She heard him say, "You two clean up and get us some chow. We're not going anywhere today. I hope you enjoyed yourselves last night because it was the last time."

She knelt next to the body and gently rolled Bowen onto her back. Riley didn't need to do much investigating to diagnose the cause of death. It was a combination of too many nights of too little food, too much booze, and too much heat. It was a tragic way to go, but Riley couldn't seem to summon sympathy for the women. Bowen had treated the three of them like dirt since leaving the border camp, had partied with abandon, and brought death upon herself. All the same, Riley always hated to see such a pointless loss of life.

She pulled a blanket over the body when Russo came in and stood over her with his arms folded.

"Thank you for showing respect, Doctor. There's no need for a diagnosis. I'm fully aware of what killed Bowen. I'm partially responsible for her death, and I'm ashamed. I'll admit as much to my superiors when the time comes. In the meantime, we'll bury her and say a few words tonight after sunset."

"Yes, Sergeant," she said, stunned by his admission of responsibility.

He gestured with his head for her to follow him out of the tent. He stopped outside the door and said, "I'm not sure what happened with you and Boone last night, but I appreciate you treating his wound. How is Holtz?"

Riley had forgotten Lou in all the commotion. "I haven't had a chance to check on him yet this morning, but he'll survive. A day of rest is all he'll need to be stable enough to ride in the wagon."

"Go to him now. Let me know if there's anything you need. I'll have Ayers bring your breakfast."

Riley nodded and turned to go, grateful that Bowen's death

had been good for at least one thing – Russo's apparent change of heart. She wasn't happy about another delay in getting to Julia but was sure the Sergeant would pick up the pace after his ban on the nightly drunken blowouts.

The temperature inside their tent was suffocating by the time she got back. Harper was rubbing a wet cloth on Lou's bruised and swollen face, but it couldn't have been doing him much good.

"Let us help you out under the trees," she said. "There's a breeze, and it's ten degrees cooler in the shade. Can you walk?" Lou nodded slowly. "Good. We'll take our time. There's no rush."

As they got Lou to his feet and moving, Riley told them about her encounter with Russo.

When they had him settled on a flat patch of ground in the shade, Harper said, "I never would have guessed. He's been a pain in the ass since day one."

"Being responsible for someone's death will do that to you," Riley said. "The upside is we'll make it to Oklahoma City sooner than we thought yesterday morning."

"But as prisoners," Lou said quietly. "I had a moment's taste of freedom. I want more. Once I'm stronger, we should give it another shot."

Harper clicked her tongue at him. "Did Boone beat all of the sense out of you? Look what the last try earned you."

Lou moaned as Riley poked and prodded him, checking for broken bones or internal bleeding. When she finished, he said, "We learned what not to do. Worth it."

Riley sat back on her heels and shook her head. "Looks like you're going to pull through, Lou, but we'll reach OKC before you're strong enough to even walk, let alone mount a horse. We have a plan in place. Nico will get us out. You just rest and focus on getting better. We'll need you strong when the time comes."

———

Riley was relieved when Russo didn't force them to attend the memorial for Bowen. It would have been difficult to feign grief, and her death had nothing to do with the three of them. The guards were subdued after the service and kept to themselves. As much as Riley was itching to get on the road, she was grateful for the much-needed reprieve.

She'd expected to be out in minutes when she climbed on top of her sleeping bag at eleven but was still wide awake more than an hour later. Lou was snoring quietly on the far side of the tent, and Harper had dozed off not long after he fell asleep. Riley's brain whirled with thoughts of her children, Coop, and her family in Colorado and Oklahoma. She would see Julia soon but had no way of knowing how long it would be before she reunited with the others. There were times when she longed for Coop and the kids so much it hurt, but she knew that given a chance, she would make the same decision to go after Julia. Everyone, including her husband, had questioned the wisdom of her actions, but they weren't her and had no right to judge. She was doing enough of that for all of them.

After failing to relax with breathing exercises and meditation, she got up to look outside the tent. She was surprised to see Russo was sitting in a chair a couple of yards outside the prisoners' tent. She asked Russo if she could stretch her legs. He agreed if she stayed in his line of sight. She grabbed her flashlight and headed out into the darkness. It was a cloudy, humid night, and the air hung like a straitjacket around her. Flicking on the flashlight, she walked out in front of her tent.

"I couldn't sleep. Thought I needed some air. I'm not trying to escape."

Russo gave a quiet laugh. "Good to know. Nowhere to go anyway," he said. "Join me for a moment?"

Riley's muscles tensed as she walked toward him, dreading what he might want from her. When she reached him, he gestured for her to take his chair while he stood. He unclipped his rifle from the sling across his chest and laid it pointing away from her on a small folding table.

"How was the memorial?" she asked when he hadn't spoken for a full minute.

He rubbed his face with both hands. "Short and brutal," he said, avoiding her eyes. "I've seen too many comrades die but never in such a senseless way. We all feel the weight of her death, but I'm ultimately responsible. Honoring Bowen with our meager words did little to ease that burden. I'll live with this shame for the rest of my life. Despite what you've witnessed on this journey, Bowen was a good person and a good soldier. She was just like the rest of us. We grew up fat and happy. Life was predictable. Now, we're just doing what it takes to survive from day to day."

Riley hesitated before saying, "If you say so, Sergeant. I had a much different experience with Bowen. I didn't get to witness her good qualities. Besides, we don't have to be victims of our circumstances, even in times like these."

"I get that, but don't forget that we see you as an enemy noncombatant. Maybe we would have treated you with more respect if you told us that you're a doctor."

"Why should that matter?"

"You know the answer to that."

Riley considered how her first husband Zach, or Nico, or Conrad, or any of the other military people she'd known would have treated someone in her situation. She could say with absolute certainty that all of them would have comported themselves with far more dignity and respect.

"Not sure I do know," she finally said. "It's true I'm considered your enemy," she said, "but that doesn't justify the nightly debauchery that took place in that tent. You seem like a reasonable person when you're sober. I find it hard to believe you would have behaved this way in your pre-CME life."

He stroked his chin as he watched her. "You're a good

observer of people. I'll say that for you. I was a model of respectability in my past life."

She couldn't tell if Russo was being sarcastic and was about to ask what changed when a twig snapped in the woods behind them. She jumped out of the chair and turned toward the sound, expecting a wild boar or another dangerous animal to come rushing out at them. Russo reached for his weapon, but four men stepped out of the trees with rifles aimed at him before Russo could get to his. Riley gasped, trying to process the scene. All she could do was hit the deck.

The men ignored her and went for Russo. They wrestled him to the ground face down then tied his hands behind his back with expert speed. One of the men forced a rolled neckerchief between his teeth, then knotted the ends behind his head. Russo writhed on the ground and struggled to call out despite the gag.

"Quiet," the one who'd tied the gag hissed. When Russo continued to make a racket, the man cocked his fist, then slammed it into Russo's skull, and he went limp. "I said quiet!"

Riley stood frozen with her trembling hands raised as all four men turned and stared at her. She had no way of telling if they were good guys or bad guys. They wore night-vision goggles and were equipped with military gear and weapons but were dressed in civilian clothes. Kearns' people wouldn't have taken Russo down, and they didn't look like part of Simeon's cohort.

While she was still in a daze, one of the men stepped forward. Keeping his voice lowered, he said, "Good evening, Dr. Poole. My name's Darius Jordan. We're here to extract you and your two companions."

Even after his declaration, Riley couldn't make her muscles react to her brain signals. The man had used her real name and the word extract, which meant he was either an undercover agent with the WSA or a bad guy planning to turn her over to Kearns for a reward.

"You don't need to be afraid," the man continued. "We're here with Conrad Elliott."

Russo, who had regained consciousness, grunted at hearing that name.

One of Jordan's men gave him a soft kick and said, "Quiet you. I should have killed you last time we met."

Two more men stepped out of the shadows on Riley's opposite side. She didn't need NVG's to recognize one of them. His size was a dead giveaway.

"Bobby!" she cried. He picked her up and swung her around before gently setting her on her feet. "How in the world did you find us?"

Bobby pointed his thumb toward the man next to him. "This guy found me under a tree and asked if I'd like to join him on a treasure hunt to find you," he said.

Riley hugged Conrad, then said, "Lord, am I ever glad to see you! Is Dashay with you?"

Conrad gave a slight shake of his head. "No time for happy reunions now. We've got to get out of here before the rest of the guards wake up."

Jordan pointed to Russo. "Want me to take care of that, Chief?"

Riley stepped between Russo and Jordan. "Don't hurt him. He's been punished enough."

Jordan raised an eyebrow and said, "Doubtful. Orders, Boss?"

"No time to deal with him now. Riley, get your gear, then let's hoof it."

Jordan also gave the order to two of his men to gather all the horses so the US forces would be stranded in the middle of nowhere and unable to pursue. "Quietly, if possible," he said. "If any guards try to stop you, shoot them."

As Riley jogged beside Conrad toward her tent, she said, "Lou's hurt. He can't ride a horse."

Conrad opened the tent flap and gestured for her to go in

first. "Don't worry, my people are helping him and Harper into a wagon. Just hurry."

Riley stuffed her few personal belongings into her pack, then grabbed the med bag and left the rest. She followed Conrad to where Harper and Lou waited in the wagon. Conrad pointed to Ayres' horse and told her to mount up.

As Riley passed Harper, she winked and said, "I like your friends, Red."

Bobby tipped his head as he followed Riley past the wagon to get to his horse. Harper's eyes widened in surprise.

Riley gave a quiet laugh. "And I like yours."

Lou watched his friend mount up, then said, "How did that big lug end up with these spooks? He's supposed to be waiting for us across the border."

"Good thing he's not," Harper said, "but that's a story I can't wait to hear."

Riley turned to take a last look as Jordan got the rescue party moving. Murdock and Boone were rushing to untie Russo and help him to his feet. Ayers was nowhere to be seen. The three of them turned and stared as their three prisoners rode to freedom with all their horses and any hope of chasing after them. Riley smiled brightly and gave a small wave, thrilled to bid a final farewell to her heartless captors.

CHAPTER THIRTEEN

RILEY RODE beside Conrad in silence, smarting from the scolding he'd laid on her after he assured her Dashay was alive and well at a safe house ten miles from Russo's camp. Her relief at the news was immediately overshadowed by him telling her the outcome of the shootout on the bridge. Simeon and all but two of his people, including Harry, had died in the battle. According to Conrad's informant, they'd managed to take all but a few of the US guards with them, so one good thing came from the tragic debacle.

After Conrad expressed his relief at finding Riley alive, he'd lectured her for fifteen minutes on how reckless she'd been to run off from Santa Fe the way she did. He held her responsible for the trouble she'd left in her wake. She'd stopped him at that point and tried to explain why what happened to Simeon and his people wasn't her fault, but Conrad wasn't convinced.

"I tried to persuade Simeon to turn around and find another way into the US," she explained. "He refused to listen because of some 'honor among thieves' nonsense. I had no choice but to surrender before the situation spiraled out of control. Harper and Lou insisted on joining with me even though I tried to talk them out of it. People made their choices."

"None of you should have been on that bridge in the first place. If you'd been patient a while longer, my team could have gone after Julia without wasting time chasing you all over Texas."

"You couldn't make that guarantee. You didn't even know how long that other secret mission would take. By your own admission, you're only here now because Dashay convinced you to take leave and join her in the search for me. If I'd stayed put, we probably still would have been sitting there waiting for you to get around to finding my daughter."

"That's not fair. You know how much Julia's rescue mission meant to me. I'd spent two years of concentrated effort trying to find her. I wasn't sitting on my hands waiting for clues to fall into my lap."

"I'm sorry, Conrad," Riley said, shaking her head. "You know how grateful I am for the sacrifices you've done for my family and me. But honestly, it wasn't enough. I made more progress in getting closer to Julia in a few weeks than you did in years."

"Running into Nico was a coincidence. It had nothing to do with your superior tracking skills," he said in a rush. "It was just dumb luck."

Riley couldn't help missing a hint of bitterness in his tone. "But that wouldn't have happened if I hadn't taken the initiative. We could argue about this all day, but you won't change my mind. I'd do the same again, given a chance."

He gave a weary sigh. "And I thought Dashay was stubborn."

She let his comment pass and said, "Doesn't matter now. It's in the past. All we can do is go forward from here. What's your plan to get into the camp in Oklahoma City?"

Conrad grew quiet for a few moments, avoiding her gaze. "I have more to tell you."

Her gut tightened at the change in his tone. "Is it Julia? My family? Out with it."

"Julia and your family aren't in Oklahoma City. They were transferred to Wichita, Kansas."

He might as well have punched her in the gut. She gasped and tightened her grip on the reins. "You're positive? Your intel is reliable?"

He gave a quick nod. "Irrefutable. From an informant on the inside. I'm so sorry, Riley, but don't lose hope. We're ready with an ops plan to deal with this new development."

She swallowed the lump in her throat and took a breath. "But they're alive?"

"Last we heard."

"The only thing keeping me sane these past days was knowing how close my daughter was and that I would see her within days. I could almost feel my arms holding her. Now, this. Why were they moved?"

"We haven't been able to verify that. Does it matter?"

"What if Kearns' people heard we were coming? They could keep moving my family until they're on the East Coast, like some continent-sized game of chess."

"That's not going to happen. They have no way of knowing we're coming."

Riley rubbed her forehead. "There's one way."

She started to tell him about Yeager, but he held up his hand to stop her. "Bobby told us about Yeager, but that was weeks ago. He can't still be tracking you, or he'd have found you with Russo's people."

"You found us."

"We're better than Yeager. No one knows we're here. Even your friend Nico doesn't know we're on the way."

She spun around to face him. "Nico's with them? How is that possible? Is he still helping us?"

"All I can tell you is that he put in for a transfer, and it was denied. We got word he deserted after your family was moved. No one has seen or heard from him since, but we have a good idea where he was headed. We don't have anyone on the inside in Wichita to confirm he's there yet, but we're working on it."

Riley's thoughts were spinning from what he'd told her. Instead of seeing Julia in days, it could take weeks instead. She felt like forces were driving her toward Julia and barring her way at the same time. She struggled to fight the voices telling her that she'd deluded herself into thinking she could outwit Kearns and rescue Julia. What was she against an entire army?

She took a breath to quell those voices and squared her shoulders. She'd come too far to accept defeat. This is just a minor setback. Nothing more than a change of location, she told herself. "So, what's our plan?"

"My plan is to leave you and Dashay at a safe distance outside Wichita while my team extracts your family. End of discussion."

Conrad could say what he wanted, but Riley wasn't anywhere near the end of the discussion. "Have you forgotten that I'm a doctor? You don't know what condition my family's medical condition will be. I should be on hand."

"I've carried out dozens of these operations, Riley. Protocol is to get the victims to safety, then call in the doctor."

"Don't quote protocol to me. Technically, you can't stop me, Conrad. I'm not in the military, you're not a cop, and we're in a foreign country. You don't have jurisdiction here. I'll go wherever I want to."

"Technically, you're AWOL, but we'll save that discussion for another day. There's a warrant out for you. Just so you know. I'm here on orders from a WSA agency, so I'm under our government's jurisdiction even though we are in foreign territory. I'm in command of this mission. If you want my help, you have to do what I say."

He studied her to gauge her reaction. She did her best to keep her face emotionless, refusing to give him the satisfaction even though she was chafing at the irrefutable points he'd made.

He finally said, "Let's set all of that aside for a moment and remember that we're friends. With that mindset, my question is this — are you willing to jeopardize Julia's safety just to get your way?"

Ignoring his even more excellent question, she said, "There's really a warrant out for me? Who issued it?"

"What does that matter? You're dodging my question."

"Fine. You know better than anyone that I wouldn't risk Julia's safety, but I don't believe I would be. We're all basically going into this blind. I'm not as highly trained as you or your team, but you know I can handle myself in tough situations. I knocked out one of the guards with a rifle butt."

"You did what? Are you insane, Riley?"

Riley shrugged. "Quite possibly."

Conrad rubbed his forehead. "I can't argue with you about this now. I'm thrilled that you're safe, and it's great to see you again. Let's just get undercover at the safe house."

"Fair enough. Thank you for rescuing me. I'm deeply indebted to you. But just know, this discussion isn't over."

"I wasn't fool enough to think it was."

To ease the tension, she peppered Conrad with questions about Coop, her children, and the family until the safe little house came into view. It was an average stucco rancher surrounded by fields of wheat and corn. It was so unassuming that she understood why they'd chosen it.

She dismounted the instant they reached the house and pushed the door open, calling for Dashay. Her friend jumped up from the kitchen table and ran at her with her arms spread wide. The two of them clung to each other, sobbing in joy at being reunited.

"I'm never letting you out of my sight again, you lunatic," Dashay said as she stepped away, wiping her eyes. "I should never forgive you for running off like that. Our whole government is up in arms over that."

"I seriously doubt that," Riley said, then blew her nose into her neckerchief. "Thank you for talking Conrad into coming after me. I don't deserve what you've done."

"You've got that right, girl, but I'd do it again in a heartbeat." She fingered a strand of Riley's beached curls. "And what have you done to your hair now? Pick a color already."

Riley ran her fingers through the filthy, tangled mop. "I kind of like it."

"We'll see what Coop has to say about it." Growing serious, she said, "I'm guessing Conrad gave you the news about Julia?" Riley nodded and pressed on her eyes when a second round of tears threatened. "It's a gut kicker, but we can't let it stop us. We'll get our WP and take her home. There's someone else here to help."

She pointed toward the kitchen, where Bailey stood watching them. Riley hadn't seen her in over a year when she'd stopped at the farm with Conrad on their way to a mission.

Riley gave her a warm hug. "The gang's all here. How did you end up on this wild goose chase?"

"By the scenic route, but I'm glad to pitch in. It's time we get your family out of Kearns' clutches and put this to rest."

"Amen to that," Riley said. There was a commotion at the door as Harper and Bobby came in carrying Lou. "You know Bobby. Come meet my other new friends."

After introductions, Riley examined Lou and got him settled in one of the bedrooms before going to savor her first shower in ages. All that was missing to make it perfect was clean clothes to put on afterward. Washing her few remaining articles of clothing would be at the top of her morning chore list. Harper took her turn in the shower after Riley. She was in so long that Riley wondered if she'd have to go in and drag her out at some point.

She finally emerged looking sheepish and said, "I actually fell asleep leaning against the wall in there. Didn't know that was possible."

Once they were clean and settled, the group sat down to eggs, cornbread, and salad. It was a simple meal but tasted like a feast to the former prisoners. They filled their empty bellies with as much food as they could hold, then everyone crowded into the small living room to discuss strategy. Riley sat alone, silently listening. The news about Julia's transfer was a crushing blow but hearing the others planning the rescue buoyed Riley's spirits. If it were up to her, she would have plunged headlong back onto the road at dawn, but that wasn't Conrad's way. He had to plan and strategize until every piece was perfectly aligned. Riley knew that with so many lives at stake, it might be wise to exercise caution and follow his lead, just this once.

———

The strategy session lasted long into the night before Conrad sent his people to the tents they'd pitched behind the house. He assigned Lou, Bobby, and Harper the master bedroom while he and Dashay shared the next biggest room. Bailey offered Riley the third and only other bedroom, but Riley insisted on taking the foldout sofa. Anything was better than sleeping on the hard ground as she'd done since leaving the commune.

She lay awake long after the house was quiet, trying to remember the last time she'd slept for more than an hour. Conrad had declared that they'd stay at the safe house for at least two days, so she hoped to find quiet time to grab a few hours. A brisk jog in the moonlight would have done the trick, but Conrad ordered her to stray no further than the front yard. The only option left was reading. She dug her penlight out of her pack and walked to the small bookcase in the corner. Dashay came tiptoeing in while she skimmed through the titles.

"I thought I heard you wandering around out here. Can't sleep?"

Riley shook her head. "Too tired to sleep. You know how that is. Did I wake you?"

Dashay gave a silent finger snap. "I thought I'd be out like that now that you're safe, but I'm too excited at having my sister back to sleep." She took Riley's hand and led her back to the sofa bed. "I've missed our talks before going to bed."

Riley kept hold of Dashay's hand once they were reclining against the back of the sofa. "Me, too. Harper has become a close friend and was a good second, but she's not you."

Dashay kissed her cheek. "And no one will ever come close to you. What do you think of Conrad's rescue plan?"

"Let's talk about something else. Anything else. Tell me how things are with Conrad. I admit I was surprised to see you two are still together."

Dashay updated Riley on their relationship, then said, "I regret the time we wasted keeping our emotions hidden from each other. It was mostly my fault."

Riley wasn't sure how to take the news. She'd half hoped they'd split up so that Nico would have a chance with her. "I have something to tell you, but I'm not sure it matters after hearing you're in love with Conrad."

"Since when do you hold back with me?"

Riley turned to face her and crossed her legs. "It's about Nico, if you hadn't guessed. He still loves you. I told him you love him, too, because that's what you said before I left Santa Fe."

Dashay folded her arms and closed her eyes. "I thought he was dead when I said that. I don't blame you for telling him, but it does complicate things. How do you think he'll take it when he sees me with Conrad?"

"I told him about Conrad but said it was only casual. He'll be disappointed but happy for you, Dashay. He hadn't expected you to be alone for the rest of your life. He'll go home to his family in New Mexico and move on with his life. He's young and handsome. Girls will be fighting over him."

Dashay was quiet for several seconds before saying, "I've often played the 'what might have been' game. How would our lives have turned out differently if I'd stayed in Charleston with Nico? Maybe he wouldn't have been taken by Yeager. We might have caught up with you. Maybe Brooks wouldn't have died."

"His death had nothing to do with you. He would have died, either way, so stop playing 'what might have been.' It's pointless."

"I recently told Conrad the same thing, but it's hard not to wonder sometimes."

"Don't bite my head off for what I'm about to ask, but do you even catch yourself wishing you were with Nico?"

"I did in the early days, but not for a long time. I'm in love with Conrad, Riley. He's where I want to be. Nico is my 'what might have been.' Nothing more."

"That's all I needed to hear. I won't bring it up again. Tell me all about my kids. I talked to them a few weeks ago. It made me miss them more. How's my Xav?"

"More of a pistol than ever," she said with a laugh. "He'll run you ragged." She shared every detail of her time at the farm before leaving to go in search of Riley. "The kids miss you and are worried, but they're adapting. Coop's the one not taking it well. You're his reason for existing, Riley. I don't know how he'd survive without you."

Riley rubbed her temples. "I know I wounded him deeply. How will I ever make it up to him?"

"By making it home with Julia. Once he has the two of you in his arms, all will be forgotten."

"That's what everyone keeps saying, but I wonder."

"I was sad to hear they took Biscuit from you," Dashay said, changing the subject. "I miss that ridiculous horse."

"Me, too. I feel like I lost a dear friend. I could tell Biscuit anything. He never gave me lip."

Dashay chuckled. "You would have died of fright if he had."

"Getting to vent to him was good therapy, and he was good companionship when I was alone on the road. I would have died if he hadn't gotten me to Nico in time."

"Nico again. Are you trying to tell me something?"

"That was unintentional, but it's true. I miss my Biscuit buddy. I hope they'll treat him well and give him plenty of apples."

"Doubtful if he's been enlisted into the military. They probably think of him as a tool no different from a truck."

She feigned a yawn, not wanting to talk about Biscuit anymore. "I'm getting drowsy." Dashay started to get off the bed, but Riley reached for her hand to stop her. "Will you stay with me? I'd rather not be alone."

Dashay laid down and pulled the sheet over her feet. "You didn't even need to ask."

Riley curled into a ball next to her. "Thank you for coming after me."

Dashay kissed her scarred cheek. "Always."

Nico's internal clock told him it was time to wake up. He sat up on his couch bed and searched the living room floor for his jeans. No matter how much he'd resisted, Mitch and Beth had insisted on him hiding out with them after he'd recovered from his harrowing journey to Wichita. He wasn't comfortable putting the family at risk, but he couldn't deny he enjoyed the soft couch and home-cooked meals. He marveled daily at the creations Beth whipped up with the meager rations they were allotted.

It was also a comfort to be surrounded by family after so much time on his own. Since he'd deserted, the longing to return to Farmington grew stronger every day. In the meantime, he was grateful to have the Dunne's and Julia to fill the void. Julia reminded him of his little sister. That was part of what had driven him to return her to Riley and Coop.

Nico finally located his pants in the jumble of clothes on the floor and pulled them on.

Mitch came in a few minutes later and watched him lace his boots. "I don't like you going out in daylight," he said.

Nico pulled a folded note from his pocket and handed it to him. As Mitch read, he said, "Vince left that at the drop site last night. It's from Rick. I can't ignore it."

"Rick hasn't ever set up a meet in the daytime before. Could it be a trap?"

"I expect a trap every night, but this feels legit. I'll take extra care to avoid being seen."

"We don't expect you to do this, Nico. You don't owe us anything. In fact, we're still in your debt for the help you gave us in Oklahoma. You can just live here until Riley shows up. You know she won't give up until we're free."

Nico stood and put his hand on Mitch's shoulder. "Thanks, but as I've said, I feel like I've been training for this ever since the CME. I'm a good medic, and I enjoy helping people heal, but I was made for this kind of work. I'm not only doing it out of a sense of obligation. It's my calling."

"Well, we're indebted to you. When this is all over, I'll find a way to repay you."

"Not necessary," Nico said as he stood and walked toward the door. "Go back to bed. I'll be home in an hour."

Mitch dipped his head, then went down the hallway to his room. Nico quietly closed the front door behind him and stole through the shade of the trees along the perimeter fence. He kept to the shadows as he made his way to touch base with his informant as he was coming off his shift as a guard at the southwest internment area gate. Fortunately, the streets were quiet since the curfew was still in place.

In the two weeks since Nico recovered from his injuries, he'd located two men from one of his former Army units. Nico knew Rick and Vince wouldn't have any qualms about gathering information in exchange for anything from cigarettes to batteries to aspirin. His efforts had earned him maps of the camp, patrol routes, and guard schedules. He, along with Mitch and Clint, was piecing together what he'd collected to devise an escape plan. Nico was confident that soon, he'd hit on what they needed to get the whole family free of that stinking camp.

By the time he reached the abandoned aviation parts warehouse where the meet was set to take place, Rick was pacing nervously in the parking lot.

"Let's get inside," Nico said as he passed him without slowing down.

They found the side warehouse door with the broken lock, then went in and kept moving until they reached an interior office with no windows.

"What took you so long?" Rick asked as he turned on his flashlight. "My shift ended a half-hour ago. I should be wrapped up in my girlfriend by now."

Nico dropped into a rusty folding chair and rubbed his scar from the bear attack that still gave him grief on occasion. "Getting here in daylight was tricky. My quarters are on the opposite side of the internment area. I can't exactly walk exposed on the open street. I had to dodge two patrols."

"I'm taking a risk, too. Just because I'm a guard doesn't mean I'm allowed to take off whenever I want."

Nico slid a stool in front of Rick with his foot and gestured for him to sit. "I'm sorry, dude. I understand the chance you're taking to meet with me. Just remember it's for a good cause. Let's get to it. What do you have for me?"

Rick sat forward and rested his elbows on his knees. "It's big. I'm going to want more than your usual offerings in payment."

"Tell me the intel first, then we'll negotiate price," Nico said, leaning back with his arms folded. Rick's face showed he wasn't happy with that arrangement, but Nico couldn't back down. Rick constantly pushed the boundaries. Nico had to keep the upper hand, or he'd end up paying an ever-increasing price.

"Fine, but I decide what's fair." When Nico nodded his agreement, Rick said, "Some new Colonel came to the admin office asking about the Dunnes last night at the start of my shift. He wanted to know where their quarters are. What's that tidbit worth to you?"

Nico's heartbeat quickened, and his muscles tensed. "What's this Colonel's name?"

"Mosley. He said he just got in from Fort Sill."

It wasn't the answer Nico expected, so he said, "I've met Colonel Mosley before. Describe him."

Rick rubbed his chin as he glanced up at the ceiling. "He's about six-two with close-cut graying hair and steely eyes that don't miss a trick. Honestly, the guy creeped me out for some reason. Don't tell anyone I said that about a Colonel."

Nico stared at him, not knowing how to respond. The man Rick had just described was definitely not Mosley. He was five-nine at most, with jet-black hair and brown eyes. Rick's description fit another Colonel Nico knew. It had to be Yeager.

"Did you give him the Dunne's address?" he asked, hiding his apprehension.

"He didn't ask me, but no one else knew without checking. I finagled the assignment to get him the info. He told me to meet him tonight with the address at 2100 before the start of my shift. He wants to be sure the whole family will be home."

"I want to get eyes on this Colonel and verify he's Mosley. Where are you meeting?"

Rick jumped off the stool and backed away from Nico with his hands raised. "Look, I have no problem giving you scraps of information but spying on a Colonel crosses the line. You're a deserter. Guilt by association. That's too big of a risk."

Nico smiled and held his hand out toward the stool. Rick hesitated a moment before lowing himself back onto the seat. "Calm down, compadre. I'm the one taking the risk. I'm an expert at melting into the shadows, remember. The Colonel will never know I'm there. Even on the chance he notices me, he won't suspect you of revealing the meeting place." Rick still looked skeptical, so he added, "I'll double the payment."

Rick perked up at that. Nico knew he had him.

"What are you offering?"

"I just got my hands on a portable solar generator. Works like new."

Rick's eyes widened. "Ok, good enough. Throw in a pack of cigarettes, and you have a deal. Solar generators are impossible to score. Where'd you get it?"

"You know I never reveal my sources. Where's the meetup site? Please tell me it's not on base."

"No, Mosley was adamant about meeting off base. He said he'd come to the southeastern entrance. There's a small park with shrubs and a stand of trees just inside the gate. It's called Huntington Park. Perfect cover."

"I'm familiar with the spot. I'll get there an hour early to be safe." Nico studied him for a moment before saying, "You were right. This is big. Be here tomorrow. Same time. I'll bring the generator."

"Wouldn't miss it," Rick said before hurrying out of the warehouse.

Nico hung back to collect himself, knowing that was likely the last time he'd see Rick. He had no generator and no intention of paying his informant with anything else. If he was right about Yeager, he'd only have minutes to get the family out of the house and into hiding before he showed up.

When enough time had passed, Nico left the warehouse and made his way home, pondering two questions. First, why was Yeager posing as Mosley, and second, what did he want with the Dunnes? If he knew they were in Wichita, then he had to know Riley wasn't with them. The family had been in captivity for more than two years. What could they possibly have to offer Yeager?

————

When Nico arrived back at their quarters, he woke the household and told them Yeager might be on his tail. Nico made it clear he could be wrong, but even if that were the case, one of Kearns' officers was asking after their family. He told them to pack only what they could carry and be ready to vacate at a moment's notice. Holly and Julia stared at him with eyes wide in fear. He couldn't blame them. Yeager was a powerful and unpredictable force. He could destroy all hope of them getting out of Wichita.

"Go about your day as usual," he told the family. "Let's not overreact. If Yeager's in town, we'll be ready."

The three girls left for school, and Clint and Kathryn went to their jobs. Mitch said he needed to work off nervous energy, so he went out back to work in his garden. Beth retreated to her room to prepare for departure. Nico took advantage of the quiet to get a few hours of sleep. If they had to evacuate, it might be days before he got another chance to catch up on his sleep.

When he woke three hours later, he and Mitch poured over the maps of the camp, looking for places to hide until they could escape from the city. Most houses inside the internment area were either occupied or empty for a reason. Mitch suggested the warehouse where he'd met Rick, but Nico said they shouldn't use a place that could be associated with him. He pointed out an abandoned industrial area on the opposite side that could work but getting there with eight people trying to evade patrols could be a challenge.

"I'll go scope it out," Mitch said. "No one will pay attention to an old man out for an afternoon walk."

"It's a hundred degrees out there," Beth said.

"I worked on the ranch every summer for forty years in hundred-degree heat. You never said a word then."

She put her hands on her hips. "You were younger."

"I did it three years ago. If it makes you happy, I'll go after dinner before the curfew starts. It won't be much cooler, but at least the shadows will be longer."

"You'll have to hurry to make it back before curfew," Nico said.

"I need the exercise."

Beth reluctantly agreed to let him go. Nico was glad because he sensed that Mitch just wanted to be useful, and he could relate to that need. It was hard to stand by doing nothing while others languished in the camp.

After Mitch left, Nico dressed in an olive-green shirt and black pants, then said a quick goodbye to the family before heading out on his mission. He allowed plenty of time to reach the park well before Rick, and the Colonel were due to arrive. He found some thick shrubs growing against the fence that would conceal him completely. He didn't expect anyone to be in the park, but he wanted to take every precaution before he settled into a comfortable position to wait.

Feeling the weight of having to protect seven people, Nico ran through scenarios in his head for getting the family to safety. He would have given anything for Riley to charge in with the cavalry to rescue the Dunnes, but he didn't even know if she was still alive. If she had survived by some miracle, she would have gone to Oklahoma City anyway, expecting her family to be waiting for her. Finding they were gone would be a crushing blow. It was too painful for Nico to contemplate.

He glanced at the digital watch he'd found at a retro shop in Oklahoma City and was surprised to see it was five minutes to eight. Not long to go. He lifted his binoculars to his eyes and focused them in on the spot where Rick said he'd be. Right on cue, he walked up and stopped with his hands clasped behind his back. No one else who saw him would notice how nervous he was, but Nico read Rick's fear, loud and clear.

He felt a twinge of guilt for putting the man in such a precarious situation. He wasn't an evil person, and Nico had no desire to cause him trouble, but he was the only one who could give Nico what he needed. He reminded himself that Rick had allowed his greed to overcome his fear and handed over the meeting spot as soon as he knew what his prize would be. That alleviated Nico's guilt some.

He kept the binoculars pinned on Rick and was rewarded when he saw him shift his gaze to the left as someone approached. The officer stopped three feet in front of him. Nico didn't need to see his face to recognize him as Yeager. He swallowed hard a few times before reminding himself to breathe. Yeager's sudden appearance in Wichita was a worst-case scenario. He had the power to destroy all hope of Julia and the Dunnes ever getting free.

He was too far to hear what they were saying, but they only spoke for a moment before Yeager gestured for the guards behind the gate to let him enter. Nico tucked deeper into his hiding place and held his breath as they passed. Rick gave an almost imperceptible sideways glance in his direction, but Nico doubted he could see him in the foliage. When the guards finally locked the gate, Nico scrambled out of the bushes and ran through the trees along the fence until he feared his lungs would burst. All that mattered was reaching the Dunne's before Yeager.

———

Julia stopped for the tenth time to check out the living room window for Nico before returning to her frenzied pacing. Her backpack was stuffed with what she'd need if they had to bug out, and there was nothing left to do but wait. Waiting had never been her best quality. She'd tried to convince Uncle Mitch that they should get a head start before Nico got back, just in case. He'd said it would be worse to risk breaking curfew if Nico was wrong. Julia's gut told her Nico wasn't wrong.

The sound of footsteps pounding up the porch startled her out of her brooding. The door banged open a second later, and

Nico burst into the house. He stopped in the center of the room with his hands on his knees, gulping for air.

"We have to go, now," he gasped. "Grab your packs. Yeager is on my heels." When the family stared at him in stunned silence, he cried, "Go!"

They scattered to gather their evac bags, but Julia's legs refused to move. "Why is Yeager coming for us?" she whispered. "Does he think Mom's here?"

Nico straightened and rested his hand on her shoulder. "No, Julia. I think he's coming for you. Please, get your things. You've got to be brave. He'll be here any second."

It was all she needed to hear. As she hurried down the hallway, Nico said, "Mitch, any luck finding somewhere for us to go?"

Julia's heart sank when Uncle Mitch whispered, "No."

As she followed Holly and Rosie back to the living room with their packs, Clint came up behind Nico and laid a hand on his back. "We'll figure this out as we go, brother. Do you know any place we could hide out, even if just for the night?"

Nico shook his head. "I know an abandoned warehouse, but it's not close. We'll have the cover of darkness, but you've got to help me get them moving. We're out of time."

"Holly, Rosie, Julia, out the back door now," Clint said.

Julia pushed Holly toward the kitchen door that led to the backyard and the woods beyond, but Uncle Mitch stepped in front of them and held up his hands.

"Me first, then Beth and Kathryn before the girls. Clint, bring up the rear."

"Of course," Clint said, "I wasn't thinking."

Nico ran out in front of Mitch to lead the way just as they heard pounding on the front door.

"Open up," a man shouted.

Nico stopped in the doorway, urging the others to run toward the trees. "Hide in the woods the best you can. If I'm not there in five, go on without me."

"We're not leaving you," Beth said as she moved past him.

"Yes, you are. I'll be right behind you," Nico said, hurrying her onto the lawn.

"You have ten seconds to unlock this door, or we're breaking it open," the man at the door shouted.

Julia's heart pounded so hard that she was afraid she'd faint. She stopped where Nico stood and reached for his arm, but he shook his head and stepped away.

"Keep going, Julia. Run with all your might, and don't stop, no matter what you hear. Do this for your mom and for me."

Tears glistened in his eyes when she squared her shoulders and stepped onto the patio, but too late. A loud crash sounded in the house. Julia looked in through the kitchen window to see two men rushing towards them. Yeager was accompanied by a tall, lanky man who didn't look like a security type at all.

The tall man saw them first and shouted, "There, in the backyard."

Julia only made it a few steps before the men were on them.

Nico stepped between the tall one and Julia, blocking his way. "Evening, Colonel Yeager."

Yeager's eyes widened when he got a good look at Nico. "You! I should have guessed you were the one thwarting my plans at every turn. Why didn't I dispose of you in Charleston?"

"Yeager?" the other man said. "I thought his name is Mosley."

Nico ignored him and cried, "Clint, get Julia out of here!"

As Clint reached for Julia, Yeager drew his weapon and aimed it at Clint's forehead. Julia froze and held her breath, trying to figure out how to get away without letting that monster hurt Clint because of her.

"You move, I'll shoot to kill," Yeager said.

Julia shivered at the coldness in his voice. Clint tried to step in front of Julia but tripped on the edge of the patio and lost his footing. He fell into the gas grill, knocking it over with a crash.

The others stopped at the tree line and turned to see what was happening.

Julia summoned her strength and yelled, "Run!"

They ignored her and continued staring in their direction. Kathryn actually tried to run toward them, but Uncle Mitch grabbed her arms to stop her.

"Why won't they just run?" Julia whispered.

"Why didn't you?" the other man asked her.

Julia flinched at hearing him speak. She'd forgotten he was there.

"Stay out of this, Rick," Nico said.

Rick waved Nico off and stepped closer to Yeager. "What is this, sir? You said you only needed to question the family."

Yeager turned toward him and stared as if he'd forgotten about Rick, too. "I lied," he said, then swept his aim from Clint to Rick and shot him between the eyes. Rick gave him a startled look, then fell back onto the grass with a thud.

Julia screamed, and Yeager swung back to face her and Clint. Nico took advantage of the distraction and dove for Yeager's knees, knocking him off balance enough to wrestle the gun from his hand. He aimed the weapon at Yeager as he waved for Clint and Julia to go. Clint tugged on Julia's arm, but she stood rooted to the ground in fear.

"It's over, Yeager. Get down on your face with your hands behind your back," Nico said. Yeager's lips curved into a smile, but he didn't move. Nico tipped his head toward the gun. "Do you think I won't use this on you?"

Yeager gave the most chilling laugh Julia had ever heard, then ducked down and somersaulted toward Rick's dead body. Nico pulled the trigger, but the gun misfired. Yeager grabbed Rick's sidearm from the holster and pointed it at Nico as he climbed to his feet.

"You won't fire at me," Yeager said. "I know your kind. Soft underbelly." He kept his eyes locked on Nico but gestured to Julia with his other hand. "Get over here now, girl or Mendez, and your cousin die."

Julia took a step toward Yeager, but Clint still had a hold of her wrist.

"Don't do what he says, Julia. We're going to slowly back away. Nico will take care of Yeager."

Without hesitation, Yeager fired a round into Clint's right shoulder. He cried out in agony as he crumpled to the ground. Rosie and Holly screamed from the woods.

"That was a warning shot," Yeager told Clint. "Get on your feet and join the rest of your family in the woods. Julia is the one I want."

Clint yelped in pain as he got to his feet. He pressed his left hand to the wound with blood dripping between his fingers. "I won't let you have my niece," he wheezed.

Julia ducked away from him and ran to Yeager before he could stop her.

"No, Julia," Nico cried, but Yeager was already gripping her arm so tightly that his fingers dug into the bone.

"Get out of here, Clint," she whimpered with tears streaming down her face. "He doesn't want to kill me, or I'd be dead. Please, leave before you bleed to death, or this monster kills you."

Yeager jerked her arm, and she cried out in pain.

Nico pointed to the woods. "Do what she says."

Clint swayed as he stared at them, lost in a fog of pain and indecision. Mitch and Kathryn ran across the lawn, and each wrapped an arm around him to help him to the woods. Mitch gave Julia one last agonizing look over his shoulder as they moved away.

"Pathetic," Yeager mumbled before turning his attention to Nico. "You're the last loose end, Corporal." He loosened his grip on Julia's arm and said, "I'm going to let go of you, but don't do something stupid like running away. If you do, I'll kill you and your brave knight here." Julia nodded, too terrified to speak, let alone run. Yeager pulled a folded paper from his breast pocket and handed it to Julia. "Hold onto that until I tell you what to do with it."

Julia's hand trembled violently as she reached for the paper. When she had it, Yeager took for her other arm.

Nico watched them in confusion. "What's that?"

"Shut your mouth," Yeager said calmly. "Discussion over."

Julia watched in horror as Yeager slid his finger from the side of the gun to the trigger. As he fired, she slapped at his hand. The round hit Nico in the gut instead of his head where Yeager had aimed. As Nico fell, Julia struggled to free herself from Yeager's grip, but he was too strong. She grew still and cried silently as she watched the crimson stain spreading over Nico's t-shirt.

"That works, too," Yeager said, laughing. He loosened his hold on Julia's arm. "Put that message to your mom on his chest but not too close to the wound. I don't want it to get blood on it."

Julia stumbled to Nico and dropped to the ground next to him. She glanced at Yeager before gently laying the note on his chest, then stripping her hoodie off and pressing against his stomach. "This is all my fault," she said between sobs. "I'm so sorry. Thank you for trying to save me. You're a hero."

He closed his eyes and shook his head. "I'm the one who's sorry. I couldn't save you."

"You did everything you could. When I see my mom, I'll tell her what you did. Thank you, big brother. I'll never forget you."

"Love you, hermanita. Be brave and stay alive."

"I promise not to do anything stupid."

"Enough of the Hallmark special," Yeager said and pulled Julia to her feet. "Time to go."

He wrapped his arm around her stomach and dragged her into the house. "Let go of me. I'll come with you, psycho."

Yeager set her on her feet, then backhanded her across the mouth. "Show some respect. I need you alive but not in one piece."

Julia rubbed her cheek, remembering her promise to Nico.

"I'm sorry, sir. It won't happen again. Where are you taking me?"

"You'll find out when we get there. Get a move on."

Julia kept her head lowered as she walked in front of him with his gun aimed at the back of her head. She still had no idea what Yeager wanted with her. All Julia knew was that he was insane and deadly. Nico told her to stay alive, so she vowed to do what Yeager said and hold on until her mom came to her rescue. She prayed Yeager didn't snap and kill her before that happened.

They walked along moonlit streets for what felt like forever. Julia focused on her surroundings, struggling to keep her mind from wandering to Nico and Clint. They could both be dead for all she knew, and it was her fault. If she had run straight to the woods like Nico told her to, they'd all be safe.

Yeager came to an abrupt stop, then turned to face her. She glanced ahead and saw they were fifteen yards from one of the camp gates.

"These people know me as Mosley. You keep your mouth closed and go along with whatever I say. If you let out a peep, I'll take you to the woods and make you disappear. Are we clear?"

"Yes, sir," Julia mumbled.

"Good. Stay behind me."

He walked toward the gate like he didn't have a care in the world. Julia did her best to appear like she was out for an evening stroll but was terrified the guards would notice how hard her heart was pounding.

When they were twenty feet from the gate, Yeager hissed, "Wait here."

He left her staring after him as he went to have a conversation with the guards. Julia was too far away to hear what they were saying. One of the guards nodded, then rolled the gate open while Yeager jogged back to her.

"Don't make eye contact with the guards," he whispered. "Keep moving until we're in those trees across the street."

He walked beside her instead of behind, and she felt the guards eying her as they moved through the open gate. She forced herself to think about Aunt Beth's homemade bread and apple butter that they'd had with dinner. She was thirsty and hungry but doubted Yeager would feed her. She just hoped he'd give her enough water to keep her alive.

He nudged her toward the trees on the far side of the street, then led her to a tall black horse tethered to a tree. Yeager practically threw her into the saddle, then climbed up after her.

"Hold on to me," he ordered.

She reluctantly slid her arms around his waist. Touching him nauseated her, and bile rose in her throat as she fought off her tears.

He sighed in exasperation and said, "Tighter."

She took a breath and tightened her grip. I can do this, she told herself. Just stay alive. That's all you have to do. Stay alive.

CHAPTER FOURTEEN

CONRAD REINED in his horse at a small clearing surrounded by trees about a mile from Wichita. He signaled for the riders behind him to stop. Riley lifted her NVGs to let her eyes adjust to the natural light. She was close enough to Conrad to see him clearly in the bright moonlight. She'd need the goggles once they were inside the compound, but she preferred to have them off until then. Dashay rode up and waited beside her in silence for instructions.

Conrad wheeled Steve around to face them. "I'm sure I'm wasting my breath, but I'll give it one more go. Are you two sure you want to join us on this op, or do you think it would be wiser to ride back to the safe house and hang with Harper and Lou?"

Dashay let out an exaggerated sigh. "I thought we'd settled this after the twenty other times you asked during the trip here. Riley insists on going in, and I refuse to let her out of my sight. Discussion over."

Conrad looked at Riley for confirmation, but she just shrugged. "If you think there's any way I'm waiting one second longer than necessary to see Julia, you're delusional. So, what's the plan, Boss?"

He scratched his head in frustration. "If you both die, don't blame me." He motioned for the rest of the team to move in closer. There were ten of them, including Bobby and Bailey. Conrad and four of his agents wore guard uniforms, but that was all they'd been able to get their hands on. The rest wore black t-shirts and jeans. Conrad had insisted on Riley and Dashay wearing bulletproof vests along with the rest of the team even though the heat was oppressive. Bobby got off because they didn't have a vest big enough to fit him.

When they were in place, Conrad said, "My inside guys should be posted at the southern gate. If they're not, the mission is postponed until tomorrow night, and we keep trying until they're in place. We scrub after seven nights and start over with a new plan." Riley opened her mouth to protest, but he raised his hand to quiet her. "I don't anticipate that being necessary."

"They'll be in place," Bailey said with confidence. "These are two of our top-notch agents."

Riley let out her breath in relief. Having to wait even one more day would be agony. She couldn't imagine having to start over with a new plan after another week.

"What's the next step, Chief?" Jordan asked.

"The agents will provide the target address, written directions, and a map. We'll only have moments to make the pass. We can't risk being spotted at the gate by a night patrol. Our sources tell us there's cover along the perimeter fence. We'll stick to that for as long as we can before we have to cut into the open toward the target."

"Too bad it's a clear night and three-quarter moon," Riggs said. "We hardly need the NVGs."

"Can't be helped," Bailey said. "What I wouldn't give for my weather app."

"And drone reconnaissance," Jordan said.

There was a low rumble of laughter.

Conrad held up his hand to get their attention. "We'll stroll down memory lane after the op. For now, we'll make the best of it with the intel we have. The patrols are thin this time of night because of curfew. Once they pass our position, we book it to the house and extract the family through the woods behind the back-yard. Piece of cake."

"Damned straight," Riley said. She shrugged again when Dashay stared at her with raised eyebrows. "Adrenaline rush."

"I'm liking the energy, but don't get reckless, Riley," Conrad said. "And check your emotions at the door. You're a doctor, so you know what I mean. We have no idea what we'll find behind that house."

"I get it. All business," she said. "I'm ready."

"Perfect. We make our way back to the gate and run back here for the horses. We have a short window before our agents are replaced at the end of their shift. It's crucial that we're through the gate by then, or we'll have to engage in other measures, which I'm hoping to avoid. I want to avoid that at all costs and leave a microscopic footprint. Questions?"

The team was silent, but Riley could feel their energy pulsing around her. It was time to move. Conrad dismounted, and the others followed in unison. They tethered their horses, then stepped into their assigned places for the march to the compound. Jordan and Bailey took point. Riley and Dashay were sent to the back, with Bobby bringing up the rear. Riley would have preferred to be at the front but reminded herself to be glad that Conrad had let her go at all.

She thought she'd be too panicked to move, but she was remarkably calm, and her mind was sharp. She wondered if it was a genetic reaction hardwired to aid early humans in the hunt. If they'd panicked every time they faced dangerous prey, it would have meant a premature end to humanity. Whatever the cause, Riley was grateful. She wanted to be at her best when she found Julia.

Dashay and Bobby were sucking air by the end of the twelve

minutes it took to reach the hiding place across the street from the gate. Riley was too pumped to notice. She held her breath as Conrad focused his NVG's on the guard post. It felt like an hour passed before he signaled the mission was a go. The team members in uniforms crossed the street like they owned the place. The others stayed hidden in the shadows. After a hurried conversation with his inside men, they passed a packet to Conrad, and he signaled for the others to come. They crossed the street in a crouching run, then hurried through the gate to the trees along the fence.

Riley's earlier calm faded and was replaced with a mix of elation and anxiety. She was less than four miles from Julia but crossing those miles could prove the most dangerous journey of her life. She took slow, deep breaths to keep her heart from breaking out of her chest.

Bobby stepped closer to her and patted her back. "We've got this, Red. Just a little more."

"Listen to him," Dashay once she caught her breath. "Worst part's over."

Riley squeezed her hand and smiled up at Bobby. "I'm good. Let's get this over with."

Jordan expertly led them through a maze of trees, buildings, and streets until they entered a residential neighborhood backed by thick woods. From their cover across the street, Conrad checked the address twice against the notes from his agents. Satisfied they had the right house, he stood and signaled for his team to follow.

Riley ignored Conrad's orders to stay back and raced up to the house beside him. Jordan stepped forward to block her, but she ducked past him and bounded up the steps to the porch. As she reached for the door, Conrad tackled her.

While holding her down, he whispered, "This could be a setup. Let my people clear it first."

"Fine," she answered. "I promise to wait. You can get off me now."

"If you do something stupid that endangers my team, I'm calling this thing off. I mean it. Follow my instructions."

Conrad moved to the side but kept his hand on her shoulder as she got to her feet and squatted next to him. She could have broken free of his grip but knew he was right to be cautious. They had no idea who was waiting for them on the other side of that door.

Riggs moved to the window and peeked in, then shook his head. Even Riley could see it was covered by curtains. Jordan crawled behind him to the door, taking care to stay below the peephole. He studied the door handle for a moment before waving Conrad over.

"Stay," he whispered to Riley.

She made a cross over her heart as Conrad stood and walked to Jordan. They conversed quietly for several seconds, pointing at the doorknob. She had no idea what could be so interesting about a doorknob. Conrad finally glanced at Riley before pushing on the door. It creaked open without him touching the knob. That wasn't a good sign. Conrad, Jordan, and Riggs drew their sidearms and silently inched through the doorway. Riley heard voices seconds later. She was halfway across the porch by the time Conrad stuck his head out to wave them inside.

Riley pushed past him and came to a halt in the center of the room. Bobby nearly knocked her over when he came up behind her. She pulled off her NVGs and took in the scene as her eyes adjusted to the dim light. Nico was laid out on the couch, and Clint was propped in a chair with the rest of the family was gathered around, staring in stunned silence. Riley counted heads and found everyone except Julia.

"Riley Kate?" Uncle Mitch said, breaking the silence. "Is that you?" She nodded, too overcome with emotion to speak. He stepped forward and pulled her into his arms. "Oh, my dear girl. You're here. Thank the Good Lord you're here."

Riley pulled away and swept her gaze over the room again. "Where is she? Where's my girl?" Uncle Mitch turned away, shaking his head. "Not dead. Please, tell me she's not dead."

"No," Nico breathed. "Not dead. Yeager."

Riley gasped to hear him speak. From his pallid coloring and the amount of blood soaking his shirt, she'd thought he was dead. She dropped to her knees by his side and took his hand in both of hers. "Someone tell me what happened here, now." When Nico opened his mouth, she said, "Not you."

"Yeager came with one of the guards," Kathryn said in a monotone. "He killed that man, then shot Clint in the shoulder and Nico in the gut. He took Julia and left this."

Riley took the bloodstained paper Kathryn held out to her. Her blood boiled as she read.

If you want your daughter back alive, come to the address noted below. It's an abandoned charter flight hanger on the western side of the airport. I'll be waiting.

Colonel Orson Yeager

Riley shoved the note at Conrad and started for the door.

Bobby picked her up by the waist and deposited her in a chair under the window. "No, you don't, Red."

Conrad leaned over Riley with his hands on the armrests. "We're going after Julia, but not until we help these people. Remember when I ordered you to check your emotions at the door?" Riley nodded slowly. "Good. We have wounded that need attention. That's the reason you insisted on coming. Put your doctor hat on and treat your patients while we figure out a new plan."

Riley stared at him, trying to summon her earlier courage and push thoughts of Julia aside for the moment. "Fine," she said without taking her eyes off him. "Someone get me the med-pack. Dashay, assist me, please."

Conrad stepped back to let her up. She stood and searched the room for her friend. Dashay was on the floor next to Nico, gently dabbing his forehead with a towel.

"I'm here, Babe," Dashay said softly. "I found you."

Nico gave her a weak smile. "I never thought I'd see that gorgeous smile again. Is this a dream?"

"No, I'm real. I'm here, and I promise not to leave your side for the rest of your life."

Riley noticed Dashay had said for the rest of *your* life. She knelt beside Dashay, hoping she was wrong about what that meant. "I'm going to examine your wound, Nico. Dashay and I will get you fixed up in a hurry."

He slowly shook his head, grimacing in pain from the effort. "Don't bother. Your magic won't work on me this time. Save Clint. He has a chance."

Riley peeled his blood-soaked shirt from the wound. As she studied the pulpy mess that should have been his vital organs, she said, "Who's the doctor here? I'll be the one to diagnose you."

When he closed his eyes, she shook her head at Dashay, who gazed back with tears streaming down her face. Someone shoved the med-pack at her. She unzipped it and dug inside for the morphine vial that Conrad had managed to procure. Dashay raised her eyebrows at the size of the dose Riley drew into the syringe. Riley injected the medicine into his arm, then sat back to gauge Nico's reaction.

He opened his eyes and smiled up at her. She had to lean close to hear him say, "You are a magician after all. The pain is fading."

Riley smiled and squeezed his hand. "You rest now."

Dashay pressed her hand to his cheek and gave him a tender kiss. "I love you, Nico. I have since the moment I saw you in Branson's infirmary. I'll always love you."

"I love you more." He gasped a rattling breath, then said, "I need to rest a minute but don't leave me."

He closed his eyes and gave one more shuddering breath, then was gone. Dashay covered her face with her hands and collapsed onto his chest. Riley got up and kissed his forehead before locking her heart to the pain burning there. She still had patients to tend to. She glanced at Conrad staring down at Dashay. Too much anguish for one little room, she thought as she made her way to Clint.

Kathryn explained Clint's injury while Riley examined him. "He got shot trying to protect Julia."

"I'm sorry it didn't work," Clint said between clenched teeth.

"Don't apologize. I'm grateful, and I'm sure Julia is too. Is there an exit hole?" she asked. The color drained from Kathryn's face as she gave a quick nod. "That's excellent news. Your chances of recovery just doubled."

"Do you have any more of that happy juice," he asked when she sat him up to check the exit wound.

"Loads." She injected him with ample doses of morphine and lidocaine before going to work on his wound. "You're one lucky man," she said as she disinfected, probed, and stitched him. "The bullet missed your lung and bones, tearing mostly soft tissue. It doesn't look like you've lost too much blood, either. You did an excellent job packing the wound, Kathryn. If you keep this clean and avoid infection, you'll make a full recovery."

Holly and Rosie hugged Kathryn in unison, then kissed Clint's cheeks.

"We're sorry about Nico. He was a good person." Holly said to Riley. "But thanks for saving our dad,"

Riley hugged her and kissed the top of her head. "Of course. I'm glad I made it here in time." She hesitated before asking the question that had been plaguing her since she learned Yeager kidnapped her daughter. "How was Julia when Yeager took her? Did he hurt her?"

"No," Kathryn said emphatically. "She was perfectly fine and fearless. She's grown into an extraordinary young woman. You'll be proud when you see her."

"I already am." Riley wiped at her eyes as she turned to Conrad. "What's the plan?" He stared at her like she was speaking a foreign language. She snapped her fingers in front of his nose. He shook his head and ran his hand through his hair. "What was that you were saying about checking our emotions?"

"Right. Rough day. Jordan, Riggs, and Bailey are coming with us to get Julia. I have to take you along this time, so there's no need to argue. Bobby and the others will get your family back to the safe house. Is Clint able to walk?"

"He's a little dopey, but he can walk with help. Bobby, you take care of him for me."

Bobby gave her a crushing hug before saying, "You got it, Red. I'll be waiting to meet your girl."

She gave him a weak smile, then pulled Conrad aside. "What about Dashay?"

"I'm coming with you," Dashay said as she climbed to her feet. "I told you, I'm not letting you out of my sight."

Conrad put his arm around her. "I'm not sure you're in any condition to go on a delicate and dangerous mission right now."

She wiped her face on a towel and blew her nose. "I'm fine, and I'm not letting you get away either. You need me."

"Always," Conrad said and gave her a quick kiss. "That's settled, then." He glanced at Nico's body on the sofa. "I'm sorry, but we have to leave his body. We're running out of time to make it through the gate."

Dashay went down the hall and returned carrying a blanket. She kissed Nico once more, then crossed herself as he'd always done before lovingly covering him with the quilt. "Nico isn't there anymore. That's just his shell. We'll hold a memorial when the time is right, and I'll find a way to notify his family. For now, let's get out of here."

"Only take what you can easily carry," Bailey told Riley's family. "It's a long walk."

Holly lifted her pack onto her shoulders. "We know the drill.

This isn't our first forced march. Get Julia back. She's as much my sister as Rosie."

Riley looked her in the eye and said, "I will or die trying."

———

It was three in the morning by the time the entire group left the house together. They inched their way through the woods behind the backyard until they reached the fence. They turned west at the fence and hugged the perimeter as they moved along. Once they were within half a mile of the gate guarded by his men, Conrad divided them into smaller groups to exit. Riley caught him checking his watch every minute when they started moving again.

"We'll make it," she reassured him. "If not, I'll tear this fence down with my bare hands. I refuse to let Kearns keep me from Julia this time. Her schemes have killed two of my friends and seriously wounded a member of my family. Now, my own daughter's life hangs in the balance. Time's up."

Conrad patted her back. "I'm with you, but let's make it to the gate before my people finish their shifts. We need one of our plans to go right for once."

Riley was walking near the front with Conrad, so she turned and made her way back through the line, encouraging everyone and urging them to keep up. Clint was the weak link, so Bobby put him on his back in a dead man's carry. Riley was so touched by the selfless gesture that she couldn't speak. She squeezed his arm in thanks, then continued back through the line. Dashay was near the back with the girls, dragging her feet and keeping her head lowered. Riley linked arms with her as she walked beside her.

"They're all gone, you know," Dashay said, keeping her voice lowered.

"Who are gone, Dashay," Riley asked.

"Everyone who left the compound in Virginia with me. Brooks, Nico, Adrian."

Riley glanced at Dashay from the corner of her eye. "Adrian's not dead. He just moved to another state."

"He might as well be. I'll never see him again, and it's not like I can just call him."

"He knows our radio call sign. And I'll wager you haven't seen him for the last time. We should take that trip to California when this is over. He invited us. He has an orange orchard."

That brought a sliver of a smile. "Adrian must be in heaven, and a trip to Cali sounds like what we all need. Do you honestly believe that will ever happen?"

"We'll make it happen. Julia deserves it after what she's been through. We'll take time to rest and get reacquainted, then we'll make plans."

Dashay nodded and grew quiet before saying, "I have to go to Farmington first and see Nico's family. They have a right to know what happened to Nico."

"I'll join you. I've become quite familiar with New Mexico, as it turns out."

Riley was happy to see Dashay's dazzling smile in the darkness at her joke. She squeezed her arm as Rosie and Holly came to a halt in front of her.

"We're here," Holly whispered over her shoulder.

The line broke apart as they separated into their groups. Riley and Dashay moved to the front of the line with Conrad and his team. His inside men were there waiting.

"Just in time, Chief," one said. "You've got five minutes to get your people out before our replacements arrive."

"They're ready," Conrad said. He signaled for the others to follow him out. "My team, make for the trees where we waited before going in. I'll meet you there in three."

They hurried across the empty street and crouched to watch the others as they exited the compound. Bobby was the last out carrying Clint. Riley's resolve to check her emotions wavered for a moment, so she took a few deep breaths to stay in control. She was relieved to see them faded into the darkness down an adjacent street. They were free.

Conrad jogged across the road to their hiding place and ducked down seconds before the replacement guards marched up the street. "The others are on their own now," he whispered. "Six rescued, one to go. Let's go rescue target number one."

Riley followed Conrad as he retreated into the shadows before the new guards were in place. When they were safely away from the compound, he took out Yeager's note and the map. He and Bailey studied it until they had their bearings and had drawn out their route to Yeager's lair.

Bailey took the map and faced the team. "This will be a hike, and we'll have to hoof it to make it before daylight. You two up for that?" she asked Riley and Dashay.

Riley locked her eyes on Bailey. "I'd walk through fire for Julia. This is nothing."

Dashay gave a quick nod. "WP has been with that sick monster for hours. Do you need to ask?"

"Lead on," Riggs said.

"Let's cache the packs in that covered boat," Conrad said, pointing to a sailboat parked in a driveway two houses down. "We'll retrieve them on the way out."

They jogged to the boat and unloaded their packs, taking only what they needed. Riley stuffed her cargo pockets with vital medical supplies, then signaled when she was ready. Jordan took point, and they fell into line behind him. Bailey brought up the rear. They marched at a double-time pace, and Dashay was sucking air after the first mile, but she waved for them to keep going. Riley looked back and gave her the okay sign. Dashay nodded, too winded to speak.

"If you pass out before we reach the hanger, I'll carry you like Bobby did with Clint."

"Shut it," Dashay gasped. "Just running off my grief and anger."

They hit the airport at the two-hour mark. Riley was impressed that Dashay managed to keep up without keeling over. Riley wondered if she'd gotten a runner's high or if she was just beyond noticing how exhausted she was. When Jordan signaled for them to stop while he checked the map, she bent over with her hands on her knees.

"I'll never understand why people do this for fun," she said, between gasps.

Riley was walking it off with her hands locked above her head. "There's some insanity involved."

Bailey snorted a laugh but grew serious when Conrad gave her the cut it sign. Jordan took off again, and Dashay groaned quietly as she fell in behind Riley. They skirted the airport, then made a tighter circle bringing them closer to the private hangers. Jordan paused twice to check the numbers on the buildings. When he found the correct one, he ducked behind a concrete barrier and waved for the group to join him.

Once Riley was situated, she peeked around the barrier at the hanger thirty yards from their position. It was overwhelming to know her daughter was inside. She'd been disappointed once that night but knew it wouldn't happen twice. She could sense that Julia was within her reach.

She started to get up, itching to run in and save Julia, but Conrad tugged on the back of her shirt, holding her down.

"Not yet," he said in a harsh whisper. "You can't go in half-cocked with Yeager. He's a highly skilled special-ops colonel. Follow my lead. We'll get Julia out and alive in one piece."

Riley let out two puffs of air and said, "Fine. Tell me what to do."

Conrad put his hand on her shoulder. "Yeager wants you alive for some reason."

"To find Adrian," Dashay whispered. "That crazy SOB just can't let him go."

"That has to be it," Riley said. "He was asking about him in Fort Worth."

"The reason doesn't matter. It's in our favor that he wants you alive, but we'll go in first to confirm that it's clear for you to enter. He probably won't go after you either, Dashay. You're valuable to him, too."

Dashay rolled her eyes. "*Yay me*. Just what I always wanted, to be important to Yeager."

"I'm glad. It keeps you alive," Conrad said. "That's *my* number one priority."

Dashay's eyes teared up as she stared back at him, and her voice broke when she said, "I know, Babe."

"You two stay here and watch for our signal," Bailey said, getting them back on track. She took off her NVGs and tossed them in a patch of grass. "Won't need these. The sun's up, but there goes our cover of darkness." The rest pulled off their goggles and set them on the ground. "We don't need to hide now. Yeager's expecting us."

Conrad looked each of them in the eye, then said, "You are the bravest and most generous people I know. I have faith in your ability to successfully complete this op, but I just have to say it's been an honor serving with you. Let's go get our girl."

Riley and Dashay watched as the team moved from behind the barrier and split as they ran to surround the building. The youngest member of the team, a muscled twenty-something named Griffin, stayed behind to escort them inside when it was time. He kept his eyes focused like lasers on the building, waiting for the signal.

"How do they always know where to go?" Dashay whispered.

Griffin held up his fist to signal for her to be silent. She raised her eyebrows and smiled at Riley. She was glad to see Dashay coming out of her dark mood. There would be days of mourning ahead but having Conrad to help her get through them would make all the difference. Getting the rest home alive wouldn't hurt either.

"That's the signal," Griffin whispered. "Stay behind me and keep up."

They ran across the open ground between their position and the barrier. It felt like a mile to Riley. A wave of relief washed over her when they were under the cover of the awning outside the hanger. Bailey stuck her head out of a side door and waved them over. Griffin moved more cautiously as they approached her. Riley held her breath until the door was closed behind them.

"They're here, Riley," Bailey said. "Julia's here, and she looks well."

Riley gave an involuntary cry, then covered her mouth with her hands. "You're sure?" she whispered.

"Positive. They're in an office in the back. The rest of the team is in place, just waiting for you. When we get to Conrad, he'll call Yeager out."

"Show me," Riley said and started walking in the direction Bailey had pointed.

Griffin moved in front of her. "I take point," he said.

"Whatever," Dashay whispered.

They crept around small planes through the central part of the hanger until they reached smaller rooms and offices toward the back. Bailey pointed to the target room and crouched down to be below the window as they passed. Riley and the others did the same, then Bailey led them around a corner to an adjacent hallway where Conrad and the rest of the team were waiting for them.

Riley grabbed the front of Conrad's shirt. "Tell me you saw her," she said, too wired to contain herself a second longer.

Conrad gently peeled her fingers from his shirt. "She's here.

They're seated at a desk eating snacks." Bailey untied her necker-chief and handed it to Riley. "Lock your emotions, Riley. We need you sharp."

Riley dried her face and tossed the neckerchief back at Bailey. "To hell with that. Let's go get my daughter."

Conrad gave an exasperated sigh before leading the team into the hallway. He and Bailey set up on one side of the door with Riggs and Jordan on the other. The rest of the team stepped in front of Riley and Dashay.

"Ready?" Conrad whispered. When they nodded in unison, He straightened and drew his sidearm before saying, "Colonel Orson Yeager? This is Colonel Conrad Elliott of the Western States of America. I have someone here to see you."

Several seconds passed in silence before Yeager said, "It's open."

Riggs flung the door open wide, and the team members closest to the door rushed in with their weapons drawn. Seconds later, Jordan waved for the rest to enter. Riley's heart was in her throat as she walked in step behind Griffin. She was seconds away from seeing Julia.

The first thing that greeted her when she entered the office was Yeager gripping Julia's arm with the barrel of his gun pressed against the side of her head. Stopping herself from strangling the evil man threatening her daughter was the hardest thing Riley had ever had to do.

"Mom, is it you?" Julia whimpered. "I knew you'd come for me. I never gave up."

"Shut up," Yeager barked and jerked her arm.

Riley's voice broke when she said, "I know, sweetheart. You are the bravest person I've ever seen."

Yeager moved the gun from Julia to Riley. "One more sound and your girl will be an orphan."

"Listen to him, Mom. He killed Nico."

"We saw, WP," Dashay said, then turned a steely glare on Yeager. "We'll make him pay."

"If it isn't the Nubian Princess," Yeager hissed. "Glad you dragged her along, too. When I finish you off, Landry will be the only member of your subversive gang left."

Dashay raised her chin and threw back her shoulders. "I'll take Nubian as a compliment, you sick bastard, but princess nothing. I'm a Queen."

"Enough," Yeager said. "I hadn't expected you quite this soon. All the better for me."

Riley noticed beads of sweat forming on his forehead. He hadn't planned on her showing up with her own private ops team. "His swagger's an act," she whispered.

"Feel strong insulting girls and women, Yeager?" Conrad asked. "Hand Julia over, and we'll leave you in peace, or in one piece, I should say."

Yeager chuckled at that. "So, I finally meet the infamous Conrad Elliott. You've been a thorn in Kearns' side from the beginning, but I couldn't care less about that. I have one mission, to capture Daybreak and hand him over to my illustrious President. Nothing else matters, and you're all standing in my way." He turned his cold gaze on Riley. "Tell me where Dr. Landry is, and I'll give you your daughter. I'm sick of listening to her whining."

Riley took a step forward, but Conrad put out his arm to block her. "You first," he said.

Yeager put the gun back to Julia's head. "I was running ops when you were still reading Dr. Seuss books, so your tactics won't work on me. When I have what I want, I'll let the brat go. Not before."

Conrad gave him a smile that didn't reach his eyes. "Listen, old man. These people behind me are some of the best shots on the planet. Who has better odds?"

Yeager gave Julia a shake. "I have this precious jewel in my hands. Is her life worth exchanging for Landry's? If you fire on me, she'll be dead before I hit the floor."

Riley slowly raised her hands and backed away from Yeager. "I'll tell you anything. Just give me my daughter."

"No, Riley," Conrad hissed. "We've got him where we want him."

She raised her eyebrows. "Do you? All I see is his gun to my daughter's head."

Bailey and Jordan closed in on Yeager's left flank to draw his attention while Riggs and Griffin shifted to the right. As Yeager switched his gaze between them, Conrad stepped forward. Yeager lowered his finger to the trigger.

"Please, stop!" Julia cried, shaking uncontrollably. "He'll kill me. He shot his own guy in the head for no reason."

"Listen to her, Elliott. I'm crazy," Yeager said.

The tinny tone of his voice proved the strain was eroding his calm façade. Riley feared he'd snap before Conrad's team could act to take him out, but she couldn't see how they'd do that. They couldn't fire because they might hit Julia, or Yeager could shoot her before he fell.

They had managed to draw his attention from Riley. Desperate to end the standoff, she inched her way out of Yeager's line of sight, hoping to get behind him. Conrad glared at her and gave an almost imperceptible shake of his head. She froze, hoping he had some strategy for resolving the standoff with everyone walking out alive. She couldn't fathom what that would be.

"Adrian's in Denver," she blurted out.

Yeager turned his head and seemed surprised to see she'd moved around almost behind him without his noticing.

"Nice try, but that's a lie. I've done my homework. Daybreak's not in Denver or any of his other usual haunts. I know you went to see him before he left Fort Worth. That's how I followed you here. What kind of heartless mother are you to play with your daughter's life this way?"

"He's right," Riley said to Conrad. "I have to tell him. Putting Adrian's life over Julia's would make me as much of a psychopath as he is."

"Watch who you're calling psychopath," Yeager snapped. "I'm just a man loyal to his mission and unwilling to let anything get in the way of that."

"Justify it however you want," Conrad said. "You're nothing but an obsessed, cold-blooded killer."

"Is this the time to discuss semantics?" Dashay said, on the verge of tears. "I can't take this anymore. Adrian is on a citrus farm that his friend left to him west of Phoenix, Arizona."

Bailey gasped. "How could you, Dashay? You just gave him directions to kill Dr. Landry."

Dashay ignored her. "You have what you wanted. Let Julia go."

Riley was impressed at Dashay's quick thinking and wished she'd thought of it sooner. Yeager had no way of verifying the information, but it sounded plausible.

Yeager let out a laugh that froze Riley to the bone. She recalled hearing similar emotional outbursts from patients when she did a psych rotation during medical school. Reasoning with Yeager would be pointless.

"Haven't you learned yet that I'm no fool? I need her as collateral to get out of here alive. I require a twelve-hour head start, then I'll leave the girl at a designated spot. If you show up before the appointed time, my associates will put an end to all of you, including the child."

"That wasn't the deal," Conrad said. "We've met your demands, against my orders." He glanced at Dashay, who lifted her chin and crossed her arms.

"Discussion over," Yeager said.

Riley watched in shock as he released his grip on Julia but wrapped his arm around her waist. It was a rookie mistake, and Riley prayed Julia remembered her self-defense training. She glanced at Riley and gave a quick nod. Yeager was too focused on Conrad to notice.

"All of you back out of here slowly," he continued. "I'll leave directions where to find Julia once I've had time to map a route. Come back after we're gone, but remember, twelve hours."

"What assurance do we have that you won't execute Julia the second you're out of our sight?"

Yeager looked confused. "Why would I do that? She's played her part in my plan. Killing her serves no purpose unless any of you defy me."

Riley struggled to understand his twisted logic, but she didn't care what Yeager said. There was no way he was leaving that hanger with her daughter, even if it meant sacrificing her own life. She continued creeping behind him while Conrad and his people kept him distracted. She felt Dashay and Bailey's eyes on her, willing her to stop, but she was committed. Griffin glared at her as she moved behind him on Yeager's right side, but she pretended not to see.

Conrad had his eyes trained on Yeager to keep him from noticing Riley. "Then you win," he said, in his practiced soothing tone. "We agree to your terms. We'll let both of you go without interference, but please, remove your finger from that trigger. We wouldn't want any accidents now that we're all in agreement." Yeager hesitated for an instant before lifting his finger back to the side of the barrel. "Excellent. Everyone, get behind me, and we'll back out of here. No heroics or sudden moves. That's an order."

Riley sensed his words were meant for her, but she didn't care. It wasn't his daughter in Yeager's clutches. As the others cautiously moved behind Conrad, Riley edged in the opposite direction. As she took the final three steps behind him, Julia spun free of Yeager's hold and hit the deck. The swift action caught him off guard, so Riley took advantage and slammed her shin into the back of his knees. His legs buckled, and he dropped face down onto the tile. She stomped her boot on his right hand and heard the satisfying sound of his bones cracking. He released his hold on the gun but snapped back to his feet in one fluid motion, cradling his injured hand.

Riley grabbed the gun and aimed it at his forehead while Julia crawled to safety. Dashay and Bailey rushed to Julia's side and ushered her out the door behind Yeager's back.

Yeager eyed Riley with a half-grin. "That's an impressive move. I'll have to remember that one. You're smarter than I gave you credit for. Makes sense, you being a doctor and all, but you're wrong if you think you've won this battle."

She'd eyed him for a moment, then said, "Six people have guns pointed at you. How do you figure?"

In answer, he reached under his shirt and pulled another gun from a concealed holster. She'd been a fool to assume a trained assassin like him would only carry one weapon.

"Checkmate," he said as he raised the gun. "You'll do as well as your daughter to get me out of here."

Riley didn't flinch. "Again, six weapons aimed at you."

In a flash, he kicked the gun out of her hand, then spun and grabbed her with his weapon pressed against the underside of her chin. The metal was surprisingly cold. He pushed so hard against her windpipe that she could hardly breathe. He wound his right forearm around her gut and squeezed.

"I dare you to break free like your daughter did," he whispered with his hot, moist lips to her ear. He faced the others as she gasped for air. "You people never learn. Do you think I got where I am by letting tiny snits like this one get the best of me? Taking the girl would have been less trouble, but I can have more fun with the fine doctor. Same deal as before. You let me go without interference, and I'll deposit Riley bound and gagged in the sun for you to retrieve later."

"I'm afraid that deal has expired," Conrad said. "We'll need to negotiate a new one."

Riley felt like they'd been battling Yeager for hours, but only minutes had passed. She needed to do whatever it took to end it so she could get to Julia. While Conrad stalled, Riley frantically ran through what she remembered of her defense training. She took deep breaths through her nose to clear her mind, then assessed her situation.

Yeager held the gun in his left hand, which wasn't his dominant one, so that was a weak point. The pain in his right had to be excruciating, and the hand was useless to him. He had her left arm pinned under his elbow, but her right arm was free from the elbow down. She glanced at his broken hand. It was only inches from hers. As Conrad kept Yeager's sight locked on him, she inched her fingers toward his wounded hand.

"The situation hasn't changed," Yeager said, "unless you're less concerned about saving the mother than you were about the daughter. Just go. You'll have your precious doctor back by nightfall."

Riley wrapped her hand around his broken fingers and squeezed with all her might. Yeager shrieked and loosened his hold on her left arm. She jerked it free and pulled the gun away from her throat, shocked at how tightly Yeager gripped it despite his pain. Riley released his wounded hand to put both of her hands over his on the gun. As they wrestled for control, she caught Conrad and Jordan diving toward them out of the corner of her eye. The gun fired before they reached her. The deafening sound dazed her for a second before she released her hold on the burning hot metal. When she did, Yeager slid to the floor, still clinging to the gun. She couldn't be sure who'd fired the shot, but Yeager's finger had been the one on the trigger.

Conrad kicked Yeager's hand, and the gun skidded across the smooth floor to the other side of the room. Still dazed, Riley stared down at the man who'd caused her so much anguish for the better part of two years.

"Do something," he gasped through the pain. "You're a doctor. Save me."

Riley squatted over him and lifted his shirt. The round had entered in the vicinity of his appendix, likely causing extensive internal damage. If she performed emergency surgery, he'd have an outside chance of surviving if the bullet had missed his vital organs. Watching the blood as it pumped from the wound, she recalled what Yeager had done to Nico and Clint only hours earlier. She pictured the terror on Julia's face as he'd pressed the gun barrel to her skull. She felt nothing but loathing as his life force slowly drained away.

Riley had once vowed to always do whatever she could to preserve life. She'd saved Brooks when she could have let him bleed to death after he'd allowed Julia to get shot and had taken her family hostage. She'd stopped Bobby from crushing Reece's windpipe. But she wasn't the same doctor who'd traveled to that medical conference two and half years earlier. She'd learned she couldn't save them all, and this time felt no obligation to try. She owed the monster at her feet nothing but her contempt.

Yeager pressed his left hand to the hole in his gut and looked up at her with pleading eyes. "Are you going to help me?"

Riley straightened and calmly said, "No, I don't think I will."

He sucked in a breath. "You'd stand there and watch me die?"

"I'm going to go outside and hold my daughter for the first time in over two years. You'll still be alive when I leave, but not for long."

"You're a heartless bitch," he wheezed.

He looked small and pathetic, bleeding there on the cold tile. "I'm actually doing humanity a kindness. You've made your choices. Now, I'm making mine."

As Conrad put his arm around her to usher her out, Yeager said, "My death will haunt you for the rest of your life."

She turned her back to him and started for the door. "I can live with that."

Jordan and Griffin stayed behind to wait for the end of Yeager as Riley hurried out of the hanger. The rest of Conrad's team fanned out to secure the area in case Yeager hadn't been lying about having associates, as he'd called them. Riley was confident he was working alone. Otherwise, he'd have been surrounded by his goons. The fact that he was operating alone was an obvious sign that he lost touch with reality.

She squinted in the bright morning sunlight as she exited the hanger. The first thing she saw when her eyes adjusted was Julia sprinting toward her. It was the most beautiful sight she'd ever beheld. Julia nearly bowled her over when she reached her. They clung to each other with a joy that transcended anything Riley had ever known.

"Is it you?" Julia sobbed. "Are you real?" Riley was too overcome to speak. The most she could manage was a nod. Julia finally drew away and gasped at the bloodstains on Riley's clothes. "What did he do to you? Where are you hurt?"

"It's not my blood, sweetheart," she said through her tears. "Yeager's dead. Shot himself trying to kill me. That seems fitting somehow." Riley's words sparked a new round of crying from Julia. Riley stroked her silky, light brown hair as she sobbed on her shoulder. "Let it out. You deserve a good long cry."

Julia straightened and shook her head emphatically. "No, I don't want to waste time with tears. I want to smile and dance and sing." She did a twirl with her arms extended. "Look at my leg, Mom. No more limp."

"Excellent news," Riley said with a laugh. "Good thing, too. We have a long way to go." As Riley watched Julia doing her freedom dance, she was thrilled to see the ordeal she'd endured hadn't snuffed out her spark for life. Her daughter had grown from a girl with potential to a beautiful and courageous young woman. Riley felt her heart would burst with pride.

Julia stopped spinning and tugged on her hand. "Let's get out of this awful place. I want to make sure everyone else is safe. Dashay and Bailey told me where they are."

Riley wrapped an arm around Julia's shoulders. "We need to get orders from Conrad. He's still in charge."

"We're clear," Conrad called out to them. "No sign of Yeager's imaginary comrades. We'll retrieve our packs and get to the safe house before it's too hot to travel."

Riley took Julia's hand and said, "It's time to go home, sweetheart."

CHAPTER FIFTEEN

RILEY SWEPT her gaze over their camp on the banks of the Arkansas River from where she was perched on a stump above them. She'd made the short hike up the rise for a clearer view of the area and to enjoy a moment of solitude. She loved the people milling around in the camp below, but in the three weeks since escaping from Wichita, she hadn't had a second to herself. Julia had clung fiercely to her at first but eventually relaxed enough to let Riley steal off alone to relieve herself. Still, it had taken intense persuading to convince Julia to let her go alone on her little hike. Riley had handed her a pair of binoculars before leaving and promised she'd be able to keep an eye on her the entire time.

Riley closed her eyes and spread her arms as she felt the sun setting behind her. The weather had finally broken after a chain of thunderstorms had plagued them across eastern Kansas. The weather had slowed their westward progress but had also brought much cooler temperatures. That was a blessing since there were few trees for shade in that part of the country.

They'd passed Garden City two days earlier and had stayed close to the river, which afforded them plenty of fresh water. They still had to boil it for drinking and cooking, but they had an ample supply of cowpats to burn for fuel.

As she rested on that stump, coated in dust and sweat, she realized it was time for a bath in the river. She'd been leery of getting in the water after the rattlesnake incident, but the prospect of a refreshing swim was enticing enough to overcome her fear. She was sure also the others would be grateful so they wouldn't have to put up with her smell.

A glance at her watch told her she was fifteen minutes overdue in returning but decided to defy Conrad's strict schedule and give herself more time. She was grateful to him for taking charge of the trek west, even if he treated them more like soldiers than civilians on occasion. The worst had been during the discussion over which route they should take back to Colorado. Conrad insisted they should cut across the Oklahoma panhandle into Texas to reduce their time in enemy territory. The others protested that his route would add at least a week to the trip. They'd pushed for heading directly west across Kansas to shorten the travel time by almost half. Conrad had caved to their argument in the end, but he'd grumbled about it until Dashay persuaded him to let it go.

Despite the storms, Riley knew they'd made the right choice. Getting everyone home alive and as speedily as possible outweighed caution in her mind. The sooner they were home, the less chance for disaster. They'd had to dodge patrols for the first ten days but had seen little military activity since.

Conrad was baffled by the absence of Kearns' troops in the area and wondered if the fighting had shifted back to the southern border. Two days earlier, he'd sent Bailey, Riggs, and Griffin to a clandestine post a day's ride southwest to check in with their superiors and get updated intelligence. It would inform him if they needed to make any course changes and gave the others a needed chance to fish, hunt, and gather edible plants. As anxious as Riley was to get home, Mitch and Beth were exhausted, and Clint was still recovering. The two-day rest had been good for them and the rest of the group.

Riley stood with a sigh and stretched before heading back to camp. Conrad expected Bailey's party to return that night or early in the morning. That meant they'd all be back on the trail after breakfast. She hoped they'd have favorable news and that they wouldn't have to change course. They were only three days from the border. She'd finally be back in her country and in Colorado. From there, it would take two weeks to reach the farm and finally reunite her family.

Her heart soared at that thought as she reentered the camp.

Julia rushed at her the second she spotted Riley and threw her arms around her. "You're late, Mom," she said when she pulled away. "Conrad's not happy."

Riley chuckled at that. "When is he?" She turned and pointed in the direction of the stump. "I was just there. I could see all of you down here rushing around like ants."

Julia patted the binocs dangling from the strap on her neck. "I saw you, but you know how he is."

They walked to the center of camp where Dashay was sitting in a camp chair, stirring a pot of gray tinged liquid over the fire. She smiled up at Riley. "The Red Queen returns. You better tell Conrad. He's ready to send out a search party."

"In a sec." Riley leaned over the pot and crinkled her nose. "Let me guess. Catfish soup."

Dashay sat straighter and made a face at her. "People paid good money for food like this not all that long ago."

"Not food like this, but I appreciate that you're doing the best you can with what we have."

Dashay went back to stirring. "Don't patronize me." She was quiet for a moment, then said, "We sure could use Adrian. He could create something edible out of dirt."

"It's about time," Conrad called from behind them. "How was your walk?" he asked with sarcasm dripping from his voice.

Riley turned to face him and put her hands on her hips. "Necessary and rejuvenating. You need to chill, Conrad."

He stroked his stubbly chin. "I'm just not comfortable with anyone wandering away from camp under the circumstances."

Riley swept her arm in a circle with a flourish. "I had a view 400 miles in every direction. I didn't see anyone. I think we're safe."

"Good to know," he said as he peered over Dashay's shoulder into the pot. "Is that about ready? I'm starved."

Dashay stood and picked a bowl up off the folding camp table. "As ready as it's going to be."

She ladled out some soup for him and called for everyone to bring their bowls. Once they were all served, Riley and Julia carried their food to sit with Mitch and Beth.

Riley settled with her legs crossed on a small patch of grass across from them and said, "You're both looking stronger. I'll give you checkups before we hit the trail tomorrow, but you should be good for the rest of the trip."

Mitch glared at her over the top of his bowl. "Quit treating me like an invalid. I'm only sixty-eight, and I was working ten-hour days on the ranch before we were driven off."

"Speak for yourself," Beth said. "That's not the same as walking for miles for days on end. I was personally thrilled when I heard we were going to rest for a few days. How much longer will it take to reach the farm?"

Riley swallowed a spoonful of soup that was tastier than she expected and said, "Only two-and-a-half weeks. It'll be a breeze once we cross the border."

Julia's eyes glistened as she said, "I'm so excited to get home I can hardly stand it. I've been away for almost thirty-two months." She reached for Riley's hand. "That morning we left for the conference is still so vivid in my mind, but it feels like something from a movie, not my real life."

"I think we all feel that way to some extent," Mitch said. "I've often wondered what difference it would have made if we'd known what was coming."

Riley wrapped her other hand around the one Julia held. "I've learned not to let myself think that way anymore. This is the life we've been given. I'm trying to make the best of it I can, which includes coming to get you and bring you home." She looked into each of their faces, then said, "No regrets."

"Hear, hear," Mitch said and lifted his bowl.

Riley nodded, then dipped her spoon into the soup just as the sound of galloping hooves thundered in the camp. She jumped to her feet as Jordan rode past her toward the fire pit. Conrad had sent him out early that morning to scout the road ahead. Riley and Julia ran after him while the others followed at a slower pace and gathered around as he dismounted.

Conrad dropped his bowl on the table, then stood and faced Jordan. "What is it?"

Jordan rubbed his face with his hands before saying, "It's incredible. I didn't believe it at first, but it's true."

Riley moved to face him. "What's true? Spit it out, Jordan."

He stared at her with a look of awe. "The war's over."

Conrad gripped Jordan's shoulder and turned him to face him. "What? How?"

"Kearns is dead, Chief. Assassinated."

Conrad stared at him, too overcome to speak.

Dashay gently laid her hand on Jordan's arm. "Who told you that? I thought you were scouting campsites."

Jordan sank into Dashay's chair, shaking his head. "I'd ridden fifteen miles when I heard explosions before I reached the outskirts of the next town up the road. I thought it was cannon fire in a battle, but that didn't make sense. Why would we be fighting a battle so far from the border in a small town? I dismounted and tethered my horse in an abandoned barn before going the rest of the way on foot, staying hidden. When I reached the main square, I found what looked like all the residents gathered. They were celebrating, shooting off fireworks in the middle of the day. I asked an elderly man what was happening. He turned to me with tears in his eyes and told me the war was over. He said it reminded him of getting the news on VE-Day when he was a boy."

"Did you verify it with anyone else?" Conrad asked.

Jordan let out a booming laugh. "I didn't believe it either, so I verified it with everyone else. Kearns was assassinated ten days ago in Chicago on what she was calling a Goodwill Tour. You've got to love the irony of that. Her people either surrendered, are on the run, or in hiding. When the news reached her forces fighting out west, they surrendered in a minute. I actually witnessed soldiers celebrating with the crowd. Most astonishing thing I ever saw."

Conrad sank into a chair beside him. "Our undercover people in the East heard rumors Kearns people were planning to take her out, but no one believed they'd have the stones to do it."

"It's done. Done and over," Jordan whispered.

The camp grew silent for a moment, then Riley gave a loud whistle and let out a whoop. It was all the others needed to erupt into cheers. They hugged each other and danced around the fire. When they were celebrated out, they sat in a circle, quietly talking about what it all meant. Bailey, Riggs, and Griffin rode into camp and officially confirmed what Jordan had learned as the fire burned low.

"The US government is scrambling to fill the void left after the assassination and mass exodus of Kearns' cabinet and puppet leaders," Bailey said. "Word of total government collapse is already making its way west. The situation is confused at best. There are reports of rioting, and the military has turned on the central government. It's like a headless snake. We need to get out of here and fast."

Riley didn't fight her tears as she sat pondering the news with her arm around Julia's shoulder. The last obstacle to her quest to rescue her family had been erased, and the way was clear. All that was left was to put one foot in front of the other and walk through the door.

———

Dashay stood gazing west as the sun dipped below the Rockies. During her two years in Colorado, she'd become attached to those majestic peaks and was surprised at how much they felt like home.

"Awe-inspiring sight," Conrad said as he came up behind her and wrapped his arms around her waist. "No matter how many times I see that, it still takes my breath away."

"I agree," Dashay said and turned to face him. "Conrad, we need to talk."

He released her and took a step back. "Sounds serious. Should I be worried?"

Dashay took his hand and led him to their camp chairs sitting in front of the tent they shared. "It is serious, but it doesn't follow that you should be worried. I've had something on my mind since Nico died. I didn't bring it up before now because I had a lot to work out in my mind. I wanted to wait until we were almost home but before we're surrounded by the massive throng of Riley's family."

She'd kept her head lowered, so he put a finger under her chin and raised her eyes to meet his. "I've felt you holding back, but I didn't want to push. Just be straight with me, babe. Tell me what's on your mind. I might be able to take it."

She gave him a half-grin. "You asked for it. Seeing Nico stirred up feelings in me, but the circumstances were so traumatic that it took time to sort through what it meant. Nico was an amazing man, and I cared for him. I might have loved him even, but never in the way I love you. If I had, I never would have deserted him in

Charleston. I've come to realize that I never could have left you that way."

Conrad watched her for a moment, then said, "I have to admit this is not what I expected. You can't imagine how happy and relieved I am to hear this. Why was it so hard to tell me that?"

"I haven't gotten to the hard part yet." Conrad raised an eyebrow but gestured for her to go on. She took a deep breath for courage before saying, "Nico's death was a tragic reminder of how perilous this world can be. Human life has always been unpredictable, but the CME reversed our progress by a century, at least. We have to adjust our actions accordingly. I love you, Conrad, and I don't want to spend another minute of the time I have separated from you. We never know what's coming tomorrow."

Conrad brushed his lips against hers. "Are you asking me to marry you?"

"I'm hoping not to have to, but there's more to it than that."

Conrad slid from his chair and knelt in the dirt. "Doesn't matter. Dashay Robinson, please, marry me."

Dashay took his face in her hands, then kissed him passionately. "Of course. It's about time you asked."

———

Riley knelt next to Xav's crib, watching him in blissful sleep, unable to tear herself away. Throughout the entire journey from Wichita, she'd feared he wouldn't recognize her when she got home. Her worry had been for nothing. The instant he saw her when she'd stepped through the door, bleached hair and all, he'd spread his arms and cried, "Mama!" It couldn't have gone better if she'd orchestrated it herself. He'd refused to let her put him down during the emotional reunion with the rest of the family. He'd even tried to get her to climb into the crib with him. She would have if the crib were big enough.

As she watched her son, Coop came in and leaned against the

doorframe with his arms folded. "He'll still be there in the morning," he whispered.

Riley climbed to her feet and joined him in the doorway. "I just can't get enough of looking at him. I need to make up for every second I've missed."

"How about making up time with me?"

She gave him a lingering kiss. "With pleasure. Is Jared asleep?"

"Finally, and Julia is with Rosie and Holly in Emily's room. They're jabbering away like they were never apart."

Riley felt tears sting at her eyes but wiped them away with her filthy neckerchief. "That's a relief. All they did was argue the last time they were together."

"That was the old life."

Riley raised her head and studied his face. He looked and sounded so tired, and it was her fault. He'd held her so tightly when she first arrived, she thought he'd crush her. But he'd been reserved and distant since, and she wondered where the light-hearted Coop she met in that hotel lobby was hiding.

"True," she said. "We've all grown and changed, but deep inside, we're the same people."

"Feels like there are a thousand people in this house," he said, brushing past her comment. "Let's go to the stables so we can have some privacy. You can meet the foals."

All she wanted was a long hot bath and to climb into their bed with him, but in his current mood, she didn't want to argue. Instead, she pasted on her best smile and squeezed his hand. "Sounds great. Lead the way."

They walked to the stables in silence, and she grew more concerned with each step. Her children hadn't held her abrupt departure against her. They'd been overjoyed to see her and acted like nothing had happened. Emily had chattered on about helping get an internal hardwired intranet system of sorts configured at the school. It was a far cry from the internet, but she'd beamed with pride at describing how they'd gotten the computers communicating with each other. Jared talked about his part in helping deliver the foals. Jesse said that he had the makings of a skilled vet. Riley's mother and sister had welcomed her home with open arms. She hoped Coop was just holding back until they could be alone.

He gave her a tour of the new addition to the stables and showed her each of the new foals in turn. He told her how they'd only lost two and had even had three sets of twins. They'd purchased more mares, who would be arriving in a month. Within five years, he said, they'd have a thriving business.

She was glad to hear about the horses but was growing impatient. When he started telling her what was happening at the hospital, she held up her hand to stop him. "Enough, Coop. Don't you think I see what you're doing?"

She caught the first crack in his façade as he studied her. "Tell me, Riley, what *am* I doing?"

She led him by the hand to an empty stable filled with stacked bales of hay. She hopped up on one stack and patted the spot next to her for him to sit. He hesitated for a second before lowering himself down next to her.

"Look at me," she said when he avoided her eyes. He raised his chin and met her gaze. "That's better. One thing about you that annoyed me most and made me love you most when we met was your bluntness. You always said just what you were thinking, even when you shouldn't have. There was never any pretense with you. So, why aren't you telling me what's on your mind now?"

"I should have known," he whispered.

She looked at him in confusion. "Known what?"

"That I couldn't hide from you. The reason I'm reluctant to share my thoughts, Riley Kate Poole Cooper, is that they're so conflicted I'm not sure which ones should come out first."

He tried to turn away, but she put her hand on his cheek, making him face her. "All of them, no matter how painful."

"First off, you need to know that I perfectly understand the reasons behind why you went after Julia. What I don't understand or accept is the way you did it. Your mom tried to help me understand, and it helped some, but not enough. When you ran off without telling me, I felt like you didn't need me, or respect me, or trust me enough to come to me for help. I was hurt and furious, and to be honest, terrified of losing you. That isn't an emotion I'm familiar with."

His words were like a punch in the gut, but she deserved every one of them. Still looking him in the eyes, she said, "I get all of that, but hear this. I've never loved, respected, or needed anyone as much as I need you."

"Then why?" he asked, with eyes pleading to understand.

"I should have told you I was going, and I'm deeply sorry for not doing that. But all I knew was that I was straddling a chasm. You and the kids were on one side—Julia on the other. I trusted you to keep everyone safe here, but the ground was crumbling under Julia's feet, and I had to get to her before it was too late. If I hadn't gone when I did, we might not have ever seen her again. I did things I never imagined myself doing to save her. I would do the same for any of my family. Yes, even you, Coop. And for the first time since that horrific day when the CME struck, I'm whole."

As he watched her, his façade faded, and that boyish grin she loved so well broke through. Tears welled in her eyes as she said, "There's the Coop I remember from that hotel lobby the moment we met. I've missed him."

He tucked a stray curl behind her ear, then kissed the end of her nose. "All is forgiven as long as you promise there are no more madcap adventures tucked up your sleeve."

"I'm not going anywhere. I have everything I've ever wanted right here."

"Then welcome home, my Warrior Queen. Let's go make up for lost time."

ABOUT THE AUTHOR

E.A. Chance is a writer of award-winning suspense, historical and post-apocalyptic women's fiction who thrives on crafting tales of everyday superheroes.

She has traveled the world and lived in five different countries. She currently resides in the Williamsburg, Virginia area with her husband and is the proud mother of four grown sons and Nana to one amazing grand-darling.

She loves hearing from readers. Connect with her at:

https://eachancebooks.com
e.a.chance@eachancebooks.com

Made in United States
Troutdale, OR
09/17/2025

34604701R00199